Conde, Nicholas.

The religion

THE RELIGION

THE
RELIGION
NICHOLAS CONDÉ

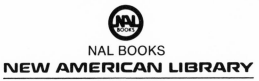

NAL BOOKS
NEW AMERICAN LIBRARY
TIMES MIRROR
NEW YORK AND SCARBOROUGH, ONTARIO

AUTHOR'S NOTE

This novel is a work of fiction. Names, characters, places, and incidents are either the product of the author's imagination or are used fictitiously, and any resemblance to actual persons, living or dead, events, or locales is entirely coincidental. It is my deepest hope that no offense is taken by those who are *yaguo*—the believers.

ACKNOWLEDGMENTS

Excerpts from *Voodoo in Haiti* reprinted by permission of Schocken Books Inc.
from *Voodoo in Haiti* by Alfred Metraux.
Copyright © 1959 by Alfred Metraux.
Introduction copyright © 1972 by Schocken Books Inc.

For information address The New American Library, Inc.

Published simultaneously in Canada by
The New American Library of Canada Limited

NAL BOOKS TRADEMARK REG. U.S. PAT. OFF. AND FOREIGN COUNTRIES
REGISTERED TRADEMARK—MARCA REGISTRADA
HECHO EN CRAWFORDSVILLE, INDIANA, U.S.A.

SIGNET, SIGNET CLASSICS, MENTOR, PLUME, MERIDIAN
and NAL BOOKS are published *in the United States* by
The New American Library, Inc.,
1633 Broadway, New York, New York 10019, *in Canada* by
The New American Library of Canada Limited,
81 Mack Avenue, Scarborough, Ontario M1L 1M8

Designed by Julian Hamer

Library of Congress Cataloging in Publication Data

Condé, Nicholas
   The religion.

   I. Title.
PS3553.04867R4   813'.54   82-2166
ISBN 0-453-00412-1   AACR2

First Printing, May, 1982

1 2 3 4 5 6 7 8 9

PRINTED IN THE UNITED STATES OF AMERICA

FOR CONSTANCE JANIS
*the only person to whom this
could possibly be dedicated*

We moderns are now living in the age of chaos. Our understanding of myth is quite degenerate, but the revelations of the new age of gods have already begun. . . .

The scientist is like an explorer climbing a mountain: giddy from the heights and thin atmosphere, he feels a premature elation and thinks that he can reach out and grab the stars. And then he climbs to the top and sees that even higher peaks await him in the distance and that the stars are so far beyond his grasp that they will never become light under the nails of his Heaven-scraping fingers.

WILLIAM IRWIN THOMPSON
The Time Falling Bodies
Take to Light: Mythology,
Sexuality, and the Origins of Culture

BOOK ONE

Yaguo

(The Initiate)

Chapter 1

"Look, Daddy," Chris Jamison said as he ran up holding out his open palm. "An arrowhead!"

Cal Jamison leaned over and looked at the object lying in the hand of his seven-year-old son. It was just an ordinary stone, burnished and worn to a vaguely triangular shape by the weather. You could find a million of them in Central Park. But Cal saw his son's eyes sparkling with excitement, and nodded approval.

"The Mohawks came through New York on their way north," Cal said. "And the Senecas."

"Lucky, huh?" Chris said. "I found it right off."

Chris plopped the stone into a paper bag he had saved from his Good Humor, then ran away to scour more of the dusty ground bordering the footpath.

Let him believe, Cal thought. The flash of enthusiasm Chris had shown at the discovery of his "arrowhead" was all too rare these days. More often the boy sat silently, morose and given to long listless spells of staring out windows or even at walls.

Had the move to New York been a mistake?

For the hundredth time since they'd arrived twelve days ago, Cal asked himself the question. Although the change of scene alone could hardly be blamed for the boy's moodiness, no doubt the adjustment was difficult. Chris had been more comfortable with the easygoing rhythms of life in New Mexico. At five he had started horseback riding, had sat in the saddle like a natural. And he had loved the camping trips to the mesas and deserts outside Taos, avidly hunting for *real* Indian artifacts. Chris could roam there, explore, have some free rein—not like in the city, where you hardly dared let a kid out of your sight for a second.

Cal glanced off to the side of the asphalt path to assure himself that his son was safely in view. There he was, kneeling under a bush, depositing another pebble in his bag. The sun had caught his face in relief, and with his light brown hair hanging straight over his forehead he looked so much like Laurie. Too much. The resemblance was almost physically painful to see—the same fair skin, the lanky too-thin build, and, more than anything, the eyes, the big wide green eyes.

Cal almost called to him, but Chris was involved in what he was doing. Well, at least this part of the day was working out.

Earlier they had gone to the zoo. Cal had thought it would make an ideal outing, a chance to show Chris the bright side of moving to a new home—give him some relief from the upheaval and the thousand-and-one chores. But Chris had reacted badly to seeing the animals. He had become sullen and withdrawn, rebuffing Cal's every attempt to cheer him with a balloon or pony ride or a box of Cracker Jacks.

Then, in front of a cage occupied by two Asian water buffalo, Chris had looked up misty-eyed at his father and uttered a single word:

"Remember?"

"Remember what, Bean?"

"You know," Chris had said, turning away.

And then Cal was struck by a long overdue awareness: the monkeys and buffalo and all the other exotic animals were reminding Chris of *her*—of past summers when they would all go together on field trips to Burma or Ceylon or the Philippines, and, while Cal gathered his data, Laurie and Chris would see the magical sights together.

Yes, he remembered. All of it. Visions of Laurie laughing when an old Magaluk tribesman showed her the tiny monkey he had trained to play dice. The frosted chocolate birthday cake she had made for Bibo, their translator in Burma, with ingredients scrounged from God-knows-where. And the way she was always befriending wonderful old characters in the markets and bazaars and the lobbies of hotels that had seen their last glory in the days of Empire. It was in fact a leftover colonial, a not-so-Great White Hunter named Eccles, who had provided the genesis for Chris's nickname. Eccles had been in the habit of calling everyone in his immediate vicinity "old bean." When he had applied the sobriquet

4

to Chris, then only four years old, Laurie had told the Englishman he was going too far—a child of four could hardly be called "old" anything. Henceforth, she had insisted with mock outrage, Chris would have to be called simply "Bean." And the name had stuck.

Cal had stopped using it for awhile after his wife's death, until one day Chris complained that he missed it. Another way of saying he missed her, of course. The name was a piece of her, too, a piece that Chris did not have to surrender for burial. So its use was revived. In memoriam.

"I remember, Bean," Cal said quietly as they stood watching the water buffalo.

They left the zoo immediately afterwards and began rambling through the rest of the park.

⊐ ● ⊏

Six months ago Cal Jamison had been professor of anthropology at the University of New Mexico in Albuquerque. With five years in the position behind him, and a growing reputation as an authority on Asian and Pacific cultures, Cal was regarded as a leading light in the anthropology department, and essential leavening on a faculty where almost everyone else was concentrating on the American Indian. He had a sabbatical coming up, and with whispers already reaching his ears that he would be voted tenure, he had no thought of ever moving elsewhere. Laurie, his wife, had been no less content. An artistically gifted woman, she had found in the umber hues of the Southwest landscape an inspiration for her watercolors, and in the last year her pictures had begun selling for prices approaching four figures. She had taken up weaving, too, translating her designs into wall hangings. In the university community she and Cal were considered the perfect couple, blessed not only with talent and intelligence and style, but also with uncommon good looks—both fair, with Cal's straw-blond hair and tall athletic build perfectly complementing Laurie's litheness. Sometimes, sitting on the porch, listening to the click of Laurie's loom and watching Chris play at her feet, Cal would wonder what he had done to deserve his luck. His marriage seemed nearly as perfect to him as it did to everyone else.

Then suddenly it was over, Laurie's life ended by what the insurance companies listed on their actuarial tables as the "leading cause of death" and called simply "an accident in the home."

Cal found it impossible to stay where he had been so content, where they had been content together. Their house was an adobe and glass design built to their specifications. The color of the land was like one of her paintings, and the views through the windows constantly taunted him with how much living she had left undone. And there was for Cal the constant thought, freighted with intolerable guilt, that the accident didn't have to happen.

There were practical considerations, too. In the sprawling environment of Albuquerque, "single parenting" loomed as a lonely and rigorous prospect. It would be easier in a big city, Cal thought, especially New York, where he could call on some help and emotional support from Laurie's older sister, Ricki.

One more overriding factor had contributed to his decision to relocate to New York. Kate was here—Kathryn Clay, the famous woman anthropologist under whom he had studied in his own undergraduate days at Columbia. Kate had inspired Cal in his choice of career, made him her protégé, then virtually adopted him as a son. After Laurie's death, Cal had turned naturally to Kate. It was late in the academic year, positions elsewhere were already filled. Kate was only a professor emeritus now, but nevertheless she had retained her clout. She had been able, in the light of Cal's excellent qualifications, to see that a niche was found for him at Columbia.

No, it wasn't a mistake to come here. You couldn't think in terms of right and wrong when there hadn't really been a choice. He was simply where he had to be—where life, and death, had put him.

∋ ● ∈

For most of the afternoon Cal had let Chris go wherever his appetite for rock collecting took him, satisfied to trail along and observe the park's teeming Sunday spectacle. Roller skaters wearing sequined shorts and hats with puffed satin wings sewn to the crown like Mercury's, joggers of all shapes and ages, a magician in clown makeup, a sidewalk juggler in baggy red pants with blue suspenders crowded the esplanade in front of the bandshell. And Jamaican musicians, their hair in the knotted braids called dreadlocks, playing "Moon River" on steel drums in front of the statue of Alice in Wonderland.

Wonderland indeed, Cal thought as he paused and listened to the song. What would future anthropologists make of this culture when they dug back into time?

Cal glanced over to the clump of bushes where Chris was rooting around.

6

His heart skipped a beat. *Gone!* Where was Chris?

Swiveling rapidly in all directions, he spotted his son about twenty yards away, snooping along the side of a path that dropped steeply between two stands of trees.

"Bean!" he called. "Wait there!"

But the music must have drowned him out, because Chris kept moving away, oblivious.

Cal started running down the slope and shouted again, but Chris disappeared around a bend in the path.

Cal ran faster and cursed himself for not laying down the ground rules to Chris before they ventured out into the park. *Stay where I can see you at all times. No wandering off.* Cal hadn't wanted to paint the city too black too soon; Chris had enough terrors to cope with at the moment without being told he'd been plunked down in a place of rampant danger and violence. So the warnings had been postponed. Foolish, Cal thought now. You couldn't be too careful. Only a couple of days ago in the *Times* there had been a story about a child who'd set out from his home one afternoon merely to walk to another apartment building across the street for a music lesson. The little boy had vanished as if into thin air. After working on the case for three months, the police had yet to turn up a single lead, a single helpful witness.

Cal rounded the bend at full steam, his mind already forming the little lecture he'd give Chris.

But the path that stretched out straight ahead for thirty yards was empty except for a woman wheeling a baby in a stroller and a pair of young girls in outrageous "punk" get-up, their hair dyed lavender.

Cal's alarm was rekindled. Chris hadn't been moving fast enough to reach the next bend in the path. He must have gone exploring in the trees. But on which side? Darting up and down the path, Cal peered between the trees on both sides, looking in vain for a flash of Chris's yellow Muppet T-shirt through the green. Then he ran to the girls and the woman with the stroller, asking if they had noticed a little boy heading away from the path—"about so high, brown hair, yellow shirt?"

No help.

Now the panic really began to build. If he pursued Chris in the wrong direction, they'd miss each other completely.

Wait a minute, Cal thought, it was Central Park, thousands of people around. Some samaritan would take a lost and crying kid under his wing and put him into the hands of the police. But being lost would still be traumatic for Chris. His mother had suddenly dropped off the earth; he was doubly dependent on having his father right there when he needed him.

Cal made a random choice and plunged into the foliage on the right side of the path.

He wasn't more than a few yards in when he saw the bushes ahead already thinning toward a clearing. A couple yards more and he could see people, a group of them, and the royal blue side-panel of a car, a spinning red light on its—

Police!

Oh Jesus no, something had happened.

So quickly?

Cal pushed frantically through the shrubbery, snagging a cuff and tearing it loose. The branch of a bush snapped back and stung his cheek.

Then he broke into the open, an area of parched and trampled grass about the size of a tennis court. The clearing was almost completely enclosed by greenery, though off to one side the bushes were sparse and a flattened swath showed the point of entry for the police cruiser parked just ahead of Cal.

Beyond the car stood a couple of policemen and a small ring of people, their attention directed toward something on the ground.

Cal charged around to the other side of the squad car.

And ran practically straight into Chris, who stood on the fringe of the crowd.

Relief and anger flooded simultaneously through Cal, and scolding words began to form on his lips. But as he reached out to grab Chris's shoulder, his glance took in the area around which the crowd had collected.

His hand froze in midair and the words died in his throat as he stared at the patch of ground.

On a bed of leafy branches lay the carcasses of several animals. The largest, a goat with a coal-black hide, had been decapitated, and the severed head had been skewered atop a short stake that was sunk into the ground at the center of the branches. Around the base of the stake lay the other dead animals—two large turtles, a gray cat, and a white rooster. All had been killed in the same manner as the goat, although their heads had simply been flung carelessly aside.

Cal cringed at the sight. Colonies of ants were swarming over the dried blood of the animals, and over a little heap of gore that Cal realized was the goat's innards. In the hot sun of the June afternoon the stench of decay was beginning to foul the air.

8

One of the two policemen had gone to the trunk of the police cruiser for some metal stanchions and a length of rope, and he was now busy erecting a cordon. The other policeman stood beside the car's open door, holding the microphone of a two-way radio.

"Yeah, yeah, the same crazy bullshit," he was saying into the mike. "With a goat this time."

An amplified squawk, unintelligible at any distance from the car, answered from the radio's speaker.

"Nah, Sarge, hours old," said the cop. "A couple of kids found it about fifteen, twenty minutes ago." He glanced toward two teen-age boys who stood nearby, holding Frisbees and shifting restlessly from one foot to the other. "Yeah, I'll do that. Will you get Sanitation on this?" There was another scratchy squawk. The cop acknowledged it and tossed the mike onto the seat of the car. Then, pulling a notebook from his hip pocket, he called the Frisbee players aside and began interviewing them.

"C'mon, Bean," Cal said, tapping his son on the shoulder. "We've seen enough."

The tableau of slaughtered animals could only be disturbing for a child; Cal was anxious to pull Chris away.

But Chris remained transfixed by the sight. "Wait, Daddy," he answered without turning around.

Cal debated. Insist? Fight it through? That might only give the incident more weight. As long as Chris didn't appear troubled or disgusted maybe it was better to let him satisfy his curiosity.

The mood of the bystanders, hardened observers of the city's excesses, became jocular and mocking as the shock began to wear off.

"Must have been quite a picnic," said a healthily tanned man who had come up behind Cal. "I've been saying for years they ought to have barbecue pits in the park."

"Whattaya think it was?" asked a small pugnacious woman holding a small pugnacious dog on a leash.

"A Board of Estimate meeting, maybe," said a gray-haired man smoking a pipe.

The policeman by the cordon waved his arms. "All right, let's break it up," he said. "Show's over." When the crowds lingered stubbornly, he raised his voice. "C'mon, c'mon, citizens. It's a beautiful day. Y'got better things to do than stare at this garbage."

The onlookers began drifting away.

"That's it, Chris." Cal laid a hand lightly on his son's shoulder.

Chris pulled away and went up to the cop. "What was it for?" he asked.

"Search me, sonny," the cop said, and moved to join his partner.

Then, from somewhere behind him, Cal heard a voice say very softly, "For the gods."

He turned around. A thin, brown-skinned man dressed in black pants and a plain white shirt, like an off-duty waiter, was standing there alone. The other bystanders were gone.

"It was done for the gods," the man repeated, as if answering Chris's question, only he was speaking too quietly for Chris to hear. *"Comprende, señor?"* He gave Cal a tightly puckered smile and walked away.

Cal's gaze followed the stranger until he disappeared into the trees. Yes, Cal thought, that was probably it—a ritual slaughter of some kind. There were all kinds of crazy cults running around these days.

He turned back to see that Chris had ducked under the cordon and was down on all fours, circling the dead animals for a closer look.

"Christopher!" Cal announced harshly. "That's enough now! Let's go!"

Chris blinked up at him, wide-eyed. But he offered no resistance. He folded his bag of "arrowheads," put it into his pocket, and came obediently to take Cal's hand.

Returning to the path, Cal waited for the questions and mentally worked through the answers that might satisfy the child's ever-present *why*.

Should he even attempt to explain cults? Chris had been exposed to enough genuine ritual on the field trips that he might grasp some of it.

But that would be taking this kind of aberrant behavior too seriously.

As it turned out, though, there was no need for explanations. Chris didn't refer to the bizarre scene again, didn't ask a thing about it. Not for the rest of the afternoon, nor on the long bus ride down to Kate's.

Not a single question.

Chapter 2

KATHRYN CLAY was twenty-four years old when she set out from New York on a tramp steamer heading for the Tokalau Islands in the South Pacific. Pictures taken by her friends before her journey showed a curly-haired young woman dressed in khaki pants and wearing a smile that seemed at once shy and determined. The Great Depression was paralyzing America, but the third-year graduate student from Sedalia, Missouri, armed only with a box of empty notebooks and undaunted curiosity, had a single goal in mind: to live in one of the world's most isolated and primitive societies and to bring back a new way of seeing how human beings lived. No one had been there before her; there were no maps, no guidebooks, no anthropological journals to tell her what she should look for, or what she might find.

Eighteen months later she returned with her notebooks full and wrote a book about what she had observed. The result was *Lessons of the Primitive: Love and Sex Among the Innocents*. She had composed a scholarly work, a study of the courtship and procreation customs of an unknown tribe in an unknown corner of the world. She hoped for the attention of other anthropologists, the sale of a few thousand copies to college libraries, and perhaps a teaching job in a world where women professors were as rare as the collection of tribal tools she had brought home.

Her modest hopes were more than fulfilled. Her vivid descriptions of a society totally free in its carnal appetites, where children were taught to be unashamed of their natural urges, promptly became a national sensation. *Love and Sex Among the Innocents* was banned in Boston, decried in newspaper editorials, and denounced from the pulpits of every major city in America for encouraging moral corruption. At the same time it was hailed by her colleagues as a landmark, a classic work of anthropology, and proceeded through nineteen printings in its first year of publication.

Kathryn Clay was twenty-seven years old—and an international celebrity.

It had always amazed Cal that Kate, starting from such a high plateau at the beginning of her career, had managed to move on to even higher peaks. Journeys to other primitive islands, to the heart of Africa and the mountain villages of South America, had yielded an entire library of observations on tribal societies. In the half-century following her first spectacular success she wrote twenty-two books, but unlike most anthropologists, who concentrated on one tribe or country or theory, Kate's interests spanned the globe. She was devoted to studying all "the innocents," as she called those whose ancient customs had survived untainted by civilization. It was Kate's thesis, stated again and again in her work, that modern civilization, in its blind march toward Progress, was guilty of ignoring and even destroying invaluable ancient philosophies and customs. "We actually think we *own* the stars," she had written, "just because we reach them with rockets. We've lost a sense of where we fit into the Grand Design." Whether or not this was true, it was a persuasive notion when the so-called progress of modern life seemed to be leading the earth toward destruction. Kate Clay believed so fervently in her ideas that she was not content merely to write books read by millions. She traveled incessantly, lectured wherever she could find an audience; she played her celebrity like an instrument, using her outspokenness as a trademark. Probably no one had done more to bring a difficult scientific field before the general public.

Of course she had her detractors, those who said she had succeeded in popularizing herself and her work only by writing and talking so much about the sex lives of natives. And both her private life and her politics had caused her some trouble. She had been an outspoken feminist before Jane Fonda was in grade school. She had campaigned for birth control and the sexual rights of women long before either cause became fashionable. And she had been through four husbands, all older than herself—a literary critic, the famous anthropologist Quentin Kimball, a university president, and a shoe manufacturer. "I'm an expert on what makes a happy marriage," she playfully told interviewers. "I've had four of them, all perfect." Of course Kate's idea of marriage was telephoning long-distance from Borneo to say she would be home in six months, and not to hold dinner.

Most amazing of all was that she seemed not to be slowing down. At the age of seventy-seven, when most people wanted to simplify their lives and warm themselves in the sun until the final darkness came, Kate had trekked halfway around the world taping a PBS series called *Cultures*. There had been a great deal of publicity surrounding the sight of this grandmotherly yet still vital and somehow sexy woman retracing her past expeditions for television, and while she was writing her companion book to the series she had called Cal in New Mexico to talk about both the work and the media attention. "I'm in serious danger of becoming a goddamn cult figure," she had complained.

Becoming? Cal could still remember the day he first saw her. It had been at the beginning of his sophomore year in college, and even then, twenty years ago, she had already become that rarest specimen of the celebrity breed: a living legend. Cal had, in fact, gone to hear her not because of a special interest in anthropology, but out of sheer curiosity about someone so famous and, reputedly, scandalous. In the lecture hall, however, he heard only her passion for her work. She had given an account of a month spent in the jungles of New Guinea with a reportedly cannibalistic tribe. She told the enthralled undergraduates that the word used by the cannibals for human prey translated as "long pig." Then she had used this simple fact for an easily understood lesson in comparative anthropology. "Not every culture has a concept of fame," she said. "It always brings me down to earth to remember, whenever I'm getting too big for my britches, when I think I'm cock of the walk, that to a Bulungundi I'm just another mouthful of long pig."

With that first exposure to Kate, Cal knew he had found his career—or it had found him. He took every course available to prepare for a degree in cultural anthropology, and worked for top grades with one mission: to go on to graduate work with Kathryn Clay. His plan succeeded more dramatically than he could have hoped. Kate had adopted him as her favorite. She had sponsored his doctoral thesis and recommended him for jobs. She had been at his wedding and was godmother to his son.

She was his teacher, his mentor, his inspiration, and his friend.

Ɔ • Ɛ

Cal stood at the center of the vast high-ceilinged space, admiring its airy modern design and the view from the huge windows that looked out on the riverfront of lower Manhattan. The room itself was more than forty feet long; it felt like a gymnasium. Kate had moved since the last time Cal was in New York and now lived in a neighborhood of old industrial loft buildings converted to apartments.

"It's so huge," Cal said. "What was it before?"

"A hat factory," Kate said. She had aged to a hefty broad-shouldered woman with blue eyes still full of wonder, gray hair cut short in a practical style, and the same shy-determined smile that had been enchanting the American people for fifty years. She was dressed in a red-patterned caftan, one of many that had become her trademark. Caftans and muumuus were fashionable now, but Kate had been wearing them for decades; she had probably helped start the trend.

"I needed more space," she went on, "for all the things I've collected in my travels, and this place has five thousand square feet. Now I have one storeroom just for my African stuff, and another for the South Pacific. I ought to run little tours down here."

Cal marveled at the size of the apartment. "Only you could find an old hat factory," he said, "and turn it into something this nice."

Kate laughed gustily. "Anybody would know you're new in town. There are so few places left to live that people are turning old *firehouses* into apartments. It's hard to believe, but this neighborhood's actually getting to be chic."

She was phenomenal, Cal thought. At her age she still had the energy to move into a new apartment; even housing was an occasion for her to find a new frontier.

Chris was wandering around the apartment staring at the pictures on the walls—a visual diary of Kate's life in hundreds of photographs. Kate bustled to the other end of the loft toward the kitchen, a large butcher-block island alongside the living room, open so that she could cook without being separated from her guests.

"Are you settling in all right?" she asked as she dumped a handful of spices into a pot of fish. "How's the new apartment?"

"It's fine," Cal said. "But New York always takes a little getting used to."

"Isn't it fabulous?" she said, stirring the pot. "There's so much to see that I always feel like I'm on a dig here. Just getting the ingredients for dinner took me to five different stores." She lowered her voice. "How's Chris taking it?"

"He has his ups and downs," Cal said. "He gets a little uncommunicative sometimes, keeps to himself. It's been hard on him."

14

"I imagine it's been hard on both of you," she said solicitously, and then shouted out across the room, "Chris, would you like something to drink? Some juice, a soda . . . ?"

Chris didn't answer. He was absorbed in examining the wall of photographs.

"You see what I mean," Cal murmured to Kate, and then, calling to Chris, "Christopher! Kate asked you a question."

Now Chris replied, not looking around. "No. I don't want anything."

Cal crossed the room to him. Chris was standing in front of an old photograph of Kate taken in a South American village. Kate was sitting in front of a grass hut, her second husband Quentin Kimball standing behind her, his hands on her shoulders, and in her lap was their young son, Scott. Of all the pictures Cal had seen of Kate, she looked happiest in this one; it was always poignant to remember that not more than a year after the picture had been taken, Scotty had died of a childhood disease. Cal thought sadly of the times when he and Laurie and Chris had been together like this. Manila, last summer. Sri Lanka the year before. Laurie and Chris, the three of them together.

"Bean," Cal said, "we're Kate's guests. She's gone to a lot of trouble for us. Try to be nice, okay?"

"Okay," the boy said a bit sullenly.

"Bean . . ."

"Okay, Daddy, okay," Chris said, and moved along down the wall.

Cal returned to the kitchen where Kate was tasting her recipe. "This is delicious," she said, licking her lips, "if I do say so myself."

Cal leaned against the edge of the counter, looking down at the tiled floor, disturbed by Chris's mood.

Kate put a hand on his shoulder. "It's difficult," she said.

Cal nodded.

"And the change of scene will help eventually," she said. "He'll come out of it."

"Sure he will," Cal said quietly.

"You sound doubtful. You don't regret the move or—"

"No, no, not at all," Cal said, trying to reassure her. "I really appreciate everything you've done. I just wish Chris . . . well, he used to be such a terrifically happy kid, bubbling over with energy. Now . . ."

Kate stirred the pot for a moment. "Cal, how are *you* handling it? Losing Laurie must've—"

Cal's head snapped up, his face suddenly taut and intense.

Kate went on. "You know, you've never talked to me about it at all. You're holding something in, Cal; it's not good for you. Laurie would've—"

"Please, Kate. Drop it. Just drop it. I don't want to talk about it."

Kate was silent, then reached out to touch him again. But he turned and walked out of the kitchen, leaving her dismayed in his wake.

⊃ ● ⊆

Dinner was a fish stew called woolliwow, a recipe Kate had brought back from one of her Pacific expeditions, and she went into extravagant detail about how the natives caught the fish and gathered the herbs. Her narrative was obviously meant to engage Chris, but the boy gave only the most cursory responses. There was not a sign of his normal eager curiosity, but Kate kept trying to reach him. She spun out tales of one adventure after another; when that provoked nothing more than meager attention she tried to excite Chris about the future—the bright side of being set down in a new place by a sad fate.

"Are you enjoying the city, Chris? There's such a lot to see, isn't there?"

"It's okay," Chris said.

Cal took up the slack. "We were up in Central Park today."

"Did you find the carousel?" Kate asked.

Chris nodded and idly played with his food.

"We also went to the zoo," Cal offered quickly.

Chris looked up abruptly. "And saw the animals," he said with curious emphasis.

Kate smiled. "Were the lions outside today?"

"No," Chris said. "Dead animals."

Kate studied him for a second, then switched her attention to Cal, mystified.

During the bus ride to Kate's, Cal had thought about the scene in the park, and now realized it might interest her, that it even had a certain anthropological significance. But before he had a chance to reply, Chris preempted him with more details.

"There were piles of them," the boy went on spiritedly. "Dead chickens and big turtles and a goat. All with their heads cut off. There was lots of blood and ants all over them and they smelled."

"It was apparently some kind of sacrifice," Cal said when Kate turned to him for confirmation. "Can you picture this? Right in the

16

middle of the city, some cult gets together under the moonlight and performs the most primitive ritual. And not for the first time. I heard one of the policeman say he'd seen it before."

Kate nodded. "I've read about this in the papers. Frankly, it doesn't surprise me. I think it's kind of wonderful."

"Wonderful?" Cal said, confused. Had he heard her correctly?

"Well, I mean that the city isn't quite the melting pot the sociologists say it is. People, even the strangest people, don't have to lose their identity here, and that's kind of refreshing. We've both seen ritual animal slaughter in primitive societies. If we were out in the field you'd think nothing of it."

Cal shook his head. "Kate, this wasn't an outdoor prayer meeting. It was a blood ritual, right in the middle of the city. Don't you find that a little shocking?"

Kate airily dismissed his concern. "Dear, nothing shocks me anymore. I've seen it all."

She excused herself to go into the kitchen and get dessert. Cal watched her cross the room, her caftan swirling around her. It was true she had seen everything, but he had to wonder at her blithe indifference. Maybe at her age she had begun to get a little eccentric.

She returned with a platter on which there was an orange confection resembling the helmet of a Swiss Guard.

"Special treat," she proclaimed. "Papaya bombe."

∋ • ∈

While Kate was clearing the table, Chris left his dessert half-finished and plopped in a corner of the living room, emptying his bag of arrowheads onto the floor.

"Chris, don't you want your ice cream?" Kate called out.

No answer.

Cal sighed and walked over with the plate. "Do you want this or not, Chris?" he asked.

But still Chris was silent, involved with his stones. Cal looked down at the pile, then at the one Chris was holding in his hand. It wasn't a stone at all, but a shell of some kind.

Chris held it up. "This belonged to Chief Black Cloud," he pronounced with authority.

Kate came up behind Cal and smiled. "He still has his imagination," she said. "That's a good sign."

"Chief Black Cloud had an army," Chris continued. "He fought wars all the time. He fought wars in the rain. In big storms."

Kate bent down and looked closer. "Can I see that a minute?" she asked. "You know, people have used shells for thousands of years for all kinds of things. The Indians used them for money, and the Pacific islanders for jewelry."

"I know," Chris said, handing her the object. "But this is a wishing shell. Chief Black Cloud left it just for me."

Cal smiled to himself at the boy's inventiveness. Kate held the shell a moment, staring at it pensively. Then she turned away and crossed the room. She stopped in front of the photograph taken with Quentin Kimball and their son. Cal thought he heard her sniffle, and saw her brush a hand across her cheek. Was she crying? What a selfish ass he'd been, worrying only about his own problems and forgetting the crushing losses that others had to bear. He had been out playing with Chris all day, and now Kate was reminded that she had been denied this parental pleasure. It was probably why she had taken Cal under her wing, and why Chris had always been like a grandson to her. But could the two of them ever completely make up for the family she had lost and would never have again?

"Daddy," Chris whispered, "is Aunt Katie going to keep my wishing shell?"

"No, Bean. Just give her a minute."

Kate turned from the photograph and came back slowly, eyes down. She turned the shell over once more in her hand, then handed it back to Chris.

For the rest of the evening she seemed distracted. Pouring a liqueur for Cal, she spilled a puddle of brandy onto the floor and stained her caftan. Later, when she was loading the dishwasher, she dropped a plate and a wineglass. The conversation was strained. She was upset, Cal guessed, by the flooding memories of her son.

For a while she seemed downright anxious for them to leave, but before an hour had passed her humor had revived. When she kissed them good night at the door, she was her old self.

"Did I tell you I'm doing the Johnny Carson show next week? Be sure to watch. I'm on with Joyce Brothers—I did Merv with her last year—and someone named Bo Derek. Tell me, dear, who in God's name is Bo Derek?"

Chapter 3

THE UNIVERSITY housing office had found him a place to live on West Twenty-third Street, in Chelsea. The apartment, occupying the entire first floor of an old brownstone, was not particularly convenient to the Columbia campus, which was much farther uptown, and Cal was irked by the high rent; there were houses in Albuquerque with three times the space for half the money. But New York was experiencing the worst housing shortage since World War II, and Cal accepted that by local standards he was damn lucky to have done so well: seven hundred dollars a month for two smallish rooms at the front, a closet-sized kitchen in the middle, and a large living room in the back that opened through French doors to the apartment's one redeeming feature, a rear garden. Cal had briefly met his upstairs neighbors—a night-court paralegal whom he hardly ever saw, and Millie and Jack Burke, a pair of retired Broadway scenic designers in the second-and-third-floor duplex.

When Cal and Chris returned from dinner at Kate's, it was a few minutes past ten. Chris immediately bolted for the television.

"Hey now, Bean," Cal said, "it's way past your bedtime."

At Kate's Chris had started watching a police series—cars chasing around in a demolition derby and the usual 2.7 violent deaths per episode. It was the kind of show Laurie had always ruled strictly out of bounds.

Chris pouted and stood his ground for a moment. "Can't I see the end?"

"Sorry, pal. You know I don't like you to watch that stuff.

You've got to be up early, remember?" Chris was enrolled in a day-camp program for the summer, and every weekday a bus stopped on a nearby corner at eight o'clock.

"Will you read to me?"

"All right. Now go on and brush your teeth."

Cal sighed. The process of endless negotiation in raising a kid could make ironing out a SALT treaty seem tame by comparison. At least it seemed that way without a partner on the negotiating team.

Cal went into the boy's bedroom. Chris hadn't made a start on undressing. He was sitting on his bed, sifting through the stones he had collected in the park.

"Jesus," Cal muttered, losing his patience. "You can play with your arrowheads tomorrow. Right now you get into your p.j.'s. Pronto!" He moved to the bed and reached out to collect the stones.

"Don't you dare!" Chris said with a sharpness that brought Cal up short—a ready-made rebuke forming on his tongue. *That's no way to talk to your father, young man.*

But Cal was arrested by his son's face, which wore an expression of fixed intensity directed toward the blanket. Cal looked back to the assortment of stones and saw that all of them had been pushed aside, isolating the shell.

Cal reached for it to take a closer look, but Chris grabbed up the shell as if to protect it. "It's mine," he declared.

"Sure it's yours," Cal said. "Finders keepers. Not every day you pick up a seashell in Central Park. The nearest ocean's fifteen miles away. Can I see it?"

Chris hesitated, then held out his open palm.

It was not the shallow flattish type from a bivalve, but a fragment of the swirled conical variety. The outer surface was etched with a row of angular markings. At first glance Cal had thought the shell was broken, but with closer examination he saw that the outer lip had been filed away, neatly baring an interior section of the shell's serrated edges so that it resembled a tiny mouth with opposing rows of minuscule teeth.

Cal handed the shell to Chris, who laid it on his pillow and undressed. As the boy was slipping into his pajamas, a thought struck Cal.

"It's interesting, Bean," he said. "Which part of the park did you find it in?"

"Somewhere. It just looked nice, that's all." The boy's face popped up through the neckhole. Something in Cal's tone had made him wary. "I can keep it, can't I?"

"Why not? I was only wondering . . ."

Cal stopped himself. It had occurred to him that the curio might have some connection with that strange tableau of dead animals. Animal sacrifice and practical uses of shells, after all, were both primitive customs. But why delve into it further? Why taint Chris's delight with a found treasure by linking it in his mind to some gory craziness?

Chris went off to brush his teeth and Cal gathered up the shirts and socks and toys strewn around the bedroom. He put the clothes into the Snoopy laundry bag hanging behind the door and stored the toys on a stand of built-in shelves. Turning down the bed, he saw the shell on the pillow and set it with the stones on the window-sill. From the bedside table he picked up the book he had begun reading to Chris a few nights ago. He gazed absently at the cover, an illustration of animals parading, two by two, into an ark.

⊃ ● ⊂

He had found the book, titled *Old Testament Stories for Children*, when he was packing up the house in Albuquerque. He had never seen it before; Laurie must have bought it with the idea of beginning to give Chris some religious awareness. Cal and Laurie had discussed the matter several times, and though there had been no rancor between them, they had found it difficult to agree. Cal's parents had been nominal Christians and loving people with high moral standards. But neither had been a serious churchgoer, and as Cal pursued an occupation that involved constant rational examination of the diverse and idiosyncratic in human customs, he had decided for himself that religion was only a form of superstition—necessary to some individuals, perhaps, but not to all. It had always been Cal's view that if Chris wanted religion in his life, he could make up his own mind when he was old enough to grapple with the complex concepts such a choice entailed.

Laurie's feelings had been quite different. Her family were German Jews, and had been among the fortunate few who were wise enough to emigrate when Hitler was named chancellor in 1933. Having survived while so many others perished, they saw the strict preservation of their religious customs as nothing less than a sacred mission. The rituals of Orthodox Judaism had been observed as a daily part of their lives. So rigid was their devotion that when Laurie came home from college to tell them that the graduate student she intended to marry was a Presbyterian from Ohio, her father had regarded it as the worst kind of betrayal. To see the blood of the family diffused by marriage into another faith was no less a loss for him than if it had been spilled in a Nazi charnel house. In response he had observed the Orthodox ritual of renunciation. He declared his wayward daughter dead; he sat *shiva*, weeping and saying prayers for her departed soul over a symbolic coffin. Neither Laurie's mother nor her sister had been willing to participate, however, in ostracizing her so extremely. Later, when Chris was born, there were visits from the women, a partial healing of the rift. But Laurie's father had died without ever speaking to her again, and had bequeathed to her none of the modest fortune he had acquired as a manufacturer of handbags. The result could have been to embitter Laurie to religion, to make her reject it for the strangling grip it could have on reason, perpetuating intolerance, destroying love between people in the name of love for the Almighty. But she had never been one to nurse grudges. She had no regrets about marrying Cal. Still, since he had no particular religious tradition he wished to perpetuate, she had asked him to let her instruct Chris in Judaism, and Cal had raised no objection.

He was reading the Bible stories to Chris now because it was what Laurie would have been doing if she were alive. The act itself gave Cal some sense of continuity with her spirit: it was his only form of prayer. In the cruel emptiness that had engulfed him after Laurie's death, he had been forced to modify his view of religion as mere superstition. For the first time in his life he wished his own background had not been so devoid of faith, and he understood the desperate need one could feel for belief in a holy purpose to human existence, a celestial plan. Perhaps he could never discard his pragmatism enough to embrace any gods, but in the absence of a belief in an afterlife, the soul, divine will, his grief had been all but unbearable. Nights of wailing, pillow crammed in his mouth so Chris, in the next room, would not wake and overhear. How could she be gone so suddenly, so unnecessarily? Could there be nothing more left of the warm flesh into which he'd planted his own than dresses hanging in a closet, flat images in a snapshot?

He yearned for an explanation of this brilliant disappearing act called death. He wanted to trust in some cosmic intelligence, with reasons for the giving and the taking away.

But he was a man of science; he couldn't allow himself the comfort.

Still, he didn't want his son to go without it, and so he had told

Chris that Mommy was in heaven. Told him, too, that it was Mommy who had bought the book for him and that, probably, when they read it together like this at bedtime, she was "up there," listening.

∋ • ∈

". . . and on the third day of their journey," he read, "Abraham saw the place in the distance. Then he said to the two servant boys who were traveling with them: 'Stay here with the donkey. The boy and I will go yonder to pray alone.' "

Cal paused, then started to close the book.

"Hey, you can't stop yet," Chris protested. "That was only one page."

Cal hesitated another moment. As usual, he had started reading at the place he'd left off last time. He had gone unthinkingly through several paragraphs before realizing exactly which Old Testament tale was unfolding. Then he wanted to stop. Hearing this story would be no good for Chris; he was already in a vulnerable state, questioning the permanence of relationships. The fable of a man asked by God to kill his own son was the stuff of nightmares.

"It's late, Bean. We'll go on with it tomorrow." Maybe he could skip past it then, start at a different place.

Chris clutched at Cal. "Daddy—please!"

There was an urgency Cal could not ignore. It had gone too far already, and Chris would be less distressed if he knew the ending, if it was explained right. Cal spread the book and his eyes searched for the new sentence.

"So Abraham took the wood for the burnt offering from the back of the donkey and gave it to Isaac to carry. Then he took the charcoal for the fire, and a knife, and he and his son went forth together. Then Isaac said: 'But father, are we not required to kill a lamb? Where is the lamb for the offering?' "

Cal halted, suddenly chilled by the coincidence—this story, the scene in the park. He glanced to Chris and saw the boy was mesmerized, anxious for more.

"And Abraham said: 'Have no fear, my son. God will provide an offering.' "

Cal read it to the end. The voice of God spoke to Abraham, commanded him to spare his son; and then Abraham saw the ram tangled in the thicket, and the animal was sacrificed instead.

"And they went down out of the mountain together," Cal concluded, and laid the book aside.

"Wow," Chris said. "That was scary. I thought Isaac was going to die."

"He was never really in any danger," Cal put in quickly. "His father loved him very much. You understand that, don't you?"

"Sure." Chris slid down under the covers. Cal studied the boy. His eyes were already closed. They could talk tomorrow if anything about the story bothered him. Cal leaned over, kissed him on the cheek, and turned off the lamp.

"Daddy?" Chris propped himself on one elbow.

"Yes?"

"Suppose, right at the end, God didn't tell Abraham not to hurt Isaac?"

"But he did, Bean. And Abraham knew he would."

"*How* did he know? He just did what God told him. He took his knife and went up the mountain alone with Isaac and—"

"But it was only . . . a kind of test. God wanted to see if this man trusted Him enough to do anything He asked. So He told Abraham to do a really hard thing."

Chris persisted. "But suppose God wasn't pretending about asking to make Isaac a . . . a sacker—"

"Sacrifice."

"Then what would Abraham do?" Chris asked plaintively.

In the dark, Cal rolled his eyes, exasperated yet somehow amused at being trapped in the web of a child's relentless logic. *If you're up there, sweetheart, give me a tip on how to get out of this one.*

Cal eased himself down onto the bed again and spoke as firmly as he could. "Listen, Bean, he would never have hurt his own son, I'm sure of that, and I'm sure he would never have to." Forget logic, Cal reminded himself; kids could why-and-how you to death. "Okay, Bean?"

"Mmmm," Chris said after a moment.

"Then snuggle down and get some sleep."

Cal gave him another kiss and tousled his brown hair. This time Chris wrapped his arms around his father's neck and hugged him tightly.

Cal was at the door when Chris stopped him again. An angry tone: "Hey! What'd you do with it?"

Cal sighed. "What?"

"My wishing shell. It was right here on my pillow."

"I put it with your arrowheads. I didn't think you'd be very comfortable lying on top of it."

Chris wasn't interested in explanations. Scampering straight to

24

the windowsill, he retrieved the shell, then scrambled back into bed.

Cal shook his head. "G'night, Bean," he said, and walked out.

Standing in the hall, smiling to himself, he felt a curious paternal pride about Chris's attachment to his new acquisition. The kid, he mused, was already showing the collecting habits of an anthropologist.

Chapter 4

THE FOLLOWING Thursday after putting Chris on the day-camp bus, Cal drove a rented van uptown through the morning rush-hour traffic to pick up his sister-in-law, Rachel Hanauer. It was Ricki, as she liked to be called, who had insisted it was high time to get his and Laurie's furniture out of the Brooklyn warehouse where it was stored. "You can't go on paying eighty bucks a month storage forever," Ricki had said in her typically hectoring tone.

She was waiting in front of her apartment building at Lexington and Seventy-third. Cal spotted her when he was still half a block away. She had black layered hair, and her trim figure was well displayed in a white V-neck pullover and tight designer jeans. She was as unlike Laurie as a sister could be—brassy and worldly-wise without a smidgen of Laurie's shyness or gentleness. Her take-charge urban toughness had, in fact, intimidated her younger sister and led Cal to dub her Queen Rachel of the Asphalt Jungle. But Ricki had been able to laugh at the remark, and that was why Cal liked her. Whatever Ricki's faults, she was humorous and generous and well-meaning. Her job as an editor at *New York* magazine gave her access to vast amounts of city lore. She knew the best dentist, the best French bakery, the best place to get quilts cleaned, and expected Cal to use them all.

"I hope you didn't get this from Hertz," she said the moment she climbed into the van. "That place I gave you charges ten bucks a day less, and you don't pay gas or mileage."

"I used yours," Cal said graciously. "Thanks for the tip."

Cal stopped at a corner as soon as the light turned amber. Ricki

26

said pointedly that she absolutely had to be back in Manhattan for a two o'clock editorial meeting. Then she turned conversational.

"So how does Chris like the camp? I know it's one of the best—Dusty Hoffman's kids went there."

"Two days ago he hated it," Cal said, adjusting the sun visor. "Yesterday he loved it. God knows what he'll think today. To tell you the truth, I don't understand him right now. It was hard enough before we moved, but his mood changes seem to have gotten worse. One minute he's cheerful and happy and talkative, and the next I can't get a word out of him."

Ricki lit a cigarette and put on her face of motherly concern. "You know what that boy needs as well as I do," she said.

Cal sighed at the opening strains of the familiar lecture.

"Well, six months *is* a long time, Cal," she went on. "You have to stop mourning. She was my sister, and I miss her, too. But if it's Chris we're thinking about . . ."

"All right, Ricki," he said.

But there was no stopping her. "I was just reading Charlotte Ford's etiquette book—we're excerpting the revised edition in our next issue—and she says three months is pushing it mourning-wise." She cast a sidelong glance at Cal. "How long has it been since you had a woman?"

Jesus, she could be irritating, Cal thought, and then had to brake sharply to avoid rear-ending a taxi. He chose to ignore her question, but Ricki continued as if he had answered anyway.

"That's the problem," she declared. Then she began listing a few of the "terrific" unattached women she knew. Someone named Muffy Danziger who was getting a law degree at NYU, and an old classmate named Sally Something-or-other.

Cal lost his patience. "It's too soon," he broke in. "I don't want a woman now, Ricki. I don't care what Charlotte Ford or anyone else says. Etiquette books have nothing to do with feelings." His voice had risen to a shout. Ricki turned away with a hurt look.

Quickly, as much of an apology as he was prepared to make, Cal added, "Give me time, Ricki. I need time . . ."

∋ • ∈

The closer Cal got to the warehouse, the more uncomfortable he was about retrieving Laurie's things. Having all the trappings of her life around him, without the person, would make her absence that much more painful.

He drove along the edges of Red Hook, a slightly seedy section of Brooklyn crowded with unused food-packing plants and deserted marine terminals. Looking at the run-down buildings, Cal recalled what Kate had said about man's conquest of nature; this riverfront must have been beautiful before industry's invasion.

"Over there," Ricki said abruptly, pointing.

Cal looked across two blocks of open parking lots and saw, painted on a high brick wall, FINE BROS. MOVING AND STORAGE, and below, PORTAGE, MARINE, CRATING. He wondered what "portage" was, and started scanning the warehouse for an entrance or loading bay. The sheer three-story wall facing him had no windows or doors.

He drove past the far end of the building and rounded the corner.

Almost at once he had to stop the van. A barricade of gray wooden sawhorses blocked the street. Fifteen or twenty people were lined up, leaning on the barriers—men with bottles in paper bags, women in drab smocks who might have left some assembly line to observe the excitement. Farther down the block stood a cluster of several fire trucks, their hoses snaking away through a large loading bay into one of the brick buildings. Beyond the trucks were a couple of police cars.

"Oh shit," Ricki said, "just what I need."

"It's not Fine Brothers, is it?" Cal said, as if wishing could make it true. He switched off the ignition and hopped out of the van. He ran to the barricade and was about to duck under it when a policeman who'd been standing at one end of a sawhorse addressed him loudly:

"Hey, you! You can't come in here."

Cal moved over to the policeman and explained politely that he had come to pick up some valuable belongings in the warehouse. He was relieved when the policeman told him that the fire was not in Fine Brothers, but in the basement of an abandoned building next door. However, the cop said, the street would have to remain closed for a while; Cal would not be allowed to bring his van in for loading until late in the day or tomorrow.

Cal took the news stoically and turned away. Ricki was out of the van now, and as she came up Cal explained the situation.

"Come back tomorrow?" she shrilled. "Are you nuts? You're not going to pay another day's rent on that van, and I'm not shlepping out here again." Hastily rummaging in her canvas totebag, she pulled out a pink laminated card shaped like a shield attached to a long chain. She slipped the chain around her neck.

"What's that?" Cal asked.

"Police press credentials. Comes with my job." Then, stepping around Cal and aiming herself toward the policeman, she murmured *sotto voce*, "I'll take care of this."

And she did.

A minute and a half with the policeman and he was pulling back a sawhorse so Ricki could pass without even having to duck under. She turned to Cal, waggled a finger for him to join her, and marched down the street toward the fire engines. A young fire marshal with a ginger mustache intercepted them, but nodded permissively when Ricki showed him her press shield.

"Can I get pictures to go with my story?" she asked the marshal. He shrugged. "Far as I know . . ."

Ricki thanked him and continued briskly toward the entrance to the Fine Brothers warehouse.

Cal was thoroughly mystified. "What was that about pictures?" he asked.

"Street smarts," Ricki said. "I'll tell them the van has the camera equipment and they'll let us bring it into the street. But first let me get the *Frères* Fine lined up so we can make a fast getaway." She winked at Cal and walked off.

He let her go alone, feeling that his naiveté might interfere with her manipulations.

Waiting in the street, his attention was drawn to the activity around the fire engines. Apparently the fire had been extinguished, because some of the hoses were being pulled out of the abandoned building, wound up again on large motorized spools. One contingent of firemen stood around a pumper truck, their heavy coats off, drinking coffee dispensed from a metal urn.

Cal strolled past the fire trucks. A fire chief's red station wagon, two police cruisers, an ambulance, and a couple of plain sedans were pulled up in a group. As Cal watched, a man dressed in everyday street clothes appeared in the doorway from which the hoses were being withdrawn. "It'll be coming out in a minute," he shouted to the ambulance driver, who was leaning against his vehicle smoking a cigarette. The driver flicked his cigarette to the pavement and went around to open the rear door of the ambulance.

Cal drifted closer. No one interfered with him. He had acquired that immunity which comes with having penetrated the territory of the privileged; he was assumed to belong because he was there.

A group emerged now from the doorway of the abandoned building. Two firemen, their cheeks sooty and their yellow slickers

29

smudged with ash, carried between them what looked like a long green plastic garbage bag. Two men in dark suits and ties walked alongside the firefighters, accompanied by a third man wearing a lightweight summer overcoat and gripping a black doctor's kit. The green plastic bag sagged in the middle, and Cal realized it was a body, and the man with the doctor's bag probably a coroner. No matter how small and easily controlled the fire had been, it had claimed a victim. Cal went closer to the ambulance, automatically reacting with the common, inescapable curiosity about death.

The body was placed into the ambulance and the firemen walked away. The other three men huddled off to one side.

"Well, doc," said the taller of the two men in plainclothes, "same business, right?"

"As far as I can tell, Lieutenant," answered the coroner. "Let me do the postmortem and I'll give you an official opinion."

"C'mon, doc, you really need a P.M.? How many homicides you get where they were killed *this* way? It's got to be connected. I'd just like you to go on record . . ."

Cal felt awkward eavesdropping on police business. The two men with the coroner were obviously detectives; the body in the plastic bag was not the victim of a fire but of a murderer. Cal wanted to retreat, but if he moved it might only make the detectives notice him more quickly and arouse their suspicion that he'd been snooping.

"Lieutenant MacTaggart," the coroner was saying, "the investigative side belongs to you. My job is to give an informed medical judgment, and before I can do that I like to have all the facts. I'll do an autopsy and give you the results."

"Okay, doc," the detective said.

"You'll have my report on your desk tomorrow," the coroner said, and left.

The shorter detective, who had been silent until now, turned to his companion, the "lieutenant." On the verge of saying something, he noticed Cal.

"Hey, bud," he demanded with an aggressive edge, "something you want?"

Cal tried a smile and backed away. "No, thanks. I'm just . . . waiting."

The lieutenant turned, too. "Waiting for what? How'd you get in here?"

"Press," Cal said cryptically, falling back on Ricki's demonstrated open-sesame.

But this time it didn't work. The lieutenant's expression darkened as he stepped forward. Tall and lean, he had a narrow face tapering to a long chin, not without warmth but with slight hollows in the cheeks. To Cal, the cop's face looked like something out of a medieval painting of an ascetic monk, the face of a man who had tested himself through some ordeal of the spirit.

"If you're a reporter," he challenged quietly, "then where's your pass?"

"Well, I'm not actually the one—"

Another man in plainclothes, sweating profusely and holding a cloth-wrapped bundle, came running up. "Just found these in the ashes, Lieutenant," he said urgently, and pulled back the corners of the wrapping. Nested in the cloth were a necklace of colored beads and a small brightly painted figurine that looked at first glance like a prize from a shooting gallery.

Momentarily forgetting Cal, the lieutenant lifted the figure and turned it around in his hands. Cal recognized it now as a plaster saint, draped in a red robe with a bland beatific face and a painted halo.

"Same goddamn thing," the lieutenant muttered, and returned the statue to the man who'd brought it. "Tag 'em and put 'em in my car."

The sweating plainclothesman hurried away.

Then, abruptly aware of Cal again, the lieutenant said roughly, "How'd you say you got in here?"

"My sister-in-law, she—"

"It's all set," Ricki said breezily, choosing this perfect moment to waltz up and address Cal as if the detective didn't exist.

"And who the hell are you?" the lieutenant said, getting even hotter.

Ricki flourished her shield again. *New York* magazine."

The detective rested a smoldering gaze on her for a long moment. "There's no press allowed in here, miss," he said then, clearly exercising control. "I'd like you to leave immediately and take your friend with you. If I see you taking notes, or asking questions, I'll have you put under arrest and I'll make sure that your press privileges are revoked—permanently."

Ricki stared back a second, lips tightly compressed, but she managed to hold her tongue. Slipping her arm through Cal's with face-saving nonchalance, she tugged him away.

"What the hell was that all about?" she murmured when they had covered half the distance back to the van.

31

"There was a murder," Cal said.

"So what else is new? But since they're so upset about it, we'd better load up extra fast."

Cal started to protest. Surely it would be wiser now to forget the furniture and come back another time.

But Ricki persisted. "Don't worry. That cop's too busy to bother with me. You'll have to learn that about the city. Threats are a way of life. But nobody ever means any harm. Now get the van, it's all arranged."

He did, and the Fine Brothers put the furniture into it, and in half an hour they were on their way as if nothing had happened.

Chapter 5

His office at Columbia was roomy and bright, with a wall of varnished bookshelves, six new metal filing cabinets, and three high windows facing the main quadrangle. In the academic pecking order it represented a solid level of achievement. The books and files he had shipped from New Mexico were waiting for him that afternoon, stacked neatly in one corner with their labels facing out. "Reference." "Lecture notes, myth." "Lecture notes, ethnology."

It took him two hours to fill the shelves. By tomorrow he would be ready, maybe, to start his book.

If anything positive could be said to have come out of the event that had destroyed his happiness, it was that now he would have no choice but to settle down and write, begin the project that would do for his career what Kate's early work had done for hers. On an expedition two years earlier to a Philippine archipelago, he had discovered the Zokos, a small tribe, a mere 137 people, who still lived in the Stone Age. Because they were such a small band, Cal was touched by their survival, their perpetuation of a way of life dating back more than a million years.

On a subsequent visit last summer he had gathered enough material for his book. The Zokos were cave dwellers and hunters, and spoke a language with barely one-tenth the vocabulary of English. Most astounding of all, they seemed to be gentle and content, utterly without violence. Cal wanted to set down in simple anecdotes the surprise and joy of his own collision with a people unaffected by the chaos of the Space Age. There was, he knew, nothing original about the theme; the French philosopher Rousseau had

33

written two hundred years ago that "nothing is more gentle than man in his primitive state." But Cal thought the message could be made new—and would be welcomed by those who felt lost and angry in a world of accelerating technology, where the only gentle being might soon be a robot. With luck, he might write a book as important as Kate's first effort, or Margaret Mead's *Coming of Age in Samoa*, or Desmond Morris's *The Naked Ape*.

What the Zokos had verified for Cal was the communality of all men. They had a classic mythology. The tribe lived in the shadow of a small and occasionally active volcano. Once, hundreds of years earlier, a tribal elder had climbed the side of the crater's shell, to live inside and understand its meaning. He had been there twelve days when the volcano chose to erupt. Immediately the tribe had a myth: deep inside the volcano, under the earth, lived a man in the form of fire—in short, a god who sent signals to those on earth. It was the myth of the vision-quest, the search for a Supreme Being. Moses went to the mountain, Jesus to the desert, Buddha to the hills, the Zoko to the volcano.

Yes, that was how he would begin his book. He might even call it *The Man in the Volcano*.

Ǝ ● Ɛ

At the end of the afternoon he had worked his way through the last of the cartons when there was a rapping at his open door.

"All moved in?" It was Kate.

Cal was surprised to see her. "I thought you'd already left on your book tour," he said. He cleared a stack of old *National Geographic*s from a chair and motioned her to sit.

"I'm leaving tomorrow," she said, "but I thought I'd better have a look in my old files and dig out a few extra yarns for Merv and Johnny." She fluttered her hands as she sat down. "I can't help worrying whenever I'm on TV that I've already told every damn thing that ever happened to me."

Cal laughed. "Katie, you could talk for a year of prime time and you wouldn't be near scraping the bottom."

She smiled. "I hope you're right. You know, I want so much to teach people about what anthropologists do, but if you want to teach these days you have to be entertaining—part salesman and part clown. I think Einstein knew it first. That hair! Those baggy pants!"

"You're not going to tell me that's why you started wearing muumuus?"

34

"No, that was to hide my fat behind. But I suppose I'd have to plead guilty to working on my image here and there, inventing myself a little bit."

There was a long pause, and Cal suddenly sensed that Kate's visit wasn't so casual. They had a piece of unfinished business, the same subject that had triggered his flare-up the other evening.

They both started to speak at once.

"Cal, I didn't want to leave without—"

"Listen, Kate, I shouldn't have been so—"

They stopped and smiled. The mutual effort was all the apology needed.

Kate was first to try again. "Perhaps I was prying where I shouldn't have—"

"No," Cal interrupted, but she silenced him with a motion of her hand.

"Cal, as close as we are, I don't have any right to trespass on your grief. If the best way to purge yourself is to grieve alone, no one should take that away from you. But it seemed to me that . . ." She checked him with a glance. She was resolved to speak after all, Cal realized—unstoppable Kate—but she was treading carefully.

"I've noticed," she went on, "that whenever Laurie's death is mentioned you steer away from the subject. I don't think that's good for you, bottling it up completely."

Cal nodded, head down like a sinner before his confessor.

"Maybe," he said.

"You know, Cal, when I was in Java last year I spent some time with the Galoum. They're a net-weaving tribe. When one of their young men or women dies, if the victim had a mate, the survivor goes to a special hut—a place that's only used for this purpose— and stays there to weep and tell all the memories of the mate he's lost, everything he can think of, everything they ever did together. The other members of the tribe take turns sitting with the mourner, listening until he's wrung dry, not a tear left. Then the mourner emerges from the hut and from that moment on never speaks of the dead again. Never even thinks about it." She shrugged her broad shoulders. "I suppose that's hitting both sides of the coin too hard, the mourning and the forgetting, but I don't think you've got the right balance either, Cal. You live alone with it too much. You've never even told me how it happened. All I know since the night you phoned is that it was an accident, and ever since then there's been . . . well, a news blackout, you might say."

A blackout, Cal thought. A blown fuse. An appropriate metaphor. He turned away from Kate and looked out the window, needing the light.

Kate went on. "It isn't really fair," she said, "to others who loved Laurie. We need to talk about it, too. That's part of the process of accepting death. And from what I've seen of Chris, I'd guess that he hasn't been given enough of a chance to get at his feelings . . . with you."

Cal stared out at the people passing through the quadrangle. He said nothing for a minute.

"You're right," he said finally, facing her. "I've wished a thousand times I could tell someone, but—" He broke off, defeated again by the shame and guilt.

"Cal, if you can't talk to me, then who? I loved her, too."

"But that's why!" he said in anguish. "That's what makes it so hard to be honest with you. Or Chris. Especially Chris."

Kate hesitated. Then she asked gently, "Why, Cal? Why don't you expect sympathy from those who loved her, too?"

The time had come. It had to be told.

He turned toward the window and looked out at the quadrangle. Suddenly the view was blurred, and only then he realized that the tears were welling in his eyes. For a moment he gripped the back of his chair as though he might fall. The memory and the guilt consumed his mind, exploding like a gas under pressure, and the imprisoned confession finally burst out of him.

"Because," he said, "I killed her."

⊇ • ⊆

They had risen late that morning. Late for them, anyway. Seven-thirty was the usual hour—Laurie to get Chris off to school, Cal taking coffee into the den before his early classes. But the night before there had been a party at the Burnetts', their best friends among the other young faculty couples. A good dinner, good conversation, and finally, when everyone was pleasantly mellow on wine, a funny game of charades with lots of the silly intellectual puns that flowed in academic circles. Jay Burnett, who taught Dramatic Lit., had contributed "Who's Afraid of Virginia Ham?" —which Cal had somehow managed to get across to his team in sixty-four seconds. With a grad student baby-sitting for them, he and Laurie had been able to stay out until three.

He remembered coming awake the next morning, a Sunday, to the feel of her hand, warm, lightly rubbing his lower back.

"Nice," he purred into the covers. And her hand moved over his hips, his thighs. He felt her long silky hair brush against his cheek, and opened his eyes. She was propped over him on one elbow, looking down, enjoying the pleasure reflected in his expression. How he adored her face, blonde bangs over feline green eyes. She put her hand between his legs, stroking, then started to slide down, her head ducking under the blanket.

Cal suddenly became aware of the sound of the television downstairs, dialogue about death-ray ships and laser beams coming up the stairwell through the open bedroom door. Chris was soaking in the Sunday morning "kidvid."

"Wait, honey," he said. "Let me close the door."

"Don't worry, he's into what he's doing," came Laurie's muffled answer from beneath the sheet. "And so am I."

Cal laughed and tried to relax. Amazing how demure Laurie appeared outwardly, then how brazen she could sometimes be about sex. He liked the combination.

"Honey, any minute he'll run up here and ask for breakfast."

"Will you shut up?" she requested softly. "He made his own already."

"Made his own?" Cal couldn't help remarking on it: a milestone. "Since when can he do that?"

Her head and shoulders shoved out into the light. "Put cornflakes in a bowl? Pour in a little milk and sugar? Cal, he's six. It doesn't take a prodigy."

"I just didn't realize he was already so . . . self-sufficient."

"He'll be asking for his own car next."

"You know what I mean. It's—I guess he's not a baby anymore."

She smiled touchingly. "No." Moving up closer beside him, she added, "Maybe that's why I feel so sexy."

"Where's the connection?"

She hesitated. "Cal, let's make another one. We've waited too long as it is."

They had discussed it occasionally, then let it slide by. Cal had grown used to having both his wife and son accompany him on field trips. A new baby would mean another hiatus. Two or three years, or maybe an end to it completely. Their kind of traveling with more than one child would be impossible. Two kids somehow worked out to ten times the distraction of one.

"It'll mean big changes," he reminded her.

"That's one thing," she said, "a woman never has to be told."

They talked a little more, but it didn't take much to convince him she was ready, her heart set on it. Two weeks ago, she admitted, she had stopped taking the pill. She wasn't thinking only of herself, she explained. "If you eased off on the globe-trotting, you'd get your book written. And if Chris had a little sister, he could be downstairs making *her* breakfast right now, instead of frying his brains on the idiot box."

Cal got up and locked the door.

After they finished, she hugged him and whispered, "You know, I have the damnedest feeling you hit a bull's-eye."

Chris was still in front of the television when they went down, though not, Cal noted gladly, watching cartoons. He had switched to a program about rare birds, a documentary with some footage in Maui. "Hey look, Daddy, we were there!" Chris exclaimed. The boy's memory amazed Cal. How old had he been when they passed through there? No more than three. Cal stood by Chris's chair to watch with him while Laurie went into the kitchen. "You deserve a real he-man breakfast this morning," she told Cal. "Juice, ham and eggs, toast and coffee comin' up."

It struck him only a minute later that she ought to skip the toast. He liked it with his breakfast—he'd never had a weight problem, was too skinny if anything—but he had brought home a new toaster two months ago and the damn thing had a flaw in the pop-up mechanism. Every third or fourth time the toast charred completely. Cal had been meaning to return it to the appliance store, but he'd been lazy about it, tolerating the inconvenience and wasted bread. Last Wednesday, however, a form letter had arrived from the manufacturer saying that a defect in this particular model had been discovered, and all buyers were entitled to a refund or free exchange. The letter also recommended discontinuing use of the toaster, since the defect created an increased risk of electrical shock. Cal had mentioned the recall to Laurie and told her he would do the exchange on Saturday. But then yesterday he had gotten tied up in conferences with a couple of his doctoral students and had neglected the errand.

He went into the kitchen. "Better skip the toast, honey. Remember that recall notice."

"No problem, it's already in and cooking nicely." She was running a mop over the floor near the counter. "Why don't you do the eggs while I clean this up."

"What up?"

"Seems our little culinary prodigy needs another lesson in preparing a bowl of cornflakes. He spilled half the milk on the floor."

Cal laughed. "But wasn't it clever of him not to bother us about it?"

He was beginning to fold the eggs into the pan when he smelled the toast burning. He glanced along the counter and saw smoke rising from the toaster. Laurie was nearer, at the sink, squeezing out the mop.

"Hey, get that, will you, honey?" he said quickly.

She hadn't noticed until now. Moving to the toaster, she pushed up on the handle that would manually lift the toast.

"Oh shit," she muttered. "It's jammed."

"Need help?"

"I've got it," he heard her say.

He was only half aware of what happened next. He heard a drawer open, the jangle of silverware. Sparing a glance away from the pan, he saw her begin fishing in the opening at the top of the toaster with the tines of the fork. He looked back to the eggs, almost done.

And then he heard the slight explosive *pop*. He spun toward it, startled, and saw her frozen in an awkward pose, leaning forward stiffly, her head bobbing up and down very slightly, eyes clenched shut.

There was another *snap*, and this time he registered the tiny blue spark crossing a gap between the smooth skin of her stomach where the robe had worked open and the metal trim on the edge of the formica counter. Now, instantly, his brain collected all the details, analyzed the problem, drew on memory, computed the odds.

Bare feet wet floor hands wet metal fork wires hot *the manufacturer strongly recommends that no further use . . .*

"Oh Jesus," he whispered. He lunged toward her and with the first quick step felt the tingle coming up through the sole of his foot where it touched the wet spot on the floor. Tied into the circuit now. If he touched her—

Was it only another second before he remembered the correct emergency procedure. Or longer? Longer, longer. But so goddamned obvious!

He yanked the cord out of the socket.

She crumpled to the floor like a flag falling with the sudden dying of a gale. Going to his knees beside her, he grasped her by the shoulders, started to pull her up and felt only dead weight. His fingers searched her wrist for a pulse, all thumbs, missing it *he was sure* only because he couldn't find the right pressure point. He bounded up and phoned for an ambulance. And as he slammed down the receiver after the call, saw the goddamn toaster. He snatched it up and hurled it with all his strength across the kitchen.

The crash brought Chris running. He froze at the threshold and stared into the room.

But Cal didn't notice. He was bent low over Laurie, trying desperately with every ounce of his breath and being to bring her back with the kiss of life.

∋ • ∈

There was a long silence when he finished telling it. He hadn't left much out, only the most intimate details. If Kate were to understand the impact on him, then she had to know everything, had to realize the craziness of fate, as he had. One moment they were planning to give birth to a new life—in the next, the very spring of that creation was destroyed. What logic could there be for such punishment?

"But why?" Kate said at last. "Why do you blame yourself?"

"Why?" Cal echoed in exasperation. It was as if she had understood nothing. "For Chrissakes, Katie, my wife didn't die from a disease or in a hurricane or from getting hit by a locomotive. She was killed by a *toaster!* I knew the thing was dangerous. I'd known for weeks, but I did nothing about it. Even after I'd been warned. I'd promised to make the exchange, but I just . . . goofed off. I left the thing sitting there like a fucking booby trap!" The guilt was pouring out, a stream he couldn't turn off. "Even then I could've stopped it in a dozen ways. If I hadn't been so casual about the recall. Why didn't I take it straight to the store? And why did I go on watching her make the toast? If I'd taken care of it myself when it started burning, if I'd moved faster . . . if—"

Suddenly he heard himself running on about it, the lethal *toast*, sounding like some nut, Queeg with his strawberries. "Good lord, can you believe it comes down to that? She died because the toast was burning. How the hell do I get used to that? The craziness . . . stupidity. Like some horror movie version of Dagwood and Blondie . . ."

He laughed, soft but with a shrillness around the edges, a hint of hysteria. Then the laughs turned into sobs and he covered his face with his hands.

"Listen, Cal," Kate said, "I can understand how horrible it must be for you. You can't help reliving it, and when you do you tell yourself that there was something more you could have done. But it's not true, Cal. Things happen . . . the way they're meant to

40

happen. If you could have saved her, you would have. It's life
. . . it's karma, that's all. Laurie's time had come."

Cal took his hands away from his face. He gazed at Kate, his
mentor, not so much comforted in his sorrow as distracted from it.
"Katie, you can't really believe that. Do you think our fate is
written down in a little black book God carries around in his hip
pocket?" He turned away. "If you want to help me, at least respect
what I feel. Don't think it'll be cured with a pat on the head and a
little pep talk."

"But I do believe in destiny, Cal." Her voice was soft, and yet
Cal could hear the profound conviction. He was astonished. He'd
never known this side of Kate at all, the woman of piety and
fatalism. She was a "doer," a force in her own right. How could
she subscribe to a philosophy that said people were not in control
of their own lives?

"I don't understand, Kate. How can you accept what's intangi-
ble, illogical, irrational?"

"Shouldn't a scientist believe his own research?" she asked.

"And in what laboratory did you prove the existence of fate?"

Kate smiled. "In every primitive society I've ever studied, the
most striking characteristic was the simple unquestioning accep-
tance of the world as it is, as it was given to us. That may not
prove empirically the concept of destiny, but it's proven to my
satisfaction the value of simply not doubting it. Primitives were—
are happier than we are, Cal. They know the limits of their power,
understand their dependence on forces beyond their control. Whatever benefits they get from the weather, the tides, the stars, they
receive gratefully—taking nothing for granted. And whatever trials
befall them are accepted without complaint. There's a"—she
paused, seemingly intent on finding the right phrase to convey her
awe of these ancient attitudes—"a sense of their harmony with the
whole universe, the contract that exists between mankind and the
powers that be. I find that enviable, Cal, and I mourn the loss of
it. We're so damn convinced we control our own fate. That's what
science has taught us . . . this egotism. All the sciences, that is,
except one. Ours, Cal. Anthropology. We have to teach the opposite—that man *isn't* all-powerful. We have to bring back the lost
lessons, and we have to remind ourselves of our place in the scheme
of things . . ."

Listening to her, Cal was transported back to the first time he'd
heard her on a lecture platform. He remembered how she had
inspired him. But he couldn't agree with her. He had his own

reverence for primitive people—the marvels of their ingenuity and imagination, the nobility of their struggle to survive. And he mourned their gradual extinction from the earth. But he couldn't say the course of progress had to be reversed. Along with primitive man's respect for the forces of nature went fear and superstition.

Kate seemed to anticipate his objections. "But goodness, dear," she went on, "I didn't come to debate anthropological theory. I was only hoping to cheer you up."

Cal was about to say he couldn't become superstitious for the sake of being easier on himself, but instead he leaned over her chair and kissed her on the cheek. "Thanks for trying, sweetheart."

She rose to her feet and they embraced, then she said good-bye and was bustling out the door, her muumuu swirling around her like a colored cloud.

Cal stood motionless for a moment, thinking. If only he could put the suffering behind him, stop the incessant reruns of that short horror film in his head.

He picked up the stack of *National Geographic*s from his desk and put them on the shelf.

Karma.

Fate.

Kate's words lingered in his brain, the promise of self-forgiveness.

Christ, yes, how nice it would be to believe . . .

Chapter 6

He put through a call to Santa Fe as soon as he got home.

"Ulrich, Haig and Markey," came the answering voice.

"Bill Markey, please," Cal said to the law firm's receptionist.

Bill Markey was the young lawyer who had agreed to handle Cal's lawsuit against the Universal Appliance Company. For their negligence in manufacturing and marketing the instrument of his wife's electrocution, Cal was seeking damages of two million dollars. He wished he could sue for a hundred million. It wasn't a matter of money; it was using numbers as a language of grief.

Markey came on the line with a warm greeting and some concerned questions about Cal and Chris and how they were adjusting to life in the "wild, wild East." Cal raced impatiently through the answers.

"What's been happening?" he asked finally. "I haven't heard from you."

Cal detected a low sigh before Markey replied. "You haven't heard from me, Cal, because they're still stalling." The company, Markey explained, had filed motions and countermotions to keep the case from going to trial. This was standard courtroom practice. Markey had warned Cal that the case could go on for six, seven years, and cost thousands of dollars to fight before Cal saw any return—if he ever did. The cost in time and energy and peace of mind could be crippling. There were people whose health had been broken by fighting giant companies, and Markey's counsel from the beginning had been to save his money and strength and go on, forego vengeance.

"So what do you want me to do?" Markey said now, prodding Cal to reconsider.

"I want you to fight them," Cal said.

"Then you're not going to toss it in?"

"I can't," Cal said. This, only this, could comfort him.

Markey warned him again that the legal bills were already high.

"Just keep going," Cal instructed him. "I'll get the money some-where." An advance on his book, maybe, if he could finish it by autumn.

"I'm not worried, Cal," Markey said. "Not about anything but you."

That made two people worried about him today, Cal thought as he hung up the phone.

Was he being self-destructive? Was Markey right? There had been an old professor in Albuquerque who had fought a plagiarism suit on one of his textbooks for seven years, who had even sold his house to pay the legal bills. And in the end he had lost.

If something didn't break soon, Cal thought, maybe he would give up the suit.

His eyes rested on the wall above the fireplace. Until that morn-ing it had been blank, but now Laurie's favorite tapestry hung there, a blue-and-gray abstract called "Weeping Willow." Next to the fireplace was her Edwardian wing chair, where she had sat for hours reading *Barnett's Looms and Weaving* and giggling at *Fear of Flying*. And next to the window, the antique child's loom she had picked up on their way back from the Painted Desert.

No, he couldn't give it up, no matter how long the lawsuit took, no matter what the cost.

∋ ● ∈

"Is time for eat," Mrs. Ruiz said, and Cal dragged himself away from his memories.

Carmen Ruiz, the housekeeper, was a chubby, good-hearted woman in her mid-fifties who lived nearby in the neighborhood. The apartment's former tenant, a visiting economics professor from Sweden, had enthusiastically recommended her, and Cal had hired her full-time. She picked up Chris from the day-camp bus every afternoon, cleaned the apartment with a thoroughness amounting to obsession, tended the garden, and several nights a week cooked spicy masterpieces that gave Cal heartburn.

At dinner Chris, surprisingly, was in an upbeat mood. Cal had thought seeing Laurie's things would throw the boy into another

44

funk. But he merrily counted to twenty in Spanish to Mrs. Ruiz's pleasure and wolfed her *ropa vieja*.

After dinner Mrs. Ruiz scrubbed the kitchen as though it were an operating room. There was something faintly comic about the way her loud print dresses accented the rolls of fat at her waist, and the constant jangle of her bracelets and earrings as she cleaned and cleaned, rubbing every surface several times and leaving the prickly smell of ammonia in the air. After she claimed her straw bag from the broom closet and packed her things, she swept around the apartment for a final proprietary check of its cleanliness. Then, before leaving, she lit a stick of incense to mask the ammonia, and went home.

Cal had trouble falling asleep that night. For half an hour he watched *Nothing Sacred* on Channel Eleven's Ben Hecht festival, but the idea of Carole Lombard having six months to live somehow failed to make him laugh. Lying in the dark, he was struck by the odd sensation that Laurie was with him in the room. The feeling was so vivid that he reached over and patted the other pillow. Nothing was there except the starchiness of the cotton. But the notion that she was lying next to him remained—so real, so keen, that he imagined he felt her hair brushing against his cheek as he finally drifted into sleep.

∋ ● ∈

Chris's whimpering woke him up. The bedside clock's digital numbers said 1:25. Cal listened for a moment, coming into consciousness. It wasn't crying exactly. Moaning. Painful moaning.

Cal threw off the topsheet and leapt up. Yanking open the door, he stubbed his toe and yelped. In the hallway he groped for the light switch.

"Coming, Bean—"

The boy was huddled against the wall in the corner of his bed with the sheet drawn over his face. "No. No, please don't," he was sobbing.

Cal pulled the sheet away and light from the hallway fell across the boy's face. His lips were quivering and he was deadly pale. "Wake up, Chris," Cal said firmly.

"Stop!" Chris shouted. Cal sat down on the bed and wrapped his arms around him, brushing sweaty strands of hair from his eyes.

"Bean! C'mon!"

Chris's eyes snapped open.

"What's the matter, Bean?"

The boy sniffled, shivering, and Cal tucked the sheet around him. The sobbing continued, tears spilling down his cheeks, and the look on his face was of terror mixed with confusion.

"It's all right, Bean, I'm here," Cal said, pulling him tighter. But Chris recoiled. His hands flew to his face, shielding his eyes, and his sobbing deepened into sharp gasps.

"Tell me what it was, Bean. What frightened you?"

Slowly the boy lowered his hands. "I was on an elephant," he began tentatively, "riding an elephant."

"Okay," Cal said gently. "What about the elephant? Where were you going?"

"You were in front of it," Chris said, "you had a rope around the elephant's neck with these . . . these big red and yellow beads on it . . . and we were going higher and higher."

"Where, Bean, where were we going?"

"Higher up the mountain," Chris said. "We were going the whole way up to the sky. It was like the elephant was flying, because then there wasn't any mountain and we were in the air."

"And you were afraid we'd fall?"

"No!" Chris said. And was silent.

"C'mon, Bean," Cal urged. "Tell me the rest of it."

Very quietly, Chris went on. "We were going to see Mommy and we were up at the top and you . . . you were holding a. . . ." He looked away.

"*What* was I holding?"

"It . . . you were going to hurt me. You were going to do something terrible to me!"

"What was I holding?" Cal asked again.

The boy said nothing.

"Bean, you know I'd never do anything to hurt you." Cal put his hand gently to Chris's face and pulled him around so he could look into his eyes. "You know that, don't you?"

"But it was so *real*, Daddy," Chris said.

Cal held his son for another twenty minutes, rocking him in his arms. Eventually, without another word, the boy dozed off.

Cal covered him with the sheet and lingered in the room in case he woke up again. But Chris slept soundly, with no sign of disturbance.

Cal walked through the living room and stepped out the garden door into the warm summer air. In an apartment on the second floor of a building across the way, a party was in full swing. Two

46

men standing on a terrace argued loudly about the president's effect on the credit markets. The garden was fragrant with flowers and herbs. Cal leaned unsteadily on the fence separating him from the yard next door. He thought about Chris's dream and doubly regretted having read the Abraham and Isaac story. He should have seen it coming. You mix in the Bible with memories of Burma churned up by animals at the zoo and add Laurie's things in the apartment—well, the kid was likely to have a nightmare. But the idea that he could dream of Cal hurting him, what could you make of that?

"There's going to be a total credit collapse," the man on the terrace was saying.

Cal turned back into the living room.

You were holding . . .

What could he have been holding, Cal wondered, to hurt his son so terribly?

From across the way he heard another voice chime in, "If you ask me, the whole damn world's coming to an end."

Chapter 7

IT WAS THE next day, quite by accident, that he saw the clues to the murder.

He had been at home transcribing notes for his book from his field journals, and he had run out of index cards. At a little after two he went out to buy some more.

Whatever the drawbacks of Chelsea, Cal enjoyed strolling through the neighborhood. Kate was right: living in the city was not unlike being on a field expedition. In Chelsea especially there was a colorful street life that had been totally absent from the homogeneous affluence of his Albuquerque suburb.

At the turn of the century, Chelsea had been a wealthy residential area, its brownstones and brick town houses inhabited by merchants and bankers. The financier Jay Gould had lived here, and Boss Tweed, and Edith Wharton. Later the neighborhood had gone into steep decline. Once gracious residences had been converted to rooming houses; the rococo apartment buildings became run-down slums. Arriving immigrants, Hispanics mainly, had settled in during the decades after the last world war.

But these days Chelsea was, as the real estate agents put it, a neighborhood "in transition." Many of its brownstones were being turned back into single-family dwellings or renovated as small co-ops. More and more restaurants and boutiques catered to the new wave of middle-class residents. Yet the ethnic character that had taken root over the years was not being summarily swept away. On the corner of Cal's block a new chrome-fronted hairdressing salon stood cheek-by-jowl with Raoul's Bodega, a dingy hole-in-the-wall grocery specializing in *chorizo*, canned *frijoles*, and hot stuffed peppers. On warm days there would always be a group of people seated on folding chairs outside Raoul's chattering in Spanish. Cal had read in the *Times* that fully fifteen percent of the city's population was Hispanic—almost two million people, more than the population of some Caribbean republics. The foreign language in the streets and the *salsa* music blaring from the tenements' open windows sometimes gave Cal the illusion of being in another country.

At the corner of the block, he paused and looked up and down Eighth Avenue. Now where exactly had he seen a stationery store —north of the savings bank? He turned uptown and found it two blocks away.

Returning home, Cal decided to take the long way around, see more of the locale.

He had just turned off the avenue onto Twenty-second Street when he passed a small storefront with an eye-catching sign hanging from a bracket over the pavement. "Botánica Del Arco Iris," it read in gold-outlined black letters over a childishly uneven painting of a rainbow. Cal glanced through the window, but the glare of the sun bounced off its almost opaquely grimy surface. What was the place? A flower shop? Cal cupped his hand over his eyes and moved up to peer through the dusty window.

A bizarre array of junk filled the casement, a demented pop sculptor's tableau: statues, feather dusters dyed garish shades of pink and purple, strands of beads in dozens of different color combinations—yellow with green, yellow with red, red and black, green and brown and white. Necklaces were they? Or rosaries? Next to them stood a row of plaster figures. Cal looked closer.

Saints.

Beads.

Cal thought back to the ascetic-looking cop standing outside the warehouse in Brooklyn. The evidence found in the ashes.

Clues to a murder.

He went in.

A bell tinkled quaintly as he pushed open the door. The store was narrow and cramped by the shelves that ran ceiling-to-floor on both sides, and standing display racks that crowded the floor. But it was brightly lit by banks of fluorescent tubes and spotlessly maintained. Not a speck of dust on the shelves. The wood floor glistened.

49

Cal scanned the merchandise. Immediately inside the door a wire rack held an assortment of crudely printed pamphlets. *Paul Benoit's Charts of the Stars, Answering All Inquiries for Health and Happiness* was stocked in great quantity. And *Numerology: Your Personal Keys to Betting, Life Problems, Illnesses*, conspicuous in a bright yellow cover with a border of numbers. Ah yes, Cal thought, add up your birth date, divide by two, add your weight, divide by three, and bet the Quiniela at Hialeah. Next to the pamphlets an adjacent rack was brimming with small jars and vials of colored liquids. Cal read the labels. "Dragon's Blood Bath Oil." "Glow of Attraction Oil." "San Isidro's Balm."

He lifted his gaze to the shelves. There were ornate bottles of more colored liquids, these labeled in Spanish. Cannisters holding dried flower stalks. More beaded strands on pegs. Bars of soap in colored wrappers. And candles—hundreds of them, maybe thousands. Bulky cylinders of wax in highball-sized glasses. The candles came in every color of the rainbow, and in white or black. And one type—the most popular seller, filling a shelf of its own—combined six or seven hues in layers. They were votive candles, Cal thought. Stenciled on the glass containers he saw the names of different saints. The side of every tumbler filled with the multicolored wax bore the words "Seven Powers Candle."

Cal turned from the shelves to the back of the store. In front of a white formica counter with a cash register stood a couple of customers, a bow-legged elderly woman in a shabby coat, and a young girl in hiphuggers and a red bolero blouse. They were being attended to by the proprietor, a matronly woman in her fifties wearing a pink cable-knit cardigan over her shoulders and rhinestone-trimmed glasses on a chain around her neck. Her black hair was pulled high on her head and wrapped tightly in a bun, held in place by several tortoiseshell combs. She was listening intently to the elderly woman, whose voice emerged in a plaintive whine Cal could hear from the front of the store.

"*Son mis venas varices,*" the old woman said, reaching down to touch the back of one of her blue-veined legs. "*Los médicos no me pueden hacer nada. Tiene la poción?*"

Cal understood enough Spanish to know that the customer was saying something about her varicose veins and the doctors not helping her.

The proprietor put on her rhinestone glasses and turned away to open a glass-fronted apothecary's cabinet behind the cash register. On the shelves were several dozen Mason jars, the kind Cal recalled his mother using to preserve fruit. The jars were marked with masking tape and filled with what appeared to be shredded weeds and wild flowers. The proprietor took down one of the jars and scooped out a cup of greenish powder into a brown paper bag. Then from another jar she added a handful of dried leaves. Basil, maybe, or oregano? Cal moved toward the counter for a better look.

Now he became aware of the saints, more plaster statues of all sizes and description crowding high shelves on the rear wall. Some were in the customary saintly garb of long flowing robes. Many had haloes encircling their heads, but others wore crowns. One figure of a young girl cradled a lamb in her arms. A mantled woman brandished a lightning bolt like a sword. Cal spotted a group of figures identical to the one he had seen the detectives examining at the warehouse. Which saint was it? Francis, Christopher? He didn't know the liturgy well enough to identify any of the figures. Yet it seemed that these were not conventional religious articles. The facial features were crudely modeled—except for the eyes, cast not in the traditional glance aimed upward toward heaven in pious supplication, but staring straight forward. Cal felt the eyes of the statues looking through him and averted his glance as if caught staring at a stranger on a bus. Then, on the shelves of a rear side wall, he noticed an array of aerosol cans. "Aerosol de Santa Barbara" read the lime green wrapper on one can. Was she the patron saint of housewives? Cal wondered. There were saints' names on all the aerosol containers. This made no sense at all. Why would spray cans be named for saints?

"May I help you?"

The proprietor had interrupted her service to the other customers, and moved along the counter to stand directly in front of Cal. When Cal was slow to answer, she said, "Is there something I can do?" And smiled.

"I'm . . . new in the neighborhood," Cal said. "I've never seen a store like this before. I was just wondering what a *botánica* is."

"We sell religious items and herbal remedies," the woman answered matter-of-factly, her smile fixed so tightly it might have been glued on. The smile was positively eerie, Cal thought. Full and sweet and charming, but at the same time unnervingly frigid. The smile said *Welcome*, but a message behind it said *You are not wanted here*. Her black eyes remained fixed on him, as though merely waiting to serve, but the tilt of her head conveyed a sense of regal superiority. Cal looked around at the shelves once more, as though trying to select a purchase, then into the cabinet of Mason jars. He could read the inked inscriptions on some of the masking-tape labels. "St. John's Wort," said one. "High John the Conqueror Root." "Five Finger Grass." "Jumbie Seeds." "Devil's Shoestring Root." "Buchu." "Job's Tears." Herbal remedies? Cal had never heard of them.

"Yes," the proprietor said, pushing her bejeweled glasses higher on her nose. "You're sure there's nothing you'd like?" The menacing radiance of her smile was undimmed.

It was all too strange for him. Suddenly he was anxious to leave.

"No, thanks very much," he said.

She was still smiling her awful frozen smile as he walked out the door.

Her face stayed in his mind, along with the saints, and the beads, and the strange names on the labels. He ought to call that detective, Cal thought, and all the way home he tried to remember the man's name.

∋ ● ∈

He came into the apartment and went to the living room where he had set out his journals on the desk by the window. He was halfway across the room when he glanced out into the garden. There, kneeling and facing the fence, Mrs. Ruiz was hunched over a flat slab of stone, probably from the old crumbling wall that ran through several of the block's backyards. She was wearing bulky rubber gardening gloves and with her left hand was holding the slab steady against her knees. In her right hand she was gripping a small stone that she scraped back and forth over the surface of the larger one. As Cal watched, she stopped scraping and brushed some powder from the slab into a plastic sandwich Baggie. Then she turned to the soil bed beside her and yanked up a sizable weed stem. Methodically she peeled off the leaves and, when she had a small pile, set about pulverizing them with her makeshift mortar and pestle. For a moment, Cal had a vision of a peasant scrubbing clothes by a river. Scrape, bend. Scrape, bend.

Again she stopped, held her plastic bag against the edge of the stone, and carefully brushed in the powder. Wiping the sweat from her forehead with the back of her arm, she began stripping leaves from another uprooted weed.

Curious, Cal went to the garden door. "What're you doing, Carmen?" he called amiably.

52

She looked up, startled. Seeing him, she stood and hastily jammed the plastic bag into a pocket of her apron.

"Escuse, escuse," she said, and came bustling into the apartment.

"What's in the bag?" Cal asked.

She halted, and ran her tongue over her lips. Her eyes darted around the room, and then down to the bag in her apron.

"*Las yerbas*," she said, almost inaudible.

"Pardon me?"

"*Solo . . . solo las yerbas*, only *yerbas*." She rubbed her hands together, nervous at her failure of language. "*Como . . . como mostaza. Entiende?*"

"*Mostaza?*" Cal said, shaking his head.

Her brow furrowed a moment. Then her face lit up.

"Moos–tard," she exclaimed. "*Yerbas*. For eat."

"Ah," Cal said. "Mustard."

"*Sí, sí*," Mrs. Ruiz nodded with relief.

Cal understood: she had been chopping herbs for cooking. But why was she so nervous and visibly flustered at being discovered? She kept looking at the floor or glancing in the direction of the kitchen, never letting her eyes meet his, and holding tight to the bag in her apron. Cal guessed that she must have planned to take the herbs home. Well, why not? She was the one who did the planting and watering of the garden, after all.

"Carmen," he said, "you know it's perfectly all right with me if you take things for yourself from the garden. You don't have to hide that from me."

She gazed at him blankly for a second. Then the strain went out of her expression. "Ah, *sí*. Is to cook for my Eduardo. You not mind?"

Eduardo was her husband, who cleaned buses at the Port Authority. "Absolutely not," Cal said, gesturing to the garden. "Help yourself to whatever you want. Take some of the tomatoes home, too. Please."

"You real not mad?"

Cal smiled. "No, I'm not mad." Poignant, he thought, that she could even imagine he would chastise her for taking away a few dried leaves.

Carmen thanked him, tidied up the kitchen, and before leaving put her *arroz con pollo* on low heat to simmer.

That night Cal went to the refrigerator to get an apple for a late snack. As he reached into the crisper, he saw behind a mound of celery a sealed plastic Baggie filled with green powder. It looked like the one Carmen had been filling in the garden. She must have forgotten it.

He wondered how much difference it had made to Eduardo's dinner.

Chapter 8

"BUY ME A CANDLE, Daddy," Chris said.

Cal had sent Carmen home early and picked up Chris himself from the Camp Hawthorn bus, a chance for a little more father-son contact. Together they had gone to the Chinese hand laundry to pick up Cal's shirts. Walking home afterwards they had passed the *botánica*.

Chris was bent forward, his nose pressed to the front window. "Please, Daddy," he pleaded. "Get me one of those candles."

"No, Bean. You don't want anything like that." Cal hooked an arm around his son to tug him away, but Chris remained pressed to the glass, squirming from Cal's grasp.

"But Daddy, look at that one up there with all the colors! Please buy it for me."

Cal resisted. The woman's off-putting smile had stayed with him. The saints and beads and jars full of strangely named substances. Devil's Shoestring? No place for a kid. He really ought to call that cop, Cal reminded himself. How did you go about calling someone if you couldn't remember his name?

"Daddy, come *on*," Chris said, and before Cal could grab him he had scampered away into the shop. Cal bounded after him.

The woman was alone behind the counter, reading the afternoon *Post* through her rhinestone-rimmed glasses. She looked altogether harmless, a woman who sold plaster saints to the devout and desperate poor. At the sound of the tinkling bell she raised her head. For a moment her face was blank, then a smile creased her cheeks, this one utterly benign. Chris had stopped in front of the wall of candles, staring up at a high shelf.

"Can I help you?" the woman said, addressing herself to Chris.

"I want a candle," Chris said eagerly.

The woman pulled off her glasses and they fell to her chest, suspended on the chain. "Of course." She started dragging a step-ladder from behind the counter.

Cal took a step forward as if to intervene, but the woman gave him a quick glance that was somehow friendly and reassuring, expressing a kindred tolerance. *Funny, the things that children want.* Was this the same woman he had seen before? There was no sign of recognition from her, and no hostility.

"Which one would you like?" the woman asked as she set up the ladder.

Chris put a fist on his chin and squinted at the shelves, one eye closed like a savvy diamond appraiser.

"How about a green one?" Cal said, a random suggestion to speed the process of decision.

"No," Chris said at last, and pointed to the top shelf. "I want that one—with *all* the colors."

The woman climbed up and brought the glass cylinder down to Chris. "It's very pretty, isn't it?" she said, handing it over.

Chris nodded and raised the candle up to the light. Again, Cal saw the words stenciled on the side of the glass container: "Seven Powers Candle." Cal didn't know why—it was only some multi-colored wax—but he didn't like the idea of Chris having it.

"I can have it, can't I, Daddy?" Chris said.

"How much is it?" Cal asked the woman.

"Five dollars."

"Oh, that's too much, Bean," Cal said. "Let's go."

"Daddy," Chris protested. "We waste five dollars all the time."

"This candle is hand-dipped, sir," the proprietor said. "Made especially for Del Arco Iris. It will burn for two weeks."

Chris clutched the candle and turned expectantly toward Cal.

He gave in. "Okay, Bean. You've got it."

He reached for his wallet and fished out a five-dollar bill. The woman took the candle from Chris, returned to the counter, and put it in a paper bag. Cal gave her the money and reached for the bag, but the woman came out from behind the counter again and breezed past him.

"The colors will be very beautiful," she said to Chris, and laid the package in his eagerly outstretched hands.

⊐ ● ⊏

They stopped and ate Kentucky Fried Chicken, and went afterward to Baskin-Robbins. Cal had a coffee cone while Chris gorged himself on two scoops of double-chocolate-chip. Which reminded him to ask Ricki who the best dentist was. She was undoubtedly on intimate terms with whoever cleaned Halston's teeth and Liza Minnelli's and Dustin Hoffman's, too.

They went home and he let Chris watch "Happy Days." At bedtime Cal went on reading the Bible stories. They were up to the Flood, but the negative side of the tale didn't seem to bother Chris. He liked the aspect of saving the animals.

When it came time to turn off the lamp, Chris said, "Light my candle, Daddy."

"Not now, Bean. You're going to sleep, and fire can be—"

"But remember the pumpkin on Halloween? You let me have that on when I went to sleep."

"Bean, this candle is in a glass, and when that gets hot it can crack and—"

"I want it *on*, Daddy," Chris proclaimed, sitting up in bed.

Cal relented. Chris was ready for sleep. An argument now would agitate him, keep him up for an hour or two.

"Okay, Bean," he said. "But only for a little while."

Cal went into the kitchen, found a book of matches, and returned to Chris's bedroom. The candle was on the windowsill. Cal lit the wick and the shimmering flame bathed the room in soft light. The seven-colored wax seemed to become luminous; the prism effect of the glass projected rainbows onto the floor and the walls.

"Thanks, Daddy," Chris said and snuggled down under the sheets.

Cal waited half an hour until Chris was sleeping soundly, then went back to the bedroom. He stared at the glowing corona around the candle on the windowsill. Creepy, that store. Cal thought for a moment of just taking the candle away, tossing it into the garbage.

But he reconsidered and, wetting his fingers, squeezed out the flame.

Chapter 9

IN HIS OFFICE the next afternoon he tried to reach the detective from the warehouse murder. It was probably foolish in a city this big to think of citizenly duty, but in Santa Fe there had been a string of murders solved by one telephone call, one man who had ignored the don't-get-involved advice of his friends.

Cal started by calling the Brooklyn precinct near the warehouse. The phone was answered by a man with a classic Brooklyn brogue. "Ninety-second. Passarella speakin'."

Cal told the policeman that he had information about the murder on Farrell Street.

"Hold on."

The line was left open while he waited, and he could hear voices in the background, mentions of "a guy on the phone," "a tip on the warehouse thing." He had visions of a trace being put on the line, an assumption that he was the killer making an anonymous call.

But the cop came back on the line quickly and said, "The man you want operates out of the Two-three Squad, Manhattan. His name's MacTaggart."

Yes, that was the name he had heard. "That's it," he acknowledged. The connection was broken before he had a chance to say thanks.

The Two-three? Cal took the numbers to be police parlance for the Twenty-third Precinct in Manhattan, which was odd. He wondered what procedural technicality determined that a crime committed in Brooklyn would be investigated by a policeman based in Manhattan.

He referred to the "blue pages" in the Manhattan phone book. The precinct, he noted as he took down the number, was on East 103rd Street.

He dialed again.

"Twenty-third, Detectives."

"Lieutenant MacTaggart, please."

"Speaking."

Cal wasn't quite sure how to go on. "Lieutenant, my name is Calvin Jamison. You may not remember me . . . we met at that warehouse in Brooklyn where someone was murdered . . ."

"Yes?" the detective said flatly. He gave no indication of recalling the meeting.

"Have you solved the case yet?" Cal asked.

"Why are you asking, Mr. Jamison?" The detective spoke politely, but somehow managed to get across in no uncertain terms that *he* was the one who asked the questions.

"I might have some information you can use," Cal said.

"And what would that be, Mr. Jamison?" There was no perceptible heightening of interest.

"I was in a shop around the corner from my apartment, and I saw some stuff that reminded me of what you were holding at"—he paused at the corny phrase—"the scene of the crime. That religious statue and the colored beads. The stuff I saw was so similar, I thought you ought to know."

"What kind of shop were you in, Mr. Jamison?"

"It's not easy to pin down . . . sort of a religious drugstore, called a *botánica*. I think they sell mainly to Spanish people in my neighborhood."

"Spanish? You mean Hispanics—like Puerto Ricans?"

"That's right."

"Okay," the detective said cryptically. "Thanks for calling, Mr. Jamison."

It was obviously a preface to a good-bye. "Don't you want the address of the shop?" Cal put in quickly. "There must be some connection. These objects were amazingly similar—"

"Mr. Jamison," the detective cut in, "please don't think the police are unappreciative of public assistance. But in case you don't know, there are hundreds of those weird little shops in this town, all selling same collection of junk to every Cuban or P.R. who's into Santeria—which amounts to maybe seven, eight hundred thousand."

"Sorry, I didn't realize," Cal said, not quite sure why he should

59

be apologizing, except that the detective suddenly sounded frazzled and weary.

"Yeah, neither did I . . . once. But now that we both do, you can see the connection doesn't narrow things down too much. But thanks for calling, Mr. Jamison. Have a nice day."

The detective hung up.

End of stint as good citizen, Cal thought.

He took some of his notebooks down from a shelf, material to review for his book. But he didn't open them. His mind lingered over the conversation with MacTaggart; he was interested in what the detective had said about the *botánica*. There were hundreds of them in the city, and their clientele were all involved with "Santeria," whatever that was. He thought of the woman behind the counter telling him there was nothing more to the shop than what met the eye: it sold herbs and religious articles. Santeria was evidently a cult of some kind, a mix of faith and folk medicine. An offshoot of conventional religion, apparently—all the saint statues were recognizably Christian. A Spanish version of Christian Science, maybe. No, not Spanish, he reminded himself. Hispanic. An anthropologist ought not to be sloppy about such distinctions.

He opened his notebook finally, but paused again.

Santeria. The word stuck with him. An ethnic cult with several hundred thousand practitioners. Odd that he'd never heard of it before, Cal thought; it sounded like a subject that should have been tackled at some time in an anthropological journal. Or was it a new phenomenon? Even a cop, who ought to be familiar with urban subculture, had confessed to being unaware of its popularity until he started investigating a murder.

Might be worth looking into further, Cal thought. If no one else had done it, maybe he'd write an article himself for the *Journal of Ethnology*.

He started reading his diary of the expedition on which he'd first encountered the Zokos. Soon he was far away from the city and living again in the Stone Age.

⊃ ● ⊆

He smelled the paint the minute he walked through the door to his apartment. With a twinge of regret, he recalled that this was the day he'd told his landlady, Mrs. Halowell, that she could come in and start painting. He stepped inside expecting the worst, total disarray.

Victoria Halowell called out a spritely "Hi!" For some reason—

perhaps the word "landlady"—Cal had expected a dumpy middle-aged woman with short silvery hair; he had spoken to her only on the phone. But she was, in fact, an extremely attractive woman in, Cal judged, her late twenties or early thirties. She was slightly shorter than he was, with long chestnut hair and sloe hazel eyes. She looked like a girl who had gone to finishing school and then spent the next decade putting back the rough edges that had been polished away. She was the kind of woman who had an aura of "class," and there she was, standing in a man-tailored workshirt and paint-spattered jeans.

She was lifting one end of a dresser, moving it back through the door into Chris's bedroom. Holding the other end was a handyman whom Cal had seen around the building, a young man in his early twenties with a dark Latin complexion, curly black hair, and a half-developed mustache shadowing his upper lip.

They disappeared into Chris's bedroom with the dresser and Cal looked around in amazement. Except for a few paint cans, a pile of speckled drop cloths, and a stepladder stowed near the door, the only signs of the day's upheaval were the expanses of freshly painted wall done in pleasing shades of beige and ivory.

Victoria Halowell reappeared from Chris's room and began folding the canvas drops by the door.

"How'd you get it done so fast?" Cal said, waving to the walls. "Witchcraft?"

She laughed. "Plain old quick-drying latex," she said. "We came in right after you left this morning. I figured we could knock it off in a day with a little extra effort." She finished folding one tarp and picked up another.

Cal told her he appreciated having the painting done so quickly.

"I was hoping to make it easier for you," she said sympathetically. "Being invaded by painters is a nuisance for anyone, but I figured after all you and your boy have been through . . ."

She had been talking idly while she folded the canvas, but now she glanced up abruptly as though caught in an indiscretion. Cal understood then that, either by way of the university housing people or from neighborhood gossip delivered by Mrs. Ruiz, Victoria Halowell knew his whole story—"the tragic widower." It was Mrs. Ruiz, after all, who had told him about the landlady's unhappy marriage and divorce.

She had finished folding the drop cloth, and filled the awkward silence by remarking on all the wonderful new products that fortunately made painting such a breeze these days.

The young handyman came out of the bedroom.

"Ricardo, have you met Mr. Jamison?"

The handyman smiled a greeting, then spoke to his boss in lightning-fast Spanish.

She turned to Cal. "He says to remind you that the paint's dry to the touch, but it needs to set so be a little careful."

Reverting to Spanish, she rattled off a stream of instructions to Ricardo, who immediately began carrying paint cans into the outer hallway.

Victoria Halowell's fluency in Spanish aroused Cal's curiosity. Maybe the name Halowell, acquired from her failed marriage, masked a Latin heritage. He was going to ask about it, but the tarps were all folded and she had started carrying them outside. Cal overheard another rapid exchange of Spanish with Ricardo in the hallway. The handyman waved a *Buenas tardes,* and left with the stepladder.

"I've got to finish rinsing a couple of brushes in your kitchen sink," Victoria Halowell said, coming back into the apartment. "Then I'll be out of your way."

"No hurry." He trailed her into the kitchen. "Anything I can do to help?"

She shook her head. "This is the last of it."

She stood at the kitchen sink holding the brushes under the tap and Cal leaned in the doorway. There was a strange intimacy in the moment, watching a woman engaged in the homey act of cleaning paintbrushes. It occurred to him that this was the first time he'd been alone in his home with an appealing female since his wife's death. It was usually couples who found themselves in this situation, married people decorating a home together.

"Can I get you a drink, Mrs. Halowell?"

"Call me Torey," she corrected, then glanced at her hands and clothes. "No, thanks," she said with a smile.

A dumb moment to ask her, he realized—her hands still slippery with water and paint. But he didn't want to see her go too quickly.

"C'mon," he coaxed. "Take the seven dwarfs' advice. Wet your whistle while you work."

She laughed. "Okay. Got a beer?"

He winced. "Sorry, I don't happen to—"

"Never mind. Anything'll do."

It turned out that all he had was an unfinished bottle of Piper-Heidsieck in the refrigerator, the remains of a housewarming gift Ricki had brought when she dropped in to give the apartment her seal of approval. He offered the champagne apologetically—"It's gone a little flat, I'm afraid"—but she accepted, and he poured two glasses. She finished cleaning the brushes and dried them on the tail of her shirt.

"Well, this seems to call for a toast," she said, picking up her glass. "But do you think it's safe?"

"Safe?"

"I mean, flat champagne. I'm superstitious about things like that. Never make a toast with water, or wine in a paper cup."

Funny the kind of people who were tyrannized by tiny rituals. Torey Halowell was so plainly levelheaded in other ways.

"I've never heard warnings about flat champagne," Cal said. "On the other hand, I'm sure they launched the *Titanic* with a brand new bottle, every bubble intact. So I'll take my chances on your toast."

She hesitated, then hoisted her glass. "To—what else? Happiness in your new home."

He bowed slightly in appreciation, and they drank. Lowering her glass, she kept staring into it. A shy avoidance? Was it so obvious that he'd forgotten how to be alone with a woman?

"Hey, you've been on your feet all day," he said. "Let's sit down."

He led the way into the living room. They took chairs facing each other, and he complimented her on her choice of colors for the walls. Then there was another lull.

"Where'd you pick up your Spanish?" he asked.

"My father was a career officer in the State Department," she said. "When I was two, he was posted to Havana as chargé d'affaires at the embassy, and we stayed twelve years. Then Castro took over and chased out all the Americans."

Cal's mind raced through the arithmetic. Castro's revolution: 1959. She had been fourteen then. She was thirty-six now, though she looked much younger.

"I've never really cut the ties completely," she continued. "It's why I liked this neighborhood when I moved to New York. I feel at home here—doing business in Spanish, that kind of thing."

"Cuba had that much of an influence on you?"

"It was an exciting time in my life," she said. "Growing up in a foreign country left me with a certain nostalgia, and," she added with a provocative smile, "a taste for the Latin temperament—you know, all that fire and spice."

On the surface, he thought, she was cool and practical, but

underneath was a hint of volatility. Or was he reading too much into her remark—was he overly sensitive after his long hiatus from sex?

"It's an interesting neighborhood, all right," he said, mentally sifting conversational gambits. "I've had the feeling walking around here that I could be in a foreign city. There's this spooky little store around the corner, they sell religious articles and herbs and—"

"The *botánica*," she said.

"Yes, I've never seen anything like it."

He hadn't interjected it idly into the conversation, he knew after it was out. From what she'd told him about her background, he thought she might be able to tell him more about the store. After talking with the detective this morning, his curiosity—more than that, really, his suspicion—hadn't evaporated.

"There's nothing unusual about *botánicas*," she answered. "Not to Hispanics, anyway. Walk through any section of the city where there are Cubans or Puerto Ricans—immigrants from any of the Caribbean islands, for that matter, or South America—and you'll find at least one or two. In the *barrio* there are dozens."

"The *barrio?*"

"It's the Spanish word for neighborhood. It's called *el barrio.*"

"Where is the *barrio* exactly?"

Torey pursed her lips thoughtfully. "Way uptown," she said. "There aren't precise boundaries, really, but I guess you'd cross into the *barrio* above Ninety-sixth Street and Park Avenue."

Uptown? Cal sensed the answer to the small puzzle he'd wondered about this morning. The precinct where MacTaggart worked was on East 103rd Street. So the cop assigned to the warehouse killing was based in a part of the city where there were dozens of stores similar to the one in which Cal had thought he'd seen clues to the murder. In some vague way it seemed to confirm his suspicion. But what did it prove except that the police were already aware of anything he might tell them?

Yet he couldn't let go of the chance to find out more, and Torey was someone who obviously knew.

"Tell me," he said, "have you been in a *botánica?*"

"Oh sure," she said lightly. "I go into the one around the corner fairly often. It's the most convenient place to buy certain things . . ."

"What things?"

She raised her glass, sipped, and lingered a moment, her hazel eyes peering at him over the rim. He felt she was appraising the motive behind his interrogation.

64

"Herbs mostly," she replied.

"What kind of herbs?" he persisted. "The stuff they sell in there has such crazy names."

She laughed. "Some of it is pretty odd, isn't it? But it's very effective folk medicine. One of the things I buy, for example, is St. John's Wort. It's a pulverized root, and the most effective stuff I've ever come across for my hay fever—clears my sinuses in a flash. And I get some more conventional things there. Like chamomile tea, which is great for an upset stomach. And they sell some lovely essences for perfume, or to put in a bath—"

Cal broke in, "They also have religious statues and candles and beads and feather dusters. It's such a strange combination of merchandise, I don't see how it all fits together." He paused, not sure how much further to pursue the subject. "Somebody told me it's involved with a . . . a cult or a religion called Santeria. Do you know anything about that?"

She examined him again, more intensely this time. "Why are you asking this?" she said.

"Because it interests me professionally. And also," he admitted then, "because that place worries me a little."

"Oh my," she sighed, and shook her head as though dismissing an ancient misconception. "I guess it could seem—what was your word?—spooky, especially to someone who's not familiar with the customs behind it, but there's nothing to be afraid of. Everything for sale in a *botánica* is to help people, some of it spiritually, some of it physically. Santeria's an old tradition among these people, a particular way of approaching their problems. That's all there is to it."

Perhaps it was wiser, Cal decided, to drop the matter. Victoria Halowell had confessed her affinity and affection for Hispanic culture. She might be affronted if he harped on a negative aspect, might regard him as narrow-minded and intolerant.

"Maybe I've been worrying about nothing," he said. "Probably I wouldn't have given it a second thought, but my son seemed fascinated by the place. The way things are . . . I mean now that I'm alone with him and completely responsible . . . well, I feel an extra . . ."

He trailed off, not sure of what he intended to say. An extra fear? Extra guilt?

Quietly, Torey Halowell said, "I understand." And Cal felt that she did.

The day outside had darkened, or the sun had slipped down behind the buildings across the garden, dimming the light in the room. Cal stared through the gloom at the woman across from him, gripped by an illusion. It was Laurie sitting there. They had rested like this together, drinking wine—she wearing jeans and one of his old shirts—after painting the nursery for Chris.

Then the illusion faded. He saw her clearly as Torey Halowell.

Or did he? Wasn't it just a physical impulse, the need for a release? As Ricki had said, he couldn't go on fucking a ghost forever. He had to have a woman, any woman, as long as she was flesh and blood.

She lifted her drink once more, drained it, then sat for a few seconds cupping the empty glass in her hands. Was she waiting for him to offer a refill?

He couldn't. He was suddenly uncomfortable with the prospect of physical intimacy. He wanted her to go. Laurie was too alive for him still. Another woman would be an infidelity. He had the crazy feeling that Laurie's ghost was *here*, a witness. And crazier still, that the ghost had a heart to break. He was on the verge of asking Torey to leave when she put her glass aside and stood.

"I ought to be on my way now. Thanks very much for the drink."

He rose with her. "My pleasure. And thanks again for making this so easy. . . ." He gestured to the fresh walls.

"If there's anything else I can do," she said as he went with her to the door, "please give me a call." She turned to him after crossing the threshold. "And don't worry so much," she added. "I'm sure you and your son are going to be fine."

He felt a rush of disappointment when she was gone. A wasted opportunity. He'd spent the time with her dwelling on foolish fears instead of getting to know her better.

But it was too soon to know her better. He went back to the living room and collected the two glasses and the bottle. A bit of champagne was left, too little to save. He was reluctant to pour it down the sink, and emptied the bottle into one of the glasses.

It was her glass, he realized as he drank. Her smell was on it, a mingling of the paint from her fingertips and a trace of some perfume, from her lipstick perhaps, or one of those essences she said she bought at the *botánica*. He liked the smell and held the glass to his lips for a while even after it was empty.

66

Chapter 10

AFTER DINNER Cal challenged Chris to a game of Monopoly. They played on the living room floor, giving themselves over to the make-believe of greedy acquisition. With the apartment painted and furniture all in place, they could begin to feel at home. Cal enjoyed the game and really tried to win, but every roll of the dice only added to Chris's stock of cash and hotels.

"It's no use," Cal conceded at last, shuffling through his pile of mortgaged properties. "I'm just beating a dead horse."

"What, Daddy?" Chris shot him a troubled glance.

Was it the mention of death? Cal wondered. He had to be more careful. There was no telling what would trigger another nightmare.

"Just a figure of speech, Bean. It means I've got no hope against your luck tonight. You're the champ."

As the price of defeat, Cal agreed to clean up the board. When he followed a few minutes later to help Chris into his pajamas and tuck him into bed, he was astonished and distressed by the sight that greeted him. Chris was seated cross-legged in the middle of the rug facing the window. On the sill the seven-colored candle was burning.

Cal stalked over to the window, blew out the flame, and whirled around. "Christopher, what the hell is going on here?"

Chris remained seated passively on the floor. "Nothing. I was just sitting . . . thinking."

"Oh, is *that* all?" Cal grabbed up the candle, a skein of smoke still curling from the wick. "Since when are you allowed to use matches? You know how dangerous that is. What ever got into you, Bean?"

Chris didn't move. "Don't be angry, Daddy," he said in a dreamy, languorous voice.

He was practically asleep, Cal realized. Tired after an active day at camp, somnolent from staring at the candle. Even the scolding hadn't roused him. Cal fought the urge to seize him and shake him awake to drum in the vital lesson of safety. He decided to settle for eliminating the danger; he'd deliver the sermon tomorrow.

Cal stuck out his hand, palm up. "Just give them to me, Bean. Now."

"What, Daddy?"

"The matches. C'mon, on the double."

Chris looked back dreamily, with seeming bewilderment.

This was too much. Cal took him by the arm and pulled him to his feet. "I won't play games about this, Chris. Give me those matches!"

"But I don't have any," Chris replied.

Cal was astounded by the boy's calm. He would have preferred some defensive whining or screeching. But carrying through with the accomplished boldness of a habitual liar—this was far more serious.

"For God's sake, Bean," Cal said, "don't make it worse. The candle was burning and I sure as hell didn't light it. Now for the last time—"

"But it was like that, Daddy. It was burning when I came in, so I sat down to watch . . ."

Where did you go from here? Into the old military discipline routine—Colonel Cal and Private Chris? *All right, young man, I don't care if it takes all night, you're going to. . . .* He'd never spanked Chris yet. Laurie had done it a couple of years ago—flown off the handle when Chris, in a burst of spite, had spilled ink on one of her weavings—but even then she'd reproached herself and sworn never to hit him again. The oath was hers, but Cal wanted to honor it. What the boy needed more than punishment, anyway, was compassion.

"Okay, Bean, I'm going to drop it for now. You broke a rule, and I'm mad as hell about it. But I'm going to hope you've got enough sense never to do it again. Will you give me your word on that, at least—no more playing with matches?"

Chris pouted and looked at the floor.

"Promise, Bean!" Cal demanded hotly, the reins on his temper slipping again.

"I promise," Chris mumbled.

"Into bed, then."

Chris shuffled slowly to the bed and climbed in as though scaling the north face of the Eiger.

Cal dispatched the nightly ritual quickly. Tuck in blanket, switch off lamp, kiss on cheek. Chris lay motionless, turned to the wall. Chastened, Cal thought. He pondered whether to complete the confiscation. But Chris had given his word, and a sign of trust could strengthen the contract. Cal tiptoed back across the room and set the glass holder down where it had been, on the sill next to Chris's shell.

∋ • ∈

Cal sat for a while in the living room, sipping from a snifter of brandy. The lie bothered him; Chris had never been deceptive in the past. Was the change another symptom of a deep struggle with unhappy realities? Or a normal lapse for a boy Chris's age, falling back on the easiest defense after being caught at mischief?

At a few minutes past eleven, he switched on the television set, though he turned the volume all the way down so he could keep a casual eye on the screen without being bothered by the sound. Kate was going to be on the Carson show tonight talking about *Cultures*, and he didn't want to miss it.

But the eleven o'clock news tugged at his attention. The silent screen transmitted pictures of bullet-riddled bodies of children scattered inside an explosion-torn building. Cut. In an orchard of fruit trees, men and women huddled together crying. Cut. An anchorman sat at his desk, talking in front of a backdrop of a huge ballistic missile frozen in flight. Was it all one story? Or three?

Cal went to the television, turned up the sound, and caught the last half of a report that a full "third-stage nuclear alert" had accidentally been set off during the afternoon at an Air Force base in Omaha; a spokesman revealed that the cause of the "incident" was a defective microchip in a computer, a part costing forty-nine cents. The Air Force had been unwilling to say how close the missile had come to actually being launched.

Cal watched one story after another, each more depressing than the last. Nothing like a dose of the evening news to put your problems in perspective. He had been worried about raising his son to tell the truth. But the malfunction of a two-bit piece of electronic hardware might soon make all the best plans extraneous.

∋ • ∈

"Did you hear about the latest nuclear alert?" Johnny Carson was saying to his audience. He glanced over at Doc Severinsen, winked, did a puckish take, and turned back to the audience waiting for the punch line.

"There was a meltdown in Dolly Parton's jumpsuit."

The audience roared with laughter and Carson chuckled with them.

Carson's guests included a television actress, a country singer, and a young comic. Cal almost never watched talk shows. He regarded the very format as sad proof of the mediocrity in modern life. What hope was there for a society where millions of people would rather listen to the chit-chat of show business celebrities than engage in the exchange of their own ideas? Yet Cal had a soft spot for Carson, who was bright and entertaining, and whose show provided a unique platform for psychologists and scientists and literary figures to reach a mass audience.

Kate came on late in the show, and Carson introduced her with respect and affection.

"Phenomenon is one of those words that I suppose has been overused," he said, "but it's really the only way to sum up this next lady. She's been exploring the world for fifty years, and I think there's no doubt she's one of the most interesting and important women in the country. Would you please welcome—Kathryn Clay."

Doc Severinsen led the orchestra in a spirited chorus of "He's Got the Whole World in His Hands," seemingly meant to apply to Kate despite the difference in gender. Kate came on flashing an irresistible smile and looking cuddly in one of her formal caftans, the same old tent style but made of fabric shot through with shiny thread.

She kissed Johnny, took the seat beside him, and soon he was leading her into telling an episode from *Cultures*. This one involved a tribal wedding feast she had attended in Borneo where a cooked snake was served as the main dish of the celebration, an old marriage tradition. Carson had a knack of working the material for jokes without seeming to mock or belittle its basic interest. Then he managed to turn the whole subject a bright shade of blue that probably wouldn't have passed the censors at an earlier viewing hour. It started when Kate explained the background of the custom.

"Before the wedding all the men of the tribe go hunting for the snake, including the groom-to-be. They have a sort of contest to catch the biggest one for the feast. There's an old belief among the men, you see, that if you have a long one—especially if it's the groom's—then it means the marriage will be happy."

Johnny had only to contribute "I can see where that makes sense"—with his air of total choirboy innocence—to draw attention to the double-entendre.

"And they say the longer it is," Kate said with apparent ingenuousness, "the happier the marriage will be."

After that it took no more than one of Carson's deadpan stares to demolish the audience. When the first wave of laughter died down, he asked Kate if she happened to know the record for length.

"I don't know the record," she replied, "but when I was there the groom came in with one that was forty feet long."

"What a happy marriage that must have been," Johnny said, and the laugh that followed lasted more than a minute.

It was sophomoric and obvious, Cal thought, but he was laughing anyway. Kate did nothing to discourage the hilarity, roaring along with the rest. Her genius in the situation was to accept the jokes as a way of getting her message across.

"Well, you know, Johnny, the interesting thing about the joke is that it's absolutely on target. The association we're making is exactly what was in the minds of the ancient men who originated the custom. Eating the snake guaranteed a good marriage precisely because it did stand for virility, for sex itself. Just consider what the snake represents in the Garden of Eden. . . ."

So in the end she made her point that primitive customs were not so alien and bizarre. All men were brothers. Carson himself seemed to be having a marvelous time, not merely grinding through the interviewer's task. He obviously admired her.

"What keeps you going, Kate?" he asked. "I mean, most people at your time of life are sitting in Florida mainlining Geritol."

"I have to keep going," she explained earnestly, "because I'm in a frantic race against time. The primitive peoples of the world are dying out, Johnny—the Indians of the Amazon, the tribes of Africa and the far Pacific islands—they'll be gone soon, all of them. And I think it would be tragic if all their wisdom died with them."

"That's an interesting way of putting it," Johnny observed. "We always think of them knowing less than we do. But you talk about their wisdom . . . as if they knew more about some things."

Kate nodded. "We've been rushing ahead so fast toward our own self-destruction, never stopping to look back, that we've lost some important truths. It's one of the reasons I think our world is in so much trouble."

Carson hesitated momentarily, in his thoughtful mode. "But you're basically an optimist, aren't you, Kate?"

"Oh, dear, Johnny, I try to be. But these days it seems to me so much has changed . . . even the future ain't what it used to be."

Carson chuckled and, knowing a good tag line when he heard it, announced the final commercial break.

Cal switched off the television set and started for bed. No mystery about Kate's success; she knew her subject and how to sell it, right down to coining the catchy slogan. Study the past, everyone, because the future ain't what it used to be. Recalling the horrors he had seen on the news, Cal had to agree it was a great line, perfect for its time. He had his own nostalgia for a simpler world, but he wondered what Kate had meant when she spoke about the lost truths of the ancients. Was it anything more than salesmanship? The problem was that now people would buy what she had written, perhaps, for the same reason they bought the diet books and the looking-out-for-number-one tracts. For answers, methods, solutions. They would read about Kate's journeys in the hope of finding out how the future could again be what it had once been —a machine that was supposed to work.

But what did Kate really think the primitives knew that offered any solution, any hope, for reversing the terrible destructive momentum of the nuclear age?

Chapter 11

ALL THE FOLLOWING week the American Anthropological Association was holding its annual conference at the Waldorf. The only session Cal wanted to attend was the Wednesday luncheon, where Peter Beecham, the great mythologist, was to be the principal speaker.

Cal arrived early and mingled with the large crowd having drinks in the foyer outside the Grand Ballroom. He picked out a number of old acquaintances—Hugh Kerner from Princeton, who had been a graduate student of Kate's; roly-poly Gilbert Hunsecker, entertaining a crowd with his new theory of Japanese family structure—and moved around the room sharing the gossip of the anthropological community. He was crossing the foyer to the bar for a second vodka-and-tonic when he heard a voice behind him rise slightly above the babble and utter a word that immediately trapped his attention.

". . . and the Puerto Ricans call it Santeria . . ."

Santeria? The cult mentioned by the cop.

Cal spun around and searched for the source. In a group standing nearby he saw a pale and reedy man holding forth to three others. He was on the young side, in his late twenties, Cal guessed, with a tight-lipped deaconish face and round gold-framed glasses.

". . . and in Miami, of course, with the Cubans—theirs is called *lucumi*. What's fascinating is that they all seem to be the same thing. The one we've got in New Orleans, Obeah, isn't much different from the rest."

One of the others in the group gestured toward the speaker with his cigarette. "John, you seem to consider this a real religion."

73

"Oh, sure, absolutely," the speaker said. "Voodoo is definitely a real religion."

Voodoo?

Cal moved closer to the group and stood on the edge of the discussion, listening and trying to read the speaker's name tag.

"How many forms of it are there?" another member of the group asked, this one a short older man with bushy white eyebrows.

"It's hard to say," said the speaker. "Maybe half a dozen in South America, as far as I know anyway. The Haitian branch is called *vodun*, and there's Brazilian *mayombe*, and *shango* in Trinidad. I don't know them all offhand. I was going to study it seriously, but I ran into some resistance from the department and. . . ." He shrugged.

Cal was instantly sympathetic with him, wherever his department was; he understood the dispiriting effect such resistance could have on research.

The deaconish type went on. "When you get into the slave migration aspect of it, and the way the Catholic saints became Voodoo gods—"

A white-jacketed waiter passed through the foyer ringing a gong and summoning the crowd to lunch. The group Cal had been listening to broke up and drifted toward the dining room. Cal lingered a moment, then stopped the man who had been talking so knowledgeably about Santeria and introduced himself. The other man turned out to be a junior Tulane faculty member named John Viner, who with a self-deprecating smile described himself as a "young Turk." Viner recognized Cal's name at once.

"It's a pleasure to meet you, Professor Jamison," Viner said respectfully. "I read your piece in the *Journal of Ethnology*, the piece on the Zokos. It's very impressive. I'm looking forward to reading the whole story."

Cal thanked him, sincerely flattered, and asked if he had heard correctly. Did Viner say Santeria had something to do with Voodoo?

"They're the same thing," Viner said. "Santeria's just one form of Voodoo."

"But Voodoo is *African* religion."

"Originally it was," Viner said, "but from what I understand it's all over the world now."

"I couldn't help overhearing," Cal said, "about your department's discouraging you. How did you find this out?"

"It was sort of an accident," Viner said. "I was talking with this

74

Creole guy who runs the Xerox in our mail room. He's into the fringes of Obeah—that's the Voodoo we have in New Orleans— and then I started asking questions."

Two of the men from the coterie Viner had been with earlier beckoned and called out, saying they would save him a seat at their table.

Cal said, "I'd like to talk with you more about this."

They agreed to meet after lunch, and Viner went in to the dining room and joined his friends. For a moment, Cal stood thinking about what Viner had told him.

Voodoo.

Santeria was Voodoo and it was being practiced right here in New York.

ᗡ ● ᗴ

"I'm sort of in a hurry," Viner said after lunch as they rode down in the elevator. "I promised my wife I'd take her on the boat tour around Manhattan."

"The Circle Line," Cal said. He told Viner he had taken the same ride with Chris. He supposed all tourists did it.

"Hillary's an architect," Viner explained. "She's never been to New York before, and she really wants to *see* it. I can't be late for this or Hillary'll pop a gasket. I'm never on time."

"You'll make it," Cal promised, anxious to find out what else Viner had learned. "You can grab a cab halfway. What else can you tell me about Santeria?"

"Not much," Viner said as they came out of the hotel and started walking west. "I didn't have a chance to get into it too deeply."

"What I'd really like to know," Cal said, "is how an African religion comes to be practiced in New York, or New Orleans for that matter, by people who aren't Africans."

"That's actually the most interesting part," Viner said. "I was just starting to tell those guys about it before lunch. It started when the slaves brought their religion from Africa. The slave traders— you know, the *civilized* people—they thought the slaves were a bunch of savage black heathen. Animals. But the truth of it was that the tribes from the African coast had an incredibly complex religion. Very sophisticated. Hundreds of gods—"

"Pantheistic," Cal said. "Like the Greeks."

"Oh, the Africans made the Greeks look like amateurs. Voodoo was much more complicated. For one thing, it was so much older, probably the oldest religion in the world. And it wasn't only that

75

they had all these gods, but they appealed to them directly. You know, like give us a good harvest or let us win this war, and there was a ritual for each god and each prayer, and spells to cast when you made the appeal. It's classic primitive-culture religion, only deeper than anything I've ever heard about. They had holy books and tabernacles, just like any other religion. But what Voodoo is, really, is what everybody wants a religion to be. It's an attempt to control fate by appealing directly to the gods. They believed, and they still do, that they can ask the gods directly to intervene in their lives."

"What do you mean? *Who* still believes?"

"The followers all over the world," Viner said. "That's what's so extraordinary. None of it has changed. It's just as strong as it was five thousand years ago. This thing is so strong that no matter what the local name is, no matter what country you're in, they all call it the same thing. 'The religion.' The *only* religion. They don't even acknowledge the others." Viner stopped, looked at Cal. "Hey, why are you interested in this?"

Cal thought about mentioning the warehouse murder, but decided not to get into it. "Just curious," he said. "I saw one of their little shops." They continued walking. "What confuses me," Cal went on, "is that the religion I've seen—this Santeria, which you say is Voodoo—doesn't seem at all African. The religious symbols I've seen are saints. Christian saints."

"Amazing, isn't it?" Viner said. "It blew me away, too." Cal could see Viner's pleasure in being able to inform someone older and with more substantial credentials. "When the slaves were brought from Africa the first thing their owners did was try to kill off their religion. Why? Because the colonies were Catholic countries—the Louisiana Territory, the Caribbean. French and Spanish cultures. But the last thing the slaves wanted to do was give up their religion when they needed it most. So you have the church trying to eradicate their beliefs and being pretty brutal about it. They passed laws against Voodoo, and the punishment was death. And they literally tried to beat the devil—what they thought of as deviltry—out of the Africans. The French weren't even subtle; they just drove the slaves into the churches under the lash and whipped them until they agreed to become Christians."

"Which they did eventually," Cal said.

"And they didn't," Viner said. "Outwardly they were Christians, worshipped the Trinity, the whole thing. But they really kept worshipping their own religion. I guess you could say they put their own gods in disguise."

76

Now Cal thought he understood what he had seen in the shop. "You mean, every saint actually represents a Voodoo god."

"Exactly. In fact, Santeria means 'the worship of saints,' " Viner said, then nervously looked at his watch. "Say, are you sure I'm going to make this boat?"

"With time to spare," Cal assured him. "So let me get this straight. When someone goes into a store that deals in religious items for Santeria, if they buy a saint figure . . . it's actually the representation of an African god."

"Yes and no," Viner said hesitantly. "The way I understand it, the statue is both—the saint *and* the god. It's a form of syncretism, two religions mixing together into one. It's conventional Western religion, and it's Voodoo at the same time. Claude—he's the guy who runs the department's Xerox machine—Claude tells me his mother goes to church, prays, and then on the way out dips a little vial into the holy water so she can use it in a spell when she gets home."

"Spell? It sounds like witchcraft."

"It's not, though. Not at all. A spell in Voodoo isn't a hex, it's a prayer—an appeal to a god to make things happen or not happen. Mix some holy water with a few herbs, and maybe one of the gods will arrange for you to get a job, or for your worst enemy to die."

They were at the corner of Forty-ninth and Seventh Avenue, brushed on all sides by heavy pedestrian traffic. The heat rose in waves from the pavement. An Italian ices vendor hawked his wares from a metal cart.

"Something cold?" Cal offered, rummaging for change.

"No, thanks," Viner said. "I guess I'd really better run. When Hillary gets mad . . ." He started scanning for a taxi, then spotted an empty checker and flagged it.

"Here you go," Cal said as the cab pulled over, and held the door open. "Thanks very much, John. You've been very helpful."

Cal's hand stayed on the door. Viner got into the taxi, and they made the usual promises to meet again someday. Cal thought for a moment of other questions he wanted to ask—Who else could he ask about Santeria? What books should he read?—but Viner was clearly growing restless and Cal closed the door.

The cab pulled away, and Cal stood watching it until it had turned a distant corner.

⊐ ● ⊏

It was a big night for Chris, his first "grown-up" meal in a restaurant.

Ricki had invited them to the Russian Tea Room to meet her fiancé, Wayne Millman. He was a Wall Street lawyer who looked just like one: thinning blond hair, slightly pudgy, and outfitted by Brooks Brothers from his gray vested suit to his black wing tips. He seemed stuffy at first—the glasses he put on to read the menu were "Ben Franklin" half-lenses that Cal had always seen on much older people—but he had an understated confidence and an easy way with Chris, and Cal warmed to him as the meal went on. When they had finished and the waiter was clearing the table for dessert, Ricki told Cal how she had met Wayne while interviewing him for an article on the rash of corporate takeovers. Wayne looked expectantly at her as he ordered a bottle of champagne.

"Go on," he said. "Tell them."

Ricki beamed. "Tonight's a celebration. We've set a date for the wedding."

"That's great," Cal said with a big smile. He kissed her and shook Wayne's hand.

"Can I be the best man?" Chris asked unabashedly.

Cal was embarrassed, but Wayne and Ricki laughed. Wayne apologized that the job was already filled, by his brother, but Chris seemed content when told he could be an usher and wear a flower in his buttonhole.

"Five weeks from this Saturday at the St. Regis," Ricki said. "Supper and dancing afterwards."

"You're getting married in a hotel?" Cal asked. "Why not in temple?" He had not forgotten the pious objections of the Hanauer family to his own marriage to Laurie.

"It's just easier this way," Ricki said, "doing it all in one place. But of course it'll be a religious ceremony."

The discussion of religion reminded Cal of his talk with John Viner, and when there was a lull after the excitement of Ricki's announcement died down, Cal asked if they had heard that Voodoo was being widely practiced in New York.

"Voodoo?" Wayne set down his coffee cup, shaking his head. "Is that right?"

"Oh sure," Ricki said. "I've heard that. Somebody proposed an article on local Voodoo for the magazine. Not our kind of thing, though."

Chris looked up from his chocolate pastry. "Voodoo. That's where they stick pins in dolls. Like in *You Only Live Twice*."

"There's a little more to it, Bean. It's a religion." He turned to

Wayne and Ricki. "I was talking about it with someone today at the conference. He said it's probably the oldest religion in the world. I thought it might make a good subject to research."

Ricki looked at him wide-eyed. "For *you* to research?"

"How'd you get interested in that?" Wayne asked.

"By accident, really. Remember that warehouse fire, Ricki?" Cal recounted the sequence of events that led up to his discussion with John Viner: seeing the ritual articles in the hands of the detectives, recognizing similar items in the *botánica*, calling the cop who had mentioned Santeria.

Ricki said, "Why do you want to get involved with a murd—" She shot a glance at Chris and saw him contentedly digging into his pastry. "That's nothing for you to get mixed up with, Cal. Let the cops investigate."

"Ricki," Cal said, "doing research on this doesn't mean I have to get 'mixed up' with the warehouse case. In fact, it was obvious when I called the cop he wasn't at all interested in any outside contributions." Cal paused. "I almost got the feeling, frankly, that he didn't like discussing the case—whether or not I *could* help him."

Wayne took two cigars from his breast pocket and offered one to Cal, who declined with thanks.

"I can understand where the cops would be touchy," Wayne said, stripping the cellophane from his cigar.

"What do you mean?"

"First Amendment," Wayne said, the words coming out garbled as he clamped his lips around the cigar to light it.

"Thirsty mending?" Ricki repeated what she thought Wayne had said.

Chris giggled.

Wayne finished lighting his cigar, holding his gold Dunhill lighter half an inch below the tip so as not to scorch the wrapper.

"First Amendment," he said again, and recited dramatically: " 'Congress shall make no law respecting the establishment of religion or prohibiting the free exercise thereof.' Now, from what Cal says, there's some religious connection to this murder. That means the police have to be extremely careful how they investigate. They have no right, for example, to interrogate people about religious practices. I imagine the restrictions could make this kind of case pretty frustrating, and you can see how they wouldn't be too anxious to discuss it on the phone with a stranger."

Cal hunched forward over the table. "But we're talking about a murder here. How careful would they be if it means solving a case?"

"Extremely careful," Wayne said. "The Supreme Court's been as firm on this as any constitutional issue: you have the right to worship the way you want to worship." Wayne examined the tip of his cigar to be sure it was burning properly. "Of course it does make for some problems enforcing the law. Religions are tax-exempt, right? So now we have these groups who'll ordain you as a minister so you can avoid paying income taxes. Send in a hundred dollars and they give you a piece of paper that says you're a priest and your house is a church, and then you can claim all kind of deductions and tax breaks. Or take these love cults that haul kids away to country retreats and indoctrinate them in their beliefs. The Moonies went to court in England after a newspaper accused them in print of kidnapping and brainwashing kids. The Moonies sued for libel—and *lost*. And let me tell you, English courts are tough on libel. There must have been real evidence of brainwashing, because the accusation was upheld. But in this country it's not enough to call the Reverend Moon and his followers dangerous kidnappers. You won't get the police or the FBI to go into one of their retreats and bring out a kid whose parents say he was stolen from them."

Cal shook his head. "Still, where a murder is involved—"

"I'm sure the police are doing everything they can to investigate," Wayne said. "I'm not saying they don't want to solve *every* case. But they have to work within some very narrow limits."

Ricki had obviously heard enough on this gloomy subject. "Hey, there's some more champagne," she said, lifting the bottle from the bucket. "Let's kill it."

"Can you kill champagne?" Chris asked earnestly.

Cal suddenly regretted all the talk of murder that had gone on in front of the boy. "How about another one of those pastries, Bean?"

Chris's eyes brightened, and Wayne offered to take him up for a look at the dessert cart.

"So," Ricki said when they were alone, "have you found a woman yet?"

At another time Cal might have lost his patience, told her once and for all to lay off. But something else was on his mind, and he merely shook his head.

Chapter 12

A DETECTIVE with a raspy voice answered the phone and informed Cal that Lieutenant MacTaggart was out on an investigation but was expected in the squad room later in the morning.

"I'll call back," Cal said, declining to leave his name or number for a return call.

He returned to the metal café table in the garden, where he'd been having breakfast, and drank the remaining half-cup of coffee. It was probably just as well that he hadn't gotten through to the cop. The proposition he'd wanted to make was a hasty ill-conceived whim, best forgotten. This was no time to go chasing off in new directions. He had his book to write. He had his work cut out for him.

But the idea wouldn't let go. It had been in his head when he woke this morning, fully formed as if in a dream: to research the uncharted territory of an ancient tribal religion—possibly the world's oldest—that was flourishing here in the hub of a world ruled by technology. Discovering the *botánica*, meeting John Viner, hearing about syncretism and how the most pagan religion had assumed a disguise—it was a curious chain of coincidences, the kind reputations were made on.

Yet all of that had prompted no more than idle wondering. It was Wayne Millman's mention of the constitutional restraints on investigating religion that was the real catalyst for calling the detective. In doing his research, Cal thought, he might be able to help the police. And it could work both ways: if he helped the police, they should be willing to share whatever information they had about Voodoo in the city.

That at least was the plan. In the first waking rush of inspiration he was ready to put any other project aside. This new research could relieve the restless frustration he felt at being tied down this summer, unable to travel. There was no need to fly off to a jungle halfway around the world. He could launch an expedition right here.

Cal leaned back in the sun and indulged a fantasy of achieving the kind of recognition that had come to Kate with her early work. Was this his real motive? Sheer ambition? A chance to seize on a sensational subject? He knew he should write about the Zokos, do the work Laurie would want him to do—his memorial to her.

During the rest of the morning he tried to concentrate on his field journals. He made notes, even tried to draft a paragraph or two for his opening chapter. But he couldn't stay with it. He kept glancing at the clock.

At eleven-thirty he called the Twenty-third Precinct again, and was switched through to MacTaggart.

"Yes, Mr. Jamison," the detective said. "You have some new information for us?"

The policeman's quick recall of their earlier conversation impressed Cal, but he couldn't tell if there was a trace of mockery in MacTaggart's question—dismissing the caller as another tireless crank.

"No new information, Lieutenant," Cal said, "but I might be able to get some for you."

"And how might you do that, Mr. Jamison?"

"It's *Professor* Jamison," Cal answered, bridling at the policeman's too-tolerant, patronizing tone. "I'm an anthropologist and I've been thinking about doing some research into Santeria. I thought my findings might be useful to you. Can we meet to talk about it?"

There was a short silence. MacTaggart was obviously considering how much weight to give this stranger's approach. "Anthropologist," he said dryly at last. "Okay, Professor, I'm on duty until four. It's a little tight around here now, but come in near the end of my shift and I'll listen."

∋ • ∈

The taxi driver tossed a dubious glance over his shoulder when Cal announced his destination as East 103rd Street. But without a word the driver started the meter running and wheeled out into city traffic.

Cal had seen little of the city since arriving five weeks ago. There had been too much to do: moving into the apartment, getting Chris into camp and a school for the fall, attending faculty meetings. Except for occasional outings with Chris, most of his experience with the city was confined to shuttling between his apartment and his office. But it wasn't necessary to be familiar with the city to know that a vast portion of the uptown area was a ghetto, a place those who did not belong were unwise to enter.

Yet he had no hesitation about venturing into the *barrio*. In the taxi ride uptown he felt the anticipation of a tourist on an excursion to the quaint old quarter of a foreign city. He was always interested in seeing how different ethnic groups decorated their environment, reproduced the rhythms of the native territories they had left behind. From its name, Cal imagined the *barrio* would offer the same tantalizing taste of another culture as a trip to Chinatown. He gave no thought to the question of safety. Ricki had provided a quick survival briefing on where in the city one did and did not go, which methods of transportation to use, and how the time of day affected both lists. But Cal didn't think he was heading into forbidden territory; MacTaggart's precinct headquarters was located only a few blocks away from the fine residential sections of upper Fifth and Park Avenues.

For the latter part of the ride, in fact, the cab traveled straight up Park. Cal looked out the window at the passing phalanxes of prewar luxury apartment buildings, all with uniformed doormen standing guard. Where did all the money come from? In this part of town, he had heard, the cost of a co-op apartment with two or three bedrooms started at three hundred thousand dollars. Along the side streets stood rows of town houses priced at an average of a million dollars. From avenue to avenue they ran, the golden towers, block after block, from Central Park to the river, from midtown upward through streets numbered in the sixties, seventies, eighties, nineties . . . Who were they, the people who populated such prime real estate? The world-beaters, yes, the insiders, the corporate executives and Wall Street lawyers. But Cal had always thought they were a select group. Riding through this part of the city you learned otherwise. There were tens of thousands of kings and king-makers, and their palaces filled acre after acre, surrounded by boutiques and expensive restaurants and exclusive health clubs populated only by the very wealthy. Between Eighty-eighth Street and Ninety-third alone Cal figured he must have passed at least twenty long limousines parked at the curb.

And then, suddenly, the world changed before his eyes. It was as though his taxi had been suddenly lifted from the street and set down in another city, as though the handsome prince had been instantly transformed by the spell of a fairy-tale witch into a loathsome frog.

The realm of the rich vanished and a different vision took its place. Cal blinked as one might to clear a mirage.

But the vision stayed: a landscape of filth and desolation. The cab had no sooner crossed Ninety-sixth Street than blocks of dingy tenements with broken windows lined the avenue, overlooking railroad tracks that had emerged from underground.

Cal glanced back over his shoulder. Through the cab's rear window the tall luxury buildings could be seen receding on the other side of the intersection.

Cal was stunned. It was as if he had crossed a frontier.

He turned around to the oncoming view, and found that with each passing block it became even more dismal. The *barrio* reminded him of a war zone. Tenements were not merely dilapidated and poorly maintained, but already half-destroyed and abandoned. In some the windows were completely broken out and the gaps closed up again with sheets of cardboard or tin. There were overturned garbage cans spilling refuse everywhere; pillaged car hulks sat burnt out and ignored. Doorways were sealed by cinderblocks, giving the dead slums the look of huge mausoleums. Yet, scanning their gruesome facades, Cal saw that even these sealed buildings had been penetrated by squatters. Where the cardboard had been punched out, or the tin peeled back from windows on upper floors, it was possible to catch a glimpse of laundry drying on a line, the scrawny wizened face of an old man staring out blankly, a woman cuddling a bawling infant. A block or two deeper into the neighborhood and the decay became even more depressing. Between the skeletons of surviving structures yawned empty lots like bomb sites, where only the broken fragments of walls still stood amid dust and rubble, the climax of neglect.

Berlin, Cal thought. Not since he'd passed through there on a student tour of Europe seventeen years ago had he seen a similar collision of warring societies. But there the glittering plenitude was separated from the deprivation and ugliness by the Wall. Here it was stranger, with no tangible line of demarcation. Though just as surely a boundary existed: Cal felt that he had passed through an invisible checkpoint into another country. Even the signs that appeared over the small shabby stores here and there were written in another language. Among the stores, in the space of only a few blocks, he saw half a dozen identified as *botánicas*.

The square modern design of the precinct headquarters re-inforced the impression of having entered an alien world. The ar-chitecture—no windows at street level, an entire square block of concrete and brick—brought to mind the fortress garrisons of the Foreign Legion, something out of old black-and-white movies like *Beau Geste*. Inside the street-level entrance a prominently displayed sign read: ALL VISITORS STATE YOUR BUSINESS AT THE DESK. Cal stopped at the reception counter tended by a uniformed policeman and asked for MacTaggart. He was directed up a flight of stairs to the detective squad room on the second floor.

The squad room was a wide open space, brightly lit by large fluorescent fixtures set flush into the ceiling—not the cramped messy scene Cal had been led to expect from television police shows. The windows that ran along one side of the room, though small, admitted a flood of sunlight, and beside the windows was a row of unoccupied desks. The squad room was deserted.

Then from a glass-walled cubicle at the far end came a muffled gust of laughter. Cal crossed the room and looked in. Gathered behind the glass were five men in plainclothes, one of whom Cal recognized as MacTaggart. The detectives were enjoying them-selves immensely, breaking up at wisecracks that were inaudible through the door, though Cal could well imagine their content from what he saw: MacTaggart, standing in front of a desk, was wearing not trousers with his shirt and tie, but a blue-and-green plaid kilt.

Reluctant to interrupt the camaraderie, Cal waited at the door another minute. The faint laughter rolled out of the office contin-uously, MacTaggart's audience gesturing to his exposed legs. And then MacTaggart went into a rather authentic-looking and graceful fragment from a Highland Fling that put a stop to the jokes and reduced the circle of hecklers to appreciative spectators. At the end of the dance they applauded.

Cal knocked hesitantly on the door. All the detectives turned, startled, but it was MacTaggart who walked over to open it; of all in the group, he seemed the least abashed.

"I'm sorry to butt in," Cal said, "but I had an appointment . . ."

MacTaggart recognized him. "Right, Professor," he said without a trace of embarrassment. Wearing his kilt with the proprietary composure of a laird at the gate of his ancestral domain, he turned to the other detectives. "Okay, gentlemen, the show's over. Any of you want an encore, you buy your tickets."

The others filed out. MacTaggart closed the door to a fresh outburst of laughter. Crossing to a coatrack, he said, "There's a police dinner next week and I'm part of the entertainment. That was my dress rehearsal—no pun intended." A pair of gray flannel slacks and a rumpled jacket were thrown over the rack. "Just give me a second to get back into uniform."

"Is that the real thing?" Cal asked as MacTaggart unhooked the kilt and folded it neatly.

"Aye, lad, it is," the detective said, playfully laying on a thick Scots burr. "Tartan of the clan MacTaggart."

"I'd heard the New York police force was loaded with Irishmen. No one ever mentions the Scots."

"Why should they? I'm the one and only clan Scotsman on the force."

MacTaggart finished zipping up his trousers and sat down behind his desk, pointing Cal to a chair opposite. "Now let's see if I have this right, Professor. You want to assist us on a murder case. You're offering to give us information—if and when you get any. Not a thrilling offer as it stands, but it's the thought that counts, isn't it? It's real public-spirited. But what I'd like to know, Professor, is why. What's your angle?"

Cal met MacTaggart's hard stare with his own. He fought down the impulse to rail against the detective's implication that the offer of help was selfishly motivated. He did, after all, have an "angle."

"I've become professionally interested in studying Voodoo in an urban environment, the variety of religions that seem to have a common origin in African tribal—"

"We're not in your classroom, Professor. Knock off the academic bullshit. You're turned on by Voodoo, is that it?"

Cal was puzzled by the detective's apparent need to put him on the defensive. Turned on by Voodoo? As if he was looking for thrills? No. But MacTaggart was giving notice that he wasn't fooled by academic phrases; he was no dumb cop automatically bowled over by experts.

"I'm fascinated," Cal said. "I want to research the subject, find out how widespread it is. But I'm not looking for kicks. What attracts me is the amazing fact that a religion conceived by savages —men who actually believed that the sun was a flaming torch carried across the sky by a superhuman being—that their religion appears to be thriving here and now. People who drive fast cars and eat fast food can worship gods who are supposed to be able to

86

turn the sun on and off. Why are people reaching so far back for something to believe in?"

MacTaggart bobbed his head slowly. "So what do you want from me?"

"Frankly, I was hoping you'd cooperate with me, be one of my sources. From investigating that warehouse murder you must have learned—"

"How do you know Voodoo's linked to that murder?" the detective cut in sharply, as though some secret had been leaked.

"Lieutenant," Cal replied evenly, "I saw the things you found with the body, and now I know those saint figures are representations of African gods. The murder was in Brooklyn and you've been assigned to investigate it, even though you're based in the *barrio*. Which means it's not just a simple murder case. I thought we could strike a deal. You share what you know with me, and I'll feed back my research data. I might even come across something that helps your case." Heading off the attack on amateur sleuthing the cop was bound to make, Cal added, "I'm not unaware of the problems the police have when it comes to investigating a religion."

MacTaggart put his head back and arched one of his bushy eyebrows. Now he looked less annoyed than bemused. "And you think it'll be easier for you? Professor, our problems don't begin or end with the fact that this is a religion. It's much more than that. You don't know what you're dealing with. You don't begin to understand it by walking into one of those freaky stores. Ask the people who go in and out—hell, they won't even admit it exists. 'Voodoo? What's that?' The only way to really find out what goes on inside is to join up, become a believer."

Cal was surprised to hear the cop express such hopelessness. Wasn't it his business to track down information no matter what the difficulties?

"Does that mean you're giving up on your investigation?" Cal asked, and instantly knew it was a mistake.

The detective's long thin face grew even harder; his skin took on the gray cast of chiseled stone. MacTaggart was clearly a man who gave up on nothing. But he offered no defense. The silent reaction said it all.

When he spoke again, there was no edge to his voice. Very quietly, looking down at the green blotter on his desk, he asked, "How do you think this research of yours can turn up more than we can?"

"I have an advantage over you," Cal said. "I'm not a policeman. People won't start with their barriers so high."

There was a long silence, though not a restful pause. Cal sensed a quickening rhythm as MacTaggart lifted his eyes and examined him once more, an unheard crescendo building to a decision.

Finally MacTaggart shook his head and dragged in a deep breath. "Forget it, Professor. Find something else to study. Didn't you see what you had to pass through to come here today? The local headhunters aren't as easy to make friends with as the ones in Pago-Pago or Bora-Bora or wherever the hell you've been before. Just go home. You don't know what kind of crazy shit you'd be stepping into."

"Look, I know Voodoo is extraordinary," Cal said, "even bizarre. But I'm an anthropologist. Whatever human beings can think up, however they behave, has meaning for me. There aren't any human ideas or beliefs that I'd ever run away from or put down as crazy shit." He heard himself getting up on his high horse, yet couldn't help venting his passion for knowledge—and a bit of disgust with the cop's apparent bigotry. But Cal knew that his outburst had blown the connection to the cop, and he rose to leave.

MacTaggart rose with him. "All right, Professor," he said grimly. "You want cooperation? You've got it."

The policeman stalked out of his office. Cal followed as if yanked along by an invisible tether.

Striding across the squadroom, MacTaggart called to a man bent over one of the desks. "I'm going downtown, Pete. You and Chico take the lineup on that grocery rip-off."

MacTaggart stopped at a pegboard near the door to pick up his keys. "Let's go, Professor. Time to start your research."

"Where will you be?" the other detective called out.

MacTaggart shouted back, "The morgue."

Chapter 13

THE CAR had no police markings and MacTaggart used no siren or flashing lights, but he raced downtown along the East River without regard for the speed limit, simply hitting the horn to blast slower traffic out of his path. Hunched over the wheel, jaw set, he obviously meant to rule out further conversation. Cal was baffled by the intensity of the detective's reaction.

In ten minutes they were in lower Manhattan. MacTaggart veered onto an exit ramp and drove a few blocks to a side street not far from the river. He pulled up in front of a building faced with white brick, joining a cluster of other vehicles—police cars, an ambulance, and a van with CITY OF NEW YORK, OFFICE OF THE MEDICAL EXAMINER stenciled on the side.

Cal trailed MacTaggart into the building. The cop made a quick round of the various offices, engaging in murmured conversations with secretaries and a man in a white surgical smock. At last he took Cal in an elevator down to a basement corridor. Dull fluorescent light bounced off the walls of gray ceramic tile and a linoleum floor of a shade too neutral to classify. A place without colors, like death itself. Near the elevator door, a couple of young men in white uniforms were laughing together; beside them stood two stainless steel trolleys. On one a body was laid out, its bare bluish feet protruding from under a covering sheet.

Just as Cal and MacTaggart stepped onto the floor, the two morgue attendants parted, wheeling their trolleys in opposite directions. The one with the body bumped into Cal, and the sole of the dead foot brushed his hand.

"Sorry, Jack," the morgue attendant said blithely, and moved on.

The touch of the corpse lingered on Cal's skin. But he didn't try to rub it away; he almost welcomed it as a kind of vaccination against the shock of death, preparation for whatever MacTaggart was taking him to see.

MacTaggart led the way to double doors at the end of the hall, pushed through, and held one open for Cal. They entered a large chilly chamber with rows of body lockers lining the walls. Another attendant was leaning over a long stainless steel table in the center of the room and scanning the sports pages of the *Daily News*. He glanced up as MacTaggart entered, then looked back to his reading.

MacTaggart waved a slip of paper. "Sorry to break the monotony, Freddy, but would you pull—"

"You think I don't know which one by now, Lieutenant? Four-eighty-one, right? What else do you come to see these days? Four-eight-one, comin' up."

The attendant pushed himself up off the table and ambled over to a row of lockers. He pulled out one of the long drawers, and sauntered straight back to his newspaper.

MacTaggart had been leading all the way. Cal expected now to be escorted forward. But the detective wasn't moving. He stood back, arms folded, and nodded toward the open locker.

"Go ahead, Professor. Look and learn."

Cal hesitated, trying to fathom the reason for the cop's bitter challenge. MacTaggart nodded again at the open drawer.

Cal went to the side and looked in.

He had thought he was prepared. Maybe if there had been nothing but a simple death, a simple murder, it wouldn't have hit him so hard. But this was something else: an atrocity. Gritting his teeth, gouging a thumbnail into the skin of his index finger curled over it, Cal suppressed the nausea that mushroomed up from his gut into his chest and throat.

Look and learn. Christ.

In the middle of the small naked torso was a gaping cavity. A large slab of the flesh and muscle from the abdomen had been jaggedly cut away and the innards completely taken out, like a melon scooped down to the rind. Heart, stomach, intestines, liver, all were gone. The mutilation was far greater than a postmortem would have left in its aftermath.

But there was something even more horrible than the victim's ravaged body. The young boy was no more than seven or eight years old. He was beautiful, too—slender, perfectly proportioned, with clear unblemished skin and silky light brown hair cut in bangs over the closed eyes. The face, untouched, had all the chaste nobility of a death mask taken from some ancient boy-king. But most shocking of all was the expression on the boy's face in repose. There was no hint of pain or terror; not the slightest misalignment of a muscle to remind an observer that the victim must have endured the most extreme mental and physical suffering leading up to his death. The appearance of the child conveyed a pure beatific contentment, some mystical ecstasy arrived at only beyond earthly life. The effect was disorienting; it was impossible to believe that this face could be part of the same body that had been butchered with such hideous savagery.

"So what do you think, Professor?" MacTaggart asked coolly. He had not moved from his place several yards away. "Are you still so fucking impressed by everything human beings do? You wouldn't put this down as crazy?"

Cal glared at the detective. "*This?* Of course I can see this is the act of a psychopath. But I didn't come to you because the murder itself interested me. I only came because I thought you'd be able to tell me something about the subject I want to study."

"But that's what I'm doing, Professor. I'm *showing* you most of what I know about the subject. This is the body we found in the warehouse."

"We're not talking about the same thing, MacTaggart. I want to research a religion. An anachronism—a primitive invention, maybe, but a true religion, as much as Buddhism or Judaism or any of the rest. But you're on the trail of a maniac, obviously some Manson-type blood cult."

MacTaggart grunted. "I'd like to believe that, too. But unfortunately it works out different. From the little we've been able to piece together, we think the way this kid was killed is absolutely a part of what you're calling a true religion."

Cal shook his head dumbly, uncomprehending.

"Of course I'm not an anthropologist," MacTaggart went on in his hard sardonic tone, "but even I have my ancient history down well enough to know this kind of murder used to be very big on the religious scene. Yes, Professor, I suppose it would be right up your alley—research-wise."

Cal turned to the body again. There was another second of confusion, not ignorance so much as a refusal to accept. But even as he heard MacTaggart speak again, Cal realized the full horror of what was being suggested.

"From your point of view," MacTaggart said, "I can see where it would be fascinating, all right. Right here in little old New York, we've got a bunch of people who believe in human sacrifice."

Cal went on looking at the body, unable to wrench his eyes away.

He felt a hand laid lightly on his shoulder.

"You've seen enough, Professor." The voice was unexpectedly gentle, shaded by its own vulnerability. "Let's get the hell out of here and leave this unlucky little bastard in peace."

Perhaps it was the result of the deadening acoustics in the cold empty room, but it seemed to Cal that MacTaggart's voice broke on the final word.

∋ ● ∈

They went to a bar around the corner from the morgue. It was the old style of saloon, gloomy and indecorous, no brighter by day than by night, with a long counter where a half-dozen scattered silhouettes sat staring into glasses that were eternally half-empty. Evidently a common stopping-off place to recover from the ordeal of meeting corpses. "Been to the freezer again?" MacTaggart was greeted by the bartender, who needed only to hear Cal order a Jack Daniels before setting up two drinks at the bar; for MacTaggart he poured a double vodka.

They carried their drinks to the rear of the room and sat down in a booth.

"I hope you'll accept my apology, Professor," MacTaggart began. "I shouldn't have thrown that at you without a little more preparation."

"Don't apologize," Cal said. "I asked to come in on this."

"Yeah, you did," the lieutenant agreed ruefully. "I guess that's what really made me want to put the needle in. Ever since I caught this case I've been wanting to run away from it. I never felt that before. I like my work, I always have. But this time . . ." He shook his head, as though surprised by his own revulsion. "So imagine how it feels when you, a goddamn civilian, show up out of nowhere and say you want to help. That's why I came down so hard on you. But it wasn't right."

"Forget it," Cal said.

They drank together, as though to seal an understanding.

Cal asked, "What makes this case so hard on you?"

"Everything about it, starting with what we just saw."

"But you must've seen violent deaths before."

"I've seen a few hundred stiffs," MacTaggart said, "plenty

bloodier than this one. But it isn't just the blood and gore, it's what goes with it. Like the look on that kid's face."

"Yeah, I'll remember that myself for a long time," Cal said quietly, and it floated whole into his mind.

"I'd settle for just remembering," MacTaggart said. "But I dream about it. I never saw anything like the faces on these kids. The M.E. tells us they had to feel terrible pain—not a trace of drugs in the blood. But they die looking *happy*." MacTaggart swigged the rest of his double vodka and called loudly for a refill. Then he noticed Cal's disapproving expression. "I went off duty at four," he said.

But Cal hadn't been frowning at MacTaggart's drinking. "These *kids*," he repeated. "You're saying there's been more than one case like this?"

"Three. Or three that we know about. No telling how many more. We wouldn't even have found what we did without dumb luck. The one in the warehouse was sheer accident. Some lighted candles were left in the basement—that's a kink in all these killings —and one must've tipped over and torched the place. Fire Department responded, saw it was 'an unusual,' and called us. That's how we got to the body only a couple of hours after the murder. Otherwise the corpse could've been down there forever. That part of the building wasn't used at all." His second drink had been brought quietly to the table. He pulled off half in one swallow. "The other two kids were also found in abandoned buildings. The first in a tenement up in the *barrio*, that's what brought me in, and then another up in the East Bronx. But the bodies weren't so fresh. The one in my part of town was the oldest, dead seven or eight months, so we know it's been going on at least that long." He hoisted his drink, but then paused to stare into the glass as though into a vast and bottomless sea. "Makes you wonder how many might've been done. One a month? One a week?"

His shoulders moved, as much a shudder as a shrug, and he drank.

So this was the city, Cal thought—the city painted in your worst dreams when you were living far away, secure in some quieter landscape like New Mexico. A jungle, a place where kids got murdered all the time. The place where he had brought his own son. Cal felt his stomach tighten, instinctive protective reflexes beginning to fire up, as though he had to be ready at any moment to save Chris from danger. Where was Chris now?

Cal caught himself. Where was his son? At day camp, of course.

Swimming, playing volleyball, making little treasures in arts and crafts. How easy it was to lose perspective. Bad things happened everywhere, and where more people were crowded together more bad things happened. But living in the middle of it you could forget that. Maybe MacTaggart had forgotten, was overreacting, too.

"Do there have to be more than three victims?" Cal asked. "Maybe you found them all."

"Professor, I told you we were led to these by chance. A wino looking for a place to sleep. A lady chasing her dog. I don't believe we're lucky enough to get the full score by the same route. There's wastelands in this city with so many empty hellholes we could never search them all. We've had a couple of cases lately with kids reported missing and we couldn't ever trace them, not a clue. One minute a kid is walking to meet the school bus, next minute he's gone and that's the last anybody knows."

"And you think those disappearances should be added to the tally?"

"Can't rule it out. Though as M.P.'s they don't fit the pattern."

"M.P.'s?"

"Missing persons. The children we found weren't."

"Weren't what? If they were dead they had to be missing."

"Right. Except that they weren't *reported* missing."

"Lieutenant, you said that one of these children had been dead more than six months. Are you telling me in all that time no one ever noticed—"

"I'm telling you there was no report. None of the M.P. descriptions in our central computer, not even in the national register of runaways, matched up. Not for any of the bodies."

Shyly, as though drawing conclusions would be trespassing on the detective's prerogative, Cal said, "But that ought to tell you who the killers are."

"Oh yeah," MacTaggart said, too blithely, "the same people who should've made the report, who should have at least wanted a body to cry over instead of an empty grave. Nails them for accomplices, anyway. Trouble is"—the cop's tone darkened—"we don't have a single fucking lead on who the kids belonged to—mothers, fathers, aunts, uncles, neighbors. No way to know. The bodies were found naked, stripped of anything that could be used for identification. They weren't old enough to have the kind of dental work that might help us track the usual John Doe. One was decomposed beyond the point where we could go for a visual I.D., like canvassing neighborhoods with a photograph. We're doing it with the

94

latest one, but so far *nada*, as the P.R.'s say." He took a swig of his drink and hammered out the word with rising fury. "*Nada. Nada. Nada.*"

"What about publishing the picture in the papers?" Cal suggested. "I've seen that done with missing persons."

"You won't see it done with this one," MacTaggart said heavily, as though taking a vow. "Once we bring in the media, we won't be able to limit the information they get. And I hate to think what'll happen if anybody says the police in this city are working on the premise that a particular group of its citizens is sacrificing children. Things are wound up tight enough in this town as it is."

"I suppose you'd be attacked by the Hispanic community just for suggesting the idea."

"Have been already," MacTaggart said. "Every time I send a couple of men out to ask questions, anything that touches on these cases, it feeds back to some community honcho who gets on the blower to the commissioner, or the mayor." MacTaggart took a breath. "So I go on tiptoe, quiet as a little mouse. And get *nada*." He picked up his glass again. But this dose of alcohol had a different effect than the last. When MacTaggart rapped his tumbler down on the table, Cal perceived a subtle change in the atmosphere. This drink had braced MacTaggart, had begun to dull the frustrations he confessed, stoke the fire that drove him to do his public duty regardless of the private battles. He didn't call for another refill, but sat turning the glass pensively. He needed to talk, Cal felt.

"You're absolutely certain," Cal said, "that the killings were done as some kind of ceremony."

"Not *some* kind," MacTaggart shot back. "*One* kind. The families were into a cult, religion, whatever it is, that required them to do this, and they did what they were told. That's why no one admits to noticing these kids disappear. It all fits, Professor, it all fits." MacTaggart stared directly across the table, and in the eyes of this man sworn to uphold the law Cal was chilled to see the flash of a wild unharnessed rage that belonged more to the eyes of a murderer.

"Those poor little bastards we find with the smiles on their faces," the detective said then, "those kids we find looking so goddamn *glad* to die . . . those kids were sacrificed."

Chapter 14

SACRIFICE.

Could MacTaggart understand all the implications of what he was suggesting? Cal wondered.

Human sacrifice. Being done here in New York. Children being slaughtered as offerings to . . . to what? Ancient deities, Voodoo gods.

Cal thought back to the little speech he'd spouted off back in MacTaggart's office—how there was something to respect in all the customs of mankind. The anthropologist's credo. He could understand now why MacTaggart had blown a fuse, had felt the urge to confront Cal so brutally with that child's mutilated body.

Yet even now Cal felt no urge to retract what he had said earlier. No anthropologist aware of the origins of the custom could dismiss sacrifice as merely insane. The ritual had been born in the cradle of great civilizations. Had anyone ever denied the greatness of the Aztec people because their religion called for ripping the hearts from the bodies of their finest warriors as offerings to their gods? The Aztecs were acknowledged as one of the most creative peoples in history. And Polynesian islanders, whose societies were studied as models of tranquility and fulfillment, had in times past regularly thrown their most beautiful virgins from the highest cliffs into the sea, because their gods demanded this tribute in return for good fortune. Offering human lives to appease wrathful deities was a custom that had roots deep in primitive tradition.

But it had belonged to a time when a logic existed, however

cruel, in which blood rituals were seen as part of the struggle for survival. What logic could justify human sacrifice now?

"You have any solid evidence to support this theory of yours?" Cal asked MacTaggart.

"Plenty," MacTaggart replied. "You've already seen some of it."

"The beads and the statue."

MacTaggart nodded. "The beads were clutched in the victims' hands, and those little saint figures were at the foot and head of the body. Same every time, except that in each case the statues were a little different. Then there was other stuff. Little heaps of fruit here and there. And, of course, the body itself, the way the killing was done—evisceration, the M.E. calls it, pulling out all the vital organs. That *is* how sacrifices were done in the good old days. Right, Professor?"

"Some were," Cal allowed.

"Then there's the way the bodies were laid out. Flat on their backs, naked, lying on a raised platform made out of a kind of rare wood."

"What kind?"

"Don't know. We shipped samples over to the Botanical Gardens in both Brooklyn and the Bronx, but nobody's been able to identify the tree it came from."

Cal pondered a moment. "But couldn't any nut buy some stuff in a *botánica* and use it to camouflage another kind of murder, say a sex killing?"

"The kids weren't touched that way," MacTaggart said gruffly, giving Cal a lingering sidelong glance. "You know, Professor, I'm beginning to get the feeling you don't want to believe me."

Cal shook his head. "It's just very hard to accept that these children were genuinely sacrificed."

"Genuinely." MacTaggart spat out the word mockingly. "What the hell does that mean? They're genuinely dead, that's for damn sure."

Cal nodded patiently. "But the killers had to be psychopaths. They couldn't be people who believed sacrifice was a meaningful act—people acting, you might say, in good conscience."

MacTaggart squinted at Cal as though trying to distinguish recognizable shapes through a heavy pall of smoke. "Killing people is murder," he said flatly. "Always has been."

Cal shook his head. "You're missing the point. To understand human sacrifice, Lieutenant, you've got to remember what kind of world people were living in when it was really done. In primitive societies people lived totally at the mercy of nature, and their religions reflected their absolute dependence. They had gods who controlled the sun, the moon, the earth, the rain, the tides—hundreds of gods in charge of every aspect of the universe. To influence those forces, they were willing to do anything. Human sacrifice was their way of showing ultimate devotion to the heavenly powers, winning favors from them. Actually, it shows how much the primitives *respected* human life—believing that a god could be flattered only by this most precious gift. As they saw it, offering one life could persuade the gods to grant victory in a war, say, or cure a plague that would claim thousands of lives. Not really a very bloodthirsty notion. More like a form of self-defense."

"Thanks for the history lesson," MacTaggart rejoined tartly. "But we're not talking about the good old days here. These kids are being killed now."

"That's my point exactly. When human sacrifices *were* done, they were a sincere attempt to control the forces of nature. But it's pretty hard to imagine that anybody who knows rain can be made by seeding clouds, or who's ever seen a moonshot on television, could still think that spilling human blood was a way of controlling human destiny."

The squint lines around MacTaggart's warm brown eyes smoothed out slowly. "There's a whole lot of things done in the name of one religion or another that I can't buy," he said. "But they're done all the same, all in the name of somebody's idea of good. With most, it's nobody's business to say what's right or wrong. But this one *is* my business. I don't have to believe it, or study it, or understand it. But I do have to *stop* it.". He leaned across the table to Cal. "That's why I accept your offer, Professor."

Cal was caught off guard. Though the detective had been willing to share confidences in the limbo of a gloomy bar, Cal had taken it as no more than a symptom of battle fatigue in a hard case—a visit to the confessional before going on to solve his problem alone. And the more he learned about the case, the more Cal wondered if it wasn't better to be left out of it. Studying "urban primitivism" was fine as an abstract notion, but then he hadn't expected to be involving himself in a whole series of bizarre and grisly murders. Suppose he did pick up some significant information, mightn't he become a target himself? This was no time to be doing anything dangerous. Chris needed him, had no one else.

And Chris was all he had, too, Cal thought. Wasn't it possible that by probing into the murders of children he would expose his own child to some heightened risk? The risk of—

The thought was so horrible Cal wouldn't allow it to form. He took a swig from his drink and did a silent run-through of the excuse he would give MacTaggart to retreat from the offer he himself had made.

Yet he did not offer it. He kept weighing the perils against something else, the prize of knowledge. Suppose human sacrifice had been done—not in a burst of crazed religious fervor but by calculated design, not once but repeatedly, not by a madman but by a congregation of truly religious, God-fearing people. To understand how it could happen would be to probe to the darkest center of the nature of man.

MacTaggart had been gazing at him, waiting for a response. Now he spoke. "You know, Cal—it must be Cal they call you, can't imagine it would be Calvin—I really could use your help. This Voodoo stuff we're investigating—it's not just a religion. It's more like . . . like a secret society. Like the Mafia was thirty or forty years ago. You found the bodies left and right, and you could never pin down who made the hits. Same with this Santeria thing. We know it exists, and we can find plenty of people who are into it, groups of a hundred or more who get together and worship their Voodoo gods. Families, the groups are called—even *that's* like the goddamn Mafia. But it doesn't matter what we know. When we try to put the big picture together, all we see is smoke. There's even a language barrier to keep us out."

"But aren't there Hispanics on the force?" Cal asked.

"Sure, a couple right under me. But ever since it became clear what we're hooked into, all our Latins have backed off. They're afraid. And sometimes I am, too."

"Of what?"

MacTaggart snatched up his glass and, finding it empty, turned away as if to call to the bar. But he was silent, and after a few seconds turned back to Cal.

"I told you about the families. At the head of each one there's a kind of priest, called a *santero*. We managed to get the names of a few—they're known all over the Hispanic neighborhoods. Well, a couple of my men went to see one of these guys, and while one detective kept him talking, his partner was able to sneak into another room and do a quick search. He found a knife—unusual thing with a curved blade, engraved wooden handle—that looked like it had dried blood on it. So he put it in his pocket." Cal arched his eyebrows, and MacTaggart noticed. "Of course, taking possible evidence without a warrant could've wiped out our ability to use it in court later. But my man was frustrated, like we all were. We wanted answers no matter how we got them. By the time we got a warrant the blood could've been washed off. So we snatched it. The man swore later there was no way the swipe could've been noticed. The *santero* was in another room, facing away to a wall. But when the interview ended and the detectives were leaving, this little monkey-faced P.R. says: 'I know what you have done.' That's all. No demands, no threats, no curses. But when my men told us about it later, they both said they were terrified. And Letzke—the one who actually had the blade on him—said as soon as the *santero* spoke he was sure he felt a painful burning on his hip, like the knife in his pocket was red-hot."

There was a pause. Cal said, "Not so amazing, actually. There was probably a mirror on the wall the santero was facing, and as for the burning, that might've been guilt at work, a psychological reaction—"

"Wait," MacTaggart said softly, "there's a little more. We did lab tests. The blood came from a bird of some kind, probably a chicken. After that, Letzke didn't know what to do with the knife to clear his conscience. He could've thrown it away or let it sit in the property room, but Letzke thought it ought to be returned. So finally he put it in an envelope and left it in the glove compartment of his car, thinking he'd just mail it back the next time he passed a post office. For a week he forgot about it. Then one night, after working a late shift, he was driving out to his house on Long Island, it was raining, and he went into a skid." MacTaggart faltered and winced. He took a breath then, and raced through the rest, words tumbling out. "And he hit a telephone pole, hit it hard, a real accordion job, and Letzke was pinned so fucking bad, half crushed, that to get him out alive the paramedics had to take off both his legs above the knee, cut them off right there on the spot."

Cal let the silence last, giving MacTaggart a chance to mourn the fate of his colleague.

"Lieutenant," he said at last, "you're not suggesting—"

"No, I'm not!" MacTaggart fired back defensively. "The man was tired, the road was wet, there are thousands of car accidents every day—no reason why it shouldn't happen to a cop." MacTaggart brought his voice down. "But since the accident, the whole squad has eased off the case. They blame the rest of their caseload, but it's just an excuse. I know because I'm fighting the same thing. It's like something is holding us all at arm's length—like when magnets are turned backwards. We know the truth is there, but we can't reach it. So we're turning away."

Cal was overwhelmed by the depth of need MacTaggart had suddenly revealed. The cop was confessing that a solution to the murders might depend on Cal. The amateur was being begged to pick up the ball the pros had dropped.

"Listen, Lieutenant," Cal started to protest.

"Dennis," MacTaggart put in amiably.

"Dennis, I'm not sure I can do what you want."

MacTaggart's gaze clouded with confusion. "You came to me, Cal," he said.

"I know. But, you see, I have a young son myself. My wife died not long ago and he needs me. We need each other. If this thing gets dangerous—"

"You'd have full police protection."

"It can't be allowed to get to that point. I'm not withdrawing my offer. I told you I want to do a serious study of Santeria and that I'd share anything I learn that might help you. But that's the limit of what I can do. I can't afford to get involved in playing under-cover man for the police. I won't swipe evidence or—"

MacTaggart smiled. "Good enough, Cal. Just do your research. I agree completely with what you said before: people who shut out the cops just might open up to you." He paused. "I assume you won't mind, though, if I steer you to a source or two."

MacTaggart took a notebook from his pocket. He scribbled a name and address, tore out the page, and passed it over.

Cal read: *Oscar Sezine.* The address was on East 107th Street, in the *barrio.*

"Sezine runs an organization called the Asociación Cooperativa para. . . ." MacTaggart wrestled with the pronunciation of the Spanish, then gave up. "Para something-or-other. It's sort of a clinic and school combined. Takes in young Hispanics who are wrecked on dope or just beaten down in general, cleans them up, and runs classes to put them back on the street as good citizens."

"Why should that interest me?"

"Because," MacTaggart explained, "Sezine makes no bones about the fact that he uses Santeria in his work. He teaches it as a positive force like any other religion, uses it to put the kids straight."

"Then why wouldn't Sezine talk to you?"

MacTaggart shook his head. "Says the whole investigation is a smear job. He makes a pretty good argument, too. Points to his own good works as proof that Santeria is harmless. Reads the statistics on his rehab program. They're damned impressive—a ninety-two percent recovery rate in hard-drug cases. He's turned around a lot of bad kids, which makes our job easier. So there's a whole bunch of reasons not to push Oscar too hard. But," Mac-Taggart added slyly, "if he could be reached without pushing . . ."

As Cal folded the paper and put it in his pocket, the detective smiled. It was a smile of appreciation, but Cal caught a glimmer of guile in it. MacTaggart had gotten exactly what he wanted out of their meeting, Cal realized. He wondered then if the whole routine —the shock tactics, followed by the breast-beating and buddy-buddy confidences—hadn't been designed to manipulate him into covering this one gap in the investigation. MacTaggart was a veteran, after all, certainly not above any strategy that might help solve a murder case.

But Cal chided himself for such suspicions. Hadn't he made the approach to the detective? Weren't they using each other? Why should he suddenly have the feeling that he was being manipulated, that he was taking this on not entirely of his own free will?

They argued over the tab. Guilty over his final thought, Cal was the more insistent and paid for the drinks.

Outside the bar, MacTaggart said he was heading back to the precinct and asked if he could drive Cal anywhere.

"No, I'm heading home, and it would be out of your way."

"Least I can do," MacTaggart pressed. "You're a lifesaver—maybe literally."

Cal assured him he didn't want the ride, that he could walk to Chelsea, practically straight across town.

"Chelsea," MacTaggart said. "Lots of Latins there, too."

"That's how I got into this, remember—passing a *botánica.*"

MacTaggart nodded and smiled again. They parted with Cal's promise to check back as soon as he had any information that might bear on the case, and MacTaggart's urging that Cal must call without hesitation if he felt any need for assistance or protection.

Cal walked west. The sun was on its lowering arc, round and golden; its rays, like the broom of heaven, swept the streets of the city clean. Cal ambled past the windows of shops and forced himself to stop and examine the contents. The fabric in an upholstery store, the colored gewgaws of a gift boutique.

He looked at everything, but it made no difference. Wherever he lingered, whatever he saw, the vision of a mutilated little boy floated in his mind, blotting out everything else.

And even more than the slaughtered carcass, there was the face —that horrifyingly unreasonable expression of the purest bliss.

Perhaps it was only a failure of memory, or some perverse inner wish to torture himself, but at moments Cal thought the exquisitely sweet smiling face in his vision looked almost exactly like the face of his own son.

Chapter **15**

THE NEXT MORNING Cal went to Columbia's Low Library and searched the card catalog. There was not a single entry under "Santeria"; the word did not appear in the files. Cal went next to search the microfilm index, the ethnological journals, and the inter-library loan listings. There was nothing.

It was strange, he thought. You would've supposed that some-body had written something about the religion. Then Cal realized his mistake, and looked under "Voodoo." Half a dozen titles were listed, a couple of them stocked in multiple copies. Surely one of them would have information on Santeria.

He went upstairs to the stacks, used his new faculty identifica-tion card to pass through the checkpoint at the locked wire-mesh gates, and began looking for titles. Only one was on the shelf, a book titled *Voodoo in Haiti*, by Alfred Metraux. Not much, Cal thought, but a start.

At the front desk he checked out the book, then gave the librar-ian the other titles and asked her to put them on reserve. The librarian moved to a computer terminal, punched in the index numbers and reserve code, and waited a moment.

"I'm sorry," she said, turning from the terminal and shaking her head. "I can't reserve any of those for you."

"But I'm on the faculty," Cal said, reaching for his card.

"Oh, there aren't any restrictions," she said. "It's just that there's such a problem these days with books being stolen, and all the titles you gave me are missing."

"Missing?" Cal said.

"Stolen," the librarian said.

As he walked across the quadrangle, Cal thought of how fanatically, according to Dennis MacTaggart, the religion prized its secrecy. *We know it exists, but all we see is smoke.* Was their secrecy strong enough to lead to the stealing of books? Could there be some organized effort to suppress any knowledge that had been written down?

No, Cal thought; after all, he had found one book on the subject, and the rest must have vanished at random. As the librarian had said, it was a common problem these days.

After putting Chris to bed that night, Cal poured himself a glass of jug wine and went out to the garden with the book. Taking a sip of the wine, he stretched out on the folding chaise, propped *Voodoo in Haiti* on his knees, and scanned the biographical notes at the beginning. Alfred Metraux had led the kind of life most anthropologists dream of. The Frenchman's early career had taken him to the High Andes to study Peruvian Indians, to the lowlands along the coast of South America, to Easter Island. And then, just after World War II, to Haiti, on a mission for the United Nations to study the peasants and help improve their nutrition and general welfare. Metraux had been to Haiti once before, helping the government set up its Bureau d'Ethnologie, but it was on this second trip that he paid closer attention to the country's folk religion, and began to discover the pervasive influence of *vodun* in the lives of the natives. Metraux became absorbed in the religion, even obsessed, and promptly abandoned all his other interests to spend the next fifteen years studying only Voodoo.

Cal looked up from the book. It was encouraging that another serious anthropologist had found Voodoo sufficiently worthwhile to lay aside other work—as Cal would be doing with his research on the Zokos.

But Metraux's fifteen years in Haiti were to be the last he would have for any kind of work. He had finished his book in 1963 and seen it published in France as *Le Vaudou Haitien;* it was recognized as his greatest achievement. Shortly thereafter, as though the book had settled some final account with life, Metraux had died.

Cal turned to the author's foreword. "Certain words," Metraux wrote, "are charged with evocative power. Voodoo is one. It usually conjures up visions of mysterious deaths, secret rites, or dark saturnalia celebrated by blood-maddened, sex-maddened, god-maddened natives."

His intention, Metraux continued, was to dispel such prejudice and superstition. Voodoo was a true religion, he said, worthy of serious study. Even so, Cal saw as he read on, Metraux anticipated criticism. Others had told him that Voodoo was dangerous, or diabolical, or black magic, that the anthropologist himself might be seduced by pagan superstition. But Metraux was confident that a scholar could "throw cold light on the facts, and make this religion emerge from its cloaking shadows and free it of the nightmares which it still inspires in many honest but·misinformed people."

Groping at the side of his chaise as he read, Cal found his wine glass, brought it to his lips, and sipped—all without taking his eyes from the printed page. He was hooked.

It was all quite fantastic, more complicated than any primitive religion he had ever heard of—myth upon myth, bizarre tales and folklore. The Haitian natives believed not only that plants and herbs had souls, but that the souls could be captured and used to chase away evil spirits responsible for human illness. It was as though penicillin or aspirin had a soul. The natives believed they could control their destiny through spells and potions and blood rituals—offering slaughtered jungle beasts as sacrifices to the gods. Ancestor worship was common, but was more than a mere abstract idea of respect for the dead: the natives believed that the spirits of their departed relatives were always present, and could communicate with the living through dreams.

The reasons for the religion's survival in Haiti were just as John Viner had explained. The slaves brought from Africa had held onto their customs, despite the Church's effort to stamp them out. And the very word Voodoo had come from the Dahomean language—*vodun*, an all-encompassing word meaning god, or spirit, or sacred object.

The most intriguing parts of the text were Metraux's experience in the field, those occasions when, after spending years to gain the peasants' trust, the anthropologist had at last been invited to actually witness Voodoo ceremonies, secret rites never opened to any but the faithful. Cal gripped the book more tightly as he read:

The rituals are held always at night in a cloistered place, "shut off from the eyes of the profane." A priest and priestess take up their positions by an altar containing a caged snake. After various ceremonies, believers approach and tell the snake what they most desire. The snake is then put on top of the altar and everyone brings it an offering. A goat or other large animal may be sacrificed and the blood, collected in a jar, is then touched to the lips of all present, in token of a pledge to suffer death rather than reveal anything of the ceremony, or even to inflict death on anyone who would break the vow.

Cal admired the Frenchman's eye for detail, but what came next showed more than a talent for observation. At some of the Voodoo ceremonies, Metraux reported, the body of a believer was entered by the spirit of a Voodoo god. Not a devil, which many religions believed in, but a god. A *benign* possession, one that was good, and not to be feared—a startling idea:

The phenomenon takes place at special feasts to the gods. Spirits are believed to take part in the homage, and actually receive the sacrifices offered. They attend and witness the worship through the medium of possession.

At a point in the ceremony when ecstasy has been induced through magic and dancing, the possession occurs. Suddenly one of the believers will feel total emptiness, as though he were fainting. He becomes not only the vessel of the god, but the instrument of the god. From now on, it will be the god's personality, not his own, that he will express. The look of his features, the sound of his voice, all his actions will reflect exactly the character of the god who has descended and entered him.

The explanation of the mystic trance given by the disciples is simple. A god moves into the head of a man after first driving out "the good angel"—one of the two souls everyone is believed to carry within himself. The eviction of this soul is responsible for the trembling and convulsion which happens at the beginning of a possession.

Cal read on, racing through several descriptions of possessions Metraux had witnessed. With each one the tone became more convincing, the description more thorough. It seemed to Cal that Metraux had begun to believe what he was describing—that possession was not an act. Cal wondered if he could ever be persuaded to believe that the spirit of a god could inhabit the body of a man.

By one in the morning he had read through much of the book—accounts of Voodoo equivalents of communion and baptism; of sophisticated, well-educated white people living in Port-au-Prince who were convinced that sorcerers could raise the dead and swore to having witnessed it; of the wrath and anger of divine spirits.

And Metraux wrote, too, that there had once been human sacrifice.

But this had all happened in a foreign culture. Laying the book aside, Cal gazed up at the rear windows of the buildings hovering over the garden. He tried to imagine how city dwellers might still subscribe to a set of primitive beliefs born in the jungle and nurtured in a rural way of life. That would be the lure of this research, he thought: to find out how Voodoo had survived in a world of concrete and computers and Cadillacs.

∋ ● ∈

The next morning Cal got a call from Harvey Rayburn's wife Ellen. He was beginning to make friends on the faculty, and Harvey, whose field was the development of languages, had been especially helpful in getting him settled. The Rayburns were having a dinner party, and wanted Cal to come. "It'll be informal," Ellen Rayburn said. "Morris Bassani's coming with Georgia, and Dick Berman and Leo Stone. You'll know everybody." When Cal gladly accepted, Ellen offered to fix him up with a date. It was inevitable, he supposed: the eligible widower in a city full of eligible women. But Cal said he had a friend he'd like to bring along.

He called his landlady, Torey Halowell. It had been so long since he had asked a woman for a date that he was more than a little nervous, and actually had to stand by the phone for a few minutes before dialing. To his relief, she responded warmly. "I'd be delighted," she said with obvious pleasure. "It sounds like great fun."

So he had not been wrong about the undercurrent of attraction on the day he found her painting his living room. He liked her, and she liked him.

She met him at the door of her apartment that night wearing a white silk dress and a linen jacket. With her chestnut hair let down over her shoulders, she was even more alluring than he had remembered. She invited him in for a drink and gave him a tour of her apartment, which she proudly announced she had renovated herself. The downstairs was a two-story living room with eggshell-white walls and big sofas covered in rouch cotton. Upstairs, off a balcony overlooking the living room, were three bedrooms, the largest an office for her business as an art consultant to corporations. The smell of scented candles burning in the master bedroom filled the air. Half-open crates, overflowing with fluffs of straw, lined the upstairs hallway. Against one wall was a Coptic cross—from Egypt, Cal guessed—and on the other, several bulky African masks with long black faces, eyes rimmed in orange, and jagged beak-like noses. The whole collection, Torey explained, had been imported from Ghana for the lobby of an electronics company in Connecticut.

Downstairs, she served him paté and crackers and a glass of kir, asked who would be at the party, and generally put him at ease. She sparkled while she talked, she was a pleasure to be with, and Cal could not help thinking she was just the sort of intelligent, self-assured woman he could fall in love with someday, if only he could get over the loss of Laurie.

∋ • ∈

"We live in an age of fear," Harvey Rayburn was saying as his wife served an appetizer of cold spaghetti *pesto*. "The world's in terrible shape and people don't know what to believe in any more. So they'll believe in anything."

The Rayburns' spacious living room was fashionably modern and unacademic. There were Stella prints on the walls instead of the usual painted-by-friends art, and the view over Riverside Drive toward the Palisades was breathtaking. Modular couches of brown velour were arranged around a low table in the center; an upside-down wastebasket from the Paris subway had been turned into a lamp table with a glass top.

Cal and Torey had arrived at eight o'clock, Morris and Georgia Bassani a few minutes later. "The baby-sitters on the West Side are now getting *three* dollars an hour," Georgia announced. In the kitchen Dick Berman and his wife, Kiki, were arguing politics with Harriet Stone, who at age forty-three was seven months pregnant. Ellen Rayburn broke off from her serving to introduce Torey—"Torey Halowell, Dick and Kiki, Leo Stone, watch out for him, he's a letch"—and took her into the den to show off her collection of Chinese dolls.

"It's the modern condition," Morris Bassani said, holding court in the living room. "The atom bomb has changed all our ideas about life. Lifton says it destroyed our idea of immortality, the hope that our work will live after we're gone."

There was talk of divorces among the younger faculty, the threatened strike by the sanitation men, the ludicrous rent situation in Manhattan. Plates of food were ferried from the kitchen to the living room, heaped with lamb in a tomato sauce, rice pilaf, and an escarole salad. Torey recommended her herbal hay-fever cure to Kiki Berman.

"You and Harriet are courageous to have another kid," Harvey Rayburn said to Leo Stone as he cleaned gunk from his pipe. "It's hard to think about bringing kids into a world that's falling apart."

Ellen Rayburn bustled in from the kitchen carrying fresh bottles of wine. "Doomsday talk again," she said disparagingly, leaning over to fill Cal's glass. "How's your book on the Zokos coming? Getting any work done?"

"I've gotten interested in something else," Cal said, balancing his plate on his lap while holding up his glass.

"Professional hazard," Dick Berman called out, coming in from the kitchen. "If you're smart, you'll finish that book quick. What are you letting distract you?"

"Voodoo," Cal said. "Voodoo in the city."

Torey turned from the serving table, wine bottle in hand, and stared at Cal for a moment, then looked away and refilled her glass.

"You're kidding," Harvey said. "Voodoo?"

"I've been thinking I might write about it," Cal said. "Something about urban primitivism, the survival of ancient African traditions in the middle of modern everyday life. Apparently it's common all over the South. There are hundreds of thousands of believers, Hispanics from the Caribbean, and they have these little stores where—"

"Doesn't sound like serious anthropology to me," Dick Berman cut in.

"Me neither," Harvey said. "You want to watch yourself, Cal. You've got good field work behind you, and you ought to write it up while it's still fresh. Leave Voodoo to the journalists."

"Listen, Harvey," Cal protested, "Metraux thought it was serious enough to write a book about. Have you read it? He actually believed in possession."

"Possession?" Georgia Bassani said. "Like in *The Exorcist?*"

"No," Cal replied, "that was possession by the Devil. In Voodoo the idea is completely different. A person gets taken over not by a devil or an evil spirit, but by a god. Metraux actually saw it happen; he believed it. And it could be happening here, around us. If that's not the material for something interesting, I don't know what is."

Harvey Rayburn puffed on his pipe. "Metraux was writing about an entire culture," he said curtly. "Not about Puerto Ricans in New York."

"Harvey," Cal said. "You sound like a bigot."

"Voodoo," Kiki Berman said, scowling. "Isn't that about sticking pins into dolls and cutting up animals in Central Park?"

Ellen Rayburn sat forward. "That's right. I saw it in the *Post.* They have these ceremonies in the park where they kill animals. And what about that woman in the Bronx who put her baby in the oven—didn't she say some witch doctor told her to do it?"

"Hey, that's not what it's about," Cal said, raising his voice. "African religion is probably the oldest in the world. Look, Jung took the *I Ching* seriously enough to write an introduction to the Princeton edition, and that's a Chinese book of fortune-telling. Voodoo's been around a lot longer, and it's more complicated than anything the Chinese had, or the Greeks for that matter. The Africans had a pantheon of more than a hundred gods, each with a defined purpose." Cal turned to Harvey. "You're the language expert, Harvey. Do you know where the word 'zombie' comes from? It derives from an African word, *zombi*. Z–o–m–b–i. It means literally a wandering spirit of the dead. How many words are there in English, Harvey, that come from an *African* language? I'd say this is a fairly significant culture, and worth studying."

There was an uncomfortable silence for a moment. Harvey Rayburn emptied his pipe again. Everyone's eyes shifted around the room, trying to focus on something other than Cal. Harriet Stone came in from the kitchen eating a bowl of ice cream. Ellen Rayburn told a joke about ice cream and pickles, Dick Berman told a story about his mother-in-law's trip to the Wailing Wall, and the tension in the air disappeared.

In a corner Leo Stone was standing with Torey. Whatever she was saying was making Leo, normally staid and pompous, laugh volubly. A moment later he caught Cal's eye and mouthed *She's terrific, where'd you find her?*

$$\ni \bullet \in$$

When dessert was served Cal and Torey were standing by the window, contemplating the view across the Hudson. Ellen Rayburn passed by with a tray of after-dinner drinks; they each took a brandy, clinked glasses, and drank.

Then, with a glance toward the others, Torey said softly, "They're kind of stodgy, aren't they?"

"They loosen up when you get to know them."

"Oh, I didn't mean socially," Torey answered quickly. "They're all very friendly. I meant about your work. They came down pretty hard on you for saying you might want to study something a little . . . unusual."

Cal shrugged. "It's a little problem we seem to have among academics. The only things you're supposed to want to study are the things that everybody else takes seriously—and about which almost everything has already been learned."

Torey laughed. "Well, from what I heard you're onto something worthwhile."

"You really think so?" It was nice to hear, Cal thought, after the bombardment of criticism from the academic conservatives.

"What I mean is, some people let themselves get stifled by convention, by what other people think of them, and you don't seem to be like that. If you think something's interesting, you'll pursue it and not let anyone discourage you. That's a nice quality."

Cal gazed at her a moment, and suddenly she glanced shyly away. Her response to what the others had said was so genuine that he was unexpectedly moved. Torey was attuned to how he thought of himself. He had always counted on that kind of support from Laurie—but then, she'd been his wife.

Torey was looking at him again now, smiling.

Georgia Bassani came up behind them. "Hot in here, isn't it? It's just murder to air-condition these big apartments."

Then Harriet Stone joined them and the conversation turned to the dangers of raising children in the city, Torey saying she was nevertheless looking forward to having her own someday. Harvey Rayburn got slightly tipsy, and Ellen Rayburn eventually took a seat at the piano and played old folk songs from the 'fifties.

Later, when Cal and Torey were on their way out, Harvey pulled Cal aside. "Try not to waste your time on this Voodoo thing," he said, throwing an arm over Cal's shoulder. "You don't need to fool around with this boogie man stuff. Stick to what you know best. We all want you to make it here. Finish your book."

Ellen Rayburn held the door open and said good night. "You're now official members of the anthropology department's Doomsday Club. Feel free to come back any time for more."

∋ • ∈

They took a cab downtown to Torey's apartment and stood awkwardly on the front steps. The night was mild and balmy and the wind blew through her hair.

"I had a wonderful time," she said, taking his hand. "Do you want to come in for a minute, for a nightcap?"

Cal hesitated. He sensed that she was inviting him in for more than a nightcap. "No, I think I . . ."

She smiled. "You're a very attractive man," she said, her disappointment obvious, "and I really enjoyed being with you tonight. But you're not ready for this, are you?"

Cal, touched, shook his head. "No. I guess I'm not. But I wish I were."

She looked a little sad as she let go of his hand.

"I'm preoccupied," he said. "It's just been, well . . ."

"Don't explain. I understand," she said, bending down from the first step and kissing his cheek. "Good-night, and thank you."

She climbed the steps and slipped through the door into the house. Cal remained on the steps for a second, then turned and walked across the street.

⊃ ● ⊂

She telephoned two days later to invite him to a gallery opening, and then over the weekend for a neighborhood movie. He turned her down both times, almost wanting to say yes but knowing he would feel disloyal to Laurie—and, even more important, knowing he lacked the desire for another woman.

On Monday she called once more. At the last minute, she said, a friend had given her two passes to the screening of a new film.

He said no, maybe some other time, but they had a nice talk.

It was possible, he knew, that she wouldn't make the attempt again, and he found it hard to imagine when he would be able to make it himself.

Chapter 16

It was July Fourth and the kids in the neighborhood were going crazy with firecrackers and cherry bombs. Sitting at the table in the living room with Chris as they ate their evening meal, Cal almost missed the knock on his front door because of the echoing racket from outside.

The first thing he saw when he opened the door was a tiny sun floating in front of his eyes, throwing off sparks. Then behind it, he saw Torey Halowell. She was dressed in white slacks and a candy-striped blouse, and her shining hair was tied back with a red, white, and blue bandana. Surprised to see her, Cal also felt a surge of pleasure, a kind of tingling adolescent thrill. How beautiful she was, he thought, and how foolish he'd been to ignore her.

"Hi," she said, and grinned self-consciously at the sparkler in her hand. "I thought I'd try spreading around a little Spirit of Seventy-six."

"Glad you did. Come on in."

There was a pause and they looked at each other until the sparkler burned itself out. She stepped over the threshold then, but lingered near the door.

"I didn't want to stay," she said. "I'm going over to watch the fireworks on the river. They have them every year—they're spectacular, and I thought you and your son might like to come along."

"Hey, that sounds great," Cal said. He called back to the living room where Chris was dawdling over his hamburger. "Hey, Bean, how about going to see some fireworks?"

Chris appeared from around the corner and moved slowly toward the door, eyeing Torey.

"Who's she?" he asked warily.

"This is Mrs. Halowell. She's our—" He looked back to Torey. "Do you mind being called a landlady?"

She shrugged. "It's what I am—though I guess these days, strictly speaking, it should be 'landperson.' "

"Sounds like something out of a sci-fi fantasy," Cal said, and Torey smiled. Cal turned to Chris again. "Well, Bean? Go get a jacket, it might be windy on the river."

Chris was frowning, his eyes still on Torey. "I'm not going," he said flatly.

"Hey, Bean." Cal worked to keep it light. "It's July Fourth. America's birthday party. You've got to go out and see fireworks, it's a patriotic duty. Now go—"

"I won't," Chris erupted in a shout. "I won't go. I don't want to go anyplace with *her*." He aimed an angry scowl at Torey, then ran away to his bedroom.

Cal took a step after him, determined to drag him back and extract an apology, but then threw up his hands. Allowances had to be made. He turned to Torey.

"Look, I'm sorry. He . . . well, he hasn't gotten over—"

"You don't have to apologize, Cal," she said quietly. "Neither of you does." She smiled and backed toward the door.

He opened it slowly, reluctant to see her go. "Maybe some other time," he said. "Really. Don't give up on us."

"I won't," she said, and was gone.

Cal went to Chris's bedroom. The lights were out, Chris was in bed. Cal went over to him. "Bean . . . you didn't have to act like that. I wouldn't have made you go if you didn't want to."

Chris hadn't moved. Cal bent over and saw by the glow of the hallway light that his eyes were closed. Just pretending, of course. But what could be said to him now, anyway? *You can't hate another woman just because she's not Mommy, because she's alive and Mommy's not.* Fine. Those were the rules. They were easy to say, but he wasn't doing so well with the rules either. *Life must go on.* What was wrong with being attracted to Torey Halowell?

Nothing. He would call her. Laurie would have to understand. It was time . . .

Christ, why did he still feel he had to apologize to her spirit?

⋑ ● ⋐

There was a stack of condolence notes in the desk drawer. He had answered them all soon after the funeral with at least a line or two—"Thank you for your kind expression of sympathy at this sad time in my life." But there were friends who deserved a more personal reply, and he went through the stack to pick out a few.

He wrote a six-page letter to Fernando Palaru at the University of Colombo in Sri Lanka, and another to Duke Mather, a high school friend from Akron with whom he had remained close. Tired and melancholy after finishing with Duke's, Cal considered getting into bed. But he looked at his watch, saw it was only ten, and went on with the letters. He wanted to be done with them, with all the business of grief. He picked up a letter from Carl Hessing, a German who'd been visiting professor at Albuquerque for two years before returning to Heidelberg. How *did* all these people hear about Laurie's death?

He laid another piece of stationery in front of him and started to write.

Dear Carl,
    It was so kind of you to get in touch with me after my wife's death. At the time, I couldn't give you the kind of answer your gesture deserved. For a while, I guess I was a basket case

He scratched out "basket case," thinking the slang might be unfamiliar to Carl, and, mulling a substitute, looked absently out the window toward the far end of the garden.

The leaves of a rhododendron by the far wall rustled faintly, and he saw her standing behind them. Smiling, naked, waiting for him to come to her.

He rubbed his eyes, and the vision disappeared.

Tiredness. He looked back to the condolence note and wondered whether to finish.

The phrase came:

    . . . I guess I was completely numb. But now I'm getting back to normal, and working again on

There was a loud bang outside. Cal turned to the window as the sky suddenly lit up. Someone had fired a roman candle off the roof of a neighboring building and colored sparks billowed outward from a small dying star. His gaze followed a green ember downward, then caught another movement from the garden.

She was lying on the chaise at this end of the yard, not more than fifteen feet from where he was sitting. The chaise faced away, the backrest propped up, so he could not see her face, only her long legs, tanned the way they always were in summer, and the tawny hair between her thighs neatly shaved to a triangle. He remembered thinking it was somehow risqué that she shaved there, that it was something only strippers or Playboy pin-ups did. But when he'd remarked on it the first time he saw her nude, she had merely asked if he liked it. He'd said yes, and she'd told him it was just a habit of hers, she had always done it.

At the memory he felt himself getting hard, and he didn't try to blink away the vision this time. Watched as she raised her legs slightly, so the pink cleft could be seen through the hair, and with one hand she began touching herself. Then the hand dropped away, moved out to the side of the chaise and seemed to beckon.

He was completely aroused.

So *real.*

Springing up from the chair, he went out into the garden, folded up the metal chaise and propped it against the fence.

Another roman candle, like a miniature missile, was launched from somewhere nearby and exploded in space. The flash of light lit the garden, exposed its emptiness.

But he wanted her now, longed to make love to her. He was still excited, hardness throbbing in his pants.

Jesus, jesus, he needed her.

Or did he just need *someone?* Perhaps it was the appearance of Torey Halowell at his door that had left him agitated, sexually raw.

He stepped back inside and looked at the telephone. Thought of calling her, inviting her over. Have a drink, shoot the breeze, get her into bed. Get into her—

You never think this way! You've never been so callous about women.

You can't go on fucking a ghost.

· Maybe that's all it was. It had just been too long since . . .

But he was tingling with the need, his whole body sensitized. He could feel the fabric of his underwear making contact, and kept imagining another kind of touch.

He walked to the desk and grabbed up his address book, found Torey Halowell's number.

This isn't me, he thought.

And dialed.

"Hello?"

"Hi, it's Cal Jamison."

"Oh, Cal . . ."

"How were the fireworks?" he asked, trying to sound cool and normal, and thinking he could hear the tremble in his voice. *She could hear—*

"Incredible," she said. "I'm really sorry you missed them. And Chris would've—"

Couldn't stand the small talk. So impatient. "Listen," he said, "I've just finished doing . . . a little work, and I wondered if . . . if you'd like to join me for a drink."

A few drinks. Soften her up. For a fuck.

He almost apologized for calling—thought of inventing a sudden headache and hanging up.

"I'd love that," she said. "Would you like to come here?"

Your place or mine. More conducive if his son wasn't sleeping in the next room.

"Let me see if I can get Mrs. Ruiz to come over and stay with Chris," he said. He told her he'd call back, and then phoned Mrs. Ruiz.

"Ees no prollem," she said. "I be right over."

He called Torey back and said he'd be over in ten minutes, then went out and walked around the garden, trying to cool himself off. A drink with her would be nice. But the way he felt now, he was afraid he'd throw himself on top of her the second she met him at the door.

Mrs. Ruiz arrived, letting herself in with the key. "Hokay, you go!" she called, spotting him in the garden. He excused himself for calling so late, but she told him she'd been fighting with Eduardo and it was a perfect time to get out of the house; Cal could stay out all night if he wanted, she was in no hurry to get home.

He went into the bathroom and threw cold water on his face, then considered a cold shower. Not too late to call back, make apologies . . .

He wanted her.

He hurried out the front door and down the steps.

∋ ● ∈

Walking to her apartment, he felt that everything around him had subtly changed. The streetlight falling on the limestone porticos, the dappled texture of the concrete, even the distant driving rhythms of *salsa* music echoing from a tenement window. All of it was the same, and yet different, full of urgency, as if the street, the whole city, were vibrating to the beat of his own heart.

He reached the door of her building, raised his hand to push the button on the intercom, and stopped. Even his own skin looked different, the flesh pinker than normal, and oddly luminous. I'm flushed, he thought, like an adolescent expecting his first complete experience with a woman.

No, this was something much stronger: a sensation of being swept away by his own sensuality, of being caught in a whirlpool of sexual need, as though his entire body and mind were being propelled, out of all control, toward a single goal.

His finger hovered over the button for half a minute. Then he pressed.

The answering buzzer sounded almost immediately and he pushed through the door.

She was waiting for him in the open doorway of her apartment on the first floor. She had changed out of the outfit she'd worn earlier into a white skirt and a blouse of filmy pale green chiffon. Through the diaphanous material, Cal saw the outlines of her breasts, the shadow of her nipples. Was he staring? He forced his eyes to her face, and even there he could focus only on what seemed sexually ripe, her lips, soft and shining as she spoke.

"That was fast," she said.

"One of the benefits of visiting a landlady who lives across the street."

He brushed lightly against her as he passed by into the apartment, and the touch was electric. He felt himself growing erect again and kept his back to her as she closed the door.

She came up beside him, and took his hand as though to lead him into the living room, but now he held back, fighting the whirlpool. She walked farther around in front of him, and looked intensely into his face. An overhead spotlight sent a shaft of light down upon her, crowning her with a radiant halo.

He wanted to take her right there in the hallway, hoist her up against the wall and enter her.

"Well," she said, her voice betraying a breathy quaver. "Shall we go in?"

In.

Was it only his skewed vision of the moment, or was she as nervous and keyed up as he was?

Neither one moved for a moment. The hallway was quiet as an empty tunnel.

Her hand went restlessly to touch the top white button of her blouse, turned it in her hand like a pearl. He stared at her long tapering fingers, imagined their touch on him. A red jewel studding the ring on her index finger glittered. His senses heightened, he was overcome by a whiff of her musky perfume.

Then he could not stop himself. He reached out, pulled her forward and kissed her. The touch of her lips shocked him, made him shiver, and he felt her arms tighten around his shoulders as though to steady him. She was with him, pressing her body against his, rubbing, her mouth open, tongue licking his. The vortex of need sucked him down. He pushed into her, too, and they reeled backward against a wall.

With the collision, he broke away. Afraid of himself, he held her back.

"Torey . . . ," he stammered. "I don't . . . don't know what's happening to me. Maybe . . . because it's been so long since—"

She put her hand to his cheek, caressed the line of his chin. "It's all right, Cal. There's nothing wrong about this."

Holding his hand, she led him up the stairs.

∋ ● ∈

Standing by her bed, she started to undress. Unhooking the band of her skirt, she let it fall to the floor and stepped out of it. Then she undid the first button of her blouse.

But he was already naked, waiting, his cock reaching out in the darkness for the warmth. And he couldn't wait anymore. He found himself rushing to her and clawing at her buttons.

No, be tender, he pleaded within himself.

But then the blouse was in his hand, torn. He flung it away and bent his lips to kiss her breasts, wide and full and tumescent.

He pushed her back onto the bed, and gripped the band of her panties, pulling at them. She moaned.

My god, I'm raping her.

He held still, lifted his mouth from her nipple.

"Torey, I—"

"No, no, go on Cal, go on," she panted. "I want you."

He thrust himself up into her, felt the wonderful warm slick wetness pulling him in. God.

"Go on, go on," she kept whispering.

Deeper and deeper he went, a hot burning piston. Harder and wilder. Fucking as he had never fucked before. Fucking the deepest hole. Her muscles gripped his cock, contracted, expanded, tightened again. He wanted to go deeper still, fill her up with himself, split her apart. This isn't me, a voice whispered in a corner of his mind. Not this way. But he banged himself down upon her again and again and again. He heard her moan, subside, and moan louder, a long rising tone. Wait, not yet, not . . . Her hand cradled his balls, then traced the base of the long hard muscle. Waves of heat and cold passed through him all at once. He opened his eyes and saw vaguely through the darkness her swirling hair, plumage, then a mask of colors. *This is a dream.* And it began to spurt out of him, so hot, volcanic. A spasm went through him and he shot again, shot like a bull. Then she shuddered violently and screamed, "Oh my god my god my god ohhh OHHHH!" and she collapsed beneath him.

He rolled back beside her.

They lay together soundlessly for several minutes.

"Nice," she said finally.

Nice? "Heaven," he said. Not his usual vocabulary, too gushy. But somehow it was the only word that seemed right for this.

She nestled against him, her hand on his chest. "It's been a long time for you," she said.

"That can't be the only reason. This was different. It's never been like this."

Never. Was that true? He'd certainly had no shortage of women before Laurie. And though she had started marriage with her share of inhibitions, she had gotten over most of them. The sex had been very good.

But not like this.

Never.

Ɔ • Ϲ

They lay together only a little while, then he wanted her again, and he grew hard. He had not been erect again so quickly in years.

He felt a danger in all of this, the same danger one felt in the face of all unforeseen eruptions. It was like waking one morning to find a geyser spouting steam in your backyard. Too real to ignore, and too mysterious to believe.

Torey was looking at him quizzically, eyebrows turned downward, asking silently what he was thinking.

"I'm scared," he said. "I mean, I scared myself. I don't know why I had to—"

"No more apologies, Cal," she said gently but firmly. "I liked it. I *loved* it."

"But I came in here and attacked you."

"I should've called the police," she said lightly, and she put her mouth against his ear and whispered. "Help, police. Save me."

They made love again, slower this time, but climaxing no less magically.

In the quiet aftermath, they kissed each other everywhere, and when they were ready again they used their mouths and came that way.

Wanting more, still more, she let him do what Laurie had never been willing to allow, and it felt good, and natural.

And over and over, he kept being amazed with himself, and with her, and the two of them together. Kept having to remind himself that it was real.

⊇ • ⊆

The clock radio beside her bed showed three-thirty when he said, "I have to go."

She lay stretched out nude, watching him and smiling while he dressed. At last, she threw on a terry robe and went down to the door with him.

He held her hand awkwardly.

"Christ—it's crazy, but I feel like saying . . . thanks."

She laughed. "You're very welcome," she said.

"I'd like to see you again."

"Soon, I hope."

They kissed once more, and he was ready again. Incredibly. But he would have to be at home when Chris woke up, and he had really taken Mrs. Ruiz too much for granted already.

"Good night," she said, standing in the doorway to watch him go. "Sweet dreams."

This was the dream, he thought on the way home.

Chapter 17

HE ARRIVED HOME still dazed. It was the kind of thing that happened only in movies. Tracy looks at Hepburn, whammo—it's love.

He opened the door and tossed his key ring onto the front hall table. Then he noticed the smell, an astringent odor of air freshener.

Cleaning the apartment? At this time of night?

Cal heard water running in the kitchen and, stepping down the hall, he saw Mrs. Ruiz hunched over the sink, furiously scrubbing at a baking dish, her fleshy arms working circles with a Brillo pad. Why was she cleaning at this hour? She had left the place spotless at five o'clock.

"Carmen, I'm sorry I'm so late."

She turned at the sound of his voice, obviously startled. Quickly, she said, "Ees no prollem, I tol' you."

Cal moved up to the sink. "You didn't have to clean tonight, Carmen. I only wanted you to baby-sit."

"Oh, mus' be done," she said. "Clean houses ees clean soul. The house mus' be clean for the—" She stopped abruptly.

"For what, Carmen?"

Her gaze fell to the dish in the sink. She stopped scrubbing and lifted a wet hand from the dish, touching her lips in concentration. Then she looked up at him again, a bit fearfully.

"Misser Jamis'," she said. "Christopher he have dream. The spirit come to him."

Now Cal was alarmed. "What was the dream about?"

"*Madre*."

"His mother?" The aftermath of Chris's blow-out at Torey, Cal thought.

"*Sí, madre*," Carmen said, a tremor in her voice. "The spirit she come, wake him to tell story."

"He woke up? You mean he had a nightmare," Cal said, "a bad dream?"

"No bad dream. The boy see *madre* and he ees *dichoso*."

Cal shook his head and Mrs. Ruiz tried again.

"*Contento* . . ."

"Happy?" Cal said.

"*Sí*. He see *madre* . . ."

"And you're sure he was happy," Cal said dubiously. "He wasn't upset?"

"*Sí*. But when he wake and I tell him you out, then he very worry. I give him de *sopa*," she added, gesturing to the bowl in the sink. "Soup ees warm. I sing to him, he sleep soon. And then I clean."

Cal paused uncomfortably. "Clean for what, Carmen?"

She looked away and mumbled, "For the spirits."

Now Cal understood. Carmen was a believer in Santeria, or something related to it, and that would include ancestor worship. To her, dreams were manifestations of spirits coming to visit the dreamer. No wonder she had exaggerated the importance of Chris's dream and started to clean; the Voodoo believers obviously had their own version of "Cleanliness is next to godliness."

"What happened in the dream, Carmen?" he asked. "Did Chris say?"

She picked up the pan again. "No," she said very quietly, "he no say."

She finished drying the dishes and gathered her straw pocketbook from the kitchen table. Cal tried to press ten dollars into her hand, but she pushed it back at him. "No, you pay me by week," she said. "Ees enough. I like for you and Chris working."

After he let her out, Cal stood by the door. He considered the possibility that she might be dangerous to have around Chris. Should he call in the morning, tell Carmen not to come in anymore? Then he upbraided himself for such knee-jerk racism. Just because Carmen Ruiz was Hispanic and believed in Santeria didn't mean she was anything less than perfectly capable. In fact, Cal realized, she might make a valuable source for his research.

He tiptoed down the hall to Chris's room. A rare summer breeze floated across the sill and rustled the drawing Chris had done at camp, tacked to the wall above his bed. Chris was sleeping motionless, pillow lodged in the crook of his arm, one hand dangling over the side of the bed. He shifted restlessly then, turning toward the wall. As he did, the fingers of his extended hand opened, and something he'd been clutching caught the light from the hall. Cal looked closely. It was the shell he had found in the park.

Cal felt bad about having left him, but Chris seemed fine now.

∋ ● ∈

A sound in the hallway woke him at a little past four.

"Hey, Bean," Cal called softly. "That you?"

The boy walked right past Cal's open door without stopping.

"Bean?" Cal called a bit louder.

But Chris kept walking, the sound of his footsteps retreating down the hall. Cal straightened wearily and reached for his bathrobe, on a chair beside the bed. He guessed the boy must be headed for the bathroom, and wanted to see him, reassure him.

Cal shuffled out into the hallway and turned toward the bathroom. Then, by the ambient light coming through the doors from the garden, Cal saw the silhouette of his son, standing at the center of the living room. His arms were raised slightly from his sides, dangling like loose streamers. Cal went toward him.

Now Chris moved away, languidly. He bumped into a chair, but didn't stop, edged around it.

"Bean," Cal said again.

Chris went to the garden door, stood facing it for a moment, then turned around.

His eyes were closed, Cal saw.

Chris was sleepwalking.

Cal took a step backward and bumped into the edge of his desk, accidentally tipping over a stack of books. They thumped to the floor. But Chris remained undisturbed, eyes closed in—in what? A trance? His arms had dropped flat against his sides and his head was cocked to one side as though listening to some noise coming through the ceiling.

Cal didn't know what to do. Hadn't he read somewhere that it was dangerous to wake sleepwalkers?

"I do," the boy murmured suddenly.

Cal stepped carefully toward him. The eyes were still closed.

"I remember," Chris said plaintively. "It was broken."

A *conversation?* What did he remember?

Chris's head remained at the same angle, tilted up. He went on mumbling sleepily, slurring some of his words. Cal strained to hear.

". . . but I know he didn't mean to . . . I don't blame him. You used it a lot before and it was all right . . ."

Cal gasped. Chris's dream companion was Laurie! She was telling him about the accident.

Chris went on, "I will . . . Promise. But when are you coming back? Always?" Chris's voice cracked. Then, abruptly, he giggled. "Oh, sure I will. I love you, too . . ."

Cal's heart sank. His eyes burned with tears that would not flow.

The conversation was over. Chris turned, arms rising to feel his way past obstacles, his eyes still shut. He glided across the carpet, out into the hall, and turned into his bedroom. Cal tiptoed after, watched Chris slip into his bed, and pull up the covers. For a long time, Cal leaned in the doorway, listening to the faint sound of his son's deep even breathing.

Then he returned to his own room and sat down on the bed. It was not in his nature to think of his son as sick. Other people's children were sick or neurotic. Not Chris. Other people's children were bedwetters or tantrum-throwers or pathological liars. Not Chris.

Sleepwalking. Talking to his dead mother.

He needed help.

Maybe they both did.

Chapter 18

SOPHIE GARFEIN was the best, or so Ricki said when Cal phoned her first thing in the morning.

"Listen, Cal, don't wait until this gets out of hand," Ricki advised. "Call her today and say it's an emergency. She's supposed to be brilliant, sees all the fucked-up kids from the best families in the city."

Cal distrusted psychiatrists in general—a bias he knew was absurd—and believed good parents should be able to raise their children without professional help. But he made an appointment for two o'clock that afternoon.

Sophie Garfein's office was in a high-rise building on Central Park South, occupying a corner suite next to a gynecologist and a dentist. The psychiatrist was in her early forties and slender, with prematurely graying brown hair. She might have been a cosmetics executive, or one of those jet-set women on the *Times*'s society pages. She took Cal alone into her office while Chris was left with some toys in the reception room.

"You're not what I expected," Cal said as Sophie Garfein closed the door.

She smiled as if she were used to hearing it. "Not all child psychiatrists are grandmothers with European accents." She motioned him to an Eames chair. "On the phone you said something about sleepwalking?"

Cal told her about the incident; then she asked some questions about Chris's general behavior. He described the radical mood swings, the outbreaks of anger, the odd little defiances. The psychiatrist inquired then about his own problems with Laurie's death, and Cal admitted his long period of self-enforced celibacy —neglecting to mention its termination the previous night. Sophie Garfein seemed to ponder all this a moment, asked a few more innocuous questions about his work, and then went to bring Chris into the office while Cal waited outside.

The time was agony for Cal. What did a psychiatrist ask a child? What if she decided he was an awful parent?

After forty minutes, the door to the inner office opened and Chris appeared. He walked out jauntily, holding a coloring book. "Just going to talk to your daddy again for a few minutes," the doctor said to him, and gestured to Cal.

He took the Eames chair again, and looked around at the litter of toys on the floor that had not been there before—model cars, trains, and a black plastic pistol.

Sophie Garfein sat down across from him. "Do you mind if I smoke?" she asked, laying her hand over a pack of cigarettes on a side table.

"Not at all."

She lit her cigarette. "I can't do it when I'm with the children, and it gets hard after an hour."

Small talk? "Well, what's wrong with him?" Cal blurted.

She smiled. "Why are you so sure there's something wrong with him?"

"Isn't there?"

"Professor Jamison, I think Chris is basically a very healthy child."

"Who sleepwalks and talks to his dead mother," Cal said, "and has nightmares that I'm going to hurt him."

Sophie Garfein rested her cigarette in a crystal ashtray and leaned forward. "He's a very sweet boy, and very bright. You should be proud of him. He's also been through the most difficult experience a child can have. A mother dying could be traumatic at any time. There are fifty-year-olds who can have trouble dealing with it. But at Chris's age, well, it's cataclysmic. Chris doesn't want to accept his mother's death—*won't* accept it. It'll take time before he does, and meanwhile he's going to act out his need to believe she's alive. His nightmare of being hurt by you is extremely common. He's afraid of being deserted by you, abandoned, the way he feels his mother did." She picked up her cigarette again.

"But why the sleepwalking?"

The psychiatrist gave him a sympathetic look. "You have every right to be concerned, but don't overreact. Let's look back at last night. I don't think it's an accident that this happened on a night when you weren't home."

"He didn't even know I was out," Cal said.

"But he woke up and you weren't there," she countered. "Then he went back to sleep feeling deserted, left alone. And his mommy came to keep him company."

"Are you saying I shouldn't go out?" Cal asked.

She smiled indulgently. "Certainly not. You need a life of your own. I do think it's best if you *tell* him you're going out, and tell him why." She inhaled on her cigarette. "Would I be guessing correctly that you were out with a woman?"

Cal hesitated, strangely embarrassed. "Yes, I was," he said. "But it was the first time since my wife died."

Sophie Garfein just looked at him, waiting.

"I guess I do feel a little guilty about it," he said.

"You shouldn't. In fact, you're probably sending Chris a message with your guilt. Children have amazing radar even if they can't articulate it."

Cal sighed audibly.

The psychiatrist gave him a very direct look. "Professor Jamison, to what degree do you think you still haven't accepted your wife's death?"

He thought about it deeply, and caught himself chewing hard on his lip. He shrugged. "Are you saying my problem is causing his?"

"Of course not. I was just asking a question. I'm not here to condemn you."

She took a piece of paper from the side table and passed it to Cal. On it Chris had drawn with crayons a scribbled figure of a woman with a halo. Around her were shafts of red, blue, and green representing rays of emanating light. To the right was a larger figure, amorphous and darker, drawn with streaks of yellow and orange and hazy gold eyes. The dark figure seemed to be wearing a swirling black robe.

"I asked Chris to draw his mother for me," the psychiatrist explained. "This is what he drew."

"What's this black and yellow thing?"

"Chris told me it was someone he calls 'Chief Black Cloud.' "

"Who's he?"

"You, I think."

"Me?"

"Partly you—and partly his idea of God. He had a dream, remember, in which you hurt him. He sees you as having the power of giving and taking life. It's possible that he does blame you for his mother's death, maybe because he picked this up from you— because you blame yourself. Talking with her in the dream last night, his mother telling him not to blame you, that seems to me a picture of the conflict he's in. Last night he acted it out. Today he drew it."

Cal thought about this. He would have to be more sensitively attuned to the boy's feelings, more careful about his own behavior.

"Dr. Garfein, everything you say sounds reasonable. But how did he know about the toaster—that it was defective? I never told him." He paused. "I was . . . ashamed of my . . ." He trailed off.

But she seemed not to notice. "Children are more attentive than we think. They pick things up and store them away. He might have heard you talking on the phone. Didn't you tell me you'd talked to a lawyer?"

"Yes, but never when Chris was around."

"Back in Albuquerque, Chris might have heard any number of people talking about the accident, and registered all of it."

"You're making this all sound pretty normal," Cal observed.

"It is," she said.

"Do you think he needs therapy?" Cal asked.

"Perhaps. But first let's wait. Give Chris a little leeway in exploring his feelings. It may work itself out." She stood, and he rose with her. Before opening the door she added, "Don't blame yourself for so much, either. Being a single parent is hard for anyone."

In the waiting room Chris was playing with a set of wooden trains. All of a sudden, Cal thought, this object of his fears, this difficult child with nightmares and moods and sleepwalking, looked very fragile and alone. Cal walked over, picked up his son, and hugged him.

Chris held tightly to his neck, hugging him back, and Cal wondered: how could Chris ever have dreamed he would hurt him?

⊃ • ⊂

He called Torey Halowell that night.

"I'd like to see you again," he said. "Soon."

"I'm glad," she replied. "I feel that way, too."

"I hope you won't mind," he said then, "but to start with I'd like to bring my son along, plan an outing for the three of us."

"I don't mind at all," Torey said. "But what about Chris's feelings? He shouldn't be forced to like me, Cal."

He appreciated her patience and understanding, and wondered for a second if it wouldn't be better not to force the issue. What if Chris made another scene like last night? But he realized then that he might be seeing a lot of Torey. It was best to abide by Sophie Garfein's prescription and clear the relationship with Chris.

"Torey," Cal said impulsively. "I like you very much, and I want to be honest with Chris about that. Of course he can have time to make up his own mind—if he needs it. I'm betting he'll come around—"

As quickly as I did, he was going to say, and was suddenly embarrassed, remembering how he'd behaved last night.

"—as soon as he gets to know you," Cal concluded.

"I hope so," Torey said. "I certainly want the chance."

They talked for a few minutes more about all the places in the city that a boy Chris's age might enjoy going, set a date for Saturday afternoon, and then said good-bye. There was no mention of the passions unleashed the night before.

Would Chris like her? Cal wondered. *As soon as he got to know her?*

Thinking about it as he stood by the phone, Cal realized how little he knew about her himself, and thought again about how strangely and suddenly he'd been swept away.

Chapter 19

CAL STEPPED OUT of the taxi and paused at the curb, examining the pair of renovated brownstones. A lot of effort and expense had gone into converting these slum dwellings into a single building. The stoops had been removed and one central entrance installed at street level, the rotten window sashes replaced, the masonry sandblasted and completely repointed. A conspicuous act of faith in this neighborhood—*El Barrio*—where rapid rot and destruction were the odds-on future of everything.

A long painted sign hung over the main entrance: ASOCIACIÓN COOPERATIVA PARA HABILITACIÓN Y EDUCACIÓN, bright yellow letters on a black background. At each end an emblem had been painted —a tree, artfully designed so that its larger branches formed the main initials of the organization, A.C.H.E. The acronym amused and surprised Cal. Was it supposed to ironically suggest the desperate yearnings of the *barrio* dwellers for a better way of life? What might it indicate about Oscar Sezine, the man whom Lieutenant MacTaggart had praised as a savior of drug-ridden ghetto youth? Evidence of a sense of humor, perhaps. Or were the letters just initials, with no meaning to be read into them?

Cal started toward the entrance. A pair of young women strolling along the sidewalk chattering in Spanish turned in just ahead of him. Both were attractive Latin types in their late teens, with creamy mocha skin, bright black eyes, and shining black hair pulled back neatly. They wore no makeup and were rather primly dressed in white blouses and plain dark skirts cut below the knee. Each had a number of books cradled in her arms; except for their surroundings they could have been coeds strolling across a green campus on the way to class.

Cal entered a bare compact lobby. The only wall decorations were bulletin boards quilted with printed signs and hand-lettered notices. Most were in Spanish, but several were in English or both languages: "Block party on 109th St. Saturday night." "Lost: 1 pr. sunglasses, blue plastek frames." Could this place really be tied up somehow with Voodoo?

"Lo puedo ayudar, señor?"

Turning, Cal saw a young man seated behind the counter of a cubicle near the entrance. Like the others, the receptionist was also neatly dressed and groomed.

"Sorry," Cal said, dragging out his minimal Spanish, *"Yo . . . no comprende . . ."*

"Excuse me," the receptionist said in flawless English. "I asked if I could be of assistance."

"I have an appointment to see Mr. Sezine," Cal said, and gave his name.

The receptionist nodded and plugged a cord into a switchboard. He announced that a Professor Jamison had arrived, pulled the plug, then pointed to the stairs. "Go right up, please. It's on the fourth floor."

The stairwell rose through the center of the building. At each landing, corridors ran off to the left and right. Noises drifted out of some of the open doors—a man's voice giving a lecture, the whine and buzz of what sounded like tools in a machine shop, the clatter of a metal locker being closed. The ordinary sounds of a school.

As Cal took the turn in the stairs midway between the third and fourth floors, he saw Sezine waiting for him on the landing above. He was a big man, statuesque, with a large head set on broad shoulders. His dark face was arrestingly handsome, drawn sharply in light and shadow by a strong, prominent bone structure. His coarse black hair, closely cropped, receded partially to leave a nar-row peninsula across the top of his head, and his mouth and chin were wreathed by a carefully trimmed short beard and mustache. His large round eyes, behind gold-rimmed aviator glasses that made them seem even larger, were colored the pale green of shallow Caribbean waters.

Sezine seized Cal's hand when he reached the landing and pumped it vigorously.

"Hello, Professor Jamison. Welcome." Oscar Sezine boomed out the hearty greeting as though Cal were an old acquaintance rather than a complete stranger.

Cal rationed the warmth of his response. He didn't want to be won over too easily. "How do you do?"

Sezine said, "Let's go where we can be comfortable and talk."

He led Cal down one of the corridors and into a large airy room. For a silent moment they stood eyeing each other like duelists before counting off the paces. Cal judged Sezine to be about his own age, perhaps a year or two older, though his clothes had a youthful aura: gray slacks, blue-striped seersucker jacket, white button-down shirt and maroon rep tie, a "preppy" look more common to Ivy League students than ghetto social workers. It could almost be a costume, Cal thought, for playing the role of the academic innocent. Sezine's outfit was complete right down to his white buck shoes.

"Shall we sit down?" Sezine motioned Cal toward a couch and easy chairs surrounding a marble-topped coffee table. A door at one side of the room stood ajar, allowing Cal a partial view of a bed and a night table piled with books. Evidently Sezine lived "over the store."

Cal sat at one end of the couch and Sezine took an easy chair opposite him.

"It's nice of you to see me so quickly," Cal said.

"But why shouldn't I?" Sezine responded brightly.

Cal thought a moment. He was amazed that there was no wary questioning to certify his intentions. Either Oscar Sezine had nothing to hide, or was confident of his ability to conceal whatever needed to be hidden.

"Well," Cal finally said, "I don't know how much your secretary passed along about my reasons for wanting to meet you, but the fact is, I'm trying to study a subject that seems to be shrouded in secrecy. Frankly, I wasn't sure you'd see me at all."

Sezine's sea-green eyes stared back impassively. Cal felt relaxed by them, as he would from gazing across a smooth lagoon on a cloudless day.

"I understood your message perfectly," Sezine replied. "You want to learn more about Santeria, and somewhere you've heard that I'm a responsible authority. Under the circumstances, I have no reason at all not to make myself available. Quite the contrary, Professor Jamison. I'm eager to share what I know—to have more people aware of my work, and the religion."

Cal was struck by Sezine's matter-of-factness. He hadn't even bothered to ask where and how Cal had heard about him. Was he fully aware of his notoriety? Or had someone working under MacTaggart—a believer—known about Cal's liaison with the detective and alerted Sezine to expect a visit?

"Your attitude is certainly refreshing," Cal said. "I've heard that your believers don't like talking to strangers."

"Does that really surprise you?" Sezine asked. "Almost anyone of any faith might be put off, even offended, by having a stranger walk up and say, 'Tell me about your religion.' There's no more sensitive topic among strangers than the way one chooses to worship. But the problem is even greater where Santeria is concerned." He paused for a second. "You do know, don't you, that another name for the religion is Voodoo?"

Cal nodded, relieved that the word had been introduced. "I can't deny that's the source of my fascination—the whole business of syncretism, the mingling of newer faiths with the ancient African traditions."

Sezine smiled sympathetically. "There is much to interest an anthropologist," he agreed. "Unfortunately, too few respectable scientists have turned their attention to the subject. Metraux did his work in Haiti, but that was more than two decades ago. Except for him, most of what has been written about Voodoo is shameful nonsense. Ask any man on the street what it is, he'll say it's witch doctors sticking pins in dolls. The result of such ignorance, of course, is hostility. Our believers today suffer much the same stigma the Christians did in the time of Pilate, or the Jews only forty years ago." Sezine sighed. "Perhaps it's just our turn. There have always been times when one religion or another was cast out of the house of God, so to speak, and put in the doghouse. You can't blame those who feel a need to protect their belief by refusing to speak about it."

Cal was impressed by Sezine's measured rationality.

"But you don't feel the need for that protection?"

"Oh, but I do," Sezine said. "Most definitely, from some quarters. But not from you."

Again that odd tone of affectionate familiarity. Cal found it vaguely disquieting from a man he'd never met before.

Oscar Sezine read his reaction and smiled. "You didn't think I'd accept this appointment without checking your credentials? My secretary went to the main reference files of the Public Library. She tells me that your contributions to anthropological literature are substantial. So I know you'll listen with an open mind, and I can be confident you will accomplish what you were sent to do."

Sent! Cal stared back, fighting to conceal his dismay. Hadn't

Sezine just uttered proof that he knew Cal's visit was a maneuver in a murder investigation? What hope was there of learning any truths unless he could dispel Sezine's perception of him as a police spy?

"It's not because anyone sent me that I'm here," Cal said forcefully. "I came for my own reasons. Because I want to learn."

"Yes, yes, no doubt," Sezine said. "I'm sure that's true. But if you wish to learn about the religion, the first thing to understand is our belief that nothing, absolutely nothing in life, occurs without the planning and intervention of the gods. And by that rule, if you are here now, then it's also because you were meant to be—to fulfill some design of theirs." Sezine gestured upward as casually as a New York tourist guide pointing to a skyscraper. "When I said you were sent, I meant by them."

So Sezine didn't know about MacTaggart. Still, it was jarring to hear someone as articulate and obviously intelligent as Oscar—a man, Cal thought, not unlike himself—speak of deities who looked down from the heavens and manipulated humans like puppetmasters. Yet Cal clung to the detachment of the researcher, his will to comprehend without making judgments.

"Do you have any idea of what the purpose is," he asked, "what divine mission I'm supposed to carry out?" He hadn't meant to sound scornful, but it came out that way.

Oscar showed no offense, however. "The best I can do is give you an informed opinion," he said.

"Go ahead."

"We live in times when people everywhere are confused, wracked by doubt about the future, about the very survival of this planet. More than ever we need to be in touch with the gods, to be able to call on their infinite power and wisdom. And the way exists: *our* way. But too many ignore it. Now," Oscar concluded portentously, "the gods can no longer tolerate being ignored. They want the unknowing to be educated."

It was another moment before Cal understood. Then he was unable to suppress a giddy amusement, as if he'd heard his name called out as the winner of a car or an all-expenses-paid trip to Paris.

"Through me?" he exclaimed, slapping one hand over his heart. "You think I've been chosen to . . . spread the gospel?"

Oscar's gaze held steady. "Don't you intend to write about what you learn? Isn't that what you've always done before? And when you write, it will be read."

136

"Yes, but—"

But what? Cal stopped. How did you argue logically against the dreams of the faithful? Was it enough to say that the circulation of the most popular anthropological journal totaled no more than fifty or sixty thousand readers?

"You asked for my interpretation," Oscar said.

Cal gave a self-effacing chuckle. "Listen, it's flattering to be told I'm part of a heavenly plan to keep humanity from committing suicide. I'd *like* to believe it myself. But the facts are much simpler."

"What are the facts?" Oscar asked flatly.

A cop gave me your name.

Cal reached further back for a safe answer that was not a lie. "I passed a little store around the corner from where I live," he said, "a *botánica*. That got me curious about Santeria, I started looking into it . . . and one thing led to another."

"As things do," Oscar said. "But what do you think made you walk past that store?"

"I've just moved into the neighborhood. It was inevitable I'd pass it sooner or later."

"But why did you chose to move into the neighborhood?" Oscar persisted. The voice was soft, but the purpose firm.

Cal was becoming exasperated. "Look, I didn't choose it. Things happened that made me come to Columbia, and I took the apartment the university found for me."

"And what things happened that made you come to the city?" Oscar continued the assault.

Her name shot through Cal's mind like a blue spark, and he looked away.

Oscar must have seen the distress; he sounded apologetic when he resumed. "Of course, the rational man will say these are merely foolish mind games. It's all too easy to pretend after the fact that random events had a conscious causality. Nevertheless, my friend, this is a touchstone for understanding the religion. As we see it, the universal clockwork, the sequence of events from day to day, from moment to moment, is controlled by the gods."

Then where, Cal mused, did the sequence begin for him? On the day he was born? He played with the idea. Had he been destined from the moment of his conception to sit in this room, meet this man? Or did it start with Laurie's death—leaving him at loose ends, looking for a faith of his own to fill the vacuum of despair? Had a pantheon of African gods sat around in their Valhalla, Olympus—whatever their heaven was called—and decided that Laurie must die?

Maybe it was crazy to be here. Oscar Sezine was just one more religious fanatic, peddling the most hotly sought—and the cheapest—commodity in the streets of the poor: hope.

Suddenly Cal felt a frantic urge to retreat, a need to prove to Sezine, to *himself*, that his will was his own. No divine force had steered him here, and none could keep him from leaving.

But before Cal could move, Sezine said, "I don't know how much you've already learned from your research, Professor, but I thought the best way I could add to your knowledge would be to show you how I've put the religion to work. So if you'll accompany me," he announced, rising to his feet, "I'd like to show you around the Aché."

He made a word of the acronym, Cal noted. Not the familiar English synonym for pain, however. A softer sound with an accent at the end, as in café. Ah-*chay*, like a Frenchified sneeze.

Sezine was already at the door, holding it open, waiting. Cal stood and moved toward the threshold. The urge to leave had passed, overwhelmed by his curiosity. No need to doubt that it was anything but professional fascination that had brought him here. No gods pulling strings. One thing had simply led to another.

As things do.

Chapter 20

OSCAR LED Cal along the corridor and stopped outside an open door. Inside a couple dozen boys and girls, all Hispanics in their late teens, were sitting behind school desks attentively facing a blackboard. At the board a bespectacled young man in a dark suit stood chalking notations while commenting in rapid Spanish.

Cal glanced over the words written on the blackboard.

aleyo yaguo iyalocha okoni moddu cue

"This is one of our Yoruba language classes for beginners," Oscar explained. "The Yoruba were the dominant tribe in the coastal region of Africa from which the slave ships drew their cargo. Having been given the task of bringing the religion across the seas, their dialect remains the special language of all Voodoo."

Given the tasking of bringing . . . The phrase spoke volumes. By Voodoo writ, Cal understood, even the slave trade was seen as predestined. That shameful period of history when black men had been sold to white men as chattel had been interpreted as another strategy of the gods to export the religion from Africa. A turnabout on the usual line about bringing the Word to the heathen.

"What do they mean?" Cal asked, nodding toward the chalked words.

Sezine ran down the list. "*Aleyo* is what we call a nonbeliever. *Yaguo* means an initiate, someone entering the religion, as are these young people. *Iyalocha* is the word defining a female practitioner. *Okoni* means teacher, and *moddu cue* means thank you."

The instructor had finished writing another word on the blackboard, *orisha*. Now, on another line, he wrote it again, breaking it down into components: *O / ri / sha*.

"And that?" Cal said.

"The Yoruba deities, the gods of Voodoo, are called the *orishas*. Señor Bentarez is explaining the probable derivation of the word. In Yoruba *ri* means 'to see,' and *sha* 'to choose.' So the word defines our gods both as those who see and choose our fate, and as the means through which mortals may see it and make choices of their own. A lovely language, isn't it?"

They remained at the door another moment. The students listened to the instructor with rapt attention, jotting notes.

The door of the next room was closed, but a small glass window permitted Cal a glimpse of a similar class in session.

"An advanced group," Sezine said and passed on, heading for the stairs. "Language is a basic part of our program."

"Then Yoruba is sort of what Latin is to the Catholic liturgy?" Cal said.

"Not exactly. It's much more than a matter of tradition with us. In the Voodoo ceremonies, the *orishas* are often spoken to directly —a kind of dialogue may actually take place between the supplicant and the *orisha*, who enters an earthly body as part of the ceremony. Of course, the *orishas* are all-knowing, and thus capable of understanding any language spoken on earth. But we believe that they are especially gratified by hearing the Yoruba tongue, more easily soothed and propitiated by its sounds."

They descended the stairs and emerged onto the lower floor just as a bell sounded somewhere and the hallways began to fill with students. Classes had broken. The kids swirled past—neat, orderly, spirited but not raucous. Slum kids? Oscar Sezine was doing a hell of a job. Even in the hectic tide of movement, Cal noticed many of the students go out of their way to acknowledge him.

"Hey, Oscar!"

"How's it going, man?"

"Oscar baby!"

The greetings were invariably delivered in street-talk, loose and affectionate. Oscar responded in kind—suddenly Cal, too, could think of him only as Oscar—a flashing smile, a nickname called out, the scat slap of hands. Oscar was totally accessible to his flock, like the beloved favorite counselor at some terrific summer camp.

The halls cleared, the tide of students ebbing away to other activities.

140

Cal shook his head. "I have to force myself to remember that all this is somehow tied up with Voodoo," he said.

"And I never forget for an instant," Oscar replied soberly. "Without the religion, Professor, I could have accomplished nothing. These nice kids you've seen, they've all come from lives of drug-taking and drug-dealing, thieving and conniving, whoring, pimping—the pointless brutal existence of the underdogs. But with the religion I've finally given them something to change it. They know that with the help of the gods *they* control their fate. That's the magic of the religion, Professor. It offers them a ride out of hell—express."

Cal heard the tremor of conviction in Oscar's voice. If at first he had been tempted to regard him as no more than a religious fanatic, Cal felt now that the characterization was mean and foolish. Whatever you might think about his strange creed, Oscar Sezine had undoubtedly coupled it to a positive vision, a burning wish to do good.

⊃ • ⊂

They poked briefly into other classrooms where various aspects of the religion were being taught: the details of African mythology and the pantheon of Yoruba deities, the history of the religion's dissemination in the Western Hemisphere. In one darkened room, slides of African carvings were being projected on a screen. "Art appreciation," Oscar whispered.

They descended one more floor and Cal found himself being steered into the sterile white surroundings of a large dispensary. This was the part of the Aché that was more clinic than school. Tiers of long shelves held copious stocks of the same kinds of herbs, roots, chopped leaves, powders, and organic oils that Cal had seen in his neighborhood *botánica*. Almost all of these substances, Oscar explained, were in the pharmacopoeia of African folk medicine; many were indispensable in combatting drug dependence and easing the agonies of withdrawal.

"And they are also used," Oscar added, "for making potions and casting spells."

"Spells?" Cal said incredulously. Oscar talked of such ordinary things most of the time; it continued to slip Cal's mind that the fundamental elements of his work were completely illogical.

"But you must know," Oscar said patiently, "that magic is as basic to the religion as . . . as the saying of the rosary is for Catholics."

"Yes," Cal replied, "but it's still hard to get my bearings with you. Just when I get accustomed to thinking of you as simply the ghetto Albert Schweitzer, you'll say something that could only come from Merlin the Magician."

Oscar laughed. But he said nothing to make comprehension easier.

⊃ ● ⊂

And then came the black madonna.

On the ground floor, along with a library and offices, was "the chapel," as Oscar called it, where members of the Aché met to perform Voodoo ceremonies.

It was a plain functional auditorium: rows of folding chairs, a platform on which there were two more chairs and a table, a large wardrobe-like cabinet with the doors standing open. Inside the cabinet was a life-size carved wooden figure of a saint or madonna.

Cal went forward for a closer look. The detail work on the figure was exceptionally fine, the folds in her robes so intricately etched and polished that the cloth looked real; in the faint wafting of air through an open window the robe almost seemed to flutter.

The most unusual feature of the madonna was that it had been carved of ebony. It was entirely black, a step beyond the usual Christian saint as stand-in for the Voodoo deity. Here the level of disguise had been stripped away. With its black face, this figure looked like an African god swathed in a mourning madonna's black cloak.

An odd trio of items lay on a shelf extending from the cabinet at a level with the madonna's feet. A bowl of water, an egg, and in a saucer a cigar with the first quarter-inch smoked down to silver-gray ash. Cal couldn't help noticing the band still around the butt end of the cigar: a Montecristo, prime Cuban, several bucks a throw.

"These are basic offerings," Oscar said as Cal's gaze rested on the shelf. "On special feast days, or on occasions when special favors are asked of the gods, more elaborate gifts may be made. But each and every day, without fail, at least these three things must be offered."

"Why these?" Cal asked.

Oscar moved up beside Cal. "They're self-explanatory. The water for thirst, the egg for hunger, and the cigar," he shrugged, "for pleasure."

"You mean she enjoys smoking imported Havanas?" Cal remarked lightly.

"We believe the gods do have earthly tastes," Oscar said. "Favorite colors, foods, styles of dress. Of course the cigar is only a symbol, representing our willingness to appease these desires. And in this case, by the way, more appropriate than you think. This god," he glanced to the madonna figure, "is a man."

"But the statue shows—"

"Yes, it's a representation of Saint Barbara. But in Santeria the boundaries of sex are insignificant. In that way you could say we're more modern than primitive. A female saint may often represent a male god—as it does here. This is one of the gods we call the Seven African Powers—Chango, the patron god of the Aché."

Again Cal experienced the difficulty of accepting the coexistence of these bizarre ideas with such mundane surroundings. The plain auditorium watched over by this woman-man-saint-god—the mute lifeless recipient of a tribute of food, drink, and a contraband cigar.

⊐ • ⊏

Finally Oscar took him down to the basement.

Cal had been wondering where Oscar got the funds to run an establishment the size of the Aché, and here he found at least part of the answer.

The entire basement area had been converted to a workshop where a range of articles used in the practice of Santeria was being produced. At long ranks of tables young people sat assembling necklaces of colored beads, filling jars with herbs, or working with molds to make wax candles and plaster saints in every size and color. The output of this cottage industry was sold wholesale to suppliers of *botánicas*. The balance of the budget, Oscar said, came from private donations.

It would have been easy, Cal thought, to regard the business skeptically—to suspect Oscar of enriching himself by manipulating impressionable youngsters. But Cal had seen enough of the *barrio* to know that the kids who'd survived there were too savvy to be conned. Looking over the workshop, he saw no sign of discontent. A radio in the background played a Mets game. Spirited conversations were going on between some of the workers.

As Oscar made a circuit of the basement, Cal spotted a table where half a dozen girls were tying bunches of feathers to wooden shafts. He was reminded that he'd seen Mrs. Ruiz using a feather-duster when she cleaned up around his apartment.

"Is that a ceremonial item?" Cal inquired. Anything was possible if a sacred symbol could be made of a cigar.

"Not strictly," Oscar replied. "But cleanliness is extremely important in the religion, and there are many specific customs relating to the way we clean our houses and ourselves."

Cal thought of Mrs. Ruiz cleaning the apartment the night he returned from Torey's.

They started to move on, but then Oscar halted abruptly and glared at one of the girls assembling the featherdusters.

"Teresa!" he said sharply.

The girl looked up, and the rest of the basement went suddenly quiet. Oscar's eyes locked with the girl's and he barked something in Spanish. The girl answered in a contrite manner, but whatever she said only enraged Oscar further. Striding around the end of the table, he seized the girl roughly by the arm, pulled her up from the workbench and hauled her into a corner.

The workshop remained frozen in silence until Oscar called toward the benches, ordering work to resume. The youngsters returned obediently to their tasks.

Cal watched Oscar and the girl from across the room. She was young, fourteen or fifteen, and extremely pretty. Her large dark eyes were turned up to Oscar in fearful supplication. What could she have done to incur his fury?

Now, through the sounds of the workshop, the sibilant hiss of Oscar's scolding whisper cut like the escape of scalding steam. The girl stood before Oscar with her head bowed and her shoulders slumped in shame.

At last Oscar's angry whispering stopped. The girl raised her hands and put them to the back of her neck. Unhooking the clasp of a chain she was wearing, she pulled it off and dropped it into Oscar's waiting palm. The wrathful Oscar was now replaced by the kindly counselor; he reached out and stroked her head in a gesture of affection and forgiveness, then prodded her back to her bench.

Climbing the steps to the main floor, Oscar said nothing. Cal glanced down at him and saw his brow furrowed, his lips compressed in a troubled frown. He kept the hand with the girl's necklace jammed into his pocket.

As they reached the landing, he caught Cal's sleeve, holding him back before they went out into the lobby. "I think you should know what that was about," he said, his voice husky with remorse. "It will increase your understanding of the religion."

Cal hadn't expected to be told. But as MacTaggart had hoped, Oscar seemed willing to impart secrets he would have withheld from the police. He withdrew his hand from his pocket and raised high the necklace. Dangling at the end of the thin gold chain was the petrified claw of a small bird.

"The talon of a sparrow," Oscar said. "It's a talisman worn by followers of *mayombe*." He stared at it scornfully another second, then returned it to his pocket. "I've told you honestly that the Voodoo we practice here is wrongly perceived as evil. But it is also true that not all Voodoo is so well-intended. Santeria is a force for good, yes, but there is also *mayombe*—a malevolent form that seeks to harness negative powers in the universe for evil purposes."

Cal was puzzled. "But that girl seemed completely content here."

"I think she is," Oscar agreed. "But there's a paradox with many of these children. They've had to become hard and cunning to manage their own survival, and yet they can be dangerously naive about other things. Teresa was a prostitute before she came to me. She told me that she often turned twenty tricks in a day and that, in an instant, she could size up whether a customer was safe or sadistic. But this understanding of human character doesn't help her comprehend the distinctions between one form of Voodoo and another. So she can be tempted to cross the line."

"By whom?" Cal asked. An evil form of Voodoo? This could be the lead that MacTaggart needed.

Oscar shrugged. "I can't say. Of course I asked Teresa where she got the necklace. She told me it was given to her for luck by a friend, someone she thought was a Santerian."

"But the 'friend' was actually into *mayombe*."

"Or was equally unaware of the significance of the talisman. Deception is often used to attract new followers. The *mayomberos*, their priests, may even pretend to be *santeros*. Someone like Teresa may unknowingly take on more of the trappings and rituals of *mayombe* . . . until she is lost. Her very soul may be captured by the sorcerers." Oscar's hand swooped through the air. "Carried away like a lamb in the claws of an eagle."

It was odd, Cal thought, but as Oscar spoke about *mayombe* it was not so much a new level of strangeness that was revealed, but rather parallels between Voodoo and more civilized religions. Didn't they all represent the same needs—to define man's place in the scheme of Creation, to give people faith in their own worth, to restate in mythic terms the dilemma of survival, the battle between Good and Evil? How much difference was there, really, between the struggle for souls waged within Voodoo and the eternal contest of God and the Devil?

And spells? Was it really so strange to believe in them? What, after all, were prayers?

⊐ ● ⊏

They went to Oscar's office, a plain room off the lobby with a window facing a dark rear alley and metal office furniture that looked as if it had been acquired second-hand. Pictures covered the wall behind the desk. Cal scanned them: Oscar shaking hands with the mayor; Oscar lined up with community leaders in front of the unrenovated Aché buildings; Oscar, much younger, with a group of other young men wielding machetes in a sugar cane field.

Seated across a desk from Oscar, Cal said, "There's still so much I'd like to know. About the mythology, the rituals . . ."

"I'd like to answer all your questions," Oscar said, with a glance at his watch. "But in a couple of minutes I have a class to teach. I think I can arrange, though, for you to learn more."

"How?"

"By attending a ceremony or two."

"I'd appreciate that," Cal said.

"We'll see if the opportunity arises," Oscar said. "For now, is there anything else?"

Suddenly there was only one question left in Cal's mind. It was, he realized, the one he had really come to ask. But how did you ask a man if human sacrifice was part of his religion?

He led up to it carefully. "I've wondered how closely the Voodoo currently practiced follows the ancient rituals. How much have they been watered down by the syncretic process and the passage of time?"

"They're identical," Oscar said. "The rituals, after all, were dictated by the gods."

"And what about sacrifice?" Cal asked at last. "In the past weren't live offerings made to the gods, killed as part of the ceremonies?"

Without a trace of regret or shame, Oscar answered, "They still are."

There was a silence. Cal was unsure how to follow up.

Oscar said, "I know this is the aspect of the religion that is always most shocking to the *aleyo*."

Nonbeliever, Cal recalled.

"But without it," Oscar went on, "there would be no religion. The gods expect it, demand it. Sacrifice represents mortal recognition of their divine right to ask for life to be taken, as they have

146

given it. Deny them that . . . and we break the contract with them by which we survive."

God giveth and God taketh away. That much came right out of the Bible.

"In our way of worship," Oscar added, "ritual slaughter is absolutely essential."

Cal still couldn't find the right words.

Then Oscar laughed, short and light. "But Cal, surely you wouldn't condemn us for that—you of all people. You must have seen this kind of thing done somewhere, a chicken or pig killed as an offering. Good heavens, it's done every day in thousands of villages around the world."

Animals! Oscar had been talking of nothing more. Why had it taken so long to penetrate? The image of the boy in the morgue had been hanging in his mind, curtaining his perception.

Yet was the truth Oscar had confessed any more reasonable?

"I know it's done in jungles," Cal said, "by men living under the most primitive conditions. It *belongs* there. But here . . . it's out of place."

The change in Oscar's expression was slight, but enough for Cal to regret his comment. To do research properly, he ought to remain detached. By offering judgments he might easily forfeit Oscar's trust.

"And not here, you think." Oscar's voice was calm and reasonable, though now Cal heard an undertone of scorn. "I suppose the idea of blood rituals is bound to offend ordinary city dwellers. The dead flesh of animals is only something to buy at the supermarket, wrapped in plastic at the meat counter. City people have no conception of the continuum, the natural links between life and death. So I must not blame them if they judge us harshly." Oscar's tone hardened. "But how different are their rituals? Don't they insist on their Christmas turkey—isn't the bird killed to satisfy their idea of tradition? And aren't there Jews whose meat must come from animals slaughtered according to ancient law, by men specially ordained to say prayers over the flesh? Surely that is ceremonial killing, whether or not it is witnessed by all the believers. Really, what right does any man have to pass judgment on how others worship?"

Should he retreat now, Cal thought, or did he dare press for a direct answer to the question still nagging at him?

Cal went ahead cautiously. "Everyone has a right to his own beliefs," he said, "but if those beliefs conflict with civilized laws and customs, you can't expect a whole society to just . . . turn the other cheek."

Oscar nodded and smiled. "So you would say that religion must conform to the law. But who decides when the law is only a weapon to discriminate against forms of worship that are feared? The kings of England made laws against the Pilgrims, the French against the Huguenots, Hitler outlawed the Jews. Who was right, Cal? Tell me. The laws of men cannot be allowed precedence over the laws of the gods."

"And what about human sacrifice?" Cal blurted out, unable to restrain himself a moment longer. "If your gods demand that, do you obey?"

Oscar's head jerked back slightly, like a boxer taking a jab. He stared at Cal, his body rigid. Then he leaned back in his chair, very slowly, his back arching like a bow being pulled to release an arrow.

"Look, you said the religion hasn't changed," Cal said, trying desperately to get the discussion back on the level of academic debate. "You and I both know that human lives were offered as part of ancient rituals. And in the course of my research, I've come across . . . rumors . . ."

"Yes, I understand," Oscar said softly. "It would be impossible to keep something so sensational completely quiet. Especially when you consider the number of sacrifices we do. Every Tuesday and Friday, regular as clockwork. Babies, mostly. At midnight, of course. We drain the blood and drink it. Good to the last drop, and absolutely first-rate for curing certain diseases of the nerves and migraine."

The delivery was all the more chilling for being so muted. But Cal understood instantly that such corrosive sarcasm could only be born of the most soul-shaking rage.

"Listen, Oscar, it wasn't an accusation. A researcher has an obligation to—"

The dam broke, Oscar's self-control failing. "For heaven's sake, man!" he roared. "What fucking obligation do you have to ask a question like that? I've spoken freely, assumed you had the necessary professional perspective. And then you throw the same kind of shit at me as we get from any downtown double-breasted bigot! After all I've shown you, all you can make of it is that we're a bunch of murdering savages!"

"No, Oscar," Cal protested. "I swear to you I . . . hell, I don't know, the way you were talking about the rest of it, well, it didn't seem like a crazy question. I mean, I could imagine how the old ways might be carried that far . . ." He stopped. He'd meant to apologize and was just restating the insult. He pushed back his chair and stood up. "You've been very fair to me, Oscar. I'm sorry it had to end on a sour note."

Oscar studied him for a long time, then rose and came around his desk. "I should apologize, too. I'm not unaware of the rumors floating around. I shouldn't be so thin-skinned. The religion is strange to the uninitiated. We must be more tolerant of *their* ignorance." He looked off through his window with the dreary view and sighed. "But just at the moment this stuff about sacrifice is a particularly touchy subject." He explained no more, but turned again to Cal and they clasped hands. "I'm pleased to have met you, Cal. I still think the gods sent you . . . and they chose wisely. I'll be in touch with you."

He glanced at his watch then and, with excuses called over his shoulder, dashed out the door.

Oscar's secretary appeared a moment later and said she'd show him the way to the street.

"That's all right," Cal said. "I can find it myself."

He had to laugh when he thought of what Oscar would say. He didn't have to find it by himself. The gods would show him the way out, just as they'd shown him the way in.

BOOK TWO

Nganga

(The Spell)

Chapter 21

THE DECKS of the schooner *Wavertree*, a 293-foot square-rigger docked in the East River, were crowded with tourists speaking German, Japanese, and what sounded to Cal like Serbo-Croatian.

He and Torey had settled finally on the South Street Seaport for a Saturday outing with Chris. When Cal first told him about it, mentioning ships and sails and a picnic, Chris had lit up. But when Cal added Torey to the picture, Chris objected strenuously, repeating his unwillingness to go anywhere with her. Only after Cal threatened a loss of television privileges for at least a week did Chris back down and agree to go.

Torey had come by for them at eleven o'clock. Except for an initial sullen "hello," Chris would say nothing to her. During the ride downtown she tried unsuccessfully to draw him out.

"How are you liking New York, Chris?"

"It's okay."

"Have you ever been on a boat that big?" she'd tried another time, describing what they were going to see.

"Maybe."

There was no use scolding him about it, Cal thought. Anger would only make matters worse.

But when they arrived downtown Chris's mood began to change. At the base of one of the schooner's tall masts, he paused and arched backward, craning to see the top.

"Why do they call it the crow's nest?" he asked, the first question he hadn't directed specifically to Cal.

"Because it's so high up," Torey said.

"Then why don't they call it the eagle's nest?" Chris asked.

"I'll bet they would have," she said, "if they'd thought of it."

Chris turned to her, his brow furrowed. He stared for a moment. Then, for the first time, he gave her a very small smile.

In the main cabins of the *Wavertree*, crammed with pictures of ships' prows and the bustling harbor of New York at the turn of the century, they ambled from display to display. After lingering before one set of old photographs, Chris tugged at Torey's sleeve.

"Why did children work on the old ships?" he asked.

She answered him skillfully, explaining that laws against child labor were comparatively recent and that even very young children had once worked almost everywhere adults did.

The next time Cal looked, Chris was holding Torey's hand as they went from one display to the next.

Torey had packed a picnic basket with home-made fried chicken, zucchini fritters, and cupcakes with mocha frosting. They ate at a wooden table overlooking the harbor. Chris said the zucchini looked "yucky" and wouldn't try any, but he liked the cupcakes, and had three.

As Torey was packing up the picnic remains, she gave Cal a how-did-I-do glance, and he winked.

Chris caught the exchange.

"You like my daddy a lot, don't you?" he said suddenly as they walked off the dock.

"Hey, Bean!"

But Torey gave him a straightforward reply. "Yes, I do. Very much."

"Good," Chris said. "He likes you, too. And so does my mommy. She told me to be nice to you."

Here we go again. Cal looked at Torey, disturbed, and attempted to tell her, by a grim shake of his head, that he didn't think this was something to tolerate.

"I'm glad," Torey said to Chris. "Your mommy's opinion is very important to me."

Cal flinched. Why was she playing out this nonsense with him? As they reached the end of the pier, he said to her quietly, "I'm not sure it's good to cater to him like that. It's not healthy to encourage that stuff about his mother."

Torey hooked her arm through his. "I'm not catering to him. Believing that the spirit of people you love survives and stays with us doesn't seem at all unhealthy to me. Why not let him work it through in his own way? It obviously makes him feel better."

Sophie Garfein had said something similar, hadn't she? Let him work it through . . . But what bothered Cal was that it sounded as if Torey believed in the spirits of the dead herself. He avoided arguing the point, though. At least Chris was warming to her; maybe she was wise enough to know just how to encourage his friendship.

They strolled downtown to the tip of Manhattan Island, detouring past the Stock Exchange and Federal Hall ("George Washington was inaugurated there," Cal said from his guidebook-reading memory), and bought tickets for the launch ride to the Statue of Liberty. On the bumpy trip across the harbor Cal recited his high school civics textbook speech on immigration and the American Experiment.

Chris's why-what-and-how curiosity continued unabated. "What does the torch mean?" and "How did they build it?" and "Why does she look like Moses?"

Except for an annoying itch Chris had developed—poison ivy, Torey guessed—the whole excursion was thoroughly and unexpectedly perfect.

∋ • ∈

When they came in the door at a few minutes past five, the phone was ringing. Chris ran to answer, said hello, and handed the receiver to Cal.

"It's a detective, Daddy."

Cal took the phone and heard Dennis MacTaggart's scratchy baritone. "How's your research going?" the policeman said.

"It's interesting," Cal said. "I've been learning a lot."

"Interesting, huh?" MacTaggart retorted, his tone strangely accusatory. "Have you got anything for me?"

"Nothing, Dennis. Frankly, I still doubt your—"

"Did you see Oscar Sezine?" the cop interrupted, talking right past him.

"Yes. As a matter of fact, he was very helpful with—"

"Helpful to *you*," the cop said, with an edge of anger.

"Hey, Dennis, the guy seems perfectly straight to me. As far as I could see, he has nothing to hide. And when I mentioned the possibility of . . . well, your theory about those kids, he practically tore my head off. He obviously believes in Voodoo, but he's not involved with sacrificing children."

There was a silence. Cal heard the cop sigh and clear his throat.

"Dennis," Cal said earnestly, "the minute I hear anything useful, I'll call you. I promise."

"Good, Cal. And I hope it's damn soon," the detective said gruffly. "Because we just found another one."

The cop broke the connection.

∋ ● ∈

On Sunday morning the poison ivy was worse. Dry red blotches had broken out on Chris's arms, welts that seemed to get scalier by the minute. Chris was cranky from the itching and from not being able to play with his friends in the street's block-party volleyball game. Cal made iced-tea compresses with dishtowels, his mother's remedy, and was on his way to the drugstore for Caladryl when the telephone rang.

It was Kate, back from her book tour.

"It was a smash," she reported. "Do you know, the day after I did Johnny, they sold out my book at B. Dalton? I brought back a present for Chris," she added. "Can I bring it over tonight?"

"Sure," Cal said. "He's got poison ivy. It'll cheer him up."

"Poison ivy?" Kate said quickly. "I'll be right there."

Cal laughed. "Kate, it's nothing serious."

"Serious enough, dear. I've got something that'll clear it up in a jiffy."

"Caladryl's fine. I was just going out to get some."

"Oh, don't do that," Kate persisted. "What I have is *much* better. Now sit tight, I'll take a cab and be there in a minute."

Good "grandmother" at her best, she arrived in minutes as promised, fresh and vigorous as a twenty-year-old despite six weeks on the road, and dressed as usual in a baroque caftan, this one in several clashing shades of pink.

"Now where do you suppose he got poison ivy?" she asked the moment she entered.

"At day camp," Cal replied.

"You'd think they'd be more careful," she remarked, bustling on into Chris's bedroom, "keep the kids away from it."

"Oh, they do," Chris piped up, "I'm the only one who got it."

Kate stared at him a moment, then pulled a white porcelain jar out of her enormous purse. "Pajamas off, duckie," she said, and began to slather on the ointment from the jar.

"Oooo, that's cold," Chris said.

"Feels good, doesn't it?" Kate said.

"It stopped hurting," Chris answered, in wonder, staring at his arms.

"What is that stuff?" Cal asked.

"A recipe I got from the Xochi Indians. I use it all the time for my prickly heat. Works ten times as fast as calamine. By tomorrow Chris should be almost better."

She finished covering Chris and told him to lie still while the ointment was absorbed. Reaching for her bag, she took out a packet wrapped in yellow tissue paper and gave it to Chris.

The present inside was a T-shirt, black with a gold-glitter thunderbolt on the front.

"Gee, it's neat!" Chris said.

"I thought you'd like it. It's just like Chief Black Cloud wears." Kate winked at Cal. "Now put it right on."

"But it'll get all greasy," Chris objected.

"No it won't, dear. The salve's sunk in now."

And it had, Cal saw. The remedy was amazing. In the fifteen minutes since it had been applied, the welts had subsided and their angry red tinge had faded.

"What did you say was in that stuff?" he asked Kate.

"Oh, I don't know—some tree bark and cactus and onion and a dash of rubbing alcohol and some leaves I get sent to me from Guadalajara. Did you hear me on Dinah's show on primitive remedies? She ate it up."

∋ ● ∈

Over coffee and croissants in the garden, Kate said, "Your roses look lovely. Gardens are so much work, I'm surprised you have the time."

"I don't," Cal told her. "Carmen does it."

"Oh, that's nice." Kate gazed around at Mrs. Ruiz's handiwork. She examined the privet and acanthus and petunias, all the while chattering about Merv and Johnny and Dinah ("She had polio as a child, you know? Isn't she a terrific dame?"), and newspaper reporters and bookstore signing parties. Cal had missed the appearance with Dinah Shore, but the subject of primitive remedies had led him to put some questions to Kate about his research.

She listened intently as he asked what she thought of his studying urban primitivism and doing "field work" in the city. And about Santeria and Voodoo? And did she think it possible, in this day and age, that there was still human sacrifice?

She set her coffee cup down on the ground and leaned toward him. "Tell me, dear, how is it that you've gotten interested in this?"

Cal started with the body at the warehouse fire, his trip to the morgue, his long talk with MacTaggart. He admitted it sounded crazy, no one could believe human sacrifice would be practiced here and now in New York; but the cop was convinced. He told her then about meeting Oscar Sezine, who convincingly portrayed Voodoo as a positive force, as something good, and who was thoroughly charming and persuasive.

"Sezine," Kate said thoughtfully. "Tall fellow? Looks like James Earl Jones?"

"That's him," Cal said.

"I've met him. We worked together on the Mayor's Commission on Ethnic Revitalization. How did you find him?"

"MacTaggart sent me to him. Sezine won't talk to the police, but he welcomed me with open arms." Cal stirred his coffee. "Kate . . . the sources are very scarce, but from what I've read . . . well, there *was* human sacrifice in Haiti as late as 1883. My God, the Panama Canal was being built then. The steam engine had been around for a hundred years. The thing is, Kate . . . maybe MacTaggart's right."

Kate meditated a moment, putting a finger to her lips in concentration. Cal had never seen her effervescence go flat so quickly. She sat for a minute, her face impassive, saying nothing.

"Kate, what is it?"

"Nothing, dear. I'm a little tired, that's all. It's been a brutal couple of weeks, and it's catching up with me." She reached over to a flower bed and pulled up a weed. "Cal, you know dealing with Voodoo isn't simply anthropology . . ."

Cal found her tone curiously solemn. "Are you telling me I shouldn't study it? I've already gotten that from the nay-sayers in the department. But I thought you'd be more open-minded, want to encourage me."

Kate got up and started pacing along the borders of the garden. "I do. It's only that I think you have to be very sure of what you're getting into. Of all the aspects of primitive culture, tribal religion is probably the hardest for us to understand. Studying it can be, well, problematical."

"I find it fascinating, and I'm going ahead with it. I'm certain I can keep my rational perspective."

She stopped and turned toward him. "You had a book you were going to write," she reminded him.

"I think this may be far more important."

She paused another moment. "Then I have something that may help you. When Quentin and I were living in New Orleans in the

158

late 'thirties, he got interested in a religion down there called Obeah. From what you've said, it sounds similar to Santeria."

Cal tried to remember if Quentin Kimball had ever published a paper on Voodoo. He was certain he had read all of Kimball's books and monographs.

"I've never seen anything of his on Obeah," Cal said.

"He planned to do a book," Kate explained, "but he never finished it. I could let you have his notes, though."

"You think they might help me?"

"I can't be sure. I've never read them."

It was hard for Cal to believe that a woman of Kate's intellectual curiosity could have left the observations of her husband untouched. "Never? Why not?"

She looked distractedly at a rosebush, touched a thorn as if she meant to hurt herself, and drew back suddenly. "I said this subject could be difficult to deal with, Cal. It was a problem for Quentin. There was . . . some confusion and unhappiness that came out of this work, and after that I could never . . ." She broke off, shaking her head.

Cal went to her. "Kate, you *are* trying to discourage me from going ahead with this."

"Absolutely not," she declared, straightening. "No, I'd be the last person to do that. I believe the more we understand about human behavior, and the more we give ourselves to the mysteries of mortal experience, the better off we all are. You're a fine anthropologist, Cal. I'm sure you'll do valuable work with this."

"Thanks, Kate," Cal said. Gratitude for her support welled up in him and he almost reached out to hug her. But as if expecting it, and embarrassed by the emotion, she turned and continued pacing along the flowerbed, head down, seemingly determined to hunt down the smallest weed.

Cal began to clear the dishes from their snack.

"Why *there* it is!" Kate erupted suddenly.

Cal turned to see Kate stepping over some bushes near the rear of the garden. She bent and inspected a low plant.

"This is poison ivy," she announced.

Cal joined her, and sure enough he saw the familiar three-leaved stem and reddish-green berries.

"Where are your gardening gloves?" Kate demanded.

"Don't bother, Kate. Carmen will take care of it in—"

"Get me the gloves," Kate said.

Cal brought the gloves. Kate pulled her caftan up over her knees and set to work tearing the noxious plants from the ground. Then she folded the uprooted plants into the hem of her caftan and carried them to the garbage.

"Well, I'm glad that's done," she said finally. Stripping off the gloves she brought them into the kitchen and dropped them gingerly into the sink. "Give them a good soak in Clorox," she instructed. "Now, I'd better be on my way. Don't forget to rub that salve on Chris tonight, and again in the morning. And give me a call whenever you want to drop over and get those notes."

After she was gone, Cal returned to the garden to finish clearing the coffee cups. The day was growing hotter by the minute, and in a neighboring yard kids were sloshing in a plastic pool. Saucer and cups in hand, Cal glanced back at the corner plot where Kate had been at work. He walked over and looked down at the freshly furrowed soil. The borders of the naked patch of earth where poison ivy had so tenaciously thrived ran in nearly a straight line.

Almost, Cal thought, as though it had been planted.

⊃ • ⊂

The poison ivy welts were nearly invisible when Cal checked them on Monday morning. Only a few dry scaly blisters remained. He applied another coating of the miraculous salve and was debating whether to send Chris to camp when Chris volunteered that he wanted to stay home and read *Willy Wonka and the Chocolate Factory*.

At noon on the dot Mrs. Ruiz arrived, freeing Cal to leave for the office. Soon, coming from Chris's room, he heard what sounded like an advanced Spanish lesson. He went in to say goodbye.

Mrs. Ruiz was kneeling in front of Chris, examining the remaining blotches on his legs and cooing in Spanish.

"It's only poison ivy," Cal said, "and it's almost—"

He stopped as he noticed that she was holding a wad of Kleenex and meticulously wiping away the salve from his morning application.

"Carmen, he still needs that. It's not healed yet." He picked up the jar of salve from Chris's dresser and scooped a gob onto his fingertips.

"It's all right, Daddy," Chris said. "It's all better. Carmen was only—"

"I think I know what's best for you, Chris." Cal moved to the side of the bed.

"No, no," Carmen said, and held his hand back.

"Carmen," Cal said shortly. "This is medicine. It'll cure—"

Carmen rose to her feet, jostling Cal away from the bed, and blocking his way. "No, *guao* to save—*guao* good."

"What the hell are you doing?" Cal said with irritation. He stepped around her and bent over Chris.

Carmen protested more vehemently. "But Misser Jamis', spirits tell, I save."

Cal paused for a glance at Carmen.

Spirits tell . . . So her religion was beginning to create difficulties.

"Carmen," he said, exercising patience. "This is a salve to cure Chris's poison ivy. Would you please move away from the bed so I can put it on?"

Carmen's mouth worked as though to speak, but then she clamped it shut and inched grudgingly aside. Cal leaned over Chris to apply the salve.

Suddenly Carmen's hand shot out and grabbed the jar of salve.

Cal whirled around, but Carmen was already running from the room. In her bright green print dress, with her waddling stride, she would have been a comic vision if Cal hadn't been so furious.

"Carmen, damn you!" he shouted, bolting after her. "Give that back! What the hell's gotten into you?"

"I save!" she called back as she darted toward the bathroom. "*Guao* good!"

He chased her down the hallway, only to be met by the bathroom door slamming in his face. He heard the bolt being thrown.

"Carmen!" he commanded. "Come out of there."

He heard the toilet flushing, one whoosh of water after another.

He leaned back against the wall. She wasn't coming out. There was nothing to do now—if he didn't kick the door down—but wait.

The toilet continued to flush. Cal paced impatiently. Turning along the hallway toward the living room, he could see through the French doors into the garden.

The poison ivy!

Of course. It was Carmen who had planted it, and now she was trying to keep the rash from being cured.

Carmen was dangerous.

The door opened. Carmen stood in the middle of the bathroom with a mournful expression on her face, eyes reflecting a plea for forgiveness and, at the same time, resolute confidence in her insubordination. On the floor lay the salve jar, empty but for a piece of toilet tissue. She had wiped out every bit of the stuff and flushed it away.

He knew he was going to explode five seconds before it happened.

"You're fired, Carmen! *Now!* Take your things and leave."

She started to protest. "But the boy—"

"The boy nothing. Just get out."

She opened her mouth as if to object again, but seeing Cal's resolute glare, she snapped her lips together and shuffled away.

She went to the kitchen, fussed around for a minute or two, then gathered her things and went, closing the door softly behind her.

Cal sat in the living room until she was gone. Suddenly he smelled something burning. He bolted to the kitchen.

On the stove, over a low flame, sat a saucepan containing a simmering mixture of water and garlic and something else Cal couldn't place. He dabbed his finger in a trail of brown powder on the counter, smelled it, hesitantly touched it to his tongue.

Brown sugar.

As he turned on the tap to rinse off his hand, he noticed the window sill. Set squarely in the center was a red candle in a glass jar, its wick burning with a steady flame.

A Voodoo candle.

Trying to cast a spell on me, huh.

He shrugged, and turned off the flame, then picked up the simmering pot to put it in the sink. The white-hot handle singed his palm mercilessly. Flinging the pot into the sink, he threw on the cold tap. You got me, Carmen, I burned myself, he thought.

Then he spotted the candle again.

In a fury, he threw the window open wide, blew out the candle, and hurled it angrily into the alley.

Chapter 22

CAL TOOK a sip of coffee and spread out the morning *Times*. The same depressing patchwork of front-page news. A group of doctors had issued a statement saying the idea of limited nuclear war was ridiculous: no one would survive the effects of radiation. Oscar Sezine had certainly been right about one thing; if ever people had needed divine help to get things straightened out, now was the time.

He leafed through the Metropolitan section and was about to close the paper in disgust when a small item on page nine caught his eye. BRONX RAID SAVES MENAGERIE, it was headlined. ASPCA SAYS ANIMALS BRED FOR RITUAL SLAUGHTER. The article that followed was terse, and rather short on solid information. The Society for the Prevention of Cruelty to Animals, with assistance from the police, had entered a home in the East Bronx and discovered dozens of live chickens, goats, and a variety of other animals. An ASPCA official was quoted: "This kind of thing is becoming more common lately. There are a number of cults in the city doing sacrifices, and there's money in raising the animals. They're supposed to be specially bred, fed certain kinds of herbs. One of these goats, full grown, sells for two or three hundred dollars, and a kid will go for twice as much." But the cults were left unspecified—no mention of Santeria, Voodoo, or any of its varieties.

Did the *Times* know what it had stumbled onto, or were they holding back because, as MacTaggart had told him, the subject was too touchy to open to wide public scrutiny?

Cal read through the article again and drained his coffee. He pinched up the last crumbs of the croissant from his plate and went for the phone.

∋ ● ∈

"That's our baby right there," said Ira Landers, the ASPCA agent quoted in the *Times*. He swerved his four-year-old Datsun to the curb, across the street from a ramshackle house with dark brown siding and a sagging front porch. Landers was fiftyish, balding, and wore a canary yellow golf shirt and a Panama hat with a multicolored band. He had described himself on the phone to Cal as the J. Edgar Hoover of animal crime, but Cal thought he looked more like a Damon Runyon racetrack habitué.

They were in a vast outlying section of the Bronx, where blocks of mammoth high-rise developments and streets of decaying wooden frame houses ran together indiscriminately. On both sides of the street where Landers had parked, the houses had small yards front and back, but it was obviously a wrong-side-of-the-tracks neighborhood, with touches of blight clinging everywhere like lichen on a rock. In the middle of the block stood the pillaged shell of an old car on rusted wheel rims. The roofs and siding of the dilapidated houses were roughly patched with tar paper, their broken windows plugged with rags. The only sign of life on the street was a mongrel dog sniffing along the gutter.

The house that had been singled out for Cal was indistinguishable from the rest except for a new chain-link fence around the yard. Forlorn and uninviting, if it was home to anyone it was obviously no man's castle.

So this was the "raid," Cal reflected. A couple of patrolmen and this one harried troubleshooter from the ASPCA. It was not mere happenstance, Landers had explained when Cal called, that another raid was about to be launched. There was, in fact, hardly a day during the past few months when the agent had not been chasing down leads to "farms" where animals were bred for sacrifice.

"If only we could trace 'em all," Landers said while they waited in the car. "We could be busting one of these dumps every day for a year. They're everywhere—the Bronx, Brooklyn, Washington Heights, Long Island. Animals being raised by the thousands. Pigs, goats, turtles, lizards, you name it. All for this sacrifice crap. I found a gazelle in a house in Queens. No kidding! A fucking African gazelle, waiting to be killed."

Landers looked over his shoulder. "They're always late, the boys

164

in blue." He popped a piece of chewing gum into his mouth. "I tell you, there never used to be so much of it around. Suddenly it's everywhere, especially in the last couple of months. You know what's behind it, don't you? Voodoo, for Chrissakes, right here in the Big Apple. All these people we got comin' in from the Caribbean, Cubans, Haitians, Jamaicans, Puerto Ricans, and each one's into a cult with a different name, but to me it's all the same creepy shit. Up in the *barrio* I hear there's something extra-heavy now, called *mayombe*. Supposedly these *mayombe* people have a shrine where they get together and chop up a couple of hundred animals at a shot. Then they drink the blood. Cute, huh?"

"Where is that shrine?" Cal asked.

"Who the hell knows? It's a secret. All I've heard is that it's there, run by some hustler they call Doctor Tata. Must be a dozen other guys like him, though, to judge from all the animals I'm seein'. It's a flood, I'm tellin' ya."

Landers railed against the sad fact that, of all enforcement bodies, only his organization had been able to do anything toward curbing the excesses of the cults.

"Pitiful," he said. "It's a religion, see, so it's anti-American to mess around with it. We don't even have a law on the books against animal sacrifice. The only thing we can get 'em on is breeding livestock on residential property—you know, the health code."

The ASPCA, Landers said, had attempted to find people in the hierarchies of the Voodoo cults, hoping to stem the animal abuses by convincing the leaders to educate their followers in more moderate forms of worship. But the leaders were unreachable; their identities were unknown to the vast majority of believers, and guarded as a sacred secret by the few who did know.

"As much as I could find out," Landers told Cal, "there's two or three high priests in the city. Got a special word for 'em—*babalao*. The poop is that these *babalaos* run the show. But since we don't know who they are, we can't find 'em. There's no way to stop this thing because there's no one to hold responsible."

They sat waiting in the car for the cops to arrive. There hadn't been the faintest sign of movement at the ugly brown house across the street; it was so lifeless it could have been a painted backdrop on a stage.

"It's hard to believe that place can be full of animals," Cal said.

"Oh, you bet your bippy they're in there," Landers hooted. "If we were downwind on a breezy day you'd get a whiff that would knock your socks off."

165

Cal stared at the house. "Mr. Landers," he said slowly, "do you think it's conceivable they could also be doing human sacrifice?"

Landers pursed his lips and pushed his Panama hat up off his brow. He looked like he was concentrating on nothing more serious than handicapping the fifth at Aqueduct.

"I've heard that one," he said at last. "This Voodoo thing is so crazy you gotta ask: where do they draw the line? But from what I hear, they can't do it."

"Can't?"

"It's officially forbidden," Landers said.

"Unlike most murders," Cal retorted.

"No, I mean by the boys at the top," Landers said. "By the *babalaos*."

"Where'd you get that information?" Cal asked dubiously. How could Landers know what was official dogma if no one outside the religion knew who was giving the orders?

"The guy at the *Times*," Landers replied, "the one who wrote that story you saw. He did a little background work and he told me about a big meeting in Havana in 1940, a convention of all the high priests from the Voodoo cults. Seems they got together to bring their policies up to date—sort of like the cardinals meeting in Rome a couple of years ago—and one of the big decisions that came down was no more human sacrifice." Landers shook his head and made a clucking sound with his tongue. "Real progressive thinkers, huh? They finally decided that sacrificing people was going too far . . . all the way back *in 1940!*"

A horn blared suddenly behind them. A police car had pulled up. The policeman at the wheel made a pointing gesture toward the house. Landers stuck a hand out the window and gave an acknowledging wave, then turned the key in the ignition.

"You just go in?" Cal said. "No plan?"

"I've done half a dozen in this precinct with the same cops," Landers said. "They know the routine."

The two cars moved down the street and pulled into the driveway of the brown house. Their arrival instantly triggered some activity inside. Cal saw a triangle of dark fabric pulled away from the corner of a downstairs window, a face flash there for an instant. The fabric dropped again as a voice was heard from within, a loud bawling cry.

"Mama! Mama!" Like a child with a scraped knee calling for comfort. Only it was a man's voice, deep in timbre, pleading with the same helplessness.

They got out of the cars. Cal smelled it then, the pungent aroma of the animals.

Landers let Cal and the two cops precede him up the steps to the porch. The odor was much stronger.

"Phew," one of the cops complained, wrinkling his nose. He looked like a veteran, face lined, wisps of gray hair around the ears. The other cop, much younger, was probably a rookie.

The veteran knocked at the door.

"Shouldn't one of them cover the back?" Cal murmured to Landers.

Landers shook his head. "They never run. Why should they? Pay the fifty-buck fine, then they can go find another pigsty somewhere and be right back in business."

The door opened. The odor rushed out, so strong it was almost palpable, as smothering as a hobo's old blanket. Cal gagged, his eyes watered. It was a moment before he could focus on the pair who had answered the door.

One was a tiny woman, very old and shrunken, the brown skin of her face parched and squashed down like a discarded paper bag crumpled into a ball. She wore a robe and slippers made of the same pink fake fur, and on her head was a black plastic tiara set with chips of faceted glass that could have been a premium from a cereal boxtop. Around her neck was drooping a necklace of brown and black beads. She was clasping the hand of an immense young man as if he were an infant being restrained. The young man had on an undershirt, a faded pair of oversized bermuda shorts, and a necklace exactly like the old woman's. He was retarded, Cal realized. They stood listening to the veteran cop.

"I have a search warrant to inspect the premises," the cop said flatly. "You have the right to accompany us. You may call a lawyer if you like."

The old woman and her son put up no resistance. Beyond the pair Cal could see a narrow central hall dimly lit by a hanging naked bulb. The hall was filthy, littered with newspapers, rags, and sacks of animal feed spilling onto the floor.

Cal and Landers waited on the porch, and in a few minutes the policemen returned from their check. The veteran grasped the tiny woman by one arm, the rookie took hold of her son, and they started to lead the two offenders away.

Then suddenly as she was going down the steps, the old woman dug in her heels, refused to move. Incredibly, she mustered sufficient strength to stop the beefy veteran cop in his tracks. He tried to pull her forward, carefully—taking no risk of being charged with police brutality—but the tiny witch remained rooted to the step. Then slowly she turned to look over her shoulder directly at Cal. Her eyes, deeply sunken in cracked brown folds, opened wide like tiny volcanoes erupting to reveal their molten cores, bright and yellowish. Parting her lips she began to keen eerily in a high squeal:

"Aguanilleo Oggun Aguanilleo Oggun
Egun Eko Mare Egun Eko Mare
Aguanilleo Oggun—"

Cal couldn't understand a word of it. But unaccountably he was terrified, pulse racing, his throat sandpaper dry.

"—Arerere Arereo Arerere Arereo
Aguanilleo Oggun—"

Distracted by her amazing show of strength and the hypnotic chanting, the policemen had remained mute and motionless, allowing the woman to continue for several seconds. But finally they reasserted themselves and pulled her away. The retarded son followed with little hopping steps that looked almost like a dance.

As the pair were shoved into the back seat of the patrol car, the old woman was still chanting.

"Jesus H. Christ," Landers said as the car backed out of the driveway. "I've never seen any of 'em do that little number before."

Cal inhaled deeply, trying to calm himself.

Landers peered at him. "You all right, pal?"

Cal puffed out the air slowly. "Yeah . . ."

Landers lingered. "You can wait out here if you want. What you'll see inside won't be any easier to take."

"I'm okay now," Cal assured him.

They went in. The blanketing foul smell became thicker at once, constricting Cal's throat.

The doors leading from the center hall were all closed. Landers pushed back the first one on the right. The room, probably a parlor in a normal house, was completely dark, the windows sealed. Only the dim light from the hallway tempered the blackness. Landers stood in the doorway waiting for his eyes to adjust, but Cal took a couple of steps over the threshold. Then his foot started to come down on what felt like a rock. He tried to shift his balance, pull back, but it was too late.

His foot settled. There was a sickening cracking sound, a sensation of softness, his sole sliding over something slick.

He froze.

168

"Wait," Landers said sharply. "I've got a flashlight in the car. I always forget the damn thing . . ."

He darted away.

In half a minute Cal heard footsteps clattering up the porch steps. Landers reappeared in the door and shone his flashlight in. The beam swept over bare walls and windows taped with tar paper, then ran down to the floor. At first glance, Cal thought it was paved in shiny black cobblestones, thousands of them in a random pattern. In places the shiny stones were heaped four and five deep. As the light paused, one of the stones budged slightly, and the whole pile adjusted around it, an avalanche in slow motion. Cal saw now that some of the stones had small outcroppings studded at their tips with black chips that caught the light like mica.

Some of the chips moved. The outcroppings shrank into the circumference of the stones.

Heads, Cal realized, pulling back into their shells.

Turtles! The room was made of them. They jammed the floor, mounded up on each other's backs to form shiny black drifts.

"Holy shit," Landers whispered.

Under Cal's foot the soft body of a dead turtle oozed from the broken shell.

Landers hurried across to a window, plowing a path through the turtles with the tips of his Hush Puppies. He ripped down the tar paper and tried to open a window. It was stuck, so he punched out a pane of glass with the metal butt of his flashlight.

By daylight the den of turtles made a strange but less menacing sight.

"Seen enough?" Landers said.

⊐ ● ⊏

They went through the rest of the house. In another room on the ground floor they found eighteen goats. The muzzled animals stood in a line, legs shackled to a heavy iron chain anchored at each end to iron rings on the wall. Their excrement covered the worn linoleum floor. In the corner under a remnant of burlap lay the decaying corpse of a baby kid, born prematurely.

On the second floor there was one room full of caged doves, another where thirty or forty cats roamed loose, a third where several white roosters sat on perches. The roosters' crowing had been silenced, Landers informed Cal from past experience, by pouring a mild acid down the birds' throats. In the attic were pigeons, monkeys, piglets, white mice, two possums, and a doe.

They went to the basement. In a pit dug from the dirt floor lay the bones and carcasses of every kind of animal, half-covered in white powder. Because the breeding conditions were so poor, Landers explained, the attrition rate was high. Dead animals were regularly thrown into the pit and dissolved with quicklime.

There was no telephone in the house, so Landers drove off to find a coin box to call for the requisite number of ASPCA vans. Cal sat alone on the porch steps, sickened and discouraged. How effectively Oscar had rationalized the custom of animal sacrifice; he'd been able to make it seem almost . . . sensible. But of course Oscar had never talked about what had to be done to provide animals for slaughter. What Cal had seen put a different slant on Oscar's clever sales talk. Could there be any comparison between these animals and those killed to satisfy other traditions?

No, Cal thought. These weren't Christmas turkeys.

⋑ ● ⋐

The morning *Times* was still on the table by the breakfast dishes when he came home. Had it been only this morning when he'd spotted the story? Plunging into the extraordinary world of Voodoo had a disorienting effect, distorted perceptions of time. Cal felt as though he might have been away a year, a century, traveled eons through another dimension, a time warp to a distant planet—the Planet of the Turtles!—only to return and find that nothing had changed.

The *Times* article was bylined George Sullivan. Cal called and reached him at his desk in the city room. He told the reporter about his research and that he had heard from Ira Landers about the Havana "Voodoo convention" in 1940. Could Sullivan add any more details?

"Sorry, Professor," the reporter replied. "I told Ira as much as I know." There was a pause. With an impatient edge in his voice, the reporter added, "Anything else? I've got a story on deadline."

"Just one more question," Cal said. "Why haven't you written more about what's happening with Voodoo in the city?"

"We gave the animal story some play, but there's a limit to how often you can write about houses full of animals."

"But there are other interesting angles," Cal said, and stopped. He'd had an impulse to mention the possibility of human sacrifice, but remembered MacTaggart talking about the need for discretion, heading off a media circus.

But the reporter's interest was piqued. "What angles did you have in mind?"

"Well, that background you gave Landers, the convention in Havana where human sacrifice was banned. That's pretty interesting stuff."

"I guess it was," Sullivan said. "That's why it made the news when it did. But that was 1940. It isn't news anymore."

Cal hesitated a second, then thanked Sullivan and hung up.

He picked up the newspaper. What had to happen, he wondered, before a human sacrifice would compete with nuclear alerts and brushfire wars for a little corner of space on the front page?

Chapter 23

THE DOOR was opened by Kate's part-time Jamaican housekeeper. In her musical patois she told Cal that "Ma'am Clay she in the back place." He made his way to the rear of the loft and entered the storage area.

He had forgotten how huge it was. There were regional museums that had less storage facility. So much stuff was piled into the cavernous space—statuary, crates, totems, trunks, her own Guinean war canoe—that Cal couldn't see her. He stepped around a pile of pottery blocking the door and shouted.

"Katie?"

A voice sang out from some hidden recess. "Over here!"

She popped into view from behind a bank of file cabinets in a far corner. Cal threaded his way toward her past native carvings of wood and ivory, boxes of Stone Age tools, assortments of vivid masks.

"I don't know why you haven't given more of this to museums," he said. "Get yourself a nice tax deduction on top of the cultural contribution."

"Dear, I've given mounds away," Kate answered. "But somehow it just keeps piling up."

Cal reached the row of filing cabinets. He walked around to the front, which faced the wall to form a small aisle where Kate was standing. There were seven of the old four-drawer metal files. All the drawers were open and many had been emptied, the dossiers pulled out and stacked on the floor. Kate was literally ankle-deep in paper, ransacking her own files. Wearing frayed jeans and a baggy moth-eaten cableknit sweater instead of her usual muumuu, she even looked like a member of a wrecking crew.

"You've gone to a lot of trouble," Cal said. "I had no idea—"

"No, no, dear, it's perfectly all right. When you told me about your project and I thought about this work of Quentin's, well . . ." She averted her eyes and spoke in a faint, distant tone. "But it's hard to dig up the past." She fell silent for a moment, then seemed to catch herself descending into a maudlin reverie, and looked up. "Quentin was the most wonderful man I ever knew. The kindest, brightest, most alive person. I suppose you could say he was the husband who deserved me most, the one I would've liked to hang onto."

She laid her hand on Cal's arm. He had never heard her express such poignant regrets. Her marital record had always been treated lightly, a topic for her own jokes. From the way she was talking now, Cal was made more keenly aware of the emotional turmoil brought on by searching for Kimball's notes.

"Kate, you're really kind to do this."

"Think nothing of it," she said, and held out a packet of papers bound in a wide rubberband. "Here they are."

Cal weighed the packet in his hand, surprised by how light it was, its ignominious appearance. At the top were some folded sheets of foolscap, two envelopes with jottings on the back, some odd scraps of paper, and underneath those a leatherbound diary.

"It's all I could find," Kate said, "but they're yours to keep."

Cal looked up. "No, Kate, I'll use them, but I can't take them as a gift."

"Please," she insisted. "In a way, I think they belong more to you than me. Maybe you were meant to take up where Quentin left off."

Cal smiled at her sentimental notion. He offered to help her straighten the files, and they began stacking them. She asked how Chris's poison ivy was doing, and he told her about Carmen Ruiz's flushing the salve down the toilet and his suspicion that she had planted the poison ivy in the garden.

"Heavens!" Kate exclaimed. "That's monstrous. I hope you fired the woman on the spot."

Cal replied that he had done exactly that, but now he was burdened with housework until he could find somebody new.

"Don't even look for anyone," Kate said. "Celestine's only here three mornings a week, I'm away and out for dinner so much. I'm sure she could find some time for you."

"It's a godsend," Cal said, and hugged her. "But only if you're sure . . ."

Kate smiled. "You know, there's an unwritten law among ladies in sophisticated circles. They can share their secrets, their hairdressers, sometimes even their lovers . . . but never, never their cleaning women. *That* leads to bad blood. But in our case, dear, I'm not worried about anything coming between us. Perhaps," she added with a grin, "only because you're not a lady."

On the way out Kate took him into the kitchen and a new schedule was discussed with Celestine. The Jamaican girl lit up with a gold-plated smile when she heard she would be taking care of Chris.

"Oh, I remember from when he come," she lilted, "one cute handsome boy."

It was a relief to stop worrying about the house being organized, Cal thought as he went down in the elevator. Thank God for Kate, always coming to the rescue. He hoped someday he'd have a chance to repay all her kindness.

∋ ● ∈

Thursday was Torey's birthday, and Cal asked if she would come over and celebrate it with Chris. They had seen each other twice since the South Street outing, once for dinner at Sandolino's in the Village, and the next night for a revival of *Flying Down to Rio;* he was amazed that she had never seen an Astaire film. Both dates had been followed by fantastic sex at her apartment. But was that all there was to the relationship? Extraordinary sex? Despite Cal's reservations and guilt over Laurie, he wanted more from Torey.

But he had carefully considered the birthday invitation. Although Chris had begun to accept her, the boy's fantasy about his mother might not be irrevocably gone. A party with Torey, just the three of them, could set off a flare-up of resentment; birthdays, after all, were celebrated with family.

Chris, however, gave no sign of objecting. He wore the new black T-shirt Kate had given him, his way of getting dressed up, and the party was a success. Torey had made a sumptuous chocolate cake ("I had to show off a little," she said), and after Chris watched Cal give her his present, a handmade briefcase Cal had bought at Mark Cross, Chris made a show of going to his room, telling them to wait. He reappeared with his own present for Torey, a ceramic ashtray he had made at camp.

Torey was touched, and when Cal went into the kitchen to load the dishwasher, Chris tugged her away, wanting to show her his arrowhead collection. The sight reminded Cal how much he yearned for the closeness of family.

He finished in the kitchen and went to join them, but found Chris's bedroom door closed. He reached for the doorknob, then stopped. It was a good sign that Chris was appropriating a private moment with her.

Cal went into the living room and picked up Quentin Kimball's notes, still in their rubber band. It was his first chance to look at them more closely, and he sat down at the secretary desk. Then he heard Torey shooing Chris into the bathroom. Getting him ready for bed? Another piece of the vacuum filled.

Cal embraced her as she came into the living room.

"So how was it?" he asked, giving her a kiss.

She laughed, tossing her head back. "I got three stars for the cake," she said. "He showed me his arrowheads, and some pictures of his mother from when you were on safari together. She was lovely."

"Field trip," Cal said a bit crossly. "Not safari."

Torey backed away. Cal was sorry he'd reacted so strongly, but she had touched a nerve; he couldn't be so casual as to talk about Laurie with her replacement, not yet.

Torey simply dropped the subject. "He showed me his big candle," she said.

"I should never have bought it for him," Cal said. "He saw it in the *botánica* and made me go in and get it for him."

"It's harmless," Torey said.

"Well, I'm not sure it's healthy for a kid to get into that stuff," Cal said, "or be around people who are. That's why I'm glad I got rid of Carmen. I think maybe she was doing Voodoo spells on him."

Torey turned away from him, looking into the back yard. "But you're studying it," she said, "and he's around you."

"I'm researching it," Cal said. "I'm not practicing it."

Chris called from the bedroom. "Tuck me in, Daddy."

Chris was already under the covers when Cal entered the room. He smoothed the blanket and kissed his son.

"Thanks, Daddy," Chris said fervently.

For a goodnight kiss? That went with the territory.

"For what?" Cal asked.

"For Torey," Chris said. "For making her a part of us—you and me and Mommy. She's great."

Cal hesitated a second. Should he let the reference to Laurie slide by without comment? Maybe. Even in spirit she was part of the equation.

"I'm glad you like her, Bean," he said. "Very glad."

Torey was standing by the front door when he came out, her overnight bag in her hand.

"You're not staying?" Cal said, disappointed. He'd counted on it —their first night together in his apartment.

"No . . . I think I'd like to go home. I'm a little tired."

"Look, you can sleep here . . ."

"I'd rather not." She paused, turned to the door, then looked back again. "We have to talk, Cal, about . . . about where we're headed. I . . . I need tonight to think. We'll talk tomorrow night. All right?"

A friend at the Public Theater had given Torey special tickets for Shakespeare in the Park the following evening, and Ricki had agreed to let Chris sleep over. It would be the first time Cal and Torey spent an entire night alone without Chris. He didn't want the romance dissipated in discussion.

"Why don't we talk now?" he said. "Chris'll be asleep in a couple of minutes and—"

She shook her head. "I really have to go. Got to be up early for a meeting anyway."

She kissed him quickly and lightly and he let her out.

He closed the door slowly behind her. She had brought her bag, he thought, had clearly intended to stay. What had changed? He didn't think he'd said anything to offend her. Had Chris? No, Chris couldn't have been nicer all evening.

Nerves, maybe. Getting deeper into a relationship was hard for everyone these days. Don't build anything, some insidious voice seemed to warn everybody, it could all be blown away. Yes, that must be it. Torey wanted a commitment from him, but she didn't know how to ask for it. He had held off, the smallest pang of guilt still nagging at him about Laurie, but he just had to go on, had to put the pain behind him and start a new life. He looked at the phone, almost called her to say he understood that she needed more from him and didn't want to pressure him.

But tomorrow would be soon enough. Tomorrow he would put all her fears to rest.

Chapter 24

HE WENT BACK to the kitchen, cut one more thin sliver of chocolate cake, then moved into the living room and sat down at the secretary desk, where he had spread out Quentin Kimball's manuscript and notes.

There was an element of adventure in being the first person to set eyes on the unpublished work of a great anthropologist. Equivalent to a musicologist finding some lost Mozart sonata and playing it on the piano for the first time, or a physicist coming across even the scantest unknown equation of Einstein's: "$G = mc^2 + T$"—enough to start a debate that would last for years.

And there was also the simple fact that a man of Kimball's stature had thought the subject of Voodoo an appropriate follow-up to his epic work *Letters in the Sand*, which had traced the history of written alphabets. Cal looked at the papers on the desk. Whatever Kate's feelings about reading Kimball's notes, her respect for their importance was evident; she had saved not only his personal journal but every relevant scrap of paper, not only the two envelopes with jotted notes, but several small slips of paper that had probably been torn from memo pads.

Cal picked up the larger of the two envelopes. It had been sent to Kimball return-addressed from a New Orleans bank and was postmarked May 1939. His monthly statement? The few lines scribbled on the back were nearly illegible, testifying to Kimball's offhandedness about the notations. Cal peered at the writing and deciphered it.

old woman in B Street sells chopped swamp grass
obeah?
voodoo, hoodoo
Saint Peter = Oggun?

The very form of the notes gave a clue to the evolution of Kimball's interest. Cal could imagine him out for a walk, spotting something that caught his attention, asking a few questions, and plucking a handy piece of mail from a pocket to record the moment.

The smaller envelope was clean on the back; it bore an English stamp and was postmarked London, June 1939. It was also addressed to Kimball, and was from the Library of the British Museum, then as now one of the world's greatest reference resources.

Inside the envelope was a letter signed by the head librarian. It indicated that Kimball had sent abroad only after failing to find reference sources closer to home.

> Dear Professor Kimball,
>
> Thank you for your letter of May 29. I regret to say that our collection contains nothing more specific pertaining to the subject of your study than you have been able to locate in American libraries. I wish we could have helped.
>
> The Director of the Museum has asked me to enquire if you expect to be in London at any time in the near future, and whether you or your wife might then be willing to lecture here. Of course with the current situation in Europe we understand the difficulty of making definite travel plans. We are encouraged to believe, however, that Mr. Chamberlain will bring us through.
>
> Kindest regards to Madame Kimball.

Cal tucked the letter back in the envelope, reflecting on the misplaced hopes of the past. *Peace in our time.* The Nazis had marched into Poland at the end of the summer of 1939. So even Kimball's motives for choosing this research matched his own, Cal thought. Easy availability. Blocked from traveling by the impending war—as Cal was by having a son to care for—Kimball had been attracted to the study of customs in his own backyard.

Cal looked next at the small slips of paper. On one Kimball had written "Marie Laveau, St. Louis No. 1." Cal had come across the woman's name in prior reading. Marie Laveau had been the so-called Voodoo Queen of New Orleans a hundred years ago, an ex-hairdresser who sold spells and herbal remedies, and had been somewhat responsible for popularizing Obeah. The reference to St. Louis meant nothing to Cal.

On a second slip of paper Kimball had noted: "worship of river spirit = baptism?" A theory he must have been playing with, extrapolated from other syncretic patterns.

Finally there was a leaf from a notepad that Kimball must have picked up in a gas station. Printed at the top was an outdated logo for Gulf Oil with a caption printed beneath: FOR THE LIFE OF YOUR CAR, GO GULF—a slogan Cal remembered hearing on the radio as a kid. Below it, in neat handwriting distinct from Kimball's scrawl, was a name and address: Raymond D'Arcandesse, 427 Pontchartraine, Phone 5487. A source, perhaps, but long gone. How many years had it been since the four-digit telephone number?

At last Cal turned to the pages of foolscap on which Kimball had drafted the opening portions of a book. They began with a sketch for the Foreword, a statement of purpose that read as though it had been composed before Kimball began his research. In an easy anecdotal style, Kimball told of being captivated by Hollywood representations of pagan African religions in films like *King Kong*, the Tarzan series, and countless others. There seemed to be, he said, a certain need in the human spirit to believe in and identify with cults of darkness and savagery. But in fact, he went on, the Voodoo he wanted to write about was a descendant of benign worship of anthropomorphic spirits—spirits that were believed to take human form—combined with folk medicine and magic. Even the practice of sticking pins into dolls had been reinterpreted by European explorers, and consequently by Hollywood, as symbolic murder, although it probably had more in common with folk healing, being a magic equivalent to the ancient Chinese practice of acupuncture.

These introductory remarks were left unfinished, but Kimball had obviously been intent on "demystifying" Voodoo. So why, Cal wondered, had Kate seemed to be holding Kimball's files back? What were the "confusion and unhappiness" that Kate had mentioned as stemming from his work? So far, Kimball's notes seemed perfectly normal, just what you'd expect from a researcher starting a new project.

The manuscript, Cal saw, was divided into two opening chapters. The first was about the migration of Voodoo from Africa via the slave trade. The outlines were familiar to Cal, but Kimball had discovered elements in the history of slaving that Cal had never known. Among the captains of slaving ships, Kimball wrote, it had been customary to establish jurisdictions from which—as an old slaver's record put it—"to harvest the merchandise." The Spanish, British, and French had all drawn their cargo from different tribes.

This accounted for the diversity of custom within the cults in different colonies of the New World and also for the variations in terminology. *Vodun*, which identified the Voodoo of Haiti, had meant spirit, but the derivation of Obeah, as the Voodoo of the southern United States was called, was in the Akan word *obayifo*.

It was now, as he read the definition Kimball supplied for this word, that Cal felt his pulse quicken.

The word *obayifo*, generally used to connote sorcerer or witch, also had a more literal meaning among the Akan tribes: "he who takes the children."

Cal's attention was riveted as he started Kimball's second chapter. Now Kimball had left Africa behind and was concerned with how Voodoo had come to New Orleans. At the end of the eighteenth century a violent and bloody slave revolt had shaken the French-held island of Santo Domingo, and thousands of escaping blacks had crossed the Windward Passage to Cuba, a Spanish colony. Napoleon's invasion of Spain in 1809 then drove the French-speaking people, both free and slave, out of Cuba. They had resettled in New Orleans, still a hybrid city, American-owned but French dominated. This cultural mix tolerated the arriving Voodoo worshippers, and the former slaves found they could practice the religion openly. Indeed, Voodoo came into vogue, adopted not only by blacks but also by many wealthy and respectable white citizens. Animal sacrifice and serpent worship became common, even publicly performed as part of group ceremonies in Congo Square.

Inevitably, of course, the pendulum swung. Voodoo adherents again became the target of suspicion and persecution. Rumors increasingly floated through the city about the kidnapping and sacrifice of children. These were never substantiated, but in 1860, when two young boys from prominent white families were found murdered and mutilated, five blacks suspected of Voodoo worship were lynched, and thereafter the religion was driven underground. Not until the advent of Marie Laveau, the Voodoo Queen of New Orleans, had anyone publicly avowed an association with the religion. Because a number of the city's power elite were among Laveau's secret devotees, she escaped persecution. In fact, the Voodoo Queen came to be regarded as a saint, and when she died she was buried as a Catholic—in St. Louis Cemetery Number One.

At this point Kimball's formally written narrative broke off. It ended in the middle of the page with a scribbled note to himself: "Cont with v's hist." He had obviously intended to write the history of Obeah through contemporary times, but had needed first to finish researching its practice in New Orleans as of 1939.

Cal was not surprised, therefore, to find that the last item included in Kimball's files—a morocco-bound, diary-sized notebook —had been kept as a journal of information Kimball had gathered day to day but never synthesized into scholarly prose. The first several entries recounted his efforts to locate sources knowledgeable about Voodoo and willing to confide in him. He had been in and out of the old black quarter of New Orleans, journeyed into the bayous to visit old women living in unheated shacks, consulted several retired policemen, and tracked one aged ex-reporter for the *Times-Picayune* who had covered a series of unsolved child murders in 1911 that were supposedly linked to Voodoo worship. Kimball had learned nothing conclusive from these early encounters.

But then came an entry dated July 19:

> It has taken me some time, but I have finally found the man to teach me. There is no other way. Too little can be learned from books. The practices have been handed down from one generation to the next. Generations that did not know how to write have told generations that have not wished to. So I will learn as they have. I will learn as the first men did, when it all began.

With the next entry, dated two days later, Kimball began recording his meetings with the man he had found for his teacher and "guide"—a man referred to in the journal only as Raymond (presumably the Raymond D'Arcandesse whose name had been jotted on a Gulf gas station notepad).

Kimball had apparently met to talk with Raymond every day for an initial period of two weeks. The first fourteen entries were similarly introduced: "Went to Raymond's," "Saw Raymond again," or "At Raymond's today." Each entry then continued with specifics of Obeah that had come out of their conversations. Every page was crammed with data in Kimball's squinched handwriting. The pantheon of African gods was listed, and the domains over which they exercised power were described. There were gods of the sun, moon, mountains, war and thunder, good luck, harvests, gardens, palm trees, doors!

Not only were there many gods, but each one had a distinct personality. (Oscar Sezine had mentioned this, Cal recalled, but had given him no idea of the degree of differentiation.) If the worshipper accepted a particular god as his patron, then he wore a necklace of beads in a particular color or combination of colors, like the beads Cal had seen in the *botánica*. Even the way the beads were arranged could be significant—three of one color followed by seven of another, and so on. When sacrificial offerings were made, these were also distinct for each deity, and dependent upon the favor being asked. A chicken was killed for this god, a goat for that one, a sheep or a pig or a duck for others. Certain combinations of animals might be killed according to the reason for the sacrifice.

As the detail mounted up, Cal realized that Kimball had luckily stumbled onto an extraordinary guide, someone who was revealing secrets no outsider could ever learn. But what, Cal wondered, was the guide's motive? Raymond had gone on to describe for Kimball the use of herbs in healing and doing spells. There were spells for health, to bring money, to win love, to succeed in a court case, to destroy a landlord—a hundred different motives. Each required mixing certain ingredients in a potion, and almost every substance in nature seemed to be employed in one spell or another: cinnamon, roses, garlic, coral, brown sugar, honey, verbena, corn, pomegranate, menstrual blood . . .

Cal wondered again about the guide's motive. What did Raymond want from Kimball? Or was the guide interested only in redeeming the religion's tarnished reputation?

Pausing at last, Cal leaned back and became aware of the stiffness in his spine. He stood up, stretched, and walked into the kitchen. The wall clock showed twenty-seven minutes after midnight. He was tired, no longer sharp. Yet he knew it would be impossible to sleep without reading further. What Kimball had written so far was only the first phase of his work, taking down another man's words. But the ultimate goal of the researcher was always firsthand observation and experience. That had to come next.

Cal rinsed his eyes with cold water from the tap and went back into the living room.

It was as though he had been tuned to some wavelength of the past, anticipating exactly when Kimball's research would change direction. The next entry began:

> Today Raymond told me we would talk no more. I have learned all
> I can from listening, he says. If I wish to continue, I must use my
> eyes as well as my ears. And after that, he says, I will be able to
> know not only with my mind, but in my heart.

Up to this point every page in the diary had been used, and almost all the entries were dated consecutively. But now Cal arrived at two blank facing pages, and when he turned past them he saw the next entry was dated in early September. What, Cal wondered, had caused the break in Kimball's momentum? Had he offended Raymond, lost his trust by speaking aloud some minor skepticism? Or had the guide conducted Kimball through some experiences that had not been transcribed?

Cal turned the page. The next entry startled him. Suddenly Kimball, the academic, was writing about something very personal.

> My concern for Scotty has kept me from concentrating on this work, but Kate insists that I am worrying too much and that the best thing for all of us would be to continue with the project.

From keeping a journal of research, Kimball had shifted abruptly into the style of a diary. Scotty was the son who had been claimed by a childhood illness. From Kimball's words, this was clearly the period when the disease had been diagnosed or had shown signs of being terminal. It was enough to explain a hiatus in his investigation of Obeah.

But as Cal read on past the sad personal note, it became evident that Kimball had instead entered the most exciting phase of his work. He had achieved the full trust of his guide and could be shown the most secret customs of the religion.

> Raymond welcomed me back. His concern for me and even for Scotty is touching. He has become a friend. He gave me a special medicine, saying he had consulted the *obeahman* about Scotty's case, and this is part of the prescribed cure. The rest of it involves taking a black cat, boiling it until the meat falls off the bones, then tying the bones in a bundle with hemp and putting them under Scotty's bed. I feel almost obliged to do it, since I know that to consult the *obeahman* on my behalf must have cost Raymond a small fortune, and he refuses recompense. But he assumes I will use the cure. He makes no distinction between my interest in *obeah* purely for the sake of knowledge, and the involvement of those who look to it for health, wealth, or power. Especially because I am distressed at the moment by Scotty's problem, it is important not to fall into the trap of believing in miracles, surrendering my scientific objectivity. However, Raymond's assumption that I am no different than a true believer has worked to my advantage. Tomorrow night he will be taking me to a Voodoo ceremony. It will be, he says, one of the rarest and most secret rites of the religion—the reading of "The Table of Ifa." He explains the T of I as the method by which priests of Voodoo divine the will of the gods, then prescribe the necessary offering to earn the favor of the deities. The Table is formed of eighteen seashells—

Cal glanced up thoughtfully, suddenly reminded of the grisly scene in the park, the seashell Chris had found nearby. He dropped his eyes to the page again.

> —specially selected and prepared. Any sixteen of these are cast by the priest onto a straw mat, then the random patterns that result are interpreted. Raymond describes the shells as looking like tiny mouths—

Yes, just like Chris's.

> —and says they are considered to be the "mouthpieces" of the gods, through which they speak to the priests. The future and the past are divined in this way, one reflecting the other as in a mirror. Raymond says the Table of Ifa is read routinely to assist believers in need of help, but the ceremony I will see is not at all routine. This is to be a divination done only once every ten years by the high priests, a reading which will tell what lies ahead in the decade to come, from which the best course for mortals to follow is prescribed.

The entry ended. Cal pondered. Seashells like mouths. The Table of Ifa must have been read at a ceremony which had taken place in the park. Routinely? It was near enough the beginning of the decade . . .

Cal flipped the page with such haste that it tore slightly at the seam, and plunged into reading the entry for the next night.

In a field on a plantation somewhere outside the city, Kimball had joined in a gathering of several dozen people to witness "the reading of the decade." By moonlight on a humid Southern night, a procession of priests garbed in colored robes had appeared, grouped themselves around a straw mat spread on the ground, and "cast the shells." Then, based on the patterns, the priests had made a series of pronouncements. Kimball quoted some, given in cryptic riddles:

> The earth will shake with great thunder and storms of fire will burn many lands.

> Bad air and flames will blow over yellow stars and the people of the desert will turn to smoke.

> The eye of the universe will fall along the people of the East and their villages will be dust.

No doubt about the general meaning, Kimball wrote: war was coming. But he perceived nothing more.

To Cal, however, the specific predictions were so apt as to be clairvoyant. The one about bad air and yellow stars and people becoming smoke: the gassing of the Jews and the Nazi crematoria. "The eye of the universe" falling and villages becoming dust: the decimation of Hiroshima and Nagasaki by the atom bomb.

But none of that had been known in 1939, and Kimball's attitude to the divination was skeptical:

Have I seen a prediction, or a trick by carnival gypsies? The reading does nothing more than echo the front pages of the newspapers. Who cannot know that war is inevitable?

In the continuing narrative, Kimball's skepticism was further challenged. Having completed their divination, the priests had pronounced measures necessary to *change* the plans of the gods. For, according to the religion, nothing was inevitable. The gods might be angry with mortals and prepared to wreak havoc on the earth, but if the proper offerings were made to them, their favor could be regained and the course of fate altered. So violent were the forces that the gods were prepared to unleash, however, that satisfying them would require the most extreme proof of mortal devotion and humility.

Cal lifted his eyes from the journal. He felt as if he had watched the ceremony unfold through Kimball's eyes, as if he had been there in the humid night. Only now was he conscious of the tension that had crept through his body, tightening the muscles across his chest and stomach, making breathing difficult. He was sweating, too, his shirt damp despite the cold air pouring from the air conditioner in the living room.

Finally he looked back to the page and read the description of the ceremony to the end.

On the basis of their reading for the decade to come, the high priests of Obeah had told their followers that a holocaust could be averted only by sacrificing to the gods the most pure and valuable human lives—the lives of children.

It was obvious that Kimball had been profoundly disturbed and confused by what he had witnessed. The journal entry, evidently written late at night, concluded:

It is evil, of course. But an evil which shimmers with a mesmerizing halo of good, an evil which professes to be done in the name of humanity. I do not know how I shall proceed from here. I have tried to sleep, and each time rise to pace through the house. Should I go to the police? No crimes have yet been committed. Would I be believed? History bears witness. But if I am believed, then what persecution will result! In 1860 when two children were killed in this city, five black men were lynched. (Raymond claims that the children were sacrificed following a reading of Ifa that foretold the Civil War; because of the lynchings the sacrifices ended too soon, so the gods' design was not altered.) For now I can only wait. But each time I close my eyes I imagine I can hear, far away in the night, the screams of a child. I walk through the house, unable to sleep, stopping again and again to look into Scotty's room and make sure he is sleeping peacefully.

Cal leaned back from the desk and closed the journal. He could read no more tonight. His eyes burned with fatigue and, strangely, a hint of another kind of strain—of tears held back. There was a slow dull churning sensation in the pit of his stomach.

Then he was overcome by an anxious need to see Chris. Standing a moment later at the boy's bedside, he felt calmer. He stayed for a minute or two, watching the boy deep in slumber, the epitome of every sweet cliché about sleeping children.

Lying in his own bed, he expected sleep to elude him. Questions dogged his thoughts as he stared into the darkness overhead.

What secrets had he unlocked by delving into Kimball's old work? Secrets of the past, or the future?

Or were they the same, as the priests believed, reflecting each other as in a mirror?

⊃ ● ⊂

The field was enormous, rolling away to a horizon on the edge of infinity, and for a moment he felt the most terrifying loneliness and isolation. Then he turned and saw the playground just behind him and Chris riding the swing, legs kicking up to the sky, laughing. He relaxed and watched the procession that came over the horizon, suddenly at arm's length, figures in long flowing gowns in shimmering rainbow colors dotted with yellow stars. He joined the procession, Chris beside him holding his hand as they climbed, the field having become the side of a mountain. A ruby corona shone around the summit, the rosy glow of a sunrise, or sunset—no, it was both at once. It seemed so far, then they were there. In Paradise, he knew, as Laurie sat up on a beach towel not bothering to refasten the top of her bikini and waved and Chris ran into her arms.

Then the sky cracked open and lightning flashed and they were both gone.

The clap of thunder lifted Cal half out of sleep. He rolled over and opened his eyes, saw the window of his bedroom with the rain dripping down over the panes of glass.

A bright soundless flash turned the raindrops for an instant to silver. He heard a low boom, the timpani pianissimo, and the fading sound played him back into the dream with no awareness that he had even closed his eyes.

The seven figures lined up facing him, wearing masks, carved primitive essences of animal and spirit, big as shields. Everything around them was a mess—crates piled up, file drawers open and spilling paper, Chris's sneakers and T-shirt on the straw mat. Cal wanted to ask the priests to move so he could straighten up around them, but they were statues. So he sat down on the picnic blanket with Torey to have a piece of chocolate cake and the figure was not a statue at all, not *that* one—but a black madonna peeking from behind one of the masks. She moved to him and gave him a knife to cut the cake. He stood up to take it and thanked her, then raised his arm and extended the knife over the altar. He felt released as he brought the blade down, exultant, as it cut cleanly through the skin, the heart and stomach and entrails revealed. Cal reached in and felt the slimy heart pulsing in his hand and Chris smiled at him as he died, a wonderful smile. From his mind, loud as a scream soundless, Cal heard Chris declare his love.

He slammed into consciousness, waking to the hard immovable reality of his darkened bedroom as though he had sprinted blindly into a wall of concrete. He was panting, each exhalation pushing a dog-like whimper from his throat. Every nerve and muscle was stretched so tight he felt bruised. He gripped the side of the bed so frantically that his thumb tore through the sheet, and he held himself up to keep from falling back into the dream.

It was minutes before he could let go and reach out to turn on the bedside lamp. Light, thank God. He inventoried the myriad insignificant sights, fixing himself in the real world. Bottle of Old Spice on the dresser, wet spot on the carpet where rain dripped through the open window, clothes flung on a chair.

The panic subsided.

Good Christ, talk about nightmares. Had he ever dreamed anything so horrible before? It had seemed so real. He knew all the dream theory, the unconscious mind giving license to act out repressed urges. But could he harbor a buried rage against his own son, a rage of such magnitude to justify a dream-murder?

Yes, if he thought about it. He could imagine the seething anger, consciously denied. Chris was the judge and jury who pronounced him guilty of Laurie's murder. It was Chris he saw as his true accuser. The feelings had come to a head, probably, because of his commitment to Torey. For all the affection Chris had outwardly displayed, there was also his continuing fantasy that Mommy was still alive. And of course reading Kimball's journal had put him in a frame of mind to act out the knife metaphor in his own way.

He didn't need Sophie Garfein to explain this one. The psychology of the nightmare was easy to grasp.

Yet that godawful moment when he had seen Chris dying, flayed open, smiling like the child in the morgue, could have haunted him no more than if it had been a memory of life, not illusion. He hated himself for having even the capacity to conceive such a dream.

It was a long time before he went back to sleep. And when he did, he left the light on like a child, to keep away the monsters.

Chapter 25

He was still tense in the morning.

"You're holding my hand too tight," Chris complained as they walked to meet the day-camp bus. Cal was almost afraid to let go.

When he returned to the apartment he took a long time over coffee in the garden. He dawdled over the *Times*, reading almost every page—accounts of quarter-final tennis matches, developments in the advertising business, letters to the editor. Halfway through an obituary of the eighty-six-year-old retired president of the Insurance Brokers' Confederation of America, he threw the newspaper aside.

This was *nuts*, avoiding Kimball's journal because of a bad dream, shying away as though he could be infected merely by reading another man's experiences. All right, granted: it was alien, disturbing, scary. But what should he do? Put Kimball's notes away in a trunk, give them back to Kate, abandon his own attempt to comprehend the enduring mysteries of primitive beliefs transplanted to the modern world? You couldn't turn your back on knowledge. You couldn't protect yourself from the truth. Might as well burn books.

He went inside, sat down at the secretary desk, and opened the journal to where he had left off last night.

On each of the next few pages, dated for consecutive days, were one-line entries.

I am waiting.

I have done nothing.

The situation is unchanged.

The confusion of Kimball's sleepless night seemed to have given way to apathy, with no will to act or analyze his own behavior or report any events in his life.

When at last a longer entry appeared, it was undated:

> The body of the boy who disappeared last week was found yesterday floating in the Mississippi below Bernardsville. I visited Raymond and he denied nothing. When I told him I could no longer keep silent, he was calm. I must do whatever had to be done, he said. But then he argued quietly that I must realize what was at stake. When I am with him, incredibly, he can almost persuade me: the course of history will depend on our bargain with the gods. God help me, he managed to lure me into an agreement, proposing to prove the magic by helping Scotty if I would not interfere thereafter. When I said yes, he brought out a small bundle of bones tied with hemp, and gave them to me to put under Scotty's pillow.

Then a short entry again:

> Scotty seems greatly improved.

Cal paused. Kimball had fallen into the very trap he had warned himself against. Desperate to believe in miracles, he had taken the first step toward belief; he had done a spell with a bunch of cat's bones. The irony was that he had pushed himself into a falsehood; Scotty had died anyway.

But that was only part of the tragedy, Cal realized when he looked at the next page and read the words scrawled large across it.

> Another has been done. I am no less guilty than if I had held the knife. Yet I am not ashamed. As I look back on it, I know that my work was my initiation. And I will do everything in my power to fulfill the

The final phrase was unfinished. Cal flipped a page. Blank. The rest of the journal was unused. Abruptly the notes had ended, as though Kimball had gotten up to answer the phone or greet someone at the door and had never come back to pick up his pen.

The uncompleted thought had the effect of freezing time at that moment in the past.

Fulfill the . . . the what?

. . . *the will of the gods.*

The phrase came whole into Cal's mind as if a ghost had whispered in his ear. It was right, he knew. Kimball had gone off the deep end.

So this was why Kate had wanted the notes forgotten. At the least she must have known Kimball had lost his objectivity, by itself enough to damage his reputation. Kimball had *known* the sacrifices were being done, and had kept silent. The sadness of it was overpowering.

Cal pushed the book away, got up from the desk, and went back to the garden, hungry for air and sunlight. He ambled distractedly along the fringe of the yard, thinking ba. ' ver the journal's references to past outbreaks of suspected sacrificial killing. Hardly incidental that the three mentioned had been in 1860, 1911, and 1939. Each had occurred just preceding or toward the beginning of decades marked by the most destructive military confrontations, with an ever increasing toll of human life. The War Between the States, the First World War, World War II. In each instance the sacrifices had begun, aroused public fury, and been cut short. *But too soon?*

That would be the Voodoo believers' interpretation, no doubt. The gods had not altered their wrathful plans only because they had been left unsatisfied.

But even more upsetting than the tragedies of the past were the crimes of the present. "The casting of the shells" must have been done again for the eighties. For *now*. Some dire prediction had been made and human sacrifice ordered to propitiate the gods, divert fate from disaster.

Was there any way that the unleashing of such powerful currents of history could be blocked? An irresistible mental game to play. Suppose in the summer of 1939, before the German army had marched into Poland, before the death trains had begun rolling across Eastern Europe—suppose the Mercedes carrying Adolf Hitler to one of his frequent weekends at Berchtesgaden had skidded on a wet patch of mountain road? Couldn't the gods have arranged that much? Wouldn't that have rewritten the scenario of history?

Madness. This was how it began! You were seduced by the notion of controlling fate—there was no more appealing mortal dream. It was, indeed, at the heart of every religion. *Believe*, and thy prayers will be answered.

And of course the dream could never be more seductive than it was now. It took no great clairvoyance to know what the shells must have told the *babalaos* who read the Table of Ifa to forecast for this decade. You didn't need "mouthpieces" of the gods to hear the oncoming rush of the Day of Reckoning. Nuclear proliferation, international terrorism, global economic decline, the concentration of vital fuel in the world's most unstable region. The scenario for ultimate disaster was inevitable.

Inevitable?

Oh yes, how tempting to think there were forces who could be petitioned for a better future, who could reweave history as casually as an old woman pulling out a line of bad stitches in her knitting. There was a powerful temptation to believe exactly as Kimball—

my work was my initiation

Cal wondered: could that happen to him?

Of course not. He and Kimball were different men, living in different times—

the future reflects the past as in a mirror

—and subject to different pressures.

A mission, Oscar had said.

Should he stop now? Giving up out of an irrational fear would only prove he had lost perspective. He was a rational man. There was only one way to treat superstitions, to make the contribution to his science. And that was to go on and study them and be unafraid.

⊃ ● ⊂

A faint peal of thunder brought him out of his thoughts. He glanced up at the sky. The sun was overhead, set in cloudless blue.

Then he heard the soft boom again. Someone was pounding on his front door, he realized, a rapid thumping as if someone had come to tell him the building was on fire. Daydreaming in the garden, he had probably not heard the bell. But who the hell was so sure of finding him at home?

He ran to the door and flung it open.

A small brown-skinned man with brilliantined hair that swept back over his head in washboard ripples was standing on the stoop. His chest heaved as though he had to fight for each breath.

"*Venga, venga!*" he gasped, and grabbed Cal's wrist, starting to pull him through the door.

Cal wrenched away. "Hey, what the hell—"

"*Favor, Señor Jamis* . . ." The man noisily sucked in enough air to continue. "Carmen eesoskinoo . . ."

Spanish? Yoruban? What language was this? He had only caught the name: Carmen. Something to do with Mrs. Ruiz.

"Look," Cal said, "I'm sorry, but I can't understand you. Just slow down and try—"

"No time essplain. She dine," the man wheezed. Again he reached for Cal, caught him around the arm. But his grasp was gentler this time and Cal didn't shake him off. "Pleace, you come.

192

Carmen ees askin' you. She much sick." Tears were brimming in the man's eyes now.

Suddenly Cal understood. Not "dine." *Dying!*

The little man tugged at Cal's sleeve.

How could he refuse?

Cal had no sooner double-locked the door than the little man darted out into the street. With only one backward glance to make sure Cal was staying with him, he hurried away down the sidewalk. Despite his short legs and chunky build, he ran amazingly fast, supercharged with adrenaline. Cal had to push himself to keep pace.

As the dash continued around the corner, then the length of one block, two blocks, three, crossing streets and avenues while dodging cars because the little man didn't bother waiting for traffic lights, Cal's lungs began to burn. How long could he keep this up?

They ran several blocks uptown, across Tenth Avenue, and past a huge taxi garage. At last, in the middle of the block, the man halted in front of a tenement building. An empty police car was pulled in at the curb in front, and a small buzzing crowd of neighbors was gathered on the sidewalk. Cal saw one of the women in the crowd reach out to the little man who'd brought him and give him a consoling pat on the back. Preoccupied, the man took no notice.

"Usstirs," he panted as Cal caught up with him, and scurried into the building.

They hurried to the rear of a long dingy hallway, and climbed three flights of stairs. The air was thick with unidentifiable smells, the walls crumbling and spray-painted with graffiti and obscenities.

Christ, what am I doing here? Carmen had probably gotten in the way of some common urban violence, he guessed, stabbed in a domestic squabble or shot by a burglar. Why, Cal wondered, were they bringing him into it?

On the third-floor landing another group had congregated, women in shapeless housecoats, men in undershirts craning to see through the open door of a rear corner apartment. When Cal arrived they fell silent and looked at him suspiciously; he saw two of the women cross themselves.

His escort led him straight through the open door into the apartment. The cramped front room had walls painted a garish turquoise; one was decorated with a large framed picture of an Indian in a feathered war-bonnet, exactly like the head of an old penny, only this one was painted on velvet in Day-Glo colors. Near the door, another anxious group of bystanders hovered, an old couple and a cluster of children of various ages. A baby and a toddler were on a sofa, but the rest stood quietly, arranged in rows almost as if to have a family portrait taken. They stared at Cal with wide sad eyes, and he stared back, confounded.

"Señor," Cal's escort hissed at him, recapturing his attention. "You go, pleace." He pointed along a narrow corridor to a bedroom at the end.

Cal stopped at the door and looked in. Carmen Ruiz lay on the bed covered with a gray blanket. Two policemen were at either side of the bed, bending over her. One, who had removed his jacket, was securing the mask of a small emergency oxygen kit over her face. Carmen writhed slightly, and muffled moans came from behind the mask.

The little man behind Cal nudged him into the room, and the policeman with the jacket who was facing the door looked up. "Yeah?" he said sharply, like a sentry demanding a password.

Cal tossed up his hands, at a loss how to explain his intrusion. "I . . . uh, she used to work for me." He nodded over his shoulder. "This man said she was asking for me."

As he spoke, Carmen rolled her head toward the door. Her eyes widened and squealing sounds came through the oxygen mask. She strained to raise herself up.

The policeman fitting the mask gentled her back onto the bed.

The other moved around the bed toward Cal. "Look, bud, you can see she's in no shape to talk now. Maybe if you—"

"She es *need* him!" the little man said, barging out from behind Cal with his hands outstretched to the policeman as though begging for alms.

The two cops exchanged a glance as Carmen pushed herself up again and shook her head so violently that she dislodged the oxygen mask. "Misser Jamis . . . ," she called in a croaking whisper. One hand came out from under the blanket and reached out to grab him, as if she had fallen through thin ice and he was the only one who could save her.

Cal went closer to the bed. The last exertion seemed to have knocked Carmen out, until a spasm went through her body and her flailing legs kicked off the blanket.

"Carmen." Cal leaned over her. "What's wrong? Why did you want me?"

Clutching at her stomach, Carmen whimpered pitifully: "*Ay, madre mia . . . las culebras . . . las culebras . . .*"

Cal glanced to one of the policeman. "What happened to her? What's she talking about?"

"Who knows?" the cop replied. "All we did was respond to a 911. We didn't stop for a Spanish lesson."

Cal looked around for the man who had brought him, but he was no longer in the room. Turning back to Carmen Ruiz, he knelt beside her, laid a hand on her arm, and shook her lightly.

"Please, Carmen. Try to tell me."

"Christopher . . . *sueño* . . . he hear . . ."

Her voice faded, and then she gave out a frail weakened scream as some agonizing pain shot through her. Her eyes flickered open, but they were dull and filmy. My God, Cal thought, she's really going to die.

Another whisper escaped her lips—something about "a broom" and "a door." Cal leaned closer, placing his ear above her mouth.

"Say it again, Carmen."

". . . *bromista* . . ."

"Carmen, I don't understand. You've got to—"

"*El engañador . . . bromista . . .*" The whisper was fainter, the eyes duller. Cal wasn't even sure she knew he was there.

There was a sudden commotion at the other end of the apartment, and a second later a team of two young paramedics in white uniforms charged into the bedroom. One carried a soft black medical bag, the other a small black suitcase. They pushed up to the side of the bed, stampeding Cal and the two policemen out of their way. The one with the medical bag pulled back Carmen's eyelid with his thumb and peered into her eye. He had long blond hair and looked very young, but there was no lack of assertiveness when he glanced to his partner and spoke: "Shock. Critical." The second paramedic, short and swarthy, had ripped open Carmen's dress from the neck, spraying the buttons, and now he set a stethoscope against her breast. He listened for only a moment. "She's arrhythmic," he said, "heart's playin' a fuckin' rhumba."

"Defib?" said the blond.

The one with the stethoscope nodded, bent to the suitcase he'd carried in, and threw open the top, revealing some kind of electric device with dials and meters. He glanced around for an electrical outlet, then pushed aside a bedside table with a lamp on it so hurriedly that the table crashed over and the china base of the lamp shattered. He plugged in his device and his hands went back to a compartment in the black case and grabbed up an object that looked like the top of an electric eggbeater, connected by long wires to the machine. Then he turned one of the dials and it began to hum.

Cal stood transfixed by the ballet of emergency. There was no logic to it, no reality. Why was he here watching Carmen Ruiz die?

One of the paramedics had gripped her by the arm, pushing her down on the mattress; the other held the eggbeater against her chest. "Ready?" he said. His partner nodded and flipped a switch.

Carmen's body snapped and stiffened, the jolt so extreme that she bounced an inch or two off the bed.

The defibrillator was turned off and her body relaxed. The paramedic who'd pinned her arms leaned over and put his ear to Carmen's chest. Then he shook his head.

The steel eggbeater was applied again.

"Nothing," said the blond when he bent down to listen for a heartbeat. The short swarthy one dropped the eggbeater and jumped onto the bed. Straddling the body, he slammed his fist down onto Carmen's chest.

The cops had been quietly watching the drama, but now they turned restlessly to Cal.

"Let's leave 'em to it," one said, and they moved out of the room, steering Cal ahead of them.

In the corridor outside stood the little man who had summoned Cal. "What es she say you?" he asked beseechingly.

Cal paused. Carmen's husband, he guessed. "I didn't understand her," he replied. "Something about *culebras . . . sueño . . .*"

"*Culebras, si, sueño,*" the man echoed grimly, supplying no translation.

In the living room the old people and kids were still huddling, immobile. It was as if they had adjusted to this death long ago, Cal thought, had been waiting all along for the funeral to begin.

Cal approached one of the cops, who was putting on his jacket. "Nothing else you can tell me?"

"It was a medical emergency," the policeman said tiredly. "That's all we know, and I'm not sure how much more we can find out before we get someone over here who speaks Spanish."

Cal drifted out into the hallway, then down the stairs and out onto the street. Dazed, he joined the crowd lingering around the ambulance, waiting to see what would happen next. It was hard to leave, to put an end to the episode without knowing why he'd ever been brought into it.

In ten minutes the blond paramedic came out of the tenement and went to open the back of the ambulance. Cal walked over to him.

"Did you save her?"

The medic turned to Cal holding a thick pack of black vinyl he'd removed from the ambulance.

"Would I be putting her in this if I had?" he replied.

"What was wrong with her?"

The paramedic closed the rear door of the ambulance and started up the stairs into the building. "No way to know without an autopsy. Right now all the cops can pry out of the others up there is some crazy story that she thought she was being eaten alive."

Cal stared. "Eaten—"

"Yeah. From the inside," the medic said. "By snakes. Got a tummyache this morning and suddenly decided her stomach was full of snakes, chewing her up from the inside out." He paused at the door. "I suppose it could happen . . ."

"What?" Cal demanded incredulously. "You can't be—"

"Oh, not the real condition," the medic cut in. "But there are cases where people talk themselves into these things. If she did, if she really *believed* it, that might psychogenically induce fatal shock." He gave a sad dry laugh and tossed his lank blond hair off his forehead. "The poor lady might have literally frightened herself to death," he added, and disappeared into the building, jauntily flinging the body bag across his shoulder.

⋑ ● ⋸

Cal walked to the corner and stood there, shaken and uncertain where to go. Home—to sit in the garden and read? Fine. You popped out on a little errand to watch a woman die a strange death, then picked up your life again where you'd left off.

But he had to know: why had she sent for him?

He walked toward the center of Chelsea, thinking he would buy a Spanish dictionary. Then, passing a small grocery store, he idly spotted a stenciled gilt sign on the window: *Habla español.*

He went in and stopped at the counter. A tall man with gray hair came to wait on him. He didn't look Hispanic, Cal thought, as he picked up a roll of mints from the rack by the cash register and gave the man a dollar.

As he was handed his change, Cal nodded at the sign in the window. "Are you the one who speaks Spanish?"

"Couldn't be in business around here if I didn't."

"Could you tell me the meaning of a few words?"

The grocer shrugged. "Do my best."

"*Culebras*," Cal said.

"Snakes," said the grocer.

"*Sueño*," Cal said.

"Dream," the grocer said.

Had she been dreaming about snakes? But she thought they were real.

"*Bromista?*" Cal said.

The grocer hesitated, searching his vocabulary. "That's like . . . like a joker, a trickster—you know, someone who plays practical jokes."

Could he have heard correctly? Carmen had murmured the word so weakly, he couldn't be sure of the pronunciation.

"What about *enganador?*"

The grocer hesitated again. This time he reached under the counter and brought out a Spanish-English dictionary. He flipped the pages, then skewered a word with his finger.

"You mean *engañador*," he said, emphasizing the rolled *n* in a way that did make the word sound different.

"I guess that's it," Cal said.

"Must be," the grocer agreed. "Means the same thing as *bromista*, just about. Somebody who plays tricks."

Cal thanked the grocer and left.

So that was it—an explanation that explained nothing. Carmen Ruiz had used her dying breath to say she'd played a practical joke on him. Or was dying of one played on her.

Chapter 26

SHELL-SHOCKED, Cal made his way through the rest of the day. Putting up a false front of cheerfulness, he met Chris at the day-camp bus and walked him home, then telephoned Ricki to say he would arrive at seven to drop the boy off for the night. But there was no escape from the pleading look he had seen in Carmen's eyes or the echoing words of the paramedic's judgment, sad and terrifying.

She frightened herself to death.

Was such a thing possible? But why—what was she afraid of? And was there a connection between Carmen's casting a spell on him, with her candles and burning garlic, and her calling him to her deathbed?

Cal didn't know, and not knowing unnerved him.

That night he tried to be good company for Torey, and sat quietly through the first act of *The Tempest* at Shakespeare in the Park. But all the frantic stage action did nothing to alleviate his private terror—the vision in his head of Carmen Ruiz gasping for breath, twitching at the electric shock to her chest, uselessly reaching out with her limp hand for understanding or solace or some inexplicable communication in the last moments of her life.

What had she wanted to tell him?

∋ ● ∈

At intermission he followed Torey to the refreshment stand, where they bought two Cokes. Cal made an attempt at normal conversation, agreeing that the outdoor special effects were wonderful and that Meryl Streep was a perfect Miranda.

Then the conversation went stale.

"What's the matter?" Torey said.

Cal looked away. He hated to ruin the evening.

"Cal? Something's wrong. You haven't paid the slightest attention to the play."

He tossed his paper cup into the wastebasket. "Carmen Ruiz died today," he said, turning back to Torey. "I saw her die."

She stared at him. "Carmen?" she gasped.

"Oh Christ, Torey, it was horrible. A man came to the door, her husband I guess, and he told me to come . . . and then I was watching her . . ."

He broke off, seeing it again, living it again. Torey took his hand.

Her touch helped him, brought him back to the here and now. "She'd asked for me to come. She wanted to talk to me."

"Why?"

"I don't know," Cal said, shaking his head. "She said some words. *Bromista*. And *engañador*—the trickster. It didn't make any sense."

Torey listened, her head bowed. For a long moment she was silent.

"I think we ought to go," she said. "I want to show you something."

∋ • ∈

Inside her apartment, she dropped her purse on the hall table. "Come upstairs, please," she said flatly.

He followed her up to the bedroom. She turned on the lamp and went to the makeup cabinet on top of the dresser. The cabinet looked Chinese, lacquered wood with cloisonné. She reached inside, took something out, and turned to him.

"I've wanted to tell you about this," she said, a hint of apology in her tone. "But I didn't know how."

"Tell me what?"

She walked across the room. "Here," she said.

He stared, nonplussed, at the object she had thrust into his hands. It was an apple.

"Why are you giving me this?"

"Look carefully," she said.

Then he saw the fine line in the apple's skin, a circle cut com-

200

pletely around just above the midpoint. He touched the top with one hand and found it was loose, like the lid of a cookie jar. He lifted the top. Inside the apple the pulp had been scooped out, and a syrupy liquid poured in. Peering into the viscous amber-colored liquid, Cal saw something blue submerged at the bottom. He looked up slowly at Torey.

"What *is* this?"

"It's honey," she said. "And a piece of paper. Take it out and read it."

He stared at her until she nodded sharply at the apple. Then he dipped his fingers into the honey and drew out a rolled-up slip of blue paper. He passed the apple to Torey and unrolled the sticky piece of paper. There was writing on it, block letters in red ink bleeding into the paper's threads. The two words written on the paper were "Cal Jamison."

He forced a smile. "Okay, I give up. I still can't figure it out."

"A spell," she said plainly. "I did a spell on you."

For a moment nothing penetrated. The words simply floated through him. The paper fell from his hand and drifted to the floor, sticking instantly to the carpet. He stared down at it.

"A spell," he echoed. "You mean . . . a Voodoo spell?" He raised his eyes to hers.

She looked at him steadily.

"No," he said. "I don't believe it. Why?"

She put a hand on his arm. "Because I was attracted to you, Cal. Oh, more than that. I felt . . . compassion for you, and I could see you were having trouble opening yourself to love. So I asked . . . for help from the gods."

He became aware of her grip on his arm, and broke away. He strode across the room. The anger was rising now, like steam through spreading cracks in the foundation of his spirit.

"I don't believe it," he said. "A spell, for Chrissakes."

"Cal, listen to me, please, it's just like some people going to church and lighting a candle, it's—"

"You did a spell," he said, "and you think I'm here because some gods—some Voodoo gods—"

"Cal," she said, her tone imploring, "give me a chance. Sit down and let me—"

"Don't tell me to sit down!" he snapped. *A Voodoo spell.* How could she believe . . . ?

"It's not so different from any prayer," she want on. "Can't you think of it that way? Cal, you're studying this. You more than anyone should—"

He whirled on her. "I'm *studying* it. But that doesn't mean I accept it."

Suddenly he felt drained. He sat down on the edge of the bed, his head sinking into his hands. "You," he said, his hands muffling his voice. "How could *you* need this?"

"Do you want to understand?" she asked quietly. "Do you even want to give me the chance?"

He could say nothing. Did he want to hear her justifying her belief in . . . in paganism? What did their love mean to her if she thought he had been awarded to her by Voodoo gods, like some kind of doorprize? What did his feelings mean if she thought they could be manipulated by gods, not expressed as a gift of his heart?

"Cal. Please listen to me."

"I'm listening," he said, his head still in his hands.

"I told you I'd lived in Cuba. A time came when I started to think about . . . some of the bigger questions: the meaning of life, eternity, creation, whether there's something up there bigger than us. Well, this was the religion in Cuba, and I was exposed to it when I was asking those questions . . . and it made sense to me. Can you understand that?"

He raised his head. "Why didn't you tell me before? If you think it's so reasonable, why did you wait until now?"

"What if I *had* told you? You wouldn't have liked hearing it then any more than you do now. But I figured if you got to know me first, then it would be easier. And you'd started to study it, too. I thought the more you learned, the more you'd be willing to accept it as . . . another concept of the universe."

"Casting *spells*," he said derisively. "Some concept!"

Torey turned away to a window. "Oh Jesus," she murmured, "I'm doing this all wrong. I should have gotten you drunk first, or told you after we'd made love all night." She turned back to him. "What we have is *good*, Cal, it's worth keeping even if you have to make room for something that's not—"

"I can't make room for this," he said.

"Why not? I did." It was a plea, not a challenge.

Cal stood up. Was this the woman he loved? Her image seemed to vibrate at high frequency—lover to stranger, stranger to lover. Which was she? *Who* was she?

"Torey," he said, his voice sounding frail as an old man's, "until ten minutes ago I was in love with you. Hell, I guess I'm *still* in love with you. But I can't see why you want to believe in this nonsense. You're bright and talented and beautiful and sensitive and good and kind—*those* are the reasons I fell in love with you. Not because you fiddled around with a gooey apple and wrote my name on a piece of paper. How can you think that could've had anything to do with *us?*"

"I'd like to tell you how," she said. "If you'd just give me half a chance."

Either he left now, or he listened.

"Go on," he said. "Tell me."

She sat down at a stool by her makeup table. "Twelve years ago, when I came to New York, I didn't have any money. I was down to two, maybe three hundred dollars. Gavin and I had been divorced for almost a year, but he still owed me money from the settlement. Not guilt money or alimony or any of that. He owed me a share of the things he'd sold when we broke up. But it was a messy divorce, and Gavin took out his anger by making me fight for every nickel. I needed a cheap place to live, and of all the cheap places available this was the one where at least I felt comfortable with the people. So I moved into a lousy cold-water walk-up for twelve bucks a week. Wonderful neighbors: five junkies, three hookers, and a gang that had a meeting room in the basement. I couldn't get a job because I didn't have any skills. Secretaries were getting a hundred a week, and I couldn't even type."

Unconvinced, Cal interrupted. "Wait a minute, you could speak two languages and—"

"And the only jobs were dead-end jobs," she said. "I decided to gamble. I asked around until I found a *santero*. You know what they are, don't you?"

Cal nodded.

"I needed a spell done for me," she said, "an *aceite intranquilo*, a spell called 'restless oils.' It's done for good luck in business. I knew people in Cuba who'd had it done, and they'd gotten wealthy. So I spent my last two hundred dollars. I'd never actually paid for a spell before, but that's what the *santeros* ask for this, and that's what I paid." She paused, her hand fidgeting with the top of a perfume bottle. "Two days later I got a check from Gavin. For six thousand dollars."

"But that was money you had coming," Cal put in quickly. "You can't believe—"

"Wait," she said firmly, "there's more. The very next day I overheard my landlord talking about selling the building to a developer. The price he wanted for a down payment was six thousand dollars, exactly the amount I'd gotten from Gavin. I persuaded the landlord to sell to me, to take the check and finance the rest."

"You were in the right place at the right time," Cal said. "Do you think that never happened to anyone before?"

Torey continued, "By the time I finished renovating the building, the neighborhood had started to turn around; developers were everywhere. The building was worth triple what I paid for it. I put it up as collateral and bought a second building, the one you're in."

Cal vented a sigh of desperation. "Torey, you're only proving what I said. You're smart and talented and you would have done just fine without your spells or—"

"Do you really think that much luck is an accident? The check from Gavin, the building being sold, being able to make a deal even though I had no assets and no prospects of getting any? Even the fact that I landed in *this* neighborhood, chose it because . . . because I felt at home here. Cal, that's not luck. It's fate, something that has a design, a kind of logic. And the design has to be made. The religion helped me do that, Cal. I did the *aceite intranquilo* and it was heard by Ayé-Shalunga, the god of fortune. After that, everything came my way."

The tremor of conviction in her voice was unmistakable. Yet he still couldn't quite absorb the fact finally and completely. Torey was a believer. A woman he had thought he knew as normal and level-headed. A woman he had fallen in love with because he had risked breaking out of his loneliness and guilt.

But she believed that his feelings, their whole relationship, had been arranged on demand by a cosmic dating service.

Cal realized that she had presented him with a stark choice. Stay and accept a woman who believed in Voodoo. Or leave, and walk out on love.

He turned toward the door. "I have to go," he said. "I have to walk around and . . . and clear my head."

She leapt from the stool and grabbed him. "Cal, don't," she cried. "Stay."

He took a step away from her, but she held on. "Cal, I love you. If you have the same feeling for me, don't throw it away. Is it so hard to accept that we were meant to be together? Meant by a force outside ourselves? Don't lovers of all kinds believe that sometimes? You don't have to believe that the gods planned for us to meet. But don't reject me because I do."

Planned by the gods.

All at once the phrase reverberated with the memory of Oscar, saying the same thing. Oscar—the picture on his wall, cutting sugar cane. Could Oscar have been in Cuba? Torey had been there too!

He turned back slowly to her, the realization sinking in. He was being entrapped by them, encircled. Meeting all these believers couldn't be mere coincidence.

"What's it all about?" he demanded. "What do you people want from me?"

Torey's face showed total incomprehension. She retreated a step. "I want your love, Cal, that's all, that's—"

"No. It has to be something else. You and Oscar, you've teamed up somehow—"

Torey shook her head in confusion. "Cal, what are you talking about?"

"The gods plan everything. The gods brought us together. You people sure do have your lines down pretty good. How does it happen that I decide to study Voodoo, and just at the same time, conveniently, the woman I . . . that you turn out to be a believer, someone who can work on me from the inside."

"Work on you?"

"It's a conspiracy, isn't it?" he shouted, pointing an accusing finger at her.

"Oh, Cal, you can't—" She shook her head more strenuously. "Don't you see a logical connection? You came to live down here because I've done business with the university housing office. Once you were in the neighborhood you got interested in Santeria. And I'd chosen to live here long ago, partly because I—"

"But you're the one who doesn't believe in coincidence. You're the one who believes it's all planned." He stepped to her and seized her by the arms. "So what's the plan? Tell me!"

She winced from the pain of his grip, and tears sprang to her eyes, but she didn't complain. "I don't know, my darling, I swear I don't. Maybe . . . maybe the gods wanted us to meet so . . . so I could help you with the work, help you understand . . ."

Cal held on another moment, his grip tightening cruelly. Anger and disbelief and disillusionment and hate flooded through him in a ravaging tide. In their wake he felt totally desolate. He thrust Torey away from him and stalked out of the room, out into the night.

⊃ • ⊆

At the corner of Ninth Avenue he stopped outside an all-night coffee shop. Bag ladies, drifters, winos, prostitutes—lost souls— all lingered hazily at the counter over dreams and coffee cups, lonely drooping figures in harsh fluorescence. Cal could not, try as he might, remember the two blocks he had walked in the previous five minutes. Everything had been blotted out by a single question. Who was Torey Halowell? The lover and friend he had thought of *marrying*, making a mother to his son? Or a spell-caster, a religious nut?

Or was she, more threateningly, the participant in a plot, some invisible scheme to use him?

It was like waking up one morning to discover the cops hauling your father away as a Russian spy, or being told your best friend dealt secretly in stolen guns. People were supposed to stay in their assigned places. They were supposed to be what they seemed.

People were never what they seemed.

He continued aimlessly past the coffee shop window up Ninth Avenue, no goal in mind, no desire to be anywhere. What had at first seemed a joke, then a betrayal, then a nightmare, now un-folded into a quilt of contradictions. The world had rotated on its axis, taking him with it. He doubted whether he could see anything clearly now.

I did a spell on you.

He kept walking. He passed a Mobil station and stared up at the illuminated sign of Pegasus, the winged horse in Greek legend whose hoof unleashed the Hippocene fountains from Mount Hel-licon. Did a horse unleash fountains? If you believed. And if horses kicked mountains, and Muslims bowed to Mecca, and Catholics swallowed the wine and wafer, then Torey Halowell could put his name on a slip of paper in a honey-filled apple and conceive love.

The rituals are absolute, Oscar Sezine had said, *dictated by the gods.*

At Twenty-third Street he turned east. As he stepped off the curb, he noticed a young Puerto Rican couple leaning against a subway entrance, necking.

"Hey, you, move!" a truck driver shouted, and Cal jumped back as the chassis brushed past. He thought again of his first night with Torey. Even then the sexual passion had seemed not quite real. Even then he had felt himself impelled by an overpowering lust he had never before known. A spell? Could magic have been at work?

Nonsense.

But the image of an apple ballooned in his mind, and he could smell the pungent-sweet odor of honey.

He walked for hours, up to Columbus Circle and down Seventh

Avenue, past the all-night grocery stores and the hard-core porn houses of the never-sleeping city. In a Burger King on Broadway he ate a hamburger and drank burnt coffee and agreed with the janitor that prices were too high. He watched pinballs clatter and ping in a penny arcade at Times Square, and of course the pinballs were like life, all chance, all random. But there was Mrs. Ruiz and her poison ivy, the ranting woman with her stinking houseful of animals, Oscar Sezine, dead children—how did they connect? A pattern, and Torey was part of it. A plan to manipulate him. But why, for what reason?

Be rational, he challenged himself. Give Torey the benefit of the doubt.

Yes, the housing office had found the apartment, and his landlord happened to be an appealingly beautiful woman, and she lived there because she was sympathetic to Hispanic culture, and living in Chelsea he could hardly miss the *botánica*, and by the sheerest coincidence make the connection to MacTaggart, who led him to Oscar Sezine.

All so logical. And somehow he had transformed these events into a sinister pattern.

But no pattern existed.

And he still loved her.

∋ ● ∈

"You look dreadful," she said, letting him in and tying the belt of her robe.

It was just past five o'clock in the morning.

"I walked all night," he said.

They stood in the doorway uncomfortably.

"I wasn't sure you'd ever come back."

"Neither was I."

She guided him into the living room.

"Torey, I love you," he began, "that's the most important thing I have to say. I love you, and I want to be with you. But it's . . . Christ, it's so hard to accept this stuff. I don't. I can't. So if you want me, if you love me, tell me you'll give it up."

She studied him curiously a moment, then turned and walked across the room to a window. For a long time she stood and watched the sun creeping up over the city's jagged crust. Then she looked back to him.

"I'll prove it," she said. "I'll prove that it works. Just tell me what you want."

"I've told you. I want you to give—"

"No, I can't give it up," she flared. "But I can prove that you're wrong to expect that from me. Tell me: what do you want from the gods!"

He said nothing. He wouldn't encourage her by becoming a partner in her make-believe.

"Tell me, Cal," she repeated. "Whatever it is I'll do a spell and get it for you."

"Why don't you just give me a lamp to rub. Bring on the genie and flying carpet and—"

She rushed forward to him. "Cal, please. Just give me a chance."

All right, he thought. Do it her way. Might be the best way to get it out of her system. "Okay," he said. "I want fame and wealth and someday maybe a Nobel Prize and—"

"Don't be flippant, Cal. I'm trying to resolve this."

A serious wish. He thought a moment. What would he ask if the genie were here? Only one thing, really. "What I want," he said slowly, "is for everyone who had anything to do with . . . with making that toaster—the thing that killed Laurie—to get sick, to suffer and die."

"It doesn't work quite that way," she said. "The gods won't grant malevolent wishes. In the religion, if you work a spell for evil purposes, then the evil gets turned back against you. Anyone who asks the gods to do evil becomes the victim of evil. You've already seen that."

"Where?"

"I think that's what must've happened to Carmen Ruiz."

"What? How do you know?"

"Because she told you," Torey said. "Those last words you told me about. *Engañador . . . bromista.* That was her confession."

Cal shook his head, not comprehending.

Torey explained. "When someone makes a malicious request of the gods and it comes back against them, in the religion we say 'the trick was turned.' One of the gods, named Legba, is responsible for punishing anyone who tries to use a spell for evil purposes. Legba is also called the Divine Trickster." Torey shrugged slightly. "I'm guessing, of course, but Mrs. Ruiz probably tried to work a spell against you because she was angry at being fired. The gods felt that whatever she wanted was wrong. So they punished her for it."

Or, thought Cal, Carmen Ruiz had merely believed she had to be punished for it. And the end was the same.

The sun had risen completely and the room was awash with

golden light. The Greeks had believed a new day arrived when Apollo pulled the sun up into the sky behind his chariot. Cal glanced around the living room. An ordinary room. He thought of the bedroom upstairs, the evidence he'd seen there of Torey's bizarre devotions—the Chinese cabinet, the scooped-out apple. The confusion had drained him, left him totally exhausted, without any will to resist the illogical.

What wish could he ask for to satisfy the demands of her gods? He still wanted Laurie's death avenged.

Perhaps if he asked not for vengeance but for *justice* . . .

He told Torey then about his lawsuit against the toaster company. Wasn't the company responsible for Laurie's death by selling a defective product? Didn't they deserve to be punished—to lose the suit?

Torey thought for a moment. "I think the gods would grant that," she said, "although it may take a few days."

Cal stifled a tired laugh. "Days? Torey, that lawsuit isn't scheduled to be heard until next *year*. And maybe not even then if they keep stalling it."

"The gods have their own schedule," she said. "You'll see."

He hesitated a moment, then went to her and put his hands on her shoulders.

"Okay, I'll give you the chance," he said. "But I want you to promise me something in return."

"What?" ·

"That when . . . if your magic doesn't work, you'll give it up, give up this religion. Now. And forever."

She hesitated only the barest fraction of an instant. "I promise," she said.

She didn't seem the least bit worried.

Chapter 27

THE HARDWARE STORE was on upper Columbus Avenue. It was newly remodeled and crammed with Saturday morning shoppers, all burdened with cans of paint, plastic dropcloths, and assorted packages of steel wool, razor blades, and scrapers. Behind the counter stood a chubby, squat coffee-colored man in a blue smock with a Sherwin-Williams "We Cover The World" patch over the breast pocket.

"His name is Voto," Torey said as she entered the store with Cal.

"What kind of name is that?" he asked.

"It means 'the voice,' " she said. "That's what we call him in the family. His real name is Ramon Suares, and he owns this place."

The man behind the counter called to a stock boy on a ladder. "A gallon of fifty-six-twenty latex, and four Peterson sevens." He ran one hand through his tight curly black hair while adding figures with the other.

Cal stared at Suares.

Him? The idea that this supplier of paint brushes and screwdrivers to young Upper West Side lawyers redoing their apartments, the idea that this baby-faced, upwardly mobile storekeeper could be a sorcerer—well, it was laughable.

No, it wasn't. It wasn't laughable at all. Not after Carmen Ruiz and Quentin Kimball. Not after last night. Nothing about it was laughable.

As they approached the counter, Suares looked up from the

order of paint he was readying for a customer. "Victoria, it's so good to see you," he said. "I'll be with you in a moment."

Torey stood by reverently while Suares finished the sale— "You'll be very happy the way this covers, one coat'll do it; you come back and tell me if it doesn't."

Suares called to the stockboy to take the register, and Cal and Torey followed him through a swinging door to a rear room where brooms and plungers dangled from wire bins. They went up a flight of stairs lit by a single bare bulb.

Suares's apartment was furnished comfortably with an over-stuffed couch, three chintz-upholstered wing chairs, two pole lamps with new white shades, and a coffee table covered with tattered copies of *Newsweek* that might have spent a few years in a dentist's waiting room. At each of the room's four corners was a door, and an old-fashioned tiled fireplace dominated one wall; on the mantel sat a two-doored lime-green cabinet the size of a hefty suitcase. Cal couldn't resist thinking that for a man with a direct line to the gods, Voto lived in a remarkably plain apartment.

On entering, Voto went directly through one of the four doors, which led down a hallway.

"He's going to wash his hands," Torey said. "We do the same."

Clean house is clean soul. He thought of Carmen Ruiz again.

Torey led him into a bathroom and when they returned Voto was waiting. His blue smock had given way to a white gold-hemmed robe; a jewel-encrusted cross hung around his neck, shimmering red rubies and fiery emeralds and topaz set in silver. To Cal the jewels looked too good to be fakes.

They sat in the three chairs around the fireplace.

"How can I help you?" Voto asked sincerely.

Torey replied, "My friend is having some trouble with a lawsuit. He'd like you to ask Ochosi for help in getting a settlement."

Voto looked from Cal to Torey and back again. "Are you a believer?" he asked Cal.

Cal hesitated. He didn't want to start by insulting the man. "I have respect for your beliefs," he said.

Voto nodded pensively. Then he rose and opened the cabinet on the mantel. A light came on inside. In the middle stood a saint statue, a man in a pink cassock clutching flowers with both hands, his eyes black and harsh and staring. Lit from behind, the figure seemed to float in space.

Torey leaned over to Cal. "That's Ochosi, his patron," she whispered.

On either side of the syncretized god there were compartments broken into shelves. Voto pulled a cigar from the middle shelf on the left, lit it and puffed, then set it down in an onyx ashtray. Without a word he disappeared into another room—the kitchen, Cal could see through the open door. Cal heard a refrigerator open and close, and then Voto returned carrying a pear and two carrots and a handful of straw. The straw he placed in a bowl next to the ashtray, and the pear and carrots on a spiked tray in front of the statue. From a shelf on the right he took a red-bound book and consulted it.

"His *libreta*," Torey murmured to Cal. "A book of spells given to him by his own priest."

"By a *babalao*, you mean?"

She stared at him, surprised by his knowledge.

The *santero* closed the *libreta* and put it down. He bowed three times to the statue. Then he took a bite of the pear, chewed it thoroughly, took the masticated pulp from his mouth, and placed it at the foot of the saint figure.

Cal watched each maneuver, his reactions wavering between pity and awe. It occurred to him that a visitor from another planet would find this no more peculiar than the Catholic Mass.

The room was clouded with smoke from the burning cigar. Odd that it hadn't gone out, Cal thought.

Voto was standing with his eyes closed as though in meditation. He stayed this way for a minute. Two. Three.

At last he opened his eyes and turned from the saint.

"Ochosi approves," he said, and hooked a finger in Torey's direction. "Come with me, Victoria."

They went into another room. Through the open door Cal could see Voto's office. On an open roll-top desk, sheaves of paper jutted from cubbyholes; hardware and paint catalogues jostled for space. Above the desk was a luridly painted Crucifixion, the figure of Christ aglow in a tangerine sky. On the opposite wall was a painting of a dark man surrounded by slaves in loincloths kneeling at an altar with a bloody goat strapped to the top. "Luis d'Andrea 1611," said the inscription on a brass plate, *"Adoración del Cabro."* Adoration of the Goat.

Voto scribbled on a small notepad, tore off a sheet, and handed it to Torey. She laid a twenty-dollar bill on the desk, and as she rose, kissed the hand that Voto held out to her. She came out, closing the door behind her, the piece of paper in her hand.

"What is that?" Cal asked.

212

"A prescription."

"And only twenty bucks," Cal said. "Not a bad price for the show."

She ignored the remark and walked to the stairs.

"What now?" he said.

"We get it filled," she replied.

⊃ • ⊂

They rode a cab uptown to the Botanica Siete Potencias on 117th Street and Lexington. Cal recognized the name—the Seven African Powers.

The store was a regular supermarket compared to Del Arco Iris, with six aisles of shelves, a platoon of clerks, and enough bottled potions to put spells on half of Manhattan. Very nice, Cal thought, surveying the operation: the witch doctors' A & P. Shrunken heads in aisle four, goat's heart in the meat department.

His desperate humor failed him. It was sad, not funny. Saddest because she was so convinced of its truth.

Torey snatched packets from several shelves and went to the front counter for the last two items, a candle and a small statue. Waiting with her while the clerk tied all the purchases into a bundle, Cal scanned the array of bottled herbs on a shelf. Cherry root, bilda, xanthan, guao, guanine—

Guao?

"*Guao* is good," Carmen had screamed at him.

Cal strained to see into the stopper bottle. It was filled with a fine greenish powder.

"Torey, what's *guao?*"

She picked up her bundle. "Powdered poison ivy," she said.

"What's it used for?"

"*Guao* is one of the strongest elements used in spells. I've never cast one that calls for it, but I do know it's used only in the most extreme situations."

"What kind of situations?"

"To dispel evil influences."

Cal paused, looking back toward the bottle. "Carmen was growing it in the garden," he said. "She used it on Chris."

Torey stared at him, perplexed. "My God," she gasped. "Why on earth—"

"I don't know. But didn't you say she died because the trick was turned against her?"

"That's what *she* seemed to be saying when she died . . ."

213

"But that god—the Divine Trickster, what's he called?"

"Legba."

"You said Legba only hurt people who tried to do *evil*. How does that fit in with using *guao?* I mean, why would Carmen die, why would the gods kill her, if she was working a spell that was meant to *ward off* evil?"

Torey stared down at the floor, thinking deeply. "I can't imagine why," she said at last. "It makes no sense at all."

The question replayed in Cal's mind. Then suddenly he caught himself: he was arguing with the logic of the religion, as though he had accepted it, as though he believed that Carmen was the victim of some divine vengeance.

Carmen had died of shock. Because she believed too much. Frightened herself to death.

The doctor said.

But there on the shelf was the *guao*, the same substance Carmen had grown in the garden, and used on Chris. Before she died.

From what evil, Cal wondered, could the woman have wanted to protect Chris?

He stood until Torey put her arm around him, steering him gently toward the door.

"Not everything the gods do can be explained," she said quietly as they left the Botanica of the Seven Powers.

⊃ ● ⊂

Cal stood over the tub in her cool bathroom and watched while she mixed some of the herbs they had bought at the *botánica* into the running water. Red powder and yellow flower buds and a green colored oil from a small vial. A sickly sweet smell rose into the air.

"This is a *despojo*," she said, "a ritual bath. Get in now."

Cal slipped off his shoes and socks and leaned on the sink in a strained counterfeit gesture of total calm.

"Would you please tell me why I'm doing this?" he said.

"The herbs and flowers in this spell are sacred to Eleggua, the god who opens and closes the door of opportunity. By getting in the water, you consecrate yourself to him in gratitude for opening the door."

"Then in Voodoo terms," Cal said, "it's a kind of baptism?"

"That's right."

Cal shucked his clothes and hung them on the towel bar. He looked into the water. Bits of green foamed on the surface. He didn't want to get in—to be baptized. Then he saw Torey gazing at him patiently, and he remembered their bargain.

I'm not getting in.

He got in.

The water clung to him like mineral oil, coating his skin.

"Put your head under for a second," she said, holding Voto's prescription slip in her hand. "Your whole body has to be immersed."

He slid down and dunked his head. When he came up she was unscrewing the cap from a small bottle. She poured the contents, an amber oil, slowly over his head.

"To the god Eleggua," she intoned softly, "guardian of the great doors, we consecrate ourselves and ask for help in opening the way to a fair judgment."

He looked at the empty bottle when she put it down on the edge of the sink and read the label, a single word: "Kyphi."

Nonsense.

But then the lines ran through his memory: ". . . thou anointest my head with oil, my cup runneth over . . ." The Twenty-third Psalm.

Reaching into her bag of supplies, Torey retrieved a bar of magenta soap. "What's the name of the toaster company?" she asked.

"United Appliance," Cal muttered.

With the tip of a tweezer, Torey carved the name on one side of the soap. "And what court is the suit in?" she said, turning the bar over.

"You're going to write it all on there?"

She sighed and repeated the question.

"Federal District Court in Santa Fe," Cal answered with a sigh. "Southern Division."

She diligently etched the letters into the soap, turning the cake on its side to squeeze them all on. When she finished she slipped the soap into the water, where in a matter of moments it began to dissolve. The water turned a wine color.

Now, in a corner behind the bathroom door, Torey positioned a figurine with a gold-leaf halo, blue robes, and what looked like a trumpet in its hands.

"Who's that?" Cal said.

"The Archangel Gabriel."

"How does he come into this?"

"He's also Eleggua," she said. "He'll stay by the door until your prayer is answered. Now," she added, "spit into the water."

His mouth was dry and he had to work to get up the saliva.

"What now?"

Torey pulled a velour towel off a rack and held it up. "You get out."

"That's it?"

"Not quite."

For a moment they regarded each other without moving. The faucet dripped noisily. A bath in greasy water, Cal thought, oil in his hair, and a disappearing bar of soap. The United Appliance Company was unlikely to respond.

He fished for the drain plug, then reached to pull the shower curtain around the tub and turn on the spray.

"No," Torey said, "you can't take a shower for twenty-four hours."

"Oh, for Chrissakes," Cal hissed, grabbing the towel and rubbing it hard over his oily hair. "I don't know why I ever—"

"But you did," she said quietly. "You agreed to try it. Dry yourself off and get dressed."

She went into the bedroom. Cal put on his clothes and glanced at his watch. It was just past two, and Ricki was expecting him to pick up Chris no later than three. She had reminded Cal a hundred times not to keep her waiting; the wedding was next weekend, and she and Wayne had a rehearsal with the rabbi today at three-thirty.

"I have to go," he called to her as he put on his shoes.

"Only a few more minutes," her voice came back.

When he came out she was sitting in front of her cabinet with a round gray stone in her hand.

She held it out to him. "This is my *otane*," she said. "Everyone in the religion has one. I found mine when I was fourteen—in a tar pit near Havana."

"What's so special about it?" He took the stone and examined it.

"Only the fact that I found it," she said, "that I felt impelled to pick it up. In the religion, we believe that the gods put an *otane* on the earth for each and every person. If they find this sacred stone, recognize its special attraction, and keep it, then they have a powerful amulet to help them with their spells. When I call on Eleggua, he invests the stone with the spirit of my enemy—or whoever will be punished with the spell, in this case the appliance company." She pointed to a spot on the floor near his feet. "Put it down."

He hesitated then set it down.

"Now kick it," she said. "Kick the *otane* around the room."

He hesitated.

216

"Go ahead," she insisted. "Kick it hard."

Cal stared down at the stone. His heart fluttered. He nudged it tentatively with his toe at first, sort of rolling it.

"Hard, Cal," Torey urged. "As hard as you can."

He let loose. The stone skittered across the floor, caromed off the baseboards, battered against every surface. He chased its path, kicking it again and again.

There was, oddly, a wonderful sensation of release; his fury at the corporate carelessness that had murdered Laurie was strangely alleviated. He thought of therapy for schizophrenics where they were put in padded rooms, given a baseball bat, and allowed to pummel the walls. And hadn't he read somewhere about executives in Japan using the technique to purge the high-pressure frustration of their jobs? Kicking a stone made as much sense—as therapy.

"That's enough," Torey said, and picked up the stone from where it had come to rest. She put it away in the cabinet and from the bag of *botánica* supplies took out a black and red candle in a tall glass column.

"When the candle burns down, Eleggua will answer your prayer." She put the candle next to the cabinet and lit the wick.

"It's done," she said wearily, and kept gazing at the flame.

What should he say now? Cal thought. Thank you?

"Well, I . . . ." Where were the words?

"Go," she said. "I think it's best if you go now."

He paused another moment, then turned and left the bedroom.

At the bottom of the steps, he halted and glanced back up toward the door. The flickering light from the candle played on the jamb.

It was so unfair! The only woman he'd been able to love after losing Laurie . . . and she had to be involved with this.

I love you.

He wanted to say the words aloud, shout to her.

But he couldn't. Not now.

Not until she was ready to keep her promise.

∋ ● ∈

Cal showered on Monday afternoon, two hours before the deadline. His scalp had begun itching furiously, and what difference did it make anyhow?

He stood motionless under the spraying nozzle and scrubbed his arms and legs, shampooed twice, and scraped some pink residue from under his fingernails. Even after rubbing the flesh on his knees and elbows red-raw, he still didn't feel clean.

He couldn't stop thinking of Torey. At what point could he call her? How long before she would accept that her gods had ignored her plea—that there were no gods?

Tuesday and Wednesday passed, and Thursday. The Dalton School called to remind him that Chris was due for orientation next week, and would he make sure the boy brought tennis shoes? Kate called to ask how Chris was feeling. "No more poison ivy?" she wanted to be assured. Ricki stopped by to pick up the wedding dress Laurie had been married in, the same one their mother had worn, and that she would use on Saturday.

On Friday morning the refrigerator conked out, which normally Cal could have called Torey to repair. He checked the fuse box, saw the fuses were okay, and twisted the temperature knob back and forth several times. In the end, he found "Refrigerator—Dlrs. & Svc." in the Yellow Pages; AAA Refrigerator Repair appeared in an hour, replaced a part in the condenser, and charged him sixty-two dollars.

He never called Torey.

And she never called him.

∋ ● ∈

That afternoon he was in his office at Columbia putting his fall lecture notes in order. His old notes had gotten scrambled during shipment from Albuquerque and the task of sorting them out was tedious and irritating. He was in a foul mood when the phone rang.

It was Oscar Sezine.

They exchanged small talk about the weather, the effect of the latest round of federal cuts on poverty programs, and the University's new building program on the edge of Harlem. Cal thanked Oscar for his tour of the Aché.

Then Oscar said, "I'm calling to invite you to a party, a fund-raiser we're having. One of my patrons is Victor Greenleaf, the labor lawyer. He's been very supportive of our work, and he has an interesting group of friends. Meeting them, I think, would do a lot to advance your understanding of the religion."

"Thanks for thinking of me, Oscar," Cal said. "But I'm not studying that anymore."

Until the words emerged, Cal had not known the decision was made. But somewhere in his mind during the past week the necessary course had crystallized: he could not continue.

"Well, I'm sorry to hear that, Cal," Oscar said. "I enjoyed meeting you. And I feel you could have done some good work . . ."

For someone who had told him previously that his involvement with Voodoo was predestined, Cal thought, Oscar was taking the news with remarkable equanimity.

"But look," Oscar went on, "why don't you take down the address, just in case you—"

"It's not necessary, Oscar. I'm sure I won't be coming."

"Yes, yes. But it can't hurt to know where it is—on the off chance you change your mind."

Cal accommodated Oscar by listening to the address and jotting it down in his calendar.

Then an afterthought struck him. "Oh, Oscar, before you hang up—I meant to ask you, don't we have a friend in common?"

"Who would that be, Cal?"

"Her name is Victoria Halowell."

There was a short silence at the other end. "No. I don't believe I know her."

"Weren't you in Cuba?" Cal asked.

"Yes, I spent a couple of months there in the late 'sixties. Why do you ask?"

"I saw that picture in your office."

"Ah, yes. I'd gone down to cut sugar cane, show support for the revolution. You know, it was that period when our generation was disillusioned."

"Well, then," Cal persisted, "you could have met Miss Halowell. She goes by the name of Torey, usually. Her father was at the embassy in Havana."

More silence. "No, I'm certain I've never met her," came Oscar's deep-voiced reply. "But then again, I was first in Cuba in 1968, long after the embassy was closed. If she's a friend of yours, though, by all means bring her to the Greenleafs' party. You'll both be welcome. Don't forget: the evening of the twenty-ninth, starting at eight. Try not to be too late."

It seemed to have escaped Oscar completely, Cal noted, that the invitation had been declined. But he let it pass.

"Thanks again for thinking of me," Cal said. "I hope you raise a lot of money for your work."

He hung up the phone.

Having decided to abandon the research, and not to go to Oscar's party, Cal found himself feeling curiously unsatisfied, and less at ease than he would have hoped.

Chapter 28

THERE WERE FACES in the Excelsior Suite of the St. Regis that Cal hadn't seen since his own wedding nine years ago. The Hanauer clan had turned out in force to see Ricki married to Wayne Millman. When Cal entered with Chris the relatives gathered around, shaking hands and fussing over Chris and gushing with memories of Laurie.

"*Such* a dolling! What a shame to die so young," said Aunt Helen from Cleveland. "Heartbreaking, that's what it is."

Uncle Heschy straightened Chris's tie. "He's got his mother's eyes—those are the Hanauer eyes. Am I right, or am I right?"

It was endless: Uncle Moe from Long Island; the Kosloff twins from Atlanta; and from Los Angeles, cousin Saul Pepper, accompanied by a platinum blond bombshell easily twenty-five years his junior—all pinching Chris on the cheek and talking about how wonderful Laurie had been.

Chris was beginning to look upset. He pulled Cal away and beckoned him to lean down.

"Daddy," he whispered, "where's Torey?"

"She's not coming, Bean."

Chris looked crestfallen. "Why not?"

Cal paused. He thought of how disappointed he had been by Chris's lie about the matches.

"She's sick, Bean," he lied. "She has a bad cold."

There were two rooms in the suite, combined by opening a partition. The Millman side of the suite filled up with Wayne's relatives, sedate older women with blue-rinsed hair and paunchy dignified men who talked quietly among themselves. At the far end was an altar with a lushly flowered *chupa*, the traditional canopy under which the couple would recite their vows. There were a hundred or so folding chairs spread wall-to-wall with an aisle down the middle. A sixtyish woman in a dark dress and white pearls, hired for the occasion, attended the door passing out prayer booklets and paper *yarmulkes* and collecting the gifts.

It showed the power of religion, Cal reflected, that in the rooms of a Fifth Avenue hotel—not even remotely a house of God—the traditional skull caps were still used, even if only made of paper.

The ceremony was brief but touching. When Ricki came down the aisle in the same creamy white gown and veil Laurie had worn, Cal squeezed Chris's hand, and had to brush away a tear that escaped from the corner of one eye. Ricki winked at him as she passed, and shot him a questioning look: *So where's your girl?* The rabbi, a cousin from Connecticut, led Wayne and Ricki in a responsive reading of their vows under the flowered canopy, and then Ricki walked seven times around Wayne—a symbolic residue of the ancient tradition that a couple should be separated for seven days before they wed. It was called the *Sheva Berochot*, Laurie had once told Cal at a friend's wedding, the Seven Blessings.

The rabbi held out a cup at arm's length. *"Yayin miseomaoch levov enosh,"* he chanted. "Wine gladdens the hearts of men." He made a blessing over the wine, and handed Wayne the cup. Wayne sipped, Ricki sipped, and they recited their vows to honor, cherish, and obey.

At the end, the rabbi placed a small bundle wrapped in a white linen napkin on the floor. Wayne raised his right foot and stomped down hard on the bundle. There was the tinkly sound of glass shattering. Tradition called for a fine crystal goblet to be broken, Cal knew (though he had seen one of the hotel employees wrapping a light bulb in the napkin for today's ceremony). Breaking the glass had symbolized, in medieval times, a warding off of evil spirits; then, later, the breaking of the hymen; and always a reminder to the faithful of the destruction of the First Temple in A.D. 76.

The bride and groom kissed. "Ooohs" and "Ahhhs" rose in hushed tones from the crowd. Cal, too, was moved—but not only because it reminded him of Laurie. It was the idea of an ancient tradition still observed. The Jewish rituals could seem strange—the flowered canopy, the paper hats, the breaking glass—but then weren't all rituals strange, particularly when they weren't your own?

What right did he have to ask Torey to give up her beliefs? All over the world, in mosques and cathedrals and synagogues and pagodas and shrines and grass huts—and in no edifice, but simply under the stars—people were worshipping different gods. Even in this hotel room Ricki and Wayne were asking to be blessed by theirs.

Would crushing a napkin-covered glass underfoot guarantee happiness any more than burning a candle before a plaster saint?

Would marching seven circles under a trellis assuage the God of Israel any more than taking a bath in herbs would win favors from the Seven African Powers?

Which homage did the gods prefer? Which symbol was their favorite choice?

Or were there any gods up there to choose?

∋ ● ∈

The champagne flowed.

A crew of hotel workers had folded up the altar, pushed the chairs back against the walls, and brought in long cloth-covered tables for the food. There were platters of filet mignon and smoked fish and steaming chicken, tables laden with chopped liver and creamed herring and bowls of fruit. The two families mingled, Wayne's brother—the best man—made a toast, and Wayne and Ricki danced a solo fox-trot to "Just the Way You Are."

Chris, dazzled by the splendor, sampled all the food, had two swallows of champagne, and danced cutely with Aunt Estelle, Heschy's wife, and Cousin Saul's blonde bombshell.

Cal had no appetite, and didn't dance.

"So how do you like your first big catered affair?" he asked when he found Chris resting on the sidelines.

"It's neat," Chris said. "But Mom thinks yours was much more fun. She says outdoor weddings are better, and it was nicer to be married under that apple tree than in a place like this."

Cal took a deep breath. "Bean. You know I don't want to hear you pretending anymore that—"

"But Daddy, it's true. Mommy says—"

"Okay, Bean," he said firmly. "Enough."

When would it stop? The relatives' talk about Laurie had obviously stirred up the boy's memories of his mother; you had to expect that, it was inevitable.

Chris gave Cal a grumpy look, then jumped up from his chair and went to the food table. Cal didn't go after him.

At eight o'clock there was a fanfare from the band, and then the clarinettist played a winding Middle Eastern riff. Soon a huge circle had formed, aunts and uncles and cousins and the blue-rinse women and all the children, dancing a vigorous *hora*—one leg behind the other, one leg over and *kick*—which went on for fifteen minutes, until Ricki and Wayne separated themselves from the merriment and the band changed to a slow rendition of "The Way We Were."

Cal poured himself another glass of champagne and sat it out.

Then he saw Chris in the center of the dance floor swaying around by himself, dancing a sort of fox-trot, arms embracing an imaginary partner.

"Isn't he adorable?" one of the aunts called to Cal from a nearby table—Leah or Ida, he wasn't sure which.

"A beautiful boy," said another.

Cal nodded and laughed, and then noticed that Chris was carrying on an animated conversation with his invisible companion. Yes, it looked adorable. But then Chris halted in mid-step, raised himself on tiptoes and kissed the air. And went on dancing.

Cal knew who Chris was dancing with. He went out onto the floor.

"Bean, who're you talking to?"

"Mommy."

"Bean, I told you I didn't want to hear—"

"But Daddy, she *is* here. She told me you can't see, but—"

"Come over here." Cal took Chris's arm to lead him off the floor.

Chris resisted, looking upward at a point in space as though appealing for assistance from the "ghost." "Show him," Chris said to the air. "Show him you're *real*."

"Damn it, Bean, not one more word!"

"But you gotta hear this, Daddy. She says—"

Cal couldn't control himself any longer. His grip tightened on Chris's arm, and he yanked at him roughly, pulling him off his feet and starting to drag him toward the sidelines. "Goddammit, Christopher, I've put up with this long enough. You're going to stop this shit right now, do you hear? Stop it once and for—"

Cal broke off, suddenly aware that people on all sides were staring, clearing a space on the floor around him. The band had picked up the tempo, was playing very loud. Aunt Helen stood with a hand clapped over her mouth.

Cal retreated from the floor, Chris in tow. Passing Ricki, he apologized, then marched Chris to a chair in the corner.

"Now you listen to me, young man," he said quietly. "This has got to end."

Chris began to cry. "But she is . . ." he sobbed.

Cal was burnt out. He sat down next to Chris and put his arm around him.

Chris went on crying softly for a minute. Cal hugged him and patted him, feeling like a complete heel.

Then between sobs, Chris said, "Please don't be mad, Daddy. Please don't . . . but Mommy wants me to tell you something."

Hopeless. "What, Bean?"

"She says congratulations. Congratulations for winning."

"Winning?" Cal asked. "For winning what?"

Chris wiped his eyes and shrugged. "For winning," he replied. "That's all she said. Congratulations for winning."

∋ ● ∈

They had to put him into a cab. He had never been this drunk in his life, not even in college. For the rest of the wedding he had done nothing but guzzle champagne, the only way he could think to get through the evening.

At his front door he fumbled over the lock. His key wouldn't go in. A knot tightened in his head, a mind-bendingly painful headache.

Chris put his hand on Cal's. "Let me help you, Daddy."

Cal reeled into the apartment and headed at once for the bathroom. Chris saw where he was going and ran ahead to open the door for him.

Cal threw cold water on his face and rubbed his eyes. "I'm sorry, Bean," he said through his fingers. "I didn't mean to yell at you tonight."

Bells went off in his head.

"It's the telephone, Daddy," Chris said. "Should I get it?"

He was suddenly ashamed of being so helpless before his son. "No, Bean, that's okay. I can do it." He staggered from the bathroom, bumped into a wall, and more or less ricocheted into the kitchen. He grabbed up the phone.

"Yeah?"

"Cal, is that you?"

"Who's 'iss?" he mumbled.

"Cal, it's Bill Markey."

He braced his hand against the wall and the room turned around him. In his boozy fog it took a moment for the name and the voice to register.

Markey. Lawyer. Albuquerque.

"Hey, Cal. You there?"

"Mmm. Hi, Bill."

"Cal, are you all right?"

"Sure, fine."

"Cal, I've been trying to get you all day. You won."

"Won?" Cal repeated. It meant nothing.

"Cal, did I wake you? You sound—"

"No. Jus' came back from . . . from . . ." Where had he come back from? "Too much to drink."

"Cal, listen to me: you won the case."

"What case?" he asked foolishly.

And then it hit. "But I can't. I mean . . . it hasn't even . . . the trial . . ."

"Look, why don't I call you in the morning and go over the details?"

"No," he snapped, abruptly focusing. "I want to hear now. Please, Bill. Go on."

"Well, okay, if you think you can grasp it. The Supreme Court just denied *certiorari* in a case very similar to yours. The circuit panel's decision was upheld. That sets the precedent for all these cases, and United wants to settle. They've made us an offer, and I think we should accept it."

"What kind . . . of offer?"

"A cash offer, Cal. Two hundred and fifty thousand."

For winning.

Congratulations.

Chris had moved into the doorway of the kitchen. He was nodding and smiling sweetly.

"Hello, Cal? Are you there?"

"Right here, Bill."

"It's a clear victory, and I don't think you'll do better with any jury. I didn't even think we'd get this far. I might be able to get United to pick up your legal bills, too. Can I go ahead and negotiate with them?"

She says congratulations.

"Whatever you say, Bill," Cal murmured.

"I'll talk to you in a couple of days. Now go get some sleep."

"Thanks, Bill."

"Goodnight, Cal. And, oh"—Cal heard the lawyer add just before hanging up—"congratulations!"

Chapter 29

ALL DAY SUNDAY he thought about calling Torey. But to call her would mean crossing the line into believing.

He didn't want to believe.

On Monday morning he went to his office and procrastinated, conferring with the department secretary, welcoming back other professors, hearing tales of their summer expeditions.

The precedent-setting case was of course a stunning coincidence, begun years before Laurie's death. That was how the law worked, after all. Disputes wended their way through the courts interminably, with motions and countermotions, appeals and more appeals. It took years. So why had the other side been defeated *now?*

Because of the gods.

Because of a pink bath and their name being written on a bar of dissolving soap.

You keep thinking like this, Cal said to himself, and you'll wind up on a sabbatical in a padded cell.

He *refused* to believe.

⊒ ● ⊑

If it had not been for Danny White, Cal might have found it impossible to call Torey.

Danny and Cal had been classmates at Columbia, and over the years they had stayed in touch with letters and phone calls and occasional visits. Back then, Danny had been a shy six-foot-four Kentucky farmboy, with a goofy smile and ugly black-framed glasses and a portable telescope. Now he was one of the world's foremost astronomers, and a candidate for the Nobel Prize for discovering a new galaxy three billion light-years from earth.

The afternoon after Markey's call about the lawsuit, Danny paid Cal a visit in his office at Columbia—Danny was in New York on his way from his base at Stanford to a Senate hearing in Washington. He was still the same shambling giant—cowboy boots, ugly glasses, goofy smile—but now it had become a purposeful "dumb hick" act, Danny's technique for not letting his extraordinary intelligence separate him from the rest of the world.

Cal was glad to see him, and over drinks at the West End Bar, only a few blocks from the campus, they talked about their work. Cal debated with himself how much he should share with Danny. He thought he had put the Voodoo project behind him. But Danny sensed his agitation, and when pressed Cal told him about the little threads of circumstance that had led him to study Santeria, and the possibility of contemporary human sacrifice. He admitted that Torey's love spell and the resolution of the lawsuit had made him begin to doubt his own sanity.

"Danny, the idea that fate can be made or unmade from one day to the next—and if we ask, in just the right way, that we could even get it made to order, well . . . shit, it's really got me kind of confused."

Danny took a meditative swig of his Chivas, dropped a ten-dollar bill on the bar, and rose from his bar stool.

"C'mon, let's go for a ride," he said.

"Where to?"

"To meet God," Danny said.

They took a cab up Broadway to the university observatory, where Danny's renown gained them entrance. The domed main viewing room was unoccupied, and Danny led Cal in. It resembled the inside of a *Star Wars* spaceship. At the center the seventy-two-inch optical reflecting telescope poked up through a slash in the roof, and on either side seven computerized panels controlled its motion. Danny sat Cal in the viewing chair, Cal pressed his eye to the eyepiece, and the central region of the Milky Way shone through, clusters of bright stars and majestic nebula and the Magellanic Clouds searingly bright.

Heaven, Cal thought. You could forget it was there. But if the gods existed, you could see why they chose it as home.

Danny put his hand on Cal's shoulder. "I don't know where that all comes from, Cal," Danny said, his voice echoing in the domed room. "But nobody's gonna tell me it didn't take *some* kind of god to assemble that little lightshow."

Cal stared for one long moment at the visible solar system, then turned to Danny. "If you think a god made that, then what's science?"

"Science," Danny said, "is our way of figuring out how God, or somebody, put together the whole thing—life. You know what old Al Einstein said: God doesn't play dice with the universe." Danny paused. "Do you know how many explosions there are in space every day? Millions. *Billions.* Stars burn up and die all the time. They collide into each other. They fall into black holes. But here we are. We're still here because our planet not only has an atmosphere that supports intelligent life, but also one that burns up all the celestial junk that comes crashing toward us. I think that's got to be more than coincidence. You have to believe it was planned that way."

"Danny, if you believe in God, which god is it?"

"I don't get into that, Callie."

"But could you ever . . . could you conceive of it being African gods?"

Danny shrugged. "Didn't you say this Voodoo thing is the world's oldest religion? Maybe their gods have some kind of priority. You know, I never get into who runs the show—first causes and that kind of thing. But I'll tell you what I do believe in. I subscribe to the Big Bang theory—that's how we respectable physicists explain the birth of the universe. And Cal, if there was a Big Bang, I'll bet my ass on one thing: somebody sure as hell had to light the fuse."

⊐ ● ⊏

When he heard her voice on the phone it was as if no time had passed. He started to apologize, then to recount the events and changes of the past few days, but she cut through it all.

"I just want to see you, Cal. I've missed you so much."

⊐ ● ⊏

He sat in a chair by the fireplace in her living room, and she listened, seated at his feet, holding his hand while he told her about Bill Markey's call and the confusion he had felt afterward.

"Of course it's only an incredible coincidence," he felt compelled to conclude, "the whole thing could fall apart tomorrow."

Even then she didn't lose patience. "It won't," was all she said, and they discussed it no more.

Cal knew how much irrationality he was accepting into his life. But what mattered was that he wanted her, and he couldn't dismiss her because of her beliefs. Danny's visit had forced him to realize that the universe couldn't be totally comprehended in logical terms. Torey was just looking for answers, like everyone else. Her answers had been around for thousands of years, and no one had yet proven them wrong. Because she worshipped in a certain way did not mean she would condone the worst excesses of fanatics who worshipped the same gods, any more than being a Catholic meant you were in favor of bringing back the Inquisition.

So Cal was ready to take her as she was, and give her the benefit of the doubt.

He was not blind to the fact that loving her could mean accepting things into his life that were strange, even a little scary. But even in the best of circumstances being in love—making that unconditional surrender of self to someone else—could require a difficult adjustment, could indeed be terrifying. There was no point in fighting his feelings. He and Torey were meant to be together, and he no longer cared by what gods their love had been planned, or for what reason.

They went upstairs, and she asked him if he'd like to take a bath with her before they made love. She meant a *despojo*, he guessed, and said no. But she took no offense. They undressed each other slowly and tenderly and lay down on the bed, and it was as magical as it had ever been. No other woman, Cal was sure, would ever make him feel as potent and passionate and soaringly unique as she did.

For a long time afterward they lay silently in the dark, holding each other. His mind was filled with things he would have to say before leaving her again tonight.

He didn't know how it could possibly work between them—his rationality constantly being tested by her kind of faith. The only answer he could give himself was that it would work because it had to. How many diversities, and perversities, had been bridged or ignored for the sake of love? Smart people fell in love with dumb people, fat people fell in love with thin people, old people with young, the beautiful with the ugly, black with white, Northerners with Southerners, communists with capitalists, the blind with the deaf; people who spoke different languages fell in love, and so did people who worshipped different gods. There were a million dif-

ferences to divide people, and love could make them all insignificant.

"I don't ever want to lose you," he said finally in the dark.

Her arms tightened around him. "You never have to," she said,
"if you'll just take me as I am."

"Gods 'n' all," he said lightly, and she laughed.

Somehow in that moment the impossible suddenly seemed easy.

⊒ ● ⊑

Now they spent time together every day, mostly in the evenings.
Sometimes they went out, saw a show or a movie, had dinner at a
place in the neighborhood. But often she came over and made
dinner and they spent a family evening at home, playing games
with Chris, then reading, talking, or watching television after he
had gone to sleep.

One evening when he was seated at his desk composing a reference letter for one of his former graduate students, Cal paused to
look across the room at Torey, curled up on the sofa with a book.
At that moment, with the stark clarity that can make the simplest
of truths seem like the most spectacular revelation, he knew that he
was *happy*. For the first time since losing Laurie, he was content,
hopeful, completely glad to be alive. A miracle. He hadn't believed
he could ever be happy again.

"What?" Torey said then.

He wasn't aware of having spoken. "Did I say something?"

She nodded. "Sounded like 'bless you.' "

"It might've been."

"But I didn't sneeze."

He smiled. "You didn't have to."

Chris, too, gave every sign of having found a new stability.
Often at bedtime he made a point of having Torey help him into
his pajamas or read him a story. At lights-out he would always give
her a hug and declare that he loved her. One night after she had
tucked him in, Torey emerged from Chris's bedroom with tears
brimming in her eyes.

"What's wrong?" Cal asked.

"Nothing," she said. "He just . . . he wanted to know . . .
whether I'd mind if he started calling me Mommy."

Touching as it was, Cal was concerned. Just two weeks ago
Chris had been acting out a fantasy that his real mother was still
hovering around him as an audible, visible spirit. Now it seemed
he was ready to forget her. The inconsistency could be a danger

signal. From everything he'd read about the problems that arose between children and potential stepparents, Cal knew that his son's quick embracing of Torey as his mother was not the norm. Might he not turn against her again?

Torey was not insensitive to these concerns. She had told Chris, in fact, that it was important he always remember and honor his real mother; he could call her Mommy as long as both understood it was a kind of honorary promotion. At the same time, she managed to persuade Cal he was worrying needlessly. She was sure Chris's affection for her was real and enduring.

In the face of her confidence, Cal asked jokingly, "Did you do a spell on him, too?"

The remark backfired. Torey was so hurt and angry that she refused to accept his apology, went straight home, and took the phone off the hook. They did not make up until Cal knocked on her door the next morning.

Except for that one instance, though, their relationship was unbelievably free of any difficulties arising from her continuing involvement with the religion—this despite the fact that she retreated not at all from her beliefs. Daily she performed the necessary rituals. But she practiced discreetly at home, and avoided the subject unless Cal raised it first. He appreciated, too, that she never made any mention of it when Chris was around.

One night when they made an appointment to meet for a movie at a midtown theater, she arrived late, and Cal pried out of her that she had been to see Voto. She was being considered for a large contract to provide decorative imports for the new headquarters of a large bank, and had wanted the *santero*'s advice on how to land the job. Cal found himself reacting with equanimity; he was annoyed that she was late, but no more than if she'd overslept from a nap, or stayed too long at drinks with a friend. By now it seemed to him that Torey's commitment to Santeria was not so different from a devout Christian's habit of stopping into church frequently, or seeking the advice of a priest on a personal matter. If he had learned she was a Buddhist and was required to spend hours seated in meditation before a stone Bodhisattva, he could have adjusted to that. So why not her commitment to an African religion? No doubt there were worshippers who became fanatics, behaved insanely and used the religion as their excuse, but that also happened in other faiths. Torey was certainly not affected by her worship in any negative way that Cal could detect.

And as he became more comfortable with her ways, he was

forced to reappraise his own professional relationship to the religion.

With the onset of the fall semester, his time taken up by teaching responsibilities, he had been able to ignore his research and tell himself it was only because he hadn't the time. Finally, though, he had to admit to himself that this was only an excuse. He had declined Oscar Sezine's invitation to his A.C.H.E. fundraiser not because of other pressing engagements, and not from a lack of curiosity. If he was totally honest with himself, he could admit he had been afraid. There had been too many shocks—the child in the morgue, Mrs. Ruiz, Kimball's journal, and then learning that Torey was a believer—and like a medical researcher tirelessly working on some bacterial culture, he had felt his resistance weakened, and knew that he might be infected by the very substance he was researching. But now, having settled down with Torey, he had adjusted to her beliefs, and his fascination with the religion was stimulated again.

It was a Wednesday near the end of September when he looked at his calendar to reschedule a graduate seminar and saw the notation he had made three weeks earlier. Tonight was Oscar Sezine's fundraiser. He hadn't missed it.

He made arrangements with Celestine to baby-sit so he could bring Torey along.

Chapter 30

THE ADDRESS Oscar had given Cal turned out to be an impeccably maintained pre-war building on the upper end of Fifth Avenue with only one apartment on each of its seventeen floors.

Waiting at the elevator, Cal and Torey were joined by two more arriving couples. The men and women were attractive and dressed in rather formal, obviously expensive clothes. A cloud of delicate fragrances hovered around them, the very perfume of success. Cal felt uncomfortably out of place in his academic-sincere tweed jacket with leather elbow patches, and regretted not having called Oscar for more details about the occasion. But at least Torey had caught the balance just right, wearing a plain but stylish black dress.

Once they were all together in the elevator, an incongruous intimacy developed, that illusion of shared secrets among strangers heading for the same destination, as though all the couples were privy to a special knowledge none could mention in public. Smiles and friendly nods were exchanged all around, and Cal recognized one of the men as a popular sports reporter on a local television news program.

The elevator opened directly onto a long carpeted gallery leading to a living room the size of a hotel lobby. The apartment had been decorated in a modern style, with no expense spared. A "floating" stairway with a swooping brass bannister led up to the second floor of the duplex. The ample spaces of the lower floor were already crowded with milling guests, and from across the hall Oscar caught Cal's eye, deftly broke off a conversation, and hurried toward them. Cal instantly felt more at ease when he noticed that Oscar was also dressed casually, right down to his white bucks.

"Cal," Oscar said effusively, "I'm so pleased you were able to make it." They clasped hands, and Cal felt the warmth was genuine. "I was frankly concerned that you might have given up your research."

"I haven't," Cal said simply.

"Good, good. As you know, I'm expecting something very special to come out of it someday." Torey had been standing by patiently; Oscar turned and gave her a wide smile. "And this is . . .?"

"Victoria Halowell . . . Oscar Sezine." Making the introduction, Cal watched closely for any hint of recognition, but there was none.

"Ah yes, Miss Halowell," Oscar said, registering the name from Cal's mention on the phone. As they shook hands, Oscar leaned over to Torey and asked in a confidential half-whisper, "This *is* the first time we've met, isn't it? I understand we share the experience of having lived in Cuba. The professor suggested our paths might have crossed before."

Torey flicked a glance at Cal, betraying the tiniest flash of ire. Then she said something to Oscar in Spanish. Oscar smiled, replied in Spanish, and Torey laughed.

Cal was unable to suppress his pique. "I wouldn't mind so much," he said, "but there's no place to read the subtitles."

Torey translated. "I told Señor Sezine that I could never have forgotten meeting a man with his charm—and he told me that he might well have tried to forget a woman who was such a shameless flatterer."

Cal realized then that she'd gone deliberately into Spanish to punish him for clinging to the suspicion of some conspiracy. But their intimacy nevertheless disconcerted him. Maybe they had no secrets, and maybe Torey had never met Oscar, but Cal was almost ready to believe that nothing was coincidence.

Oscar brought them across the gallery to meet the group he'd been talking with when they entered—Victor and Cissy Greenleaf, the host and hostess, and a couple introduced as Mr. and Mrs. Pedro Escobar. The Greenleafs looked every inch the likely owners of the penthouse: he, the high-powered labor lawyer, with perfectly barbered gray hair and a dark silk suit, his wife a sleekly coiffed brunette in a flowing designer original. The Escobars made a startling contrast. Both were short and dark, and wore off-the-rack polyester suits, clearly chosen for price rather than fit. Oscar mentioned in his introductions that Pedro Escobar was currently involved in organizing Hispanic labor against exploitation in sweatshops. It seemed to explain how the Escobars came to be hobnob-bing with a wealthy labor lawyer in his penthouse duplex.

But Cal remained puzzled. At a fundraiser he'd expected all the guests to be affluent potential contributors.

"Cal's been telling me," Torey said to Oscar after the introduc-tions, "about the way you've used Santeria for your program in the *barrio*. It's nice to hear that someone's doing something to point up the positive side of Voodoo."

Cal held his breath, assuming that Oscar must have played down the Voodoo element, perhaps had even neglected to mention it, when enlisting people like the Greenleafs to support his rehabilita-tion program.

But Oscar's quick reply made it plain that he had concealed nothing. "Thank you, Miss Halowell. I can't take all the credit, though. Everyone here is working for the same cause, to help people appreciate the religion."

"To help people, period," Cissy Greenleaf put in.

Cal understood now that the other guests were either all practi-tioners or, like himself, had come knowingly, with the intention of learning more about the religion. But as he made his way with Torey through the crowd into the living room, Cal was again per-plexed by the diversity of the guests. Along with several more downtrodden couples like the Escobars, evident representatives of the city's underprivileged, there were earnest middle-aged men in conservative suits whom Cal sized up as businessmen, doctors, and lawyers; and there was a large contingent of glossier types—models, young men in jeans and western boots, and a sampling of celebrities in addition to the sportscaster. Most of the celebrity identifications were made by Torey, who kept tugging at Cal's sleeve and pointing out guests with some claim to fame: a cele-brated pop artist, the leading man of a current Broadway musical hit, and a young real estate entrepreneur who had been in the news for announcing a planned housing development to be built in the East River . . . underwater.

At either end of the enormous living room were long tables, one with a lush display of flowers surrounded by trays of tropical fruits, the other with an unusual punchbowl that looked like the hollowed-out base of a tree trunk.

Cal steered Torey toward the drinks, and as they moved across the room, he recognized one more guest, a leggy redhead so daz-zlingly beautiful that he was brought up short at the sight of her. He knew her face—it was everywhere this year, pouting on the covers of fashion magazines, beaming from the pages of *People* and *Newsweek*, and peddling half a dozen different products on television.

"Who is that?" he asked Torey, inclining his head toward the beauty, who was leaning against the wall in conversation with a ruggedly handsome man dressed in a ruby velvet jacket and ivory flannel slacks.

"Sharon Laine," Torey said. "Don't tell me you've never seen her before?"

"Of course I have. But I couldn't think of her name."

Torey smiled and gripped his arm a little tighter. "As long as you can't remember the name of a peach like that, I guess I'll never have to be jealous."

At the bar Cal overheard snatches of conversation attesting further to the diversity of the crowd. Two men stood discussing the treatment of an "elementary frontal occlusion"—both dentists, Cal thought. But if at first it had been difficult to digest the fact that this heterogeneous group of people shared an attraction to Voodoo, seeing Sharon Laine here—this year's face—somehow put the whole phenomenon into perspective. It was just one more trend, Cal realized, the latest kick for those who were always one jump ahead of the pack. In the sixties it had been rock and acid and dropping out and "radical chic" causes. In the seventies it was rolfing and est and cocaine. And now, for the eighties, there was this: a step beyond primal scream therapy and natural healing and group sex and Eastern religions—the new primitivism. Voodoo. Another sensation, another kind of high, another item to spice up the "What's New" columns in the slick magazines.

Cal and Torey reached the table opposite the food, and the white-jacketed attendant began ladling out two servings of the dark orange liquid in the punchbowl, filling cups that were also hollowed out of wood.

Cal wasn't in the mood for a sweet punch drink. "I'd rather have a bourbon on the rocks," he told the bartender.

"I'm sorry, sir," said the man in the white jacket. "This is all we serve tonight." He held out the cups to Cal and Torey.

Cal was about to refuse, but before he had a chance Torey abruptly reached out, took both cups, and moved quickly away from the table.

"This party," she said to Cal after a moment. "Weren't you told what to expect?"

"Not exactly. Oscar said it was a fundraiser, but that it also ought to advance my understanding of the religion."

"It will," Torey agreed. "It's a *guëmilere*."

"A what?"

"A special Voodoo feast. It's usually held to celebrate receiving some great favor from the gods . . . or else on the eve of asking for one."

"Which kind is this?"

"I don't know," Torey said.

"Then how do you know it's a—"

"*Guëmilere*," Torey supplied. "I knew the minute we were given the *chekete*." She looked down at the cups in her hands, then passed one to Cal. "This drink—traditionally it's the only drink served at this kind of feast. The bowl and the cups are traditional, too. They're made from the wood of the *ceiba* tree, the sacred tree of Voodoo."

Some reference to wood stirred vaguely in Cal's memory.

MacTaggart.

The detective had told him the murdered children were found on altars of an unknown wood. Cal filed the name away, a clue worth passing along.

"Taste it," Torey said, lifting her cup.

Cal drank the *chekete*. It was sweet and bitter and pungent all at once, with a number of subtle flavors carried on the overriding taste of fermented oranges. He didn't like the first swallow, but as it lingered on his tongue the taste changed, and he could feel the natural alcohol stoking a mellow warmth in his gut.

He had another swallow while Torey told him about the ancient recipe—cornmeal, brown sugar, cane syrup, cloves, and some floral essences along with the juice of the oranges. He decided then that he didn't miss the bourbon. By the third swallow, the stuff was putting a glow on him. If Oscar was going to pass the hat, he thought, this was the right drink to put people in a generous mood.

"So you've been to a lot of these . . . feasts?" he said to Torey.

"One or two a year. But nothing ever this elaborate. Voto has them at his home, for the family."

"The last time you went," Cal asked, his eyes roaming the room, "what were you celebrating?"

Torey thought for a moment. Then, a bit sheepishly, she replied, "I think it was right after Voto enlarged his store. He was thanking the gods for making his business prosper."

Cal almost laughed; the juxtaposition of these elaborate ancient traditions with the banalities of daily modern life was sometimes so ridiculous. This religion simply didn't belong in this time and place. Voodoo priests hadn't been meant to live over hardware

237

stores and hold traditional feasts to celebrate a banner year in paint sales. This party of Oscar's suddenly seemed equally absurd. He was using the tradition to raise funds, that was all. The deities, like the guests, were being asked to pledge an infusion of new money for the A.C.H.E.

The smoke in the room had become heavy and stifling, and when someone behind Cal blew a thick plume of smoke over Cal's shoulder, he spun around in irritation. The offender, he saw, was a sultry blonde, her delicate mouth curved around the end of a newly lit cigar. Then Cal noticed that other women were also lighting up cigars along with the men. Four out of five people in the room were smoking them, in fact, plucking them from open humidors set on all the endtables.

He was surprised for only an instant. Then he recalled the significance of the cigar as a common symbol in Voodoo rites. Filling the room with strong fumes seemed to signify that some ceremonial phase of the gathering was about to begin.

He turned back to Torey to ask her about it; she was just accepting a cigar herself from a young man passing a humidor on a silver tray. The young man held a butane lighter for her, then offered the tray to Cal. He hesitated.

Torey said, "It's not absolutely necessary."

Cal declined the cigar, and the man with the tray moved on.

"What's happening?" Cal asked.

"Many of the gods are especially fond of the taste and smell of strong tobacco. Filling the air with smoke is a way of attracting them, making them want to join the party."

"Join the party?" Cal responded. "You make it sound like a god could come in here and grab his own cup of *chekete*."

Torey looked at him for a moment without speaking. Then she said flatly, "You'll see."

"See *what?*" Cal asked impatiently.

But before she could answer, the faint beat of drums cut through the babble in the room, softly at first, quickly growing louder. Everyone turned toward the sound, the entrance to the living room, as three black men walked in from the gallery carrying African drums of different sizes, but all being beaten with the same slow insistent tattoo.

A number of guests began clapping in rhythm to the drums. Then, as the three men passed once around the perimeter of the room, more and more people fell in with the clapping. When Torey took it up, Cal did too. Soon the beat had captured everyone.

After one circuit of the room, the three drummers lined up at the end near the buffet table. They ceased their drumming and the clapping stopped with them.

Then Oscar strode in from the gallery, as though from the wings of a stage—"making an entrance." To add to the theatricality he had donned a costume, a plain sky-blue gown that would have looked more appropriate at a high school graduation ceremony.

"Good evening, everyone," he said in his mellifluous baritone. "Let me start by thanking you all for coming tonight, showing your support and your interest—and of course a special thank you to the Greenleafs for giving us this lovely place to meet." He nodded to the couple, who were standing nearby, and they smiled back.

"I'm sure most of you have been to a celebration like this before. You know what it is, you understand its importance. But there are a few friends joining us for the first time . . ." Oscar's glance swept over the room, resting on Cal a moment, then passed on. "You wouldn't be here, of course, if you weren't already prepared to share in, and appreciate, one of the religion's most essential and exalting experiences. Still, I know that the first time may be difficult, even a little . . . alarming. So let me assure you now: there is absolutely nothing to fear if you behave with respect, generosity, kindness, humility—in short, if you merely demonstrate all the best qualities of human nature. The gods demand nothing more of us than that."

He paused to let the words sink in, and Cal leaned over to ask Torey what he was talking about. But before he had said a word, she silenced him with a finger pressed to her lips.

"I should, however," Oscar continued, "add a warning. If there are any here tonight who are doubtful of their courage, then it would be wise for you to leave now. If you are not comfortable, if you think there is something to fear, then you may *show* your fear —and that might be taken by the gods as an insult."

Again Oscar's eyes swept over the assembly, searching faces for signs of doubt.

When the penetrating gaze found him, Cal tried to return a stolid stare. But he felt his resolve shaken. Oscar's warning was somehow ominous, a sugar-coated command to behave or else. And Cal didn't know if he could. He had no idea what he was being asked to do, what he would be forced to witness. He was on the point of admitting his doubts aloud when he felt Torey's hand slip into his and give a reassuring squeeze.

Cal remained silent and Oscar looked away. No one in the room had taken the opportunity to leave. Finally Oscar gestured to the three drummers and they began lightly tapping the taut goatskin drumheads with their fingertips. For a minute they played the pattern in unison, then began passing solos back and forth like jazz musicians.

Torey leaned over to Cal. "Those are the *bata*," she murmured, "the ritual drums that speak directly to the gods. Right now they're playing an invocation to Eleggua, asking him to open the gate between worlds. When they finish, the call will begin."

"Call to who?"

"To the *orisha*, asking him to join us."

The rhythms grew faster, the patterns more intricate. Cal glanced around the room. The guests were attentive, yet relaxed. The sportscaster was snapping his fingers. The lovely redhead, Sharon Laine, stood with her arm around the waist of the man in the ruby velvet jacket, bobbing her head as though listening on the sidelines at a disco. Whatever rites were unfolding, however Torey had explained them, the pervading atmosphere remained that of a sophisticated New York soiree with one more new twist to entertain a crowd that liked to think it had seen everything.

Suddenly there was another lull. Oscar came forward and raised the wooden goblet he was holding in one hand. Solemnly he offered a toast:

"To Oshun, the goddess of love and goddess of gold, we consecrate ourselves tonight and plead for her divine intervention in our future. With gratitude for the gift of her *aché*, we vow on this eve of the sixth to dedicate our next offering to her."

Oscar drank from the goblet. Throughout the audience, as a kind of benediction, guests muttered "*Moddu cue*, Oshun."

Cal remembered the words—*moddu cue*—the Yoruban words for thank you that he had seen on the blackboard in one of Oscar's classrooms. But other things in the toast baffled him. Oscar had said something about the god's *aché*, linking the name of his organization directly to the god.

And there was the date: "the eve of the sixth." Today was September twenty-ninth.

Quickly Cal leaned over and asked Torey about it.

"*Aché* means power," she whispered, "the power of the gods." Cal realized Oscar must have knowingly chosen his acronym. But Torey could only shrug about the discrepancy in the dates. The eve of the sixth? It meant nothing to her.

And there was no time to discuss it. The drumming had resumed and a woman wearing a long shawl over her head, keeping her face in shadow, emerged from the crowd and took a place beside the drummers.

"She's the *akonrin*," Torey said quietly, "the caller of the *orishas*." Again Torey's mention of the call was flatly inflected, as if the ritual was banal and unspectacular—a god might actually turn up like a late-arriving guest. But Cal realized she was speaking metaphorically; the woman's singing was little different from a cantor's in a synagogue or a choir's in a church, making music to create a spiritual mood, an illusion of divine presence.

Yet just as the choirs of cathedrals sang the Masses of Bach and Handel to elicit the spirit of a civilized god, there could be no doubt from the music of this ceremony that the spirit being conjured was primitive and pagan, an ancient deity conceived in the cradle of humanity. This was music from a time when there had been no instruments but voice and drum, echoes from dark primeval valleys, a song of the cave.

The singer's low notes seemed to rise more from her belly than her chest. Coming in quick breathy bursts, they sounded like the pantings of an excited animal. The pitch rose gradually higher, changing from staccato grunts to extended howls. Then the singer opened her throat and the song became a scream. Cal had never heard such noises issue from the human mouth. It could have been a grotesque performance, but it wasn't. It was mesmerizing. Pant, grunt, howl, scream. All woven together by sliding notes that went up and down the scale. The whole of evolution, the agonies of man being born from the animal, were in the song.

And always, underneath, the sound of the drums, their tempo slowly quickening.

No fingers were snapping now, no one stood in casual poses. They were all swaying to the drums, bouncing slightly on the balls of their feet, eyes glazed, jaws slack—hypnotized by the heartbeat of the drums.

Cal could feel it happening within himself, the trance enfolding him. His mind was pleasantly dulled by the *chekete*, his breathing shallow in the smoke-laden air, his sense of time and place slipping away. Was this a sea mist around him? Or was it smoke from the fire in a cave?

The drums beat faster and his heart went with them, pounding with anticipation. Of *what?* A hunt, a feast, a carnal orgy? The echoing voice rose higher and higher and higher to a pure piercing note that seemed to go on and on, a shaft of sound traveling light-years to the distant corners of the heavens.

Cal struggled to focus on the source and found it, the singer, just as she threw her head back. The note ended and the shawl fell away. He saw then that the *akonrin* was Mrs. Escobar: the magic voice belonged to the slightly dumpy wife of a labor organizer. The trance seemed to break.

And then the man in front of Cal collapsed. Cal made a move to help him, but Torey roughly tugged him back.

"Don't," she whispered urgently. "You mustn't touch him. The saint has mounted his horse. He's the *omo-orisha*."

"What?"

"It's what we say when the god takes possession. *Subirse el santo a su caballo*—the saint has mounted his horse. The believer becomes a man-god, the *omo-orisha*."

Cal saw now that everyone had backed off to the edges of the room, forming a large ring around the fallen man. Cal let Torey pull him to the perimeter.

The singer and the drums were silent. The fallen man lay on his side, motionless, drawn up in a fetal position, eyes closed. No one made a move toward him. Then he stirred, stretched, pulled himself up on his knees. He stayed in that position for a minute, head bowed, chin resting on his chest. He was about forty, Cal judged, with graying brown hair thinning on top, dressed in a brown corduroy suit. He was one of the dentists Cal had overheard earlier.

The dentist rose to his feet. He lifted his head and slowly scanned the watching crowd.

Cal was stunned by the man's face. The features had seemed mild and inoffensive before. But they had altered somehow—thickened, sharpened, Cal wasn't sure what had changed—yet now the face was coarser, aboriginal, wild. The eyes blazed, touching everyone with a wide brilliant stare. But they were not merely savage. Cal felt in the man's gaze a cunning and imperious confidence of such glaring intensity that it bordered on the psychopathic.

Cal understood the transformation. He had read about it in Metraux—the fevered Voodoo ritual where a man became so ecstatically entranced that he believed the spirit of a god had entered his body. A form of hysterical self-hypnosis. It would last for a brief period, then the afflicted would return to normal.

The dentist finished scanning the circle of people around him. Now he bent over and slowly, meticulously, rolled his trousers up from the cuffs until they were over his knees, baring his bony calves. He looked ludicrous.

No one laughed.

Oscar stepped into the center of the circle. In one hand he held a short whip—a riding crop. Metraux had mentioned, too, that the person who appeared to be possessed was sometimes severely beaten, as punishment for pretending a false possession.

But Oscar held the whip at his side. The dentist stared coolly at him, glanced down to the whip, then exploded in a loud laugh, shrill and high-pitched.

"Oh no, my friend," he said as the laugh subsided, "you won't need the *oddaniko* for me. I *am* Oshun. I am *here*. I have truly come."

The voice, like the laugh, was a *woman's*. Not a strained falsetto, not merely a man's *imitation* of a woman. This was soft and silken, a perfect feminine purr.

Cal thought of Oscar telling him that the boundaries of gender were unimportant in Santeria. A female saint could represent a male African deity. This was only the reverse carried one step further, the female deity entering a living man.

Knowing the theory, however, made it no less shocking.

"Welcome Oshun," Oscar said ceremoniously to the *omo-orisha*. "Are you thirsty or hungry? Tell me what you want and I will serve you."

"I want nothing but to be among you," answered the possessed dentist in his sweet womanly voice. "Please, have your feast, enjoy yourselves, and I will be happy."

Oscar nodded and turned to the ring of guests, indicating with a gesture that they could disperse, the party would continue. The guests went back to talking in groups, drinking, serving themselves with food from the buffet.

It was a normal party again, with one difference: one of the guests was a god.

The dentist with his pants rolled up, accompanied by Oscar, circulated through the crowd, stopping to chat with one group or another. Occasionally the shrill high-pitched laughter cut through the room's noisy banter. The movements of the *omo-orisha* were also genuinely feminine—a sinuous feline walk, expansive yet graceful hand gestures. Cal saw the *omo-orisha* in conversation with the sportscaster, draping his hand languidly over the man's shoulder and fondling the nape of his neck.

Cal found it impossible not to stare at the spectacle, though

Torey warned him repeatedly against it. Oshun, the goddess of love, was soft and affectionate when unprovoked, Torey explained. But once offended, she was one of the most merciless and unforgiving of all Voodoo deities.

But Cal went on observing, as inconspicuously as possible, the passage of the possessed man through the room. Frequently guests presented him with small gifts, a flower from a lapel, or even a valuable piece of jewelry. This was mandatory, Torey said, whenever the god expressed an attraction to some article of adornment. But of course all the gifts would be returned after the *orisha* had departed the man's body.

Eventually Oscar and the *omo-orisha* had moved to the corner of the room not far from where Cal was standing with Torey. Cal felt a rising anxiety about the approaching confrontation. Not the anxiety of fear, but of being tempted to challenge the dentist's delusion, to try cracking through it. If ever there was any hope of freeing Torey from nonsensical superstition—and perhaps himself —the opportunity was here, in proving that this performance was nothing more than a trick. An honest trick, maybe, a trick that the mind played on itself, but a trick nonetheless.

The *omo-orisha* moved closer to Cal and Torey.

And then stopped. Sharon Laine was watching from against a wall nearby with her boyfriend. The *omo-orisha* turned slowly toward her, then walked in her direction. She gasped slightly and her boyfriend put a steadying arm around her shoulder.

"You are magnificent," the *omo-orisha* said in a cool purring voice. "There is nothing that pleases Oshun so much as to look upon a beautiful woman. For I am the goddess of love, and you are an inspiration to all lovers."

The room was silent. Everyone had turned to watch.

"Thank you," Sharon Laine responded shakily. All the poise and grace that was the successful model's stock in trade had fled from her. Awkward as a four-year-old, she stood with the sole of one foot clamped down on the toe of the other.

Sidling closer, the *omo-orisha* reached out and touched the model's blouse, a loose billowing low-cut yellow shantung buttoned up the front.

"Your plumage is beautiful, too, pretty bird," the possessed dentist said, the purr becoming softer, more seductive. Lightly he ran a fingertip up and down the buttons of the blouse, then began tracing the inside of the neckline, touching the exposed curves of the model's breasts.

244

Sharon Laine cast a glance at her boyfriend, desperate for guidance. He frowned and shook his head a little, a signal to keep calm, do nothing to offend.

"Do you think it would look well on me?" the *omo-orisha* asked, the voice turning coy.

Sharon Laine hesitated.

"You don't think so? You really don't?" Now the voice was childishly wheedling. "It's so lovely. I wish I could have it."

The boyfriend nudged Sharon Laine, but she only stared at the possessed dentist, unable to move or speak.

Finally the boyfriend spoke for her. "You've given us whatever we have, Oshun. Anything we can give in return, we give gladly." He nudged the model again. Still she didn't move. "Go ahead, doll," the boyfriend whispered anxiously. *"Do it!"*

Sharon Laine turned on her boyfriend. "Do what?" she demanded. "Take off my blouse? Johnny, I'm not wearing anything under this. I'm bare under here."

The boyfriend looked to Oscar, standing just behind the *omo-orisha*. "Look, can't she—?"

"You've been with us before, John," Oscar replied. "You know the custom."

"Honey," the boyfriend muttered to Sharon Laine, "you've got to. Yellow is Oshun's favorite color, see. And it's part of the—"

"Bullshit!" the model exploded. "I won't do it."

The *omo-orisha* laughed chillingly. "My pretty bird cannot be plucked of her feathers, eh? She would deny me . . ."

"No, no," the boyfriend said quickly. Then he put his hands to the blouse, and started undoing the buttons.

"Fuck off, Johnny," the model said, and knocked his hands away.

But the boyfriend grabbed her more roughly. "Goddamn it, Shar, what's the big deal? You did a no-top job for Avedon last week, for Chrissakes. This is just—"

"Sick!" the model screamed, fighting to tear herself away. "This whole fucking thing. Christ, Johnny, you didn't say it would be like this. You said it helped you. You said we'd meet good people." She spun on the *omo-orisha*. "Not freaks! I'll be goddamned if I can see why I should go bare so this asshole can prance around in drag."

The boyfriend had managed to maintain his grasp on the model. But now he let go and backed away from her, holding his palms up as if to ward off some lethal ray emanating from her.

Sharon Laine stared at him confused, then glanced around and saw the *omo-orisha*. The man-god stood rigid as a statue, one arm raised to point at the girl, his face a hideous mask of fury. Now, too late, the beautiful model was struck by terror.

"All right," she said hoarsely, her voice failing. "I'm sorry . . . I shouldn't have said—"

"You have denied me what is mine," the *omo-orisha* crooned eerily. "By the laws of Obatala, I give you two *irole!*"

The god said no more, but kept pointing at the model. She retreated slowly, shaking her head, unsure of what had befallen her, yet knowing it was terrible. "Please," she mumbled through trembling lips, "please . . . please . . ."

No one in the room moved or spoke. Sharon Laine looked at her boyfriend, put her arms out to him, pleading. "Johnny?"

The boyfriend turned away from her.

The model had gone to the bottom of the well of her confusion and fear. Finding no relief, no comprehension, she summoned up a last frustrated burst of anger and defiance. Clenching her fists, her tall slim body bent over with tension, she shrieked:

"You're freaks, all of you. Crazy fucking freaks!"

Then she whirled and bolted from the room, down the long gallery to the elevator, where she stood hammering on the door until it slid open. She entered, and it closed behind her.

There was a long silence, until the *omo-orisha* spoke.

"I will go now. I blame none of you here for this insult, but I wish to depart."

Oscar nodded and motioned instantly to one of the guests, who brought a chair to the center of the room. Again the crowd formed a ring, and the dentist sat down.

Pulling a large white linen handkerchief from his pocket, Oscar draped it over the head of the possessed man. Then Oscar leaned down and blew through the thin fabric into the dentist's ear while the drummers played a brief pattern. Three times Cal saw the handkerchief flutter from a gust of Oscar's breath.

The drumming ceased.

A moment later the dentist reached up and pulled the handkerchief from his head. He looked around at the ring of staring people, smiled shyly, and stood up. Noticing then that his trousers were bunched above the knees, he crouched and rolled them down neatly.

The possession was over.

The god had gone home.

Immediately the dentist was surrounded by people reclaiming pins and necklaces and other personal articles he'd collected during the possession.

"What did it mean?" Cal asked Torey. "The laws of Obatala . . . two *irole?*"

"Obatala is the father of the gods, the maker of all universal laws. *Irole* means 'day.' Oshun gave that poor woman two days."

"Two days of what? Solitary?"

"It's no joke," Torey said severely. "The god gave her two more days before something happens to her. Something awful . . ." Torey's expression mirrored a profound pity for Sharon Laine. When she realized Cal was staring at her, she turned and walked away to join a line of guests saying good night to Oscar. The party was breaking up.

For a minute Cal observed the people as they reached Oscar. Before shaking hands, many handed Oscar a slip of paper or an envelope. Checks, Cal thought. And the envelopes could contain cash. So Oscar had raised funds for the A.C.H.E. after all. Had he boosted the "take" with a demonstration of the power of the religion to possess and terrify? Showmanship, Cal thought, it might have been nothing more.

He joined Torey as she reached Oscar.

"Good night, Miss Halowell," Oscar said. "I'm glad you were able to come. Perhaps another time?"

Torey gave Cal a conciliatory glance. "Perhaps," she said.

Oscar turned to Cal. "And you, Professor, I hope you found tonight's experience enlightening."

"I suppose I did," Cal equivocated. "If you can say that there's a dark side to enlightenment."

Oscar smiled thinly. "I'm sorry if the way it ended upset you. I tried to prepare everyone at the beginning, to avoid that kind of incident. I hope, though, that you'll remember what I've shown and told you in the past . . . remember that this is all being done for a cause much larger than ourselves."

Cal said nothing. The tone of conviction was impressive, but Cal could no longer be so sure it was genuine. Oscar could simply be the leading man in a wonderfully staged and acted performance.

As they emerged from the apartment building, Cal watched the well-dressed guests climbing into their limousines. To most of them, he realized, very little of this had been new. They had been through it all before.

But this was something beyond a visit to a *santero* above a hardware store. Cal felt, inexplicably, that the evening had somehow been arranged for him, as though Oscar had meant it to be more than a learning experience, as if it were some kind of initiation.

At the curb an empty van had pulled up to take a trio of three men. They had three large cases with them, and loading themselves and their cargo into the back took some comic manipulations. The trio, Cal realized, were the three drummers with their instruments.

Torey had paused, too, studying Cal. "What are you thinking?" she asked.

"I was just wondering," he said after a moment, "if they're going home, or off to play another job."

Chapter 31

ALL THE NEXT DAY Oscar Sezine's party nagged at Cal's mind. It wouldn't be easy, he knew now, to extricate Torey from her commitment to Santeria. Or, for that matter, himself. He was more intrigued than ever. He wanted to find that dentist and interview him. He wanted to know what people like Victor Greenleaf thought of their chic infatuation with Voodoo.

And then there was MacTaggart's theory: could there really be human sacrifice?

In the second hour of a tutorials meeting that afternoon, Harvey Rayburn mentioned to Cal that he'd been appointed to the Guggenheim Fellowship selection panel. "Quite a little coup," Harvey boasted, "considering they wouldn't give *me* a Guggenheim."

Briefly Cal savored the thought of being awarded a large grant to write his book. What kind of spell, he wondered, would you cast to get a grant? Write the title of your project on a bar of soap, maybe.

The thought occurred again on Friday, just as casually. He was on his way home in the dark autumn evening when the sky opened, pouring torrential sheets of rain. The rain seemed a little miraculous; you didn't get heavy fall storms in New Mexico. Drenched pedestrians who had relied on the morning forecast scurried into doorways and under newspaper-stand awnings. Cal, too, searched for cover; the closest subway stop was six blocks away, and the rain showed no signs of letting up. He looked around for a cab, and then saw one unloading a passenger onto the Low Library plaza.

He raced to the curb. But as he reached the taxi and grabbed the door handle, the driver leaned over to lock the door.

"Off duty!" the driver shouted through the rolled-up window.

"Just take me to a subway stop," Cal shouted back.

"Forget it," the driver said, and stepped on the gas.

Cal was still holding onto the handle, and a fingernail tore as the cab sped away.

"You bastard," he screamed. "I'll do a spell on you that'll—"

Twice in two days. Thinking about casting spells on people. Cal shook his head.

On the subway platform he bought himself a hot pretzel for solace, and a *Post*. The Phillies' rookie lefthander had pitched a no-hitter, the president was coming to town to talk with the mayor, and both Pakistan and Iran, according to the CIA, were conducting nuclear tests with bombs they weren't supposed to be capable of making.

The downtown trains seemed to have stopped running, and the platform was very crowded. Cal leaned against a pillar and riffled through the front of the paper. The headline on page five leapt out at him: TOP MODEL IN BURN TRAGEDY. In the center of the page was a picture of Sharon Laine being carried out of her East Side co-op on a stretcher. The news item followed:

> In an early morning drama, the face of Sharon Laine, the $1000-an-hour model, was seriously burned when bacon fat caught fire as she was preparing breakfast in her luxurious Park Avenue duplex. Miss Laine was rushed to the burn unit of Lenox Hill Hospital, where she remains in critical condition. Asked to confirm or deny that the beauty's career may be over, a spokesman for the Femme Modeling Agency said, "No comment."

Cal looked at the photograph, then read the item again.

It was chilling. But more horrifying to Cal was the fact that he wasn't surprised.

⊃ ● ⊂

Torey came home late that night, after ten. She had been at a dinner party with some German steel executives, closing a deal to supply Peruvian art for their offices in Stuttgart.

She called from the hall. "Hi, sweetheart, how was your day?"

He didn't answer, and she came into the living room.

"Cal?"

He folded the *Post* to the item about Sharon Laine and thrust it at her.

"Look at that," he said.

"Look at what?"

"Just read it." He pointed to the story by the photograph.

She scanned it and looked up. "It's terrible," she said. "It's sad."

"Is that all you can say?"

"What do you want me to say? We knew it would happen. She brought it on herself."

"So that's what your gods do to someone who steps out of line. She said 'no' once, and now she's in a hospital somewhere without a face. If that's what Voodoo does, how can you be involved with it? What kind of gods are these anyway?"

She laid the newspaper down on the coffee table and looked at him. "They're the same gods," she said, "who sink the *Titanic* and cause wars and drop bombs on Hiroshima. And who also give life and make trees grow and rainbows shine. They do all of it—the good and the bad. And they have their reasons, which we can't always understand. But that's what gods *are*. What kind of gods would you like?"

Cal turned away from her and rested his arms on the mantel, staring at the wall. Her argument was indisputable, of course. She had merely defined the nature of divine forces. If you believed gods existed, then you accepted all that happened—accepted with grace, as the theologians put it—the miracles and the catastrophes. The gods gave light and life and the sun and the seasons—and they also let people suffer.

Cal looked back to Torey, uncertain what to say.

She spoke first. "Cal, I wish it hadn't happened. Please believe me. But what Sharon Laine did was blasphemy, plain and simple. She cursed Oshun, and she cursed Oshun's followers. I wish I could have warned her, honestly I do, and sometimes I even wish the gods weren't so powerful. But they are, and there's nothing any of us can do about it."

He wanted to reject everything she had said. Her faith, the very idea of faith itself, cried out for argument—the same argument rational man had been using since the dawn of the Enlightenment. The natural order was a scientific order, Cal wanted to tell her, not a world of gods or blasphemy or absurd notions of divine retribution.

But the protest stuck in Cal's throat. He wasn't sure how convincing the words would sound.

Torey started unbuttoning her blouse. "C'mon," she said, "I'm tired. Let's go to bed."

He followed her to the bedroom, and they crawled under the

covers. Cal switched off the bedside lamp, but remained sitting up against the headboard, staring into the darkness. Torey, in a light flannel nightgown, stayed on her side of the bed, perhaps reading his mood; it was obvious to both that neither was in the mood for sex. The strain between them was nearly palpable, and Cal craved the ability to dispel it with an affirmation of their love. But he couldn't find the strength to apologize for lashing out at her, for seeming to blame her for the accident of fate that had afflicted Sharon Laine.

He lay on his side of the bed immobile, until she whispered in the darkness:

"Aren't you going to sleep?"

"I just wanted to think awhile," he said.

And then he called out silently to her, hoping she would sense his remorse and confusion. Suddenly, as if in response, he felt her hand on his chest, and her leg against his. He rolled toward her, and they hugged, and the warm sweet smell of her, the essence that was particularly hers, helped him shed his anger. They would make it work between them.

She murmured in the dark. "I love you, Cal."

"I love you," he said, and held her tighter, his palms cupping her shoulders, his chest against the soft smoothness of her breasts. They kissed briefly, and lay entwined together, and soon he heard her measured breathing. She was asleep.

But though he felt the argument resolved, and the tension gone, sleep would not come to him. He sat up and leaned against the headboard, waiting; then, still sitting up, he finally closed his eyes.

There was a flash of light: one of those electrical impulses from a nerve-ending streaked across his retina. Then a passage from Kimball came into his mind, not as words but a picture: men in robes, casting shells in the center of a field. Then the image was cleaved by another—a gleaming knife.

Blood.

A swirling black cloud.

And, emerging from the red and the black, a glittering golden eye.

Cal's eyes snapped open.

He sat up for another two hours, listening to the wind.

⊐ ● ⊏

Dennis MacTaggart called again.

And for the same reason. Another child's body had been found, pieces of it anyway, bobbing around in the water under the Hell's Gate railroad bridge. No beads and candles this time, but the cause of death was the same: evisceration. The detective was calling because he thought Cal might have some more information. The day after Oscar's party, Cal had phoned MacTaggart and told him about *ceiba* wood. MacTaggart had passed the tip on to the Bronx Botanical Garden, and it had now been confirmed that *ceiba* was, in fact, the wood used in the altar-like platform found with the body at the Brooklyn warehouse fire. Now MacTaggart wanted to know more.

Cal said he knew nothing else of any relevance to the murder cases.

But MacTaggart was full of questions. Where had Cal learned the name of the wood? Who were the people Cal had talked to for his research—what were their names and addresses? Was Cal absolutely sure he had seen or heard *nothing*, not the smallest hint, that human sacrifice might be condoned by Voodoo believers?

Cal remained reticent, somewhat unwilling to rake through the data in his mind. He was afraid that Torey might be unfairly dragged into the investigation. He told the cop again that he had nothing to tell him.

Finally MacTaggart simply announced that he wanted to meet with Cal at once—he would drive by Cal's house in half an hour.

"Be waiting outside," he said. It sounded more like a threat than a request.

"Look, Dennis, I'm sorry, but—"

Cal's protest fell on dead air. MacTaggart had broken the connection.

⋑ ● ⋴

The car slid to a fast stop at the curb, and MacTaggart waggled his hand, indicating he wanted Cal to get into the passenger seat.

Cal stopped, stunned, as he ducked through the door and got a closer look at the detective. MacTaggart looked physically ill; deep lines were etched in his forehead, his skin had a deathly gray pallor. Cal tried to recover from staring, as he might in the presence of a man who was dying but had not been told.

As soon as Cal had closed the door, MacTaggart gunned the car away from the curb.

"Hey, Dennis, where are we going?" Cal said unhappily. He had expected they would sit in the car and talk.

"My house," MacTaggart said.

"Where's that?"

"Edgewater."

Cal looked at him blankly.

"It's in New Jersey," MacTaggart said. "Just the other side of the river."

"New Jersey? Dennis! Look, I've got—"

"It's only ten minutes through the tunnel. You'll be back in thirty, forty minutes." He gave Cal an apologetic glance. "Sorry, chum. But I've been going twenty-eight hours since the last body turned up, and I've got another shift tonight. We go a little bats if we don't take time to go home and freshen up. Do our four *s*'s: shave, shower, shine, shit. I didn't think you'd mind keeping me company."

The assumption of friendship made it hard for Cal to object.

MacTaggart slipped a Hershey bar out of his handkerchief pocket and peeled back the already torn paper wrapping. He broke off a square and put it in his mouth, then held it out to Cal. "Want a piece?"

Cal shook his head. He was reminded for some reason of police interrogations he'd seen in TV cop shows. The way they offered cigarettes, buddied up when they were trying to solicit a confession.

It was all the more unsettling when MacTaggart glanced sideways and said abruptly, "Why are you holding out, Cal?"

It was an effective moment, too, Cal thought. The car had just gone into the tunnel under the Hudson River—the feeling of being in an isolation cell. MacTaggart wanted more than company.

"Dennis, I'm not holding out. If I could tell you anything to help—"

"Listen, Professor," MacTaggart broke in, the intimate tone now gone, "I've got twenty years of reading faces and asking questions, and I *know* when a man's holding out. You're stalling me. You know more than you're giving. You went out to do research, and you're a hotshot—you're good at what you do, just like I am. You've been learning all the time. You gave us the name of that wood after our own people couldn't get it. Now I want the rest of what you know."

"Lieutenant," Cal said with irritation. "Am *I* under suspicion?"

MacTaggart grunted. "Of course not."

"Then don't talk to me as if I am, goddamnit. If I could help you, I would."

But even as he heard his convincing indignation, Cal wondered where it had come from. Wasn't he in fact holding back? Suppose he told MacTaggart about Kimball's journal, the *babalaos* predicting the events of a decade with shells, the sacrifices that had been done in the past in an attempt to change the course of fate? All of it *supported* MacTaggart's theory.

But it wasn't evidence, really. Not what a policeman wanted . . .

MacTaggart lowered his voice, sounding chastened. "Sorry, Cal. I've been going at this long and hard . . . and it just makes me so fuckin' sick to find these kids and not be able to stop it. I tell you, I'm at the end of my fuckin' rope. I'm never gonna break this case. Not unless I get lucky, and soon."

Perhaps if he mentioned Suares, Cal thought. MacTaggart had said the police already knew the names of some *santeros*, but one more lead couldn't hurt. Or maybe if the detective interviewed the Greenleafs and the Escobars and all the others who had attended the *guëmilere* . . . Who could say when and where MacTaggart might "get lucky"?

Yet Cal said nothing. And was puzzled by his own silence.

"Bastards!" MacTaggart erupted as the car emerged from the tunnel on the New Jersey side. "You know what I oughta do? I ought to just pick 'em up and sweat 'em. I oughta haul 'em in off the streets. Every one of these goddamn monkeys who believes in this Voodoo shit. They'll talk when I get through with 'em."

Everyone who believes. And where, Cal wondered, did that leave him? Christ, he *was* holding back, guarding secrets like a member of a "family." As if he was one of those worshippers Metraux had written about—who'd had snakes' blood touched to their lips at the end of a ceremony, in token of a sacred vow never to tell what they had witnessed.

MacTaggart rambled on as though Cal wasn't there. "That's what I'll do, all right. I shoulda done it months ago. Fuck all this tiptoeing around rights and amendments. It'd be worth it if I saved the life of one kid, wouldn't it? I'll round up every last fucking freak who's into this shit and put 'em in the hole, and keep 'em there and squeeze 'em until they break."

Cal looked at the detective. MacTaggart was *raving*. Was he cracking?

"Dennis, you can't do it that way."

"Oh no? Why not?"

"Because . . . you're not that kind of man."

"I didn't *used* to be. But we don't always know what we are, do we? I was hoping you'd be able to help me, Cal. But since you can't, I guess I'll have to help myself. Don't they always say those are the kind of people God helps?"

⊃ ● ⊂

MacTaggart lived in a split-level ranch house with an attached two-car garage and a reproduction gas lamp in front. It was a family neighborhood, with kids playing stickball in the street and bicycles splayed carelessly on the lawns. MacTaggart's house was not as well maintained as the others on the street, and the lawn seemed not to have been mown for weeks. When the detective drove into the garage, Cal saw that no space had been left for a second car. The empty bay was stacked with furniture and boxes, an old crib and some tricycles, and the rusted frames of a see-saw and garden swing. The happiness in this house, Cal realized, had been stored away. Perhaps his empathy with MacTaggart came from similar losses.

They entered from the garage into the kitchen, and the marks of a bachelor life were everywhere. A half-empty pot of soup on the stove, an empty beer bottle and glass on a formica counter.

"This place is a mess," MacTaggart said self-consciously. "I shouldn't have dragged you out here, Cal. It wasn't fair."

"I've seen messy houses before, Dennis."

"That's not what I meant," MacTaggart said as he prodded Cal on through the kitchen, into a hall. "I was using cop tricks on you. Get your man alone, put him off balance. You don't deserve that."

But I do, Cal thought. He resolved to tell MacTaggart as much as he knew; let the cop decide what was or was not useful.

They turned into a den, paneled in wood, its furniture upholstered in the same tartan as the kilt Cal had seen MacTaggart wearing in the squad room. A set of bagpipes hung on one wall, and a florid oil painting of a Scottish castle on another. The room was completely in order, but a fine layer of dust covered every surface.

"Lemme give you a drink," MacTaggart said, "then I'll go take a quick shower." He opened a cabinet bar in the corner and pulled out two glasses and a bottle. "Whiskey?"

Cal had no appetite for liquor, but accepted to be companionable. As MacTaggart poured, Cal looked around the room. A table under the window was half covered with pictures in plastic frames. The larger ones were family photographs, MacTaggart with a pretty blond woman and two smiling young boys, and one each of the boys separately.

MacTaggart pointed to a picture of one boy, then the other. "That's Eric, that's Peter," he said, then nodded at the woman in the group photo. "Marie. She left me two years ago." He handed Cal a glass. "Cheers."

MacTaggart put the bottle on a table, and went off to take his shower. Cal was left staring at the family pictures, the bagpipes, the bare hints of a life that had taken second place to police work. He felt sorry for MacTaggart, wanted to help him.

Cal finished his whiskey, and poured himself another.

Building courage, he realized suddenly. It was going to be hard to talk about the religion to the cop, would force him to a new level of his own belief. To be *questioned* about it.

MacTaggart came back in five minutes, freshly dressed and washed, but looking no less weary and sick.

He sat down and poured himself another drink. "So, Cal," he said casually, "you never *did* tell me. How's the research working out? Did you get what you wanted out of it?"

The interrogation was still on. Another phase, Cal realized, had gone by: the subject had been given a moment alone to meditate, arrange his thoughts. He resented MacTaggart's cleverness, his cop skills.

Resented? Why? Why not simply *tell* him . . .

"It's . . . it's been interesting, Dennis. The thing that would surprise you . . . is that the people I've met who practice the religion are all . . . all very reasonable, nice people."

MacTaggart nodded attentively. "Is that so?" he said. "What sort of people, Cal?"

There was a pause. They looked at each other for a second. Each understanding the gambit, and knowing the other understood.

"All kinds, Dennis. No crazies. People like you or . . . or me. Professionals. Dentists. Lawyers. And then ordinary hard-working types. They're not just street people. This isn't a cult. It's a religion, just as important to them, as much a part of their identity as . . ." Cal looked down, his hand rubbing the upholstery of the easy chair. "As your clan. The way you define yourself in terms of a certain tradition, a history. It's the same, in a way. The religion is their identity . . ."

MacTaggart stared at him intensely, nodded again. The room was very still. Outside on the street the kids playing stickball were yelling, and somewhere the buzzing motor of a lawn mower kicked over.

MacTaggart took a sip of his drink, then looked into his glass. He spoke very quietly.

"They've got you, don't they, Cal?"

The denial sprang to Cal's lips.

And never came forth.

"That's why you won't talk, isn't it?" MacTaggart went on. "You've gotten hooked in somehow. You! You're so ready to—Christ, how did you put it?—*respect* all the customs of men! You've just carried your respect to the point that you're standing up for the whole fucking bunch of 'em!"

"But it works, Dennis," Cal blurted. "I've—"

"Works?" MacTaggart repeated. "How, Cal? What does that mean?" MacTaggart pulled himself slowly up from his chair and walked across to Cal, stood in front of him. "How does it work?"

Sharon Laine. The possession. Spells. The honey-filled apple. The lawsuit. Congratulations. Spirits of the dead. Torey. Laurie. His head was full of it all now.

He had to tell it.

He tried to speak.

A sound filled his ears, a low rumbling voice. Like the throaty chant of the *akonrin*.

No, it was only the lawn mower passing nearer outside the window.

"How'd you like to get hauled in, Cal? I could do it to you, you know. Hold you as a material witness. Go down real well with your boss at the college, wouldn't it?"

Cal shook his head.

MacTaggart turned away with an expression of disgust and stalked to the corner of the room.

Cal stood up. *I'll tell you whatever I know*, his mind said.

His mind alone.

He couldn't make himself speak.

Then, horrified, he saw that MacTaggart was gesticulating wildly, and when he spun back to face Cal, his lips were moving. His face was red, his eyes blazing, sweat stood out at his hairline. He was screaming!

And Cal couldn't hear a thing. He had gone deaf.

No, not deaf. The sound of the lawn mower went on purring outside. Cal looked out the window. He could hear the kids playing in the street, the *thwack* of their sticks on the ball. Yet he was in some plane of time or space that separated him from MacTaggart. The detective might have been contained in an air-tight box of glass walls.

Then MacTaggart's arms fell to his side. Anger spent, frustrated by Cal's lack of reaction, the detective appeared to have given up.

"I'll give you a couple more days to think about it, Cal. Then I'll expect you to talk," MacTaggart said, and now the even voice came through with total clarity.

"Dennis," Cal said.

"Yes?" the cop said expectantly.

"Dennis, I . . . I want to go home now."

They said not a word on the ride back. Only when they stopped in front of Cal's apartment did MacTaggart speak.

"I can't figure it out, Cal. A guy like you. A man with a kid of his own. How can you hold out?"

Cal stared back, and said nothing.

"Go on," MacTaggart said, reaching across Cal's lap to fling open the door. "Get outta my sight."

Cal watched the car disappear down the street and round the corner at Ninth Avenue. And only then did he understand why he had been unable to speak a word against the religion.

Chapter 32

HE TRIED to have a normal evening.

He read articles on Charlton Heston and Lebanon in an old Sunday *Times Magazine*, but he couldn't concentrate. He watched a funny Lily Tomlin special with Torey, but he couldn't laugh.

Timmy Hackett, a new school friend of Chris's, had come for a sleepover. The night was quite warm, a bit of Indian summer, and the boys were settled in a pup tent in the garden. By eight-thirty they were in their sleeping bags with a mound of comic books, a thermos of hot chocolate, and a bag of Cheezits.

Cal and Torey lingered in the kitchen over coffee and Celestine's home-made apple pie. Torey tried a couple of times to start a conversation, but Cal couldn't sustain it. There was only one thing he wanted to talk about, but where did he begin? He had never told Torey anything about his contact with the police, about the suspicion of human sacrifice attached to the religion. Oscar's outraged response to the charge was lesson enough not to bring up the subject with Torey. But Cal was shaken after his experience with MacTaggart. The urge to confide in her, to test what could be a fragile hold on reality, had been building in him all evening.

Still, he sat picking over his pie until she gave him the opening.

"Cal, you're not listening to a thing I say. You've been like a zombie all evening. What's wrong?"

He pushed his plate away. "I had a call from a cop today," he said. "I'd met him at the warehouse when I went to get Laurie's things from storage, and then I talked to him at his precinct up in the *barrio*."

"For your research," she said.

"That's right."

There was a pause.

"What did he want today?" Torey asked.

"He wanted . . . to ask me some questions." He stopped again.

"Yes? About what."

"The case he's working on," he said. "You see, he's a homicide detective. There was a body found at the warehouse, and . . ." He forced the words out. "The police think it was a human sacrifice."

Torey looked at him, blinked, then turned away and scratched idly at the table top. Almost inaudibly, she said, "No, Cal. I don't want to hear this."

"Torey," he said. "There does appear to be . . . at least some possibility—"

She raised her head and glared at him. "Stop now, Cal. Please. I don't want to hear you tell me that my religion is killing people."

"But I have to talk about this, Torey. I can't just bottle it up. It's tearing me apart inside."

Something in his voice reached her, and the angry glare faded from her eyes. She was ready to listen.

He told her about how he had met MacTaggart, about the murdered child at the warehouse being found with the beads and saint statues and ceiba-wood altar, the trip to the morgue, the information MacTaggart had given him about the other slain children.

He told her about his own refusal to accept MacTaggart's theory that the killings had been sacrifices.

And finally, he told her how his resistance to the suspicion had begun to crumble. Told her what he had read in Quentin Kimball's diary, the record of another man's skepticism turned to guilty knowledge.

When he was done, she sat shaking her head for a minute. "Cal," she said then, "I can't imagine that you'd really believe this. If you told any of your colleagues at Columbia . . . they'd laugh you out of the department."

"I told Kate," Cal said soberly. "She didn't laugh."

"So you're convinced this is happening. You honestly think that children are being sacrificed to Voodoo gods."

"I think it's possible, yes."

"And that's what you told that detective, MacTaggart?"

Cal hesitated. "No."

"Why not? If you—"

"I couldn't."

"Couldn't?"

He bolted up from the table and gripped the sink, as though part of him wanted to run from her, from this confession, and he had to anchor himself in the room.

"I couldn't speak," he said, "because . . . because something wouldn't let me."

"Let you?"

He faced her again. "Torey, I was *possessed*."

"You—?" She shook her head, then half-smiled. "Cal. You don't really—?"

"Torey, I *wanted* to speak to MacTaggart. But it was as if something stopped me. I might've thought it was merely . . . a failure of will, or fear, or maybe doubts about implicating innocent people. But then MacTaggart started shouting at me, trying to shame me into talking, and suddenly I couldn't hear. I mean, I could hear everything else, but not *him*. And I knew he was being screened out. That I wasn't being *allowed* to hear, or to talk."

"Allowed?"

"By the gods," Cal said.

Torey rose and came to him. "Darling, possession isn't something that happens when you're standing in a room talking to a policeman. You've seen a possession. It's a religious experience . . . like a devout Christian getting 'the call,' or being born again or something. If you couldn't talk to that detective maybe it's because you respect my beliefs, because you don't want to see a faith, any faith, slandered."

"No, Torey. It wasn't anything like that. I know. I was possessed. The religion was protecting itself."

She held herself away from him, gazed at him with an expression of both concern and compassion. "Cal, that can't be true. If you couldn't talk, the problem came from somewhere inside of you, from your own—"

She stopped in mid-sentence, surprised by something behind Cal.

Cal turned around to see Timmy Hackett standing in his pajamas in the doorway. He looked absolutely petrified.

"What is it, Timmy?" Cal asked.

"Chris," the boy cried, "something's wrong with Chris. He's talking in his sleep."

Cal rushed out to the tent in the garden. The flap of the low tent was open and Chris lay sprawled diagonally across the rubber waterproof groundcloth, his sleeping bag twisted around the end

262

pole. Cal hunched down and crawled into the pup tent on his knees. He could hear Chris mumbling faintly. Cal felt around for the flashlight and found it under the other sleeping bag. He turned it on and aimed the beam at Chris's face. The boy stirred, but continued mumbling.

Cal knelt and put his ear to the boy's lips.

"I'm coming, I'm coming," came the fevered croon, a bit slurred, "coming Mommy. Help me, Chango, help me . . ."

Chango!

"Chris!" Cal shouted. "Wake up!"

But Chris went on mumbling. "Yes, Chango . . ."

Scared witless, Cal seized his son by the shoulders and started to shake him. "Chris! Wake up, damn it. Wake up!"

Torey poked her head in through the flap. Timmy Hackett was clinging to her.

"What's the matter, Cal?"

Cal didn't answer. He went on shaking Chris. "Listen to me! Chris! Chris!"

Timmy Hackett began to cry. In the small space the noise was intolerable.

Cal whirled on Torey. "Get him out of here!" he roared, and went back to shaking Chris, shouting into his ear.

But the boy didn't respond.

Cal slapped him. First the left cheek, then the right.

Timmy Hackett wailed.

"Cal! Stop it!" Torey crawled frantically into the tent.

Cal smacked the boy again harder, and again and again.

Torey grabbed Cal's shoulder to stop him. But he went on. In a frenzy.

Suddenly Chris's eyes popped open, staring, wide with shock. The boy was quiet for a moment, then he began to moan and whimper. Cal embraced him, pulled Chris's face against his own. Then Chris started to cry.

"Okay, Bean. It's all right now, everything's all right," Cal said softly, running his hands through the boy's hair. "Everything's okay."

"Give him to me," Torey said.

"No, he needs *me*," Cal snapped. He scooped up Chris's trembling body in his arms and carried him through the garden doors into the apartment. Cal sat down on the couch and cradled Chris in his lap, rocking him until he quieted.

Torey attended to Timmy Hackett, who refused to stay by himself in the tent. She took Timmy's sleeping bag into Chris's room, settled him there, then came back to the living room.

"Can I take him now?" she asked, extending her arms toward Chris's prostrate form. He was asleep again.

Cal nodded.

Torey carried Chris away to his room.

Cal remained inert on the sofa. What had come over him? He had slapped Chris, had actually hit him. To wake him? Or as punishment for dreaming . . .

Torey returned and sat at the other end of the sofa.

"What got into you, Cal?" she said. "You were . . . it looked like you might have hurt Chris."

"I was out of my mind for a second," he admitted, staring ahead. "When I realized they had him, too."

"They—?"

"He said 'Chango,' Torey. He was talking to Chango in his dreams. Don't you see what that means?" He turned and reached out to her, gripped her arm. "The gods have gotten to him, too, the same way they got me."

"What are you saying, Cal? Maybe Chris did say the name of one of the gods in his sleep. But he could've picked it up from you."

"I haven't discussed any of this research with him."

"Maybe you left your notes open on a table . . . or that journal you told me about. Chris might've seen the name there." Her voice sounded hollow and unconvincing.

"No," Cal said. "I wish the easy explanations were good enough, but they're not. It's no easier to explain this than the spells you did, or possessions. When I saw those things—when miracles happened—I didn't want to believe them. But finally I had no choice. And now I have to believe that . . . the gods are reaching into Chris, speaking to him."

"Because Chris murmured a name in his sleep? Cal, you know that Chris has been upset by his mother's death, he had other dreams—"

"And talked to his mother. I know. All of that makes sense now, I mean as part of the pattern. Laurie, her spirit, was a . . . a kind of messenger, preparing Chris to be called."

"Called? What are you—"

"Listen, Torey. Please. When I first got into studying the religion, Oscar Sezine told me that it wasn't merely by chance. He said the gods had some kind of mission for me, and that everything had led up to it. Even Laurie's death—the thing that brought me here, and freed me to . . . to love you—he said that was fated. Later, you said something similar: that we were intended to meet. I rejected all that at the time, the idea of time and history being planned, of there being any such thing as destiny, or fate, or karma. And I still *want* to reject it. Only I can't anymore. Now I've seen and felt events being controlled. Now when I hear Chris talking to a god, I know that he's the one they were after all along —ever since he stumbled on that sacrifice in the park. I know that the reason I've studied the religion is because I was *made* to study it. I was *led* to it, so I'd understand it and be ready to give the gods what they want."

He heard the rising panic in his voice, and saw that she had heard it, too. He stared into her eyes, but could find no belief in them, no sign that she agreed with him.

She asked very quietly, "What do you think the gods want from you, Cal?"

"Don't you see? They want Chris. His *life*. They want me to give up Chris to be sacrificed."

As soon as the words came from his mouth, Cal had to stop and wonder at what he was saying. It was a large leap, maybe an insane one, from hearing Chris murmur a name in his sleep to believing in gods who wanted his child's life.

He looked intensely at Torey, reading the confusion and disbelief in her face, but feeling an unspoken commitment that she would stand by him, whatever that would mean.

He clutched her arm tighter. "Maybe we should take Chris out of the city," he said, his voice growing desperate. "Maybe I should . . . should take him away. We'll go . . . we'll—"

He broke off, staring at the table. Of course the idea of running away was ludicrous. What was he running from? Did he actually believe that gods could take his son?

Torey covered his hand with hers. "Cal?"

He looked up.

"Cal, I'll go wherever you want, I'll do anything you want to do. But I don't think leaving the city is the answer. You have to . . . find a way to trust that nothing is going to happen to Chris. I'm sure there's somebody in the religion who'll tell you everything is all right, that there's nothing to worry about."

Slowly he raised his head and sighed. He felt a smile creeping onto his lips, a sad smile of irony and defeat. He had once thought he could cure her of her superstition, and now he was beginning to believe not only that her superstitions were true, but far more powerful than even she had asserted—more powerful, and more malevolent.

Had he imagined it all? Was it only a trick of the mind?

He reached out to her again. "Help me," he said, exhausted. "Help me, Torey. Help me save Chris."

She sat without speaking for a very long time, holding his hand and looking searchingly into his eyes. At last she said:

"Just tell me what you want me to do."

Chapter 33

ALL HE COULD DO the next morning was sit in his office and brood.

He believed.

But if you really thought children were being sacrificed to gods who could possess people, if you really accepted this, then you also had to believe you could appeal to them, ask for their intervention in fate, in the affairs of the world. And then you had to believe that sacrificing children would save the world.

Which meant you were insane.

Had Quentin Kimball gone insane?

Cal tried to teach his first class of the morning. But his mind kept drifting away. Several times he referred to the South Pacific islands broadly grouped under the term "Oceania," and noticed that each time he mentioned the word a restless whisper rippled through the students in the lecture theater. Finally a pretty sophomore raised her hand to ask if the word "orisha" he had been using was the Polynesian language's equivalent of "Oceania" and, for her notes, how the word was spelled.

Shocked by his unconscious lapse, Cal covered himself awkwardly. "You must have heard me incorrectly," he said.

But of course all forty-eight students had heard him. He fooled no one.

He returned to his office and told the department secretary to find two of his graduate students to take over his afternoon classes, and sat down to wait for Torey's call. She had offered to arrange a consultation with Voto. At first Cal had rejected the idea. He wanted to break away from the influence of the religion. But Torey argued that if Cal believed the gods had designs on Chris, then there was no one better than a *santero* to provide a prescription for saving him.

Her call didn't come.

At ten-thirty the phone finally rang, and he snatched it up, certain that it was Torey to tell him the appointment had been made.

It was a graduate student requesting a conference. Cal made an appointment for later in the week and hung up.

Was he really waiting on tenterhooks to find out if a man who ran a hardware store would consent to explain why the gods were visiting his son through dreams?

At eleven o'clock the phone rang again. It was Beverly Hackett, demanding to know what the hell had gone on down there last night, and was it true Cal had beaten Chris in front of Timmy, because you just didn't do that to children . . .

Cal managed to calm her by shamelessly playing on her sympathies, describing Chris as suffering one of his many terrible nightmares since becoming a motherless child. Timmy had exaggerated a bit, Cal said, there was nothing to worry about, Chris was fine, he had gone off to school this morning, happy and eager.

Wasn't Chris fine? Perhaps there would have been no clamor last night, Cal thought, if he hadn't overreacted himself. Wasn't Torey's suggestion a possibility? That Chris had inadvertently picked up the god's name, seen it in Cal's notes left open on the desk, and then incorporated it into his dream?

Possible, sure.

Only it wasn't the *possible* that happened to Chris. It was the impossible. The gods were inside Chris. They were calling to him in his dreams.

Would it save Chris if he made Torey give up the religion? Or if he had nothing more to do with it himself? Did the world—the *gods*—stop existing if you closed your eyes? Did it make any more sense to ask a hardware dealer for a prescription?

The questions were driving him crazy. He wanted to see other people, to hear Harvey Rayburn tell him that Voodoo was a waste of time, nothing serious.

Ɔ ● Ɛ

Torey had still not called by noon. He went down to the faculty dining room, and the sound of lively conversation and clattering silverware worked as an antidote to his anxiety. As he left the cashier's desk with his tray, he was hailed by Harvey Rayburn, who was sitting with Leon Farber, one of the leading lights of the department. Farber had left on a field trip before Cal arrived in June, and Harvey introduced them as Cal came up to the table.

"Cal Jamison?" Farber asked. "The young man Kate recommended so highly?"

Farber had just returned from ten weeks working in the recently excavated stone ruins at Inyanga and Dhlo-Dhlo in Zimbabwe, and was recounting his adventures. He was a short barrel-chested man with a narrow face and a high forehead capped by frizzy white hair. Cal listened to his vivid descriptions, glad to be distracted. Farber concluded his monologue with a light-hearted account of meeting a mulatto elephant hunter who claimed to be the issue of a union between a Bantu woman and Errol Flynn.

"I almost believed him," Farber said with a laugh.

Harvey stood and said, "I have to run. I've got a tutorial."

Cal was on the verge of leaving, too, when Farber turned to him. "So how are you adjusting? Kate told me about your book on the Zokos. She said you'd planned to spend the summer on it."

"Well, I'd planned to," Cal said, "but something else—"

He stopped abruptly. He was in no condition to be talking about Voodoo.

They'll laugh you out of the department.

But it was already too late.

"Yes?" Farber said curiously. "What did you do instead?"

Cal hesitated. "I've been studying primitive African religions."

"Oh?" Farber said appreciatively. "What particular aspect?"

Cal waffled and tried to avoid any mention of Voodoo. "Specifically," he said, "the way primitive beliefs have been syncretized into the religious practices of groups living here in the city."

Farber regarded him curiously. "Do I understand correctly," he said after a moment, "that you're referring to Voodoo?"

Cal was surprised how quickly Farber had seen through his attempt to hide his meaning. Then it struck him that Farber looked no different than any of the people he had seen at the *guëmilere*.

"Are you . . . familiar with the subject?" Cal asked.

"No, not really," Farber said. "I do know a fair amount about the fundamentals of African religion, of course, and I know it's filtered into the Latin American ethnic groups in the city. But I don't know the details. How did you get interested in it?"

Cal answered briefly, omitting any mention of MacTaggart and human sacrifice. Once he got into that he doubted he'd be able to say anything without sounding like a crackpot, jabbering that he was even afraid for his own son.

"I imagine it's intriguing," Farber said. "Though Kate made your other book sound so exciting. What did she say when you took up this new research?"

Farber was being diplomatic, but Cal heard the undertone of disapproval.

"She's been very supportive," Cal said, knowing that would make a difference. "In fact, she gave me some notes Quentin Kimball made when he researched something similar in New Orleans."

Farber looked at him wide-eyed. "Quentin? I didn't know he'd ever written anything on Voodoo."

With regret, Cal thought that he must have violated Kate's confidence. She had probably never told anyone else about the notes, since they could be so damaging to Kimball's scholarly reputation.

"Well," Cal said, trying to dismiss the subject, "these were just casual observations. None of it was meant for publication."

"Oh." Farber paused reflectively. "Wonderful man he was, Kimball. Brilliant mind and a very decent fellow."

"You knew him?"

"Oh yes. He was still teaching at Oxford when I went there on a Rhodes in thirty-eight. I met Kate there at the same time. They'd been married for five or six years then. Lovely couple they were, great love story. The way the legend went, they'd met somewhere out in the bush, crossed paths somewhere out in the middle of Africa, and that was it. They were never apart again." Farber shook his head. "Very sad the way it ended. Terrible tragedy."

Cal thought at first Farber must be talking about the end of the marriage, Kimball's death. But the mention of tragedy was charged with darker implications.

"What tragedy?" Cal asked.

There was a glint of astonishment in Farber's look. "I thought you and Kate were very close. Hasn't she ever told you about . . . losing the child."

"His illness, yes."

There was a silence. Farber's thin lips twitched, the reflex of the conspirator tempted to yield up secrets. "I guess she preferred to tell it that way—to save all the questions. But it wasn't an illness."

"Wasn't . . . ?" Cal murmured, incredulous. Hadn't there been something about the child's problem in Kimball's journal, his concern for his son's condition? It had certainly seemed—

Farber's voice cut through his thoughts.

270

"Nothing like an illness, in fact. The boy was a normal healthy seven-year-old."

"But he died."

"He was kidnapped and murdered," Farber said.

Cal slumped back slowly in his chair. The words fell into his mind again and again like some black hellish rain onto the waters of night, rippling out into more, and blacker thoughts.

Farber went on. "I'm really surprised you didn't know. They'd doted on the boy, only child and all that. You can imagine how hard it hit. Kate managed to hold up somehow—the woman's a phenomenon anyway, God knows. But it was a different story with Kimball. Went all to pieces. A couple of months after the body was found he got up early one morning and made himself an omelet, a mushroom omelet of all things—damnedest kind of suicide. The mushrooms were a poison variety he'd gotten somewhere, a slow painful death without any hope of saving him."

"Jesus," Cal whispered.

"Maybe he picked that way because it gave Kate a chance to pass it off as an accident—you know, eating the wrong kind of mushroom. But there was no doubt he'd been despondent since the child's death."

"Did they ever catch the murderer?"

"Never. A maniac, obviously. It was absolutely the most gruesome kind of murder." Farber shuddered, then pushed his chair back from the table, evidently preparing to leave, unwilling to dwell any longer on the crime. "Well, it was all a long time ago and Kate's obviously preferred to put the lid on. Maybe I shouldn't have said anything to—"

"Exactly how was the boy killed?" Cal insisted suddenly. His mind had been traveling down its own track.

Farber frowned at Cal, an apparent expression of distaste for a curiosity that was revealing itself as more bloodthirsty than sympathetic.

"Look," Cal pressed for a reply, "it's important that I know. How and where?"

Farber paused another second or two. "They found him in a field out in the countryside somewhere. He'd been mutilated." Farber stood up, anxious to escape his own indiscretion. "Now, if you'll excuse me—"

"What do you mean by mutilated? What had been done to him?"

"Good Lord, Jamison—"

"Tell me, please," Cal said urgently.

"Cut open, for Chrissakes!" Farber leaned forward and whispered as if over a grave. "Just split down the middle like . . . like a slaughtered animal."

"And the heart and stomach pulled out," Cal said, thinking aloud.

Farber stared at him. "Yes, I believe that's right. Now that's enough, I think. So if you'll excuse me, I have an appointment."

Ignoring the amenities, Farber hurried away, his disgust with Cal now all too evident.

∋ ● ∈

Hearing Torey's voice on the line, cool and impersonal, gave Cal no comfort. "This is Victoria Halowell. I'm sorry I'm not here to speak to you, but if you'll leave your name and number, I'll return your call just as soon as possible. Wait for the beep-tone and leave your message. Thank you."

Dutifully he announced himself for the answering machine, saying that he was at the office. He knew she carried a little remote gadget in her purse that allowed her to call in from the outside and hear her messages.

He paced the office, churning with thoughts of Kate and Kimball and what had been done to their child.

Sacrificed.

In 1940. Taken by the Obeah worshippers. They had killed the boy to propitiate the gods before they wreaked havoc upon the earth.

Obayifo: he who takes the children.

Taken by the gods?

Or *given?*

Kimball had been captivated by belief in the religion. But was it possible he had cooperated in the sacrifice of his own child? Given his flesh and blood, his most precious possession, for the sake of saving millions?

There was a kinder explanation; the journal showed that Kimball was struggling with guilt over his failure not to reveal what he had known about the earlier sacrifices to the police. Maybe he had finally reached a decision to tell what he knew, and then his own child had been abducted, to be held hostage as a guarantee of Kimball's silence.

Of course not. It made a nicer story, but it had the wrong ending. It explained only the kidnapping, not the murder. The more Cal turned it over in his mind, the more convinced he became that Kimball was implicated in the killing of his own child.

And Kate?

She had lied, had allowed Cal to believe for as long as he'd known her that the child was the victim of an illness. Farber's rationale made sense: she had not told the truth because she could not face going over all the gruesome details, reminding herself of them in any way. Wouldn't she have warned Cal away from the research if she had known what had happened to her son? If she knew how Voodoo had shattered Kimball's sanity? Evidently she was also keeping secrets from herself. She knew that Kimball had researched Voodoo, but she had blocked out the unthinkable. She could not accept the child's murder as anything but the work of a maniac. Clearly she had thought Kimball committed suicide not as self-punishment, but merely as an escape from unbearable grief.

The death of Scotty Kimball would have been horrible enough as nothing more than history, the tragic past of one of his dearest friends.

But this struck Cal deeper, pierced him to his soul. Because he knew the history of the prophecy. It was all happening again exactly as it had to Kimball.

Happening to him.

He had held back what he knew from MacTaggart.

He had become a believer.

The symptoms of mental disturbance Cal had observed in Chris must also have afflicted Scotty Kimball. Now Cal knew what Kimball must have meant when he recorded his worries about his son.

The jangle of the phone jarred Cal out of his thoughts. He grabbed up the phone as a man in a vacuum might seize an oxygen mask, his link to survival.

"Torey?" he cried without waiting. He had no words for anyone but her.

"Cal, what's wrong, darling?"

Thank God.

"You sound awful," she went on. "Even your voice on the machine—"

"I can't explain now," he broke in. "But I know I'm not wrong."

"About what?"

"Chris. He's been chosen, I'm sure of it, chosen to be sacrificed. We've got to—"

"Darling, please, nothing's going to happen to Chris. I promise you, we'll keep him safe. We'll do whatever is necessary."

He was aware of how slowly she was talking, putting great emphasis on the pacifying words as though calming a child afraid of the dark.

"Have you talked to Voto?" he said. "Will he help us?"

"He's agreed to do a reading, yes," she replied. "This evening as soon as the store closes."

"Can't he see us sooner?"

"That's only four hours from now," she said. "I don't think you could ask for more."

Yes, it was soon enough, he supposed. The gods, if there were gods, planned for decades, millennia, eternity. Four hours was no time at all on their timetable.

"All right," he said, "this evening. I'll meet you there."

"At six," she agreed. "And Cal, he said you should bring an egg."

"An egg?" he repeated. "As an offering?"

"No, it's something he needs to do this particular kind of reading."

"Then he knows what it's about."

"He knows it's for a father worried about his son's life," Torey replied. "I didn't mention . . . the rest."

"Didn't—" Cal flared. "Torey, how the hell can he—"

"Listen, Cal," she interrupted, her voice hardening. "However convinced you may be about this sacrifice idea, there are believers who'd be outraged by the accusation. If Voto can do a reading that tells you Chris has nothing to fear—that he'll grow up strong and healthy and live a long and happy life—that ought to satisfy you."

"Yes," Cal said, "that's what I need to hear."

"You will, darling," she said, softening her voice. "I'm sure you will. I'll see you at six."

As he lowered the receiver he thought he heard her add three more words. He knew what they were and they should have helped.

But they didn't.

Chapter 34

HE WAS OUTSIDE the hardware store at twenty minutes to six. He had been unable to remain cooped up in his office any longer, torturing himself with dire fantasies. Pacing the sidewalk outside the store, he caught repeated glimpses through the glass-paneled door. Ramon Suares—Voto—stood behind the counter, piling up hardware supplies for his customers and tallying their bills.

The scene taunted Cal. He asked himself again: how could he believe this shopkeeper would help Chris, that Chris even needed such help?

Precisely at six o'clock an assistant in the store flipped a card hanging behind the glass door to read CLOSED. Just a minute later Torey got out of a taxi. She looked chic in a hat with a snap-down brim and a tailored wool coat, a concession to the chilly October air. Cal wondered if she had dressed so well in deference to the *santero*, then noticed the rolled-up blueprints protruding from her tote bag and realized she had come direct from a business meeting.

"Hi, darling." She kissed him. "Been waiting long?" So casually that they could have been meeting outside a restaurant or theater, not for the soothsaying of a Voodoo priest.

"A couple of minutes," he said, not wanting to be chided for his nervousness.

But she could read it in his face. "Everything will be fine, darling," she said, taking his arm. They started across the sidewalk. "You remembered the egg, didn't you?"

He pulled up. "Damn. No." The simple chore had been crowded out of his mind by all the worrying.

"Never mind," Torey said and glanced around. "There's a superette." She nodded across the avenue. "We'll pick it up now."

"Will that fill the bill—any old chicken egg from a grocery store?"

"Is there any other kind?" she replied lightly. "All that's important is that you bring it."

They bought a dozen "Grade A Large" in a Styrofoam container. Cal took out one of the eggs and carried it in his hand while Torey put the rest in her tote bag.

They crossed back to the hardware store and Torey tapped on the glass. Roman Suares was pushing a broom along one of the aisles. He saw Torey and smiled, and let them in.

Upstairs in his apartment, they went first as before to wash their hands. When Cal and Torey returned to the small living room the *santero* was waiting for them, seated cross-legged on the floor. The wiry Puerto Rican had changed out of the denims he wore in his shop into a maroon silk bathrobe with a gaudy picture of an elephant hand-painted on the back. He looked, Cal thought, as if he might be a boxer named Kid Jumbo. Spread on the floor in front of him was a square piece of rush matting, roughly six or seven feet on each side. On the edge of the mat, just in front of the *santero*, a number of seashells had been lined up. Cal stared at the shells. He counted twelve, all very similar to the one that Chris had brought home from the park, their surfaces etched with designs and the "mouths" filed down. Off to one side was a large empty clay bowl.

The *santero* motioned them to sit down at either side of him. Torey sat along the edge of the mat to Voto's right, Cal to the left. Then Voto said to Torey, "Your friend was here before. Is he now *yaguo?*"

Cal remembered the word from the A.C.H.E. blackboard, Yoruban for "initiate."

"No, Voto," Torey answered. "He is still *aleyo.*"

A nonbeliever. Technically, anyway, that was correct, since he had undergone no ritual of initiation.

"Does he understand what I shall do?" Voto said. "If not, please explain."

Torey nodded and looked across the mat to Cal. "Voto is going to do a *registro de los caracoles*—a reading of the shells. It's the system by which we divine the will of the gods."

"The Table of Ifa," Cal murmured by reflex, thinking of Kimball's journal. The same method was used to foretell the events of the decade.

276

"Then you already know about it?" Torey said.

"A little, from my research. I know the shells are considered to be the mouthpieces of the gods, but I don't know how they speak."

Cal glanced to Voto, expecting the *santero* to participate in the explanation. But his eyes were closed, the skin of his face stretched taut over the high cheekbones. He had suggested Torey's lesson, apparently, only to occupy his client while he entered a kind of trance.

Torey lowered her voice, respecting the mood. "Voto will cast the shells on the *estera*"—she gestured to the mat—"four times. Each time they will make an *ordun*, a pattern, depending on how they fall, how many with the mouth up, how many down. Each *ordun* represents certain gods communicating with us, and is associated with a particular proverb. The four proverbs together, according to which they are, and which ones are repeated, will provide the *dillogun*—the reading."

This whole system of divination, Cal realized despite his anxiety, was remarkably similar to the *I Ching*, the ancient Chinese "Book of Changes." That one relied on casting three coins or, in a purer form, forty-nine bamboo reeds to form patterns related to specific prophecies. As skeptical as one could be about such ancient magic, it was difficult not to be impressed by the fact that two such different cultures as the Chinese and the African had both conceived nearly identical means for predicting the future.

"I am ready to begin," Voto announced sharply, and his black eyes focused on Cal. "The egg, please." He picked up the clay bowl from the corner of the mat and thrust it forward.

Cal placed the egg in the bowl, which Voto returned to the mat. But the priest continued gazing at him.

"Victoria tells me you are concerned for your son, afraid for his life. Why?"

Cal lowered his eyes. How much did he dare say?

"He's been having dreams," Cal replied at last. "He sees the gods in these dreams. Last night I heard him speak to one of them. I mean, I heard him say the god's name in his sleep."

"Which god?"

"Chango."

Voto pursed his lips, like a doctor mulling a diagnosis. "And what do you think Chango wants from your son?"

There was another silence. Voto's black eyes remained fixed on Cal.

"I don't know," Cal said finally. "I'm not sure he wants anything. Torey . . . Victoria brought me here because she said you'd know."

Voto continued to focus on Cal. For the first time Cal had the sense that this outwardly ordinary man possessed some inner fire, an ability to perceive the lies and half-truths through the unblemished lens of his own virtue. He recognized Voto as a priest.

The *santero* turned from Cal at last and with one sweep of his hand across the mat gathered up all the shells into a fist. He shook the fist like a dice-player, then opened the fingers, pressed his other hand over the open palm, and rolled the shells rapidly between the two hands. At the same time he began to chant—more of the cavelike sounds Cal had heard at the *guëmilere:*

Chango Manu Cote Chango Manu Cote
Olle Masa Chango Olle Massa Chango
Arambansoni Chango Arambansoni Chango

Cal thought the language must be Yoruban, but the only word he could identify was the name of the god. Two or three times he looked over at Torey, hoping for a silent message, or at least the reassuring contact. But her eyes were always trained on the chanting priest.

After several minutes the chant ended, and at the same moment the *santero* flung his hands apart, letting the shells scatter onto the mat. Cal started to add how many were face up, how many down. But he had barely begun when the *santero*, needing no more than a glance, announced what he had seen:

"This is the twelfth *ordun*, known as Ellila—the proverb which says: 'Man is defeated by his own crimes.' "

Cal had only an instant to speculate on how that might apply to him or Chris. Voto was chanting and quickly gathering up the shells again, rolling them rapidly between his palms. They made a loud ratcheting sound, like the noise of some monstrous cricket.

Again they were cast onto the mat.

Voto looked at the pattern only for a second. "It is the Ocana Sode," he said, "the very first *ordun* in the Table of Ifa. The proverb which says: 'The world was created by one.' "

Deftly he scooped up the shells and repeated the procedure for a third throw.

This time the *santero* did not announce the result so quickly. For a long time he stared at the scattered shells, as though the pattern was difficult to interpret. Cal made his own tally: only one of the twelve shells had landed with the "mouth" up.

"Well?" Cal prompted.

"It is the Ocana Sode again," the Voodoo priest answered, markedly subdued.

" 'The world was created by one,' " Cal recited the proverb. "So what does it mean?"

Voto said nothing. He started gathering up the shells again, but slowly now, deliberately.

Cal glanced anxiously to Torey.

"He can't tell you what any of it means until the fourth casting." She meant to soothe him, but there was an edge in her voice. Obviously she was troubled, too, by the priest's reaction.

Voto was chanting again, rolling the shells between his hands for the final toss.

Cal closed his eyes. Praying. To what or to whom he didn't know, but he was frightened. Suddenly there was an atmosphere in the room as tangibly charged as the air before a summer storm. He could almost believe that with the fourth casting, if the pattern came up wrong, lightning would shoot down from the heavens and consume them all.

The chant ended. Cal heard the ratcheting noise cease, then the soft patter of the shells landing on the rush matting.

He opened his eyes. The pattern of shells registered almost at once. They had fallen nearly in a circle, except for one at the center, and only that one was turned up, showing the mouth. For the third time it was the same *ordun*, the same proverb: *the world was created by one.*

What were the odds of twelve shells falling in the same ratio three times in a row?

Cal switched his gaze to the *santero.*

He was sitting motionless, heavy-lidded and pale as he stared at the shells.

"Tell it!" Cal erupted. "What does it mean?"

"Cal!" Torey admonished him.

The priest raised his eyes to meet Cal's. "It cannot be done," he said.

"Can't—?"

"I am not able to help you," the *santero* explained softly.

"What do you mean? You've done the reading, you've thrown the shells. You must have an interpretation. Now I want to be told!"

"I am sorry," the *santero* said, "but it is beyond my understanding." He leaned forward and started to pick up the shells, one by one as though gathering pebbles out of a tide.

Cal lunged and grabbed the man's thin wrist. "Wait a second. We came for a reading, damn it!"

"Cal," Torey said, only a faint gasp this time.

The *santero* glared at Cal. "Let go of me, señor." The voice was extremely quiet, yet somehow managed to convey a threat. Cal held on another moment, then let go.

The *santero* finished picking up the shells, went to the cabinet on the mantel, and deposited the shells in a drawer. Cal leapt up, moved in his wake. Grabbing Voto's shoulder, he spun him around.

"Look, I came to you because I'm scared, because I'm afraid the gods want my son. If what you saw proves that I'm right, you've got to tell me at least that much!"

The priest stared back implacably.

Cal struggled to control himself. An urge to violence rose in him, and he felt capable of seizing the *santero* and strangling him. "I've got to know so I can keep him safe!" Cal shouted. "I'm not going to let anything take him from me." His voice broke. He was half-sobbing in desperation.

Voto spoke. "Your son could not be safer, señor. Nobody will take him from you."

It took a moment to sink in. Then Cal realized he was being told what he wanted to hear. But perhaps only for that reason, because it would pacify him. "Then what was that big silent act all about?" he demanded. "I still want to hear the shells interpreted."

The *santero* said nothing. Cal felt the muscles in his arms tightening.

Torey was behind him now. She had her hand on his sleeve, pulling him back. He whirled on her savagely. "He's going to tell me. I won't leave until he does! He's done these readings thousands of times, right? I'll bet there's always a big song-and-dance for the customers. Well, I want mine!"

Torey appealed to the *santero*. "Can't you answer him, Voto? Why *are* you doing this?"

"Forgive me, Victoria," he replied. "I have told you everything that I can."

"Nothing!" Cal roared. "You've told us nothing!"

His voice died away in the corners of the apartment. There was no way to change the situation, he knew.

"Christ, I don't know why I ever agreed to this," he declared bitterly. "Let's get the hell out of here."

He grabbed Torey by the arm, but she stood rooted in place, resenting his rough grip and the intimation of blame. When he let go, she tossed a backward glance of apology to the *santero*, and started to follow.

Cal, halfway to the door, stepped around the straw mat, and noticed the egg lying in the bowl.

"What about the egg?" he said sharply to Voto. "Why did you ask for it?"

The *santero* shrugged. "It was not needed, after all," he said casually.

Somehow the untouched egg fired Cal's anger anew, a symbol of the pointlessness of the whole visit. Refusing to leave it behind, he bent to pick it up.

The *santero* started forward. "Never mind, señor. I will dispose of it."

He raised a hand, a pacifying gesture, and Cal saw tension in his stance. For some reason the egg was very important to the priest, a symbol for him, too. Dispose of it? Maybe it was going to be used to work a spell against Chris. Cal crouched quickly and grabbed for the white oval.

His fingers had barely touched the shell when it disintegrated, fell away, a white powder fine as talc. Bared within was a reddish jelly-like substance. It held the shape of the egg for a second, then began to ooze down into a puddle the color of blood.

Torey stared at it in disgust and whispered something inaudible.

Cal spun to face Voto again. The *santero's* face was an expressionless mask. There would be no interpretation of this either.

Cal put his arm around Torey and guided her out of the apartment.

⊐ ● ⊏

Night had come down. They stood on the sidewalk outside the store, bathed in the pink light of its neon sign, and for a couple of minutes neither spoke.

"Do you want to go home?" she said then.

"No, I can't. I've got to help Chris."

"Cal . . ." She reached for him.

He pulled away. "What?" he barked harshly. "Going to tell me again I'm worried about nothing? Goddamnit, you saw the same

281

things I did. Do you really need to have them interpreted? The gods want my son's life!"

"He said Chris was safe," she reminded him.

"He was lying. Or telling riddles. Maybe he meant safe with the gods."

"He said nobody would take him from you."

"I don't believe him," Cal muttered, then started to walk away.

"Where are you going?" Torey asked, following.

"Christ, I don't know." He ran clawed fingers through his hair as though trying to reach down into his skull and untangle the thoughts.

"Then come with me," she begged.

"Where?"

"Home. To Chris."

Cal kept walking.

She stayed behind him as they went another block. "Listen, darling," she said finally. "Maybe you're right, maybe we should go away for awhile. If it would help you feel that he's safe . . . we could take a trip, go to Europe maybe, or—"

He raised his voice to interrupt her. "How far do you go," he asked brusquely, "to get away from a god?"

"Oh Cal, really!" Her exasperation broke through. "You can't take that egg trick as proof of anything. I've seen all kinds of tricks done at ceremonies. Magic is part of the religion—of *all* ancient religions; you should know that as well as anyone. It doesn't necessarily mean that something evil is going to happen."

He stopped and faced her. "Torey, that was more than a trick. That egg was never out of our sight from the time we bought it. One of an ordinary dozen, and it turns out to be full of blood." He grasped her by the arms. "Torey, I *believe* now. I wish like hell I didn't. I wish I'd never heard of Voodoo or studied it. But I did, and now I can't erase what I've seen. I have to believe there are meanings and messages and mysteries that simply must be accepted, whether or not they can be explained. And I know what's going to happen now, because it's all happened before."

She gazed at him, drained of argument. A flickering light played over her face, shifting the planes of shadow so that one moment she looked angry, in the next loving and empathetic. Cal turned around and saw they were standing in front of an appliance store with a bank of large-screen television sets in the window, all switched on to the same image of a burning tenement.

Torey said, "What do you mean it's all happened before?"

He faced her again. "At the beginning of every decade there's a special reading of the shells by the high priests—a kind of long-range forecast. The one for this decade must have predicted some sort of terrible world catastrophe. The nuclear holocaust, maybe. Now everything possible is being done to appease the gods, change the course of fate. And children are being delivered up as offerings."

"How do you know about this special reading?"

"I read about one that was done in 1939. It predicted the Second World War, the camps, Hiroshima, all the death and destruction. The result was the same then: reversion to human sacrifice. So much of it went on that the *babalaos* denounced it, and it was stopped. I think there are some believers who say that if only it hadn't been, if they'd kept it up, the gods would have answered their prayers. And that's why they won't stop this time."

"But even if that were true," she said, "why do you think one of them has to be Chris?"

He shook his head. "I can't answer that. Any more than I could give you reasons for most of the billions of seemingly accidental events that somehow add up to history. Things *happen*. One thing leads to another and there's a pattern. Somehow Chris and I stumbled into this pattern, became part of it—or maybe we always were—and now I can see where it leads . . ."

One thing leads to another.

As things do.

The conversation came back to him: the first time he had met Oscar. It was Oscar who'd said right at the start that none of it was an accident—that Cal's interest in Voodoo was destined to serve a purpose.

Oscar had known. Then.

Cal ran suddenly to the curb and hailed an empty cab.

"Where are we going?" Torey said.

"You're going home," Cal told her as the cab pulled up. "I'm going to see Oscar Sezine, and I think it's better if I go alone."

"But I want to help."

"You will—by staying with Chris." He held the door open for her. "Please."

She kissed him and got into the cab. It pulled away, her face looking back at him framed in the rear window.

He paused, took a breath. The flickering light from the row of television sets attracted his eye again. Behind the store window a half-dozen rockets blasted off and headed toward the sky. Was this the day they sent up another space shuttle? Or was it some commentary on the new defense budget?

Man is defeated by his own crimes . . .

As he watched the missiles fly across the many screens, the *ordun* was in his head—oddly, not the one that had been repeated, but the one he had heard only once.

He turned and searched hurriedly for another cab.

It was no mystery what the gods had in store for the world if they were angry. No mystery at all.

Chapter 35

THE STREET DOORS of the A.C.H.E. were open. A melange of sounds converged in the lobby from different corners of the building. Disco music, gabbling voices, a burst of laughter, and a hollow rhythmic knocking like someone beating a primitive wooden instrument, or perhaps a dry gourd.

There was no one in the reception booth tonight. Cal made his way to the rear offices and found the door locked. He rapped on it a few times and waited, but the door remained closed.

The rhythmic *toc-toc-toc* was louder here, and he followed it, moving farther along the hallway to an open door. Looking inside, he saw it was a game room. The A.C.H.E. seemed to be fulfilling its role as a community center, keeping the local kids off the streets and out of trouble. A girl and a boy of about fifteen were at a ping-pong table, batting a ball back and forth. *Toc-toc-toc*. Some older boys were hunched over small tables playing chess.

"Anybody know where I can find Oscar?" Cal called out.

"Second floor," someone in the chess huddle replied offhandedly.

The second-floor corridor was dark except for a stripe of yellow light shining out through the glass panel of a classroom door. Cal walked to the window and stopped, instantly stunned by what he saw inside. The desks and chairs had all been pushed back against the walls, leaving a broad arena of open floor. In the center, his back to the window, was Oscar, seated astride a body of which Cal could see only the legs, clad in trousers, protruding from beneath Oscar's buttocks. Oscar was bent forward over the upper torso of the man lying on the floor so that Cal could not see clearly what he was doing. But from the set of his shoulders, and glimpses of his rapidly moving arms, it appeared he was pummeling—or *stabbing* —the man beneath him.

Twenty-odd young men and women stood on either side of Oscar, pitilessly watching him work over his victim.

Cal was transfixed by the spectacle. It was a long moment before he could think clearly. *Find a phone. Call the police. Get away from here.*

He was on the point of dashing away when Oscar leaned back, arms falling to his sides, his task completed. Then Oscar stood, and Cal could finally see the body whole, including the bland fixed expression on its painted face.

The body was a life-size dummy.

Could this have been the *demonstration* for a sacrifice?

The question had barely formed—Cal's mind stubbornly clinging to its own foolish reality—when he saw Oscar motion to one of his spectators, a young girl, to sit down on the dummy. Cal watched the girl pounding her fists on the dummy's chest—the same technique, he realized, he had seen the paramedics use when they first tried to revive Mrs. Ruiz. Oscar was providing another community service.

Cal blew out a breath of air that it seemed he had been holding in his lungs forever, then knocked sheepishly on the door.

Oscar glanced up, his brow furrowing with concern as soon as he recognized Cal. He lingered in the room briefly, pointing out various students, arranging an order for each to practice the lesson, then slipped out into the corridor.

"I'd say this is an unexpected pleasure," Oscar said, laying a hand on Cal's shoulder, "but from the way you look, my friend, I can see this visit is anything but social."

Cal's reply tumbled out breathlessly. "I'm in trouble, Oscar. I don't know anyone to ask for help except you. Though I'm not sure you can help me at all—or that you'll even be willing to."

Oscar reared back slightly, seemingly stung by the intimation that he might withhold cooperation.

"You're obviously wound up pretty tight, Cal. Let's go up to my rooms and you can have a drink while you tell me what's wrong."

As they climbed the stairs, Cal confessed that if he appeared to be in shock, it was partly the result of arriving at the classroom window and not realizing at first that he wasn't seeing a real body on the floor.

286

"Oh dear," Oscar said, "yes, I can imagine how that must have looked." And then as the vision actually formed in his imagination, he began to chortle good-naturedly. "Oh my goodness. What on earth must you have thought was going on in there?"

Cal smiled wanly.

Actually, Oscar informed him, the technique he'd been demonstrating was part of a Red Cross course in CPR training—cardiopulmonary resuscitation. "So many of our young people still have acquaintances, or even members of their family, who are heavy drug users," Oscar explained. "There's no telling when they might have to deal with someone who's overdosed. CPR can mean the difference between life and death."

⌐ ● ⌐

In Oscar's living room, Cal accepted a brandy. Despite Oscar's urging, however, he could not settle himself into a chair. While Oscar perched on the corner of a low bookcase, sipping the drink he had poured for himself, Cal restlessly paced the room.

"The first time I came here," he began, "you said the gods had a reason for steering me into Voodoo. I doubted you then, I laughed it off. But I don't any more. Now I know the reason."

Cal stopped and looked at Oscar, who was leaning forward like a student at one of his lectures. Then Cal spilled out the rest, and as he repeated the incidents he worked up a fresh fury against the forces that had entrapped him, and were endangering Chris. In telling it to Oscar, for whom the gods were not myth but reality, Cal's reasoning gained a certain momentum. There was no need to equivocate or apologize in presenting his fears, and his doubt fell away. He was inwardly convinced now that he was not in the least overwrought or muddled. He was only rightly terrified by a supernatural truth unknown to all but a few.

Oscar listened without interrupting—even when Cal spelled out his accusation that the religion was engaged in the bloodiest pagan rituals.

"Oscar, I don't know how deeply you're into that part. I suppose it's possible you've never heard anything about it—that these killings are being done by a small splinter group. I know there was a time, not too long ago, when such rituals were forbidden by the *babalaos*." He stopped pacing and faced Oscar, his voice rising as he continued. "But it's also possible that all your indignation was a complete con, that you know as well as I do that what I'm saying is true. But damn it, that doesn't matter now. I don't care if—" Cal faltered, realizing the implications of what he'd been about to say; then he went ahead anyway. "I'm not here to punish or prosecute you or anyone else for what's been done. I'll leave that to others. I want only one thing: to save my son, to get him free of . . . of the danger. And you're the only person who might be able to help."

Oscar finally took the cue to speak. Earnestly he asked, "What do you think I can do?"

"Get me the name of a *babalao*. Only a high priest would know the spell to protect Chris."

Oscar stared back. "The identity of the *babalaos* is the most closely guarded secret of—"

"But somebody has to know it," Cal shouted. "And you've built up too many contacts in the religion not to be able to find that somebody."

Oscar finished his drink and set the glass aside. He stood and walked across the room to face the window, though the curtains were drawn across it.

"You contend that these sacrifices are being done," he said, "in hopes of preventing some great catastrophe."

"Yes," Cal said firmly. "Because when the Table of Ifa was read for this decade, it predicted Armageddon."

Oscar nodded. "And if it *could* do that," he asked, his back still to Cal, "what would you say then?"

"About what?"

"About the sacrifice of a few lives for the sake of saving multitudes—of preserving all of human civilization."

Cal advanced slowly across the room. "Then you admit it. You're telling me that—"

Oscar whirled around, his green eyes ablaze, lightning crackling over the tropic lagoons. "No! You're telling *me!* And you insist I take it as the truth. All right, I will. I'll believe we're in an age as perilous as any the earth has ever known; that every means of seeing us through this peril has been called upon, even this one. But then what should I do? Choose you and your private peace ahead of everything else? Measure one life . . . or even ten lives, or twenty, a hundred, a *thousand*, against billions?"

Cal stood wordlessly, dumbfounded by the proposition as Oscar had stated it. A handful of human lives were being balanced against the survival of the entire planet. It was a monstrous absurdity. And yet if he had not become fully a believer, he would not be here at all, pleading for Chris to be spared.

Oscar was still staring, demanding an answer. Cal looked away.

"Oh God, Oscar," he murmured brokenly. "I'm lost. I don't know what's real anymore. I don't know what's right. I'm only sure that . . . I love my son. I can't give him up. If I've only imagined that he's been . . . called, then I still need the medicine, the cure, the spell—whatever it takes!—to make the nightmare go away. And if I haven't imagined it . . ."

His voice sank. He shook his head, shifted his gaze back to Oscar and added in a whisper. "I want mercy."

After a pause, Oscar said, "Let me see what I can find out. I'll speak to . . . people I know, see what I can learn to put your mind at ease."

Put my mind at ease, Cal thought. As though the problem was only in his mind. Was Oscar so quickly "believing" only because he judged Cal to be beyond rational debate?

Oscar's arm was around him now, guiding him to the door. Cal could imagine Oscar supplying the same support to one of the troubled neighborhood kids who sought his advice about more wordly matters—unwanted pregnancies, scrapes with the law.

"Don't write this off, Oscar," Cal blurted as they reached the door. "Please."

"Of course not. I'll start making calls as soon as you leave."

"And how long . . . before you might know something?"

"How can I tell you, Cal? I don't know for sure if I'll be able to find out what you want to know. All I can say is I see how much you're suffering. I wouldn't want you to suffer over this a moment more than necessary."

Oscar opened the door. As they exchanged one more glance, Cal saw in Oscar's face a compassion no less sincere and radiant than a pilgrim might see in the face of a saint.

∋ ● ∈

Oscar's call came late the next afternoon. He had found someone to prescribe a spell to protect a child from all harm.

"Even a threat from the gods?" Cal asked.

"It is a spell to guarantee that no one, man or god, will take your child from you."

Oscar would not answer directly, however, when Cal wanted to know if the spell had come from a *babalao*. "From everything you've told me, Cal, and that I've been able to tell others, this is said to be the spell you need. It comes from someone who understands your problem, and knows the cure."

The *cure*. Again a hint of ambiguity. The spell, Oscar might be saying, was merely a placebo, a device to purge imagined demons —perhaps a recommendation from some psychiatrist friend of Oscar's.

But Cal could pry loose no details about the chain of contacts through which Oscar had acquired it. "You simply mustn't press me for that," Oscar insisted. "I've done what you asked me. You must trust me."

The ceremony would consist of making offerings to the Seven African Powers, the most powerful deities in the Voodoo pantheon who together determined the most crucial matters of destiny. *Sacrificial* offerings, Oscar clarified: three animals to be killed in a very specific manner, their blood mingled in a clay cup, and drunk by whoever wished the gods' favor. There were, too, other small tasks to be carried out before the animals were killed—candles to be lit, herbs to be sprinkled over the killing ground. And it was all to take place within the boundaries of a *nefinda kilunga*—a field of death, a place where the spirits of the dead were congregated. It had to be done in the early hours of a new day, before the light and warmth of the sun dispelled the aura of the spirits.

Pencil in hand, hastily scrawling everything Oscar said, Cal listened without interruption. As though he were transcribing a recipe, he wrote down the ingredients of the spell—the names of the herbs, the list of procedures—never pausing to step back and judge the nature of what he was being told to do. *Get 1 dove, 1 turtl, 1 rstr.*

It was only when Oscar finished that the reality suddenly connected, jolting Cal as though his skin had grazed a high-voltage wire. *Go to a cemetery and sacrifice three animals!*

"I can't do this," he blurted into the phone, scanning what he'd written on the pad.

"I'm not the one who thinks you should," Oscar replied, cool and resolute. "What I've given you is to meet *your* need, not mine."

Cal could only thank him then, appreciating as well his suggestions about where to purchase the herbs, the animals, and a special knife for the killing.

For a long time after receiving the call, he debated whether to tell Torey. It was *his* problem, *his* private terror that needed fixing. He had no right to ask her to spill blood in order to purge his nightmare.

But finally he could not face it alone. He needed her. Needed her belief in the gods to shore up his own. Needed her belief in him.

Chapter 36

THE ROOSTER crowed again.

In the confined space of Torey's Chevette the sound seared Cal's nerves. It happened every seven or eight minutes. There had been a rubber band muzzling the animal's beak when Cal picked it up earlier at a poultry store on upper Amsterdam Avenue, but the restraint had somehow worked loose. When Cal tried to replace it, the large black bird had viciously nipped his finger. It had bled so much that he had to wrap his handkerchief around the wound.

"Jesus," Cal muttered, gripping the wheel as though it might dissolve any second from the heat and acid sweat pooled in his palms. "That noise is driving me crazy."

Torey turned to look at the two cages on the rear seat. Then she glanced back to Cal. "We'll be there soon," was all she could say.

They were on a broad boulevard somewhere in Brooklyn. Cal could locate it no more specifically; Torey had directed them out of Manhattan, dictating when to exit from this expressway or take a right off that avenue according to the detail map of the five boroughs lying open in her lap. Along the borders of the boulevard were ramshackle commercial buildings and used-car lots, all dark and deserted at this hour. Occasionally a diner or all-night gas station appeared, islands of garish light shattering the early morning darkness.

"Why the hell do we have to go this far?" Cal asked. "There must be one closer to the city."

She replied with exaggerated patience, refusing to be drawn into a spat. "Because it was the only one that came to mind. It's not as if I've got a list of cemeteries at my fingertips."

There was a tense pause. In a more conversational tone, working to lighten the mood, she said, "I saw a feature about it in the *Times*. It's quite historic. The rich people of New York used to bury their dead out here at the turn of the century. Still supposed to be quite pretty. You know, the article said some people still go there to have picnics and—"

"We're not sightseeing," Cal snapped. "Any one would have done. Any place we could get to quickly and get the damn thing over with."

After a moment she said, "I'm just as keyed up from this as you are, Cal. I was only trying to think of a place where . . . I might be a little less scared."

He heard the quaver in her voice. Taking one hand from the wheel, he reached out, found the bare skin of her arm, and stroked it gently. "Forgive me, honey, this is fine. I'd be going nuts no matter where it was."

She was quiet, but her free hand covered his, and the touch closed a gap between them.

The rooster crowed again.

Torey opened the glove compartment and held the map to catch the light. "It can't be far now." She raised her eyes to peer ahead through the windshield. "There it is," she said, and sat forward tensely.

He nodded.

Nefinda kilunga.

A fence of high iron bars appeared to their right, running alongside the boulevard. Beyond the fence rolling lawns sloped upward to the invisible boundary between a hilltop and the sky. In the dark, thousands of marble monuments and crypts blurred together into a faint frayed whiteness like the remnants of melting spring snows. Eighty years ago, yes, it must have been an idyllic rural setting. Now the cemetery faced across six lanes of cracked asphalt to a MacDonald's and a drive-through car wash. Both were closed for the night, though a series of giant neon arrows for the car wash blinked on and off incessantly, pointing into its black tunnel and away from the cemetery as if competing with death itself for customers.

Cal stopped the car at the cemetery's main entrance and saw that it was closed. Behind a tall iron gate stood a watchman's small stone house.

"We'll have to climb over the fence," Cal said.

"What if we bribed the watchman to let us in?"

"We'd have to pay a hell of a lot for that, and he'd still probably want to see what we're up to."

They continued driving. The fence ended its run beside the boulevard and went off at a right angle. Cal turned down a side street and continued following the enclosed cemetery property. They were on a residential street now, with a row of old porch-fronted Victorian houses set back on low knolls facing the fence. In one house a light glowed faintly behind curtains in a dormer on the third floor, but all the other houses were dark. This was the kind of close-knit neighborhood where an unfamiliar car might be quickly noticed and reported, so Cal switched off his headlights and drove slowly, reducing the motor's noise to a minimum.

They rolled past one house and a dog sleeping on the porch stood up and barked. Cal held his breath. But the dog did not chase the car and after a minute the barking subsided. No lights went on anywhere.

At a dead end, where the cemetery property took another turn, Cal cut the motor and let the car roll to a silent stop beside the iron railing.

They sat silently. Neither of them moved.

"Christ," Cal sighed at last. "Torey . . . are we crazy to be doing—"

"No, darling." She turned to place a hand softly against his cheek. "It's not crazy to believe. We'll never know what the gods are planning, but you've still got to do this—*we've* got to do it. Because when it's done, we can stop being afraid. And we can start building a life together."

He embraced her, kissed her long and gently.

Then the rooster crowed, nearly shattering any courage they had collected.

Cal glanced across at the houses. All remained dark.

"Better get moving," he said, "before that bird lets loose again."

They moved the cages of animals and the shopping bag with other paraphernalia for the ceremony to the roof of the car, then climbed up themselves. The top of the iron railing was only a few feet above them. Although each bar was capped with a spike, the fence could be easily scaled.

Cal climbed carefully, helped by rubber-soled sneakers. He found a foothold between the spikes on top, poised himself, then made the jump eleven feet to the ground. The spongy turf cushioned his landing.

Torey started passing down the shopping bag and the cages. She could reach over the fencetop, only an arm's length above her, but then everything had to be dropped, and caught by Cal. Torey saved the rooster for last, expecting it would crow when the cage fell.

But, surprisingly, the bird remained silent, stilled perhaps by fright.

Torey started to climb over. The cuff of her jeans caught one of the spikes as she was ready to jump, but she spotted it and unhooked the fabric before she fell.

"Bend your knees . . . stay loose," Cal whispered.

She jumped and toppled off her feet, but came up without injury.

Gathering up the cages and the shopping bag, they scuttled between rows of headstones until they were in a small hollow, the fence and the street lost from sight over a ridge. At the center of the hollow stood a mausoleum, its peaked roof surrounded by pillars, aping in miniature the lines of the Parthenon. An old willow grew in a small clearing beside it. Cal pointed to the ground under the tree.

"We'll set up there."

"By a Greek temple?" Torey said.

He couldn't tell if she was seriously protesting, or mocking their situation, trying to dilute the tension. Yet he could not shrug off the remark. Who could tell what might confuse the aim of their ritual, pique the vanity of the gods?

He told Torey to move on.

Religious symbols were everywhere—crosses atop the monuments, statues of the Virgin standing guard over the crypts. Finally he realized they had to stop wherever there was a patch of open ground.

They came to a small grove of trees. While Torey began unloading the shopping bag, Cal strained to read by moonlight a small metal sign stuck in the ground. "These trees are planted in memory of Lyle and Kevin Conway, twin brothers, born August 10, 1922, killed in action aboard the U.S.S. *Arizona*, December 7, 1941."

The right spot for a spell, Cal thought. If there were any spirits needed to help carry the message to the gods, he could ask for none better than ghosts of the last World War.

"Ready," Torey said, the shopping bag emptied.

They began by setting out seven large "saint candles" they had bought, one for each of the deities in the Seven African Powers.

Obatalá, father of the gods, was represented by a candle of his favorite color, white.

294

For Yemaya, daughter of Obatalá, goddess of all the seas and the waters, the candle was blue.

Orúnla, the god who "owned" and regulated the Table of Ifa, had a green candle.

Eleggua, messenger of the gods, who stands at all doorways and gates and opens or closes the way to opportunity, was represented by a red candle.

For Oggun, god of war and iron, the candle was brown.

For Oshun, goddess of love and gold, it was yellow.

And for Chango, god of fire and war and thunder and lightning, the color was black.

An eighth candle, to be burned in tribute to the Seven Powers as a unity, was made of wax layered in all the colors. Just like the one Chris had bought.

Cal positioned the candles to form a circle seven feet across, then lit the wicks with a long splint of ceiba wood ignited with a Bic lighter.

In his first attempt to light the black candle, the wick sputtered out as soon as Cal removed the splint.

The candle of Chango, the god that wanted Chris. Cal's heartbeat quickened. Chango was going to prevent the spell from being done! He glanced fearfully to Torey and she seemed to know exactly what was running through his mind.

"The wick's probably coated with wax," she said. Grabbing up the candle, she scraped the wick with her fingernail. "Try it now."

This time the wick caught, sputtered again, and then flared high in a strange surge of orange flame, as though burning up a small cloud of volatile gas in the air. Torey gasped. The burst of the flame endured only a second, then shrank to normal size and burned steadily.

But it had been there: a sign of Chango's presence.

They stood quietly in the darkness listening as if they might now *hear* another omen. But there was no sound except the dry scratch of autumn leaves wafting across the stone paths in the soft night breeze.

At last, Torey placed the cages, the packages of various herbs, two clay bowls, and a thermos inside the circle. And there, too, they seated themselves, facing each other across the limited diameter with only a small open area between them.

Cal picked up the thermos jug. It had been filled at the *botánica* near his apartment with a special goat's milk which he decanted now into one of the clay bowls. To the milk he added several herbs, pouring them in one at a time from sandwich bags, each bearing a self-stick label with the name of the herb. With the exception of powdered garlic and *guao*, the names were unfamiliar, merely part of the prescription filled from Oscar's list. Checking himself against the scribbled instructions, Cal read each name aloud as he emptied the packet:

"*Anamu . . . pasote . . . tartago . . . paraíso . . . albahaca . . . guao . . . rompe zaraguey . . .*" And finally the garlic.

The brew was to be drunk by all who participated in the ceremony. Cal went first. He held his breath as he swallowed, hoping the taste would be muted. But it was still lingering on his tongue when he inhaled, the taste activated by the air. Not really unpleasant—the milk faintly sour, with an earthy undertaste like that of bread gone moldy.

Cal hesitated before handing the cup to Torey. "It's enough that you're here, you know. You don't really have to do everything that I—"

"I'm part of it," she said, reaching for the bowl.

She drank what was left in the vessel.

Cal consulted his notes. Next he was to sprinkle over the ground within the circle a powder called *afoché*. When he'd asked for it at the *botánica*, the woman serving him had looked so dubious that he had been prompted to ask exactly what it was. *Afoché*, she told him, was made from the ashes of various animals—snakes, chickens, lizards, owls.

Having spread the fine black ash on the ground, Cal then smeared an ointment called *bálsamo tranquilo*—"peace balm"—on his right hand. This was the hand that would wield the knife for the killing, a knife with a handle of *ceiba* wood and a hammered iron blade, crude-looking but razor sharp. Also purchased at the *botánica*—this item alone had cost two hundred dollars—the knife had been packed into the shopping bag wrapped up in a dishtowel. Now Cal unwrapped it and grasped the handle in his right hand. The oily "peace balm" made it difficult to grip the knife. Perhaps that was its purpose, he thought, to hamper the killing enough so that only someone with unflagging determination could accomplish it.

And now was the time.

His heart hammered in his chest, the sound so loud in his ears that it seemed like the shovel of a gravedigger somewhere out in the dark pounding the sod flat after a burial.

"The turtle first?" she asked, prompting him.

"Right," he whispered.

296

It was in a cage with the dove. Torey reached in and removed the creature; its head retracted into the shell.

Cal hesitated before taking it from her. Staring at the turtle, contracted within its carapace by no other mechanism than a mindless instinct to survive, his will failed again.

This was the twentieth century.

He was a sensible man, a rational man, born in a world of logic and science.

How could he—

But if he did not, he knew, there would be no end to his fear. If only to close a vein of madness that had been opened by his involvement with the religion, there was no other way.

"I'm supposed to cut off the head," he said.

"Warm the shell and it will come out," Torey said, nodding toward one of the candles.

"Oh Christ." A sickness began to mushroom in his gut. Slowly his left hand moved over one of the candles, but he turned his head away, not to see. He ground his teeth together and squeezed his eyes shut, fighting the nausea. The hand holding the shell wavered and he felt the flame singe his thumb, but he did not move, suffering the scourging pain as a penance.

"You can do it now, Cal," she said quietly.

He brought his left hand down in front of him until it touched the ground. His eyes were still closed, but with the same exercise of will it might take to lift a great weight, he forced them open.

The turtle's wrinkled neck had extended fully, reaching. The beak yawned open as though the reptile were emitting a silent howl of agony.

Cal brought the blade over the neck.

He wanted to release his own cry of agony, wanted at least to say something, a prayer—felt that there should be some words to certify that this was a ceremony, not merely the tortuous mischief of twisted souls. But Oscar had given him no words, no incantations. In this religion the acts were the prayers. These bloody acts.

Sacrifice.

His arm was stone, unable to move. To kill this living thing would be, he knew, to pay tribute to ancient savage gods, to cross the last frontier into the realm of the true believer.

"I can't," he whispered.

"You must, Cal," she said. "For us. To put this all behind us. Go on."

For us, he thought. For Chris. Saying his rosary. *For Chris. For us.*

He pushed his hand down and the blade sliced through the scaly neck. The head lay on the ground, the beak still yawning. Blood leaked from the stump of meat hanging out of the shell.

"Quickly, Cal. Hold it up here." Torey was holding out the second clay bowl.

He did as she said. Automatically. His limbs felt numb now. No sensation in his body but the nausea, still controllable but growing, swelling as though it was solid, a tumor filling him . . .

The blood stopped dripping into the cup.

Then she was holding the dove, cradling it in her two hands, wings pinned, the breast upward. He started to take it from her.

"I'll hold it for you," she said.

It was easier this time. Shamefully easy. As prescribed, he plunged the tip of the knife into the dove's breast. The white feathers blossomed with red. Torey held the wound over the clay bowl already containing the turtle's blood. After a minute, she set the limp carcass of the dove beside the turtleshell.

One animal was left. Torey turned to the cage.

"Better let me," Cal said quickly. "That beak is lethal."

He paused before opening the door of the cage. The black rooster was standing sideways at the center, one golden eye staring straight back at Cal. It struck him now that the bird had not crowed—had not made a sound—since they had entered the cemetery. It was unnaturally still.

Cal inched open the door and moved his hand slowly inside. The rooster did not move. Not a squawk or a flutter as Cal's hand reached toward the neck. The golden eye did not even blink.

Cal extended his fingers, preparing to lunge.

Suddenly the rooster's head jerked to the side, the tip of the beak touching one of Cal's fingertips. Just the very point, so lightly that Cal felt it as the prick of a needle and reflexively jerked back his hand. Examining his finger, he saw that the touch had drawn no blood.

"Cal," Torey said in a hush. "Look!"

Cal shifted his eyes from the finger.

The rooster had taken two steps toward the door, left open when Cal's hand was withdrawn. The bird took a third step, reached the door, and paused. The head rotated in one direction, then the other, fixing Cal and Torey in turn with one of its gleaming eyes.

Very deliberately it raised one foot, stepped out over the sill of the door, and ducked its head as it prepared to exit the cage.

"Grab him," Torey murmured. "He'll fly."

Cal said nothing, only shook his head. The bird would not fly. As surely as he could see that its behavior was no longer characteristic of the barnyard animal—that there was something almost humanly knowing about the way it pulled itself out of the cage—Cal knew the rooster was surrendering itself to be offered.

Free now, it walked to the open ground between Cal and Torey, and settled.

There were no specific instructions on how to kill this animal. The spell had said only that it was to die last, then the heart was to be cut out, and seven drops of blood squeezed directly from the heart into the bowl. Cal knew from his research that in Voodoo ceremonies performed by *santeros*, roosters were often killed by having their head bitten off. It could not be expected of him, he thought. There had to be a limit.

The black bird perched on the ground, eyes closed now, strangely giving the impression of accepting death with grace.

Cal raised his right hand above his head, paused one more second at the apex, then swept the knife down into the black feathered body.

The bird threw back its head, eyes staring again, and from the open beak came a piercingly shrill sound, like a human scream heard at great distance, the scream of a child perhaps. The unearthly note echoed across the cemetery, bouncing off the flat stones.

"Stop it," Torey cried. "*Stop it!*"

Then the frenzy overcame him. A demon had been unleashed. He plunged the knife again and again and again and again into the bird, went on slashing at the pulp of bloody feathers long after the sound had stopped. Until her voice cracked into his consciousness.

"Cal! Enough!"

The gory mess lay in front of him on the ground. He looked at it a moment and he could no longer suppress the sickness. Lurching to his feet, he tossed down the knife to stagger away behind the corner of a small mausoleum, where he vomited.

He wanted to stop, not to go on, to leave it unfinished; and remained leaning against the cool marble until Torey called:

"Cal, they might've heard the noise . . . seen the car by now." There was panic in her voice. "Darling, if we don't hurry . . . someone might come and stop us."

No, it couldn't be left undone now. The only way he could live with what he had done already was to believe there had been a purpose.

He went back to the circle of candles and sank onto his knees beside Torey, who was already digging in the carcass of the rooster for the heart. She located it, cut it loose.

Holding it over the bowl, she squeezed it like a tiny sponge until it had yielded seven drops of blood.

She lifted the bowl, swirled it a moment, and glanced at him. When he did not reach to take it from her, she drank, setting the example.

Cal looked away. He wished he hadn't brought her. He knew that she had meant to help, but he wished he had been strong enough to do it all himself. He would hate remembering her as part of this, hate knowing that she remembered him this way. It was as if they had committed a murder together. As much as it bonded them, wouldn't it also sew the seeds of suspicion and disgust?

"Cal . . . you've got to."

He felt her touch the bowl to his chest and took it from her. Closing his eyes, he drank. The blood of the three animals he had sacrificed. Warm, slightly salty, not very different from what you tasted when you sucked at a cut finger. He tried to think of it as nothing more.

As called for by the spell, he drained the cup, then smashed it to the ground.

It was over.

He stood up and looked at the sky, feeling more hopeless and deserted than ever before in his life. He had defiled himself, his mind, his spirit, for the sake of strange gods, and now he wanted a sign from them that they had seen his sacrifice and would answer. But the stars in the sky overhead were the same as they had been for eons, flashing no messages that any man could read.

"We'd better go," Torey said. "What should we do with all this?" She looked at the evidence of their rite.

It wasn't in the instructions, but Cal knew what was to be done. Had known it ever since he and Chris had stumbled across the remains of a sacrifice, that day in the park.

"Leave it," he muttered. "Just leave it."

BOOK THREE

Asiento

(The Possession)

Chapter 37

I<small>T WAS AS THOUGH</small> he had come through a siege of malaria or some other consuming tropical fever. Everything that had been happening—for days, weeks—seemed as he looked back to be mere hallucinations, frighteningly convincing while experienced, but now, in the cool retrospect of restored health, easily seen for what they really were: tricks of the mind.

The spell had indeed been a cure. Not a magic solution, Cal thought, but an act that forced him to confront the wretched realization of how duped one could be at a vulnerable time of life. Even the morning after his immersion in the sacrificial rite, he felt his perspective had returned.

Yet his feelings about Torey remained mixed. When they had come home from the cemetery near dawn, he suggested it would be best if she stayed at her own apartment; he needed to be alone. She complied without protest, and for the next two days they did not call each other. It seemed possible to Cal that the relationship was over. He remembered reading somewhere a quote of Thomas Edison's: "Never do a friend a favor, he might not forgive you for it." Torey had done her utmost for him, but now she was associated with an event he wanted to forget. His attachment to her, the sexual release he had found with her, had softened his objections to her belief. He had already been left defenseless by Laurie's death and by worrying about the psychological effects on Chris, but it was Torey who had persuaded him of the power of the religion, and a part of him held her accountable for the extent to which it had invaded his life. If he had not fallen in love with her, perhaps all that he had learned could have remained logically isolated as research.

Their rift had gone on for three days when, at bedtime, Chris asked, "Why hasn't Torey been here? What happened, Daddy?"

Cal groped through a succession of patently unsatisfying euphemisms—"Well, Bean, things just happen between people sometimes"—until the boy's incessant probing ignited his temper and drove him to total evasion. "Go to sleep, Bean!"

Minutes later, in the living room, he heard Chris quietly crying himself to sleep.

And he missed her, too.

He waited through the night, afraid that his decision would be clouded by Chris's crying, or by thinking about their always special sexual chemistry.

But the next morning he called and asked her to lunch.

They met at a small neighborhood bistro, popular during the evening hours but blessedly empty at midday. As he came through the door he spotted her sitting in a rear corner. She was not looking in his direction, and for a minute he was able to observe her, a beautiful woman poised and at ease, simply waiting in a restaurant. In time, Cal realized, after seeing her in all the million other ordinary ways and places a man would see his wife, he would be able to obliterate the bizarre and repugnant memory of the other night.

They smiled at each other as he sat down, smiles of simple gladness, of chagrin, of pleasure in rediscovery, and their hands linked across the table.

She was the first to dare speaking. "I . . . I was tempted once or twice to . . . to do a spell that would bring you—"

"Oh please, darling, please." He would beg if he had to, literally get down on his knees. "I want to be with you, but there just can't be any more—"

"I know," she said. "That's why I want you to hear this." There was an urgency that demanded his attention. "I had the temptation, but I didn't give in. It's a crutch, I told myself. It's a way of looking at things that you can get hooked on because . . . well, when you're desperate. That's where I was when I began . . ."

Me, too, he thought.

She went on. "But I realized this time that there was only one way I wanted you to come back to me, one way it could be something to build on: if I never had to think it was because of some strange magic, if it was only because of what's truly inside you, what you feel for me. So I got rid of it all—the cabinet and the bowl and the stone, all of it. I put them in a box, and drove out to the country and buried them. And then this morning you called." Her hands squeezed tighter. "I'm not saying I can stop believing overnight, Cal, but I'll never practice it again. You're what's important to me. Only you. And Chris." She paused, breathed deeply, and looked up toward the ceiling. "And I figure if there are any gods up there, then they surely know the divinity of a good love between a man and a woman, and they'll consider forgiving whatever I've done for the sake of love." She lowered her eyes, glistening with tears and then shrugged self-consciously. "End of speech."

He tried to think of something that would speak for his heart. And then he just pulled her hand to his lips.

They ordered champagne—"to celebrate forgetting," he said— and when they clinked glasses to toast before the first sip, he said, "To us."

"The three of us," she said.

He knew then that he was a believer again—a believer in the most important faith. A faith in the future of an ordinary life, with laughter and love, and coping with everyday problems. And he knew that he wanted her to be part of it always.

When he poured out the last of the bottle he could hold back the words no longer.

"Marry me, Torey. Please."

Her eyes, already starred with tears, came up to meet his.

"Oh, Cal. I want to. But are you sure?"

"As sure as I can be of anything in this life."

The wedding could wait for a few weeks, they agreed, so Chris would have a chance to get used to the idea. They kissed across the table, and then started making plans.

϶ ● ϵ

They were together again, and there were no strains.

Chris was jubilant at Torey's reentry into his life. Afraid that he might have been responsible for her short disappearance, he was almost the perfect child, consistently cooperative, thoughtful, loving. Cal took advantage of this period of extraordinary juvenile virtue to discard the seven-colored candle. He looked for the shell, to throw it away too. But it wasn't in the bag of arrowheads, and he could find it no place else in the room. Chris had been carrying it around and, as children do, he must have lost it and moved beyond needing a security object. His attachment to the talismans had vanished along with the dreams of Laurie and of gods, or any other sign of emotional disturbance. As if he had been responding only to Cal's anxieties, after all.

Just when Cal might in fact have been roused to worry that his son had turned unnaturally good, the boy had a shouting tantrum with Torey one night, after she took the initiative in sending him to bed before he could see the end of a long TV movie.

"I take it all back about loving you," Chris screamed as he stomped out of the living room. "You're *not* my mommy and I hate you."

She came back into the kitchen as the door to Chris's room slammed, and leaned on the sink. "Thank heavens," she said. "I thought he'd never say it."

"You're glad?"

"Of course I'm glad. At last I know he accepts me—he can take *risks* with me."

A few minutes later Chris called plaintively for Torey to come and give him a good-night kiss.

A family, Cal thought gratefully. They were a real family now.

∋ ● ∈

He brought up the subject of marriage again a few days later, and this time she was willing to set a date. They agreed that Thanksgiving would be a nice time. Chris would have a break from school and they could take a trip together; a family honeymoon, Cal called it.

It was the day after, sitting in the faculty dining room, that Cal heard the scuttlebutt about Lawrence Krieger. An anthropologist of some repute who taught at Amherst, Krieger had eloped with one of his students a few weeks ago and been summarily dismissed from his job; his bride was the granddaughter of a banker who had bequeathed several million dollars to the endowment fund. A call was out on the academic grapevine for someone to fill the vacant chair.

The gossip interested Cal because Krieger's specialty was Asian and South Pacific cultures; the opportunity seemed fortuitous. His new life with Torey deserved a new beginning, a haven away from the sinister influences that had nearly spoiled their hopes.

He told Torey about the chance that evening, the beauty of the Massachusetts countryside, the pleasures of a tranquil country life, growing vegetables in the summer, watching the seasons change . . .

She laughed. "You don't have to sell it so hard, darling. I've been thinking of leaving the city, too—selling my houses. The money from that, with the settlement from your suit, would give us enough to be comfortable wherever we went. You could take a rest from teaching, work on your book." She caught his dark look. "The one on the Zokos, I mean."

They put the houses up for sale. Cal wrote to Amherst. As soon as Kate returned from Europe, where she was kicking off publication of *Cultures*, he'd ask her to send a letter of recommendation.

But when the real estate brokers came to look at Torey's properties prior to setting prices, they advised that she could expect to get as much as a million dollars for the two houses. The prospect of taking time off from teaching—perhaps traveling to the Pacific—became a steadily more appealing notion. If not so long ago fate had seemed to be dealing him a bad hand, he could have no complaints now. Everything was suddenly falling into place.

He avoided thinking about when—and how—the turning point had come.

⊃ ● ⊂

A "hot prospect" came to see the house.

Cal arrived home from the university late one afternoon the first week in November to find Torey standing in the garden with a youngish pediatrician named Weisenfeld. The doctor already owned a house on another block in Chelsea where he lived with his family, but his practice was growing and too busy to maintain in his home, so he was considering the purchase of this building to convert the ground floor into an office. Torey had been hoping for this kind of buyer so that old tenants like the Burkes could stay on.

After Torey had introduced Cal, a moment came when the doctor was contemplatively pacing the borders of the garden, evidently considering whether to make an offer. Then, quietly, Torey said to Cal, "Would you keep him happy for a minute? Offer him a drink or something. I'll be right back."

"Where are you going?"

"To touch up my face."

"Part of closing the deal," Cal teased. "The old femme fatale routine."

"Not exactly," she said, subdued. She flicked a finger toward a red spot on her cheek, so faint Cal hadn't noticed until she called attention to it. "I can't help being self-conscious. The way the damn thing itches, it feels as big as a football. I'll just put some makeup on and be right back."

It was just then, of course, after Torey left, that the doctor started asking questions about furnace depreciation, balloon mortgages, and similar matters totally confounding to Cal. He shrugged, then admitted his ignorance, and Torey was back in five or six minutes to provide the answers. But the doctor was a restless, impatient type, and when he departed without making an offer Cal felt somewhat guilty for having not come through in the pinch.

Torey told him not to worry, and her confidence was borne out on the weekend, when the real estate agents sent more than twenty potential buyers through the two properties. By Sunday night the larger house, the one in which Torey lived, had been sold by itself for $520,000, and her concern for Millie and Jack Burke proved to be unnecessary; they called to say they'd been contemplating a move to the Sunbelt anyway, and she shouldn't worry about their lease holding up the sale.

Neither Cal nor Torey mentioned to each other how she had come to live in the neighborhood, or how much she had paid for the buildings. They were quietly happy with their good fortune.

On Monday, shortly after Cal returned to his office from lunch, Torey called. She had made an appointment for four o'clock to meet a young stockbroker and his wife named Sauter; the couple had seen the building on Saturday and were returning to discuss a purchase agreement for $492,000.

"That's great," Cal told her. "Congratulations, hon'."

"Congratulate me after it's signed," she said. "There's many a slip twixt cup and lip, especially in real estate."

Cup. Lip. The image of her drinking from the potion of blood tangled his thoughts for a moment. He forced the image out, tried to concentrate on what she was saying.

"Look, I wanted to ask if you could meet the Sauters."

"I'd have to cancel a student conference. Are you sure you want me to? I'm sure your judgment about them—"

"No, I mean I can't be there. I have a doctor's appointment, and the earliest he could take me was three-thirty. I might be late for the Sauters, and I can't reach them."

"Oh sure, in that case . . ."

He was eager to cooperate, and ease her anxiety. Over the weekend the red mark on her face had become more inflamed. No bigger than a dot two days ago, now it was closer to the size of a dime. Aside from the physical discomfort, it was emotionally trying for her. With their wedding only three weeks away, she wouldn't be a "beautiful bride" if this thing wasn't cleared up.

"Do you suppose I'm allergic to marriage?" she had asked last night, bravely making light of it. But it was clear how deep her worries went when she suggested that she might stop into a *botánica* and pick up an herbal ointment. She had used these folk medicines for years, she said, and her health had always been fine.

The suggestion was obviously meant as a test. Cal begged her to avoid falling back into the old customs, even this therapeutic part. She did not fight him, and agreed to see a skin specialist.

Cal was home promptly at four to greet the Sauters. They were an unpleasant, humorless couple, and after half an hour grew visibly annoyed that Torey had not provided a real estate agent in her place to deal with the business of the house. Cal wondered if he could last much longer without offending or boring them to the point that he spoiled another deal.

Torey finally arrived at five, and from her first relaxed greeting through the settling of the purchase contract, it was obvious that her doctor's visit had put all her anxieties to rest. Within twenty minutes she was shaking hands on the sale.

Alone with him, Torey kicked off her shoes and poured two glasses of wine.

"What a relief," she sighed.

"And the doctor, that went all right, too?"

"Mmm." An ordinary boil, the doctor had said. Poulticing with hot compresses should clear it up in a few days. "I don't know what the hell I was so worried about. I guess, maybe, I thought . . ." She paused, shrugged, and laughed off whatever she was going to say.

He wanted to know. "Thought what?"

"It doesn't matter, darling. Really. Let's just think about all the good things."

And, raising her glass, she toasted their own bright future.

Chapter 38

THE FOLLOWING Wednesday night they went to Wayne and Ricki's new apartment for dinner. It was not intended only as a social evening. Cal had previously arranged for the Millmans to meet his bride-to-be, and relations were amicable enough that Torey had asked Wayne to do the contract work on her house sales. Although he knew the sales were immensely lucrative, Wayne had insisted on doing the job gratis, as a family gesture and "wedding present."

But the evening got off to a bad start. It was Ricki who let them in, and as soon as she saw Torey she shrank back from the door, staring at her cheek.

"Oh my God! What *is* that?" Ricki squawked, her gaze fixed on the boil. Torey had been diligently applying compresses, and though the doctor assured her that this was drawing the infection to the surface, to be expunged when the boil burst, the outward effect was alarming. The swelling had become a red dome the size of a silver dollar.

Extremely sensitive about her appearance, Torey blushed and covered her face.

Ricki launched at once into an awkward apology. "Oh, Torey, I'm sorry. I, well, Wayne and I have some news . . . I mean, just yesterday I learned that we're pregnant, I mean I am, and I guess my first reaction . . . well, you know, I didn't want the baby to be . . . exposed to anything . . ."

Torey recovered from her embarrassment. Ricki's concern was understandable, she said, and she explained that there was nothing to worry about.

The rest of the evening went well enough. They celebrated good news all around, and Torey went over contracts with Wayne while Cal answered Ricki's questions about parenting and whatever he could remember about Laurie's procedures when she was pregnant with Chris.

But several times Cal caught Torey looking preoccupied, and he guessed that Ricki's faux pas had started her worrying again. In fact his own concern was heightened, too. Perhaps it was only the effect of the harsh track lighting in Ricki's living room, but Torey seemed paler than usual, her eyes duller and rimmed by bluish circles. Could the infection have gotten into her system?

So he did not intervene when, for the purpose of giving advice, Ricki dared to raise the sensitive topic again at the end of the evening.

"You know, Torey, you'll have to forgive me, but that thing on your face looks like Mount St. Helens to me. If you don't mind my saying so, it's really worth getting a second opinion."

"I don't mind," Torey said. It didn't take a long acquaintance with Ricki to know that her opinion would be offered in any case. "Is there someone you'd recommend?"

And of course there was. "Well, I could send you to Peterson. Did a fabulous job on me—took off this little mole I used to have under my belly button that made me feel like a freak in a bikini. He's absolutely one of the two best skin men in the city."

Going down in the elevator Cal urged her to follow Ricki's advice. "You will call that doctor, won't you?"

"I'll see," Torey said curtly.

Though he wanted to tell her it was a good idea, he left the subject alone.

⋑ ● ⋐

When he got out of bed the next morning, she was in the bathroom. He called through the closed door.

"Torey?"

No answer. He knocked and called again.

The door opened. She paused before him, her eyes red-rimmed and frightened. Overnight the inflammation had spread to cover nearly her entire cheek, stretching the skin to a degree that seemed to faintly disfigure the proportions of her whole face.

"Where's that phone number Ricki gave you?" Cal said after one look. "We're going to get you a second opinion."

"Will it help?" she asked quietly.

Cal caught the note of hopelessness in her voice. "Of course it'll help! Look, you're having . . . an allergic reaction or something. Once the doctor can pin down what it—"

"Maybe this isn't so easy to cure," she said.

He was astonished by the tone of abject surrender he heard now from Torey, as though some terminal illness had already been diagnosed.

"Cal," she went on, "I've never had anything like this before. Never. I'm scared."

"Sure, it's scary when these things hit us. But there's nothing that can't be—"

"You don't understand, Cal. I'm scared that . . ." She hesitated.

"What?"

She moved up close to him. "That it's a spell. Someone did a spell against me."

The suggestion dangled in the air for a moment.

"Oh Christ, Torey, no," he said then, gathering her into his arms. "There's no reason at all that would be done to you. If anything, I'd be the target. So don't think that way. We're out of it now. For good." She was holding tightly to him, her face pressed against his shoulder. He stroked her hair for a minute and felt the tension in her body ease. "C'mon, let's call that doctor and start doing something about this with a little plain old modern medicine. Where's his number?"

She looked up at him, and her despair seemed to lift a little. She mustered a smile. "I know I'm being crazy," she said. Moving away to the dresser, she picked up a slip of paper. "You don't have to call for me, darling. I'll take care of it myself."

She tried the number, but it was still early and an answering service picked up. The operator said that Doctor Peterson would be in his office at ten, and Torey said she would call again.

At breakfast her spirits were a hundred percent better. She had been rattled, obviously, by the first sight of herself in the mirror after waking, but now she was back on an even keel. She also looked much better, having camouflaged the redness on her face with makeup.

When Cal left for the university at ten, he was glad to hear Torey trying again to get through to the doctor.

⊃ ● ⊂

A faculty meeting kept him late that afternoon, and he arrived home after seven. Chris was being given dinner by Celestine, who also had a message for Cal to call Torey at her apartment.

"I'll be staying here tonight, sweetheart," she told him, and gave a completely reasonable explanation. With all the time she'd put into showing the houses, other matters had slipped; there were two crates of imports to unpack for clients, and she hadn't even started looking through closets and drawers to sort out what could be discarded when she moved. Completely reasonable. But Cal heard the strain in her voice and knew it was an excuse.

"What happened today at the doctor?" he asked.

"Nothing. That is, I haven't gone yet. He must be as good as Ricki says, because he's very busy. Couldn't take me until the day after tomorrow."

Cal was alarmed. "But can you wait? How's the thing on your cheek?"

There was a pause. "Oh, Cal, I look perfectly awful." Then she began to cry. "It hurts, too."

"I'm coming right over."

"No," she said, and instantly checked her sobbing. "I don't want that. I'll be all right, and I hate having you see me this way."

"Darling, that doesn't matter. I want to be there, to help—"

"I know, Cal. But I'll be okay." A hesitation, then she added, "I just wish I could go and . . . get something that *works*."

He understood what she meant, where she wanted to go. Just a walk to the corner—but that would take her too far from him. So far, he knew, that he might never be able to bring her back.

"Don't, Torey," he pleaded. "Please don't. Just hang on until tomorrow. I'll get this Peterson guy to see you first thing in the morning, or we'll find someone else. But please don't give in to—"

"I'll try," she said, clinging to control again. "But Cal . . . I just want this to be better."

"It will, love," he promised.

He told her again he wanted to come over, but she resisted firmly, and he gave it up. He was able to persuade her, though, to take an aspirin, or a sleeping pill if she could find one, and go to bed without doing any work.

From the window of his bedroom there was a view across the street to Torey's house. After hanging up, he sat by the window, watching. He kept expecting her to come hurrying out and turn down the block toward the *botánica*. But though he watched for another twenty minutes, she did not come out of the house. He supposed she'd found a sleeping pill and turned in early.

Ɔ ● Ɛ

The clanging bell fell into his sleep like a bomb detonating over a sleeping city.

The phone.

He pulled himself up in the dark, grabbed for it as if to choke off the ringing. The lighted numerals on the digital clock said 4:27.

He hadn't even said hello before he heard her voice.

"Cal?"

"Yeah . . . what's wrong, love?" Groggy, but climbing out of it fast, he heard panic in her voice.

"Sorry, waking you . . . but can you come? Need you . . ."

He was fully awake in an instant. He could tell from the faint voice and fitful speech how weak she was. The damn infection was burning her up. Now he was frightened too.

"I'll be right there, darling," he assured her. "Just lie down and stay quiet."

"Tried not . . . bother you," she rambled on. "Know it's problem . . . get Chris watched . . ."

"Hey, I'll work it out," he said. "See you in a minute." He hung up.

What *was* he going to do with Chris? Bring him along?

The Burkes, they'd help, he thought as he grabbed up his clothes.

He was already pounding on the Burkes' door when he realized he should have called first, but he'd been too keyed up to think about it. Jack Burke answered the door in his robe and offered help even before Cal had finished asking for it. No point in waking the boy to bring him upstairs, he said, he'd go down there and sit. Cal must go take care of Torey, and not worry . . .

He had the key to her apartment, but in his haste he left it behind and had to ring her bell at the street entrance.

She was leaning weakly in the door. It was hard to believe the fever could have ravaged her so badly in the single day since he'd seen her last. Especially jarring because Torey had always before appeared so cool and in control. Now her eyes were lusterless and sunken, her sweat-dampened hair clung to her forehead and trailed in limp tangles over her shoulders, and the lithe body draped in a wrinkled satin peignoir seemed not merely slim, but wasted.

Most shocking was the swelling on her cheek. It had become grossly outsized, taking over half her face. The mound of redness rose to a hemisphere of greenish white, a collection of pus under the skin. Coming in the door, Cal had a moment's close glimpse of the horrific infection. Under the surface of its tip, a whitish secretion seemed to be moving, tumbling over, as though boiling from its own heat.

She fell into his arms, partly an embrace of relief and gratitude, yet also collapsing as if her strength had been sapped by the effort of standing to greet him. He held her for a moment as she sobbed into his neck.

He got her into bed, and told her to rest while he called the doctor.

"You won't get . . . anyone . . . no one comes at night. Cal, stay with me . . ."

"I will." He arranged the covers over her. "But someone's got to see you right away. Where's Peterson's number?"

She couldn't remember what she'd done with the slip of paper where it was written, but she remembered his first name was Howard, and motioned toward the phone book on her nightstand.

There were two listings for Howard Peterson, M.D., business and residence. Cal went downstairs to make the call.

It rang a long time. Cal was steeling himself for the inevitable outrage when the phone was answered by a man's bleary hello.

"Dr. Peterson?"

"Yes?"

Cal went into his pitch. He knew how unusual it was to ask but . . . a matter of life and death—

The Hippocratic oath was not what it used to be. The doctor fulminated wildly at being woken at five o'clock in the morning. There was nothing so serious—especially for a dermatologist— that couldn't have waited until a more reasonable hour.

But Cal bullied the doctor with a tirade of his own. The words spilled out, a description of the infection, then coaxing, begging, demanding, reminding the doctor of his humanitarian obligation. Cal refused to back down. He had lost one woman he loved by doing less than he should have, later than he should have. It was *not* going to happen again!

And somehow, he succeeded in rousing Peterson's sense of responsibility.

"Look Mr. Halowell—"

"Jamison."

"Mr. Jamison. How about if I meet you halfway? Is the woman you're calling about ambulatory? Could you get her into a cab?"

Cal said he could.

"Then bring her up to my office at seven-thirty. Normally I don't get in until nine, but I'll come in early. I think that's fair. If this is really too much of an emergency for you to wait two or three hours, then you should be calling a hospital and not me."

"Thank you, Dr. Peterson. Seven-thirty will be fine, thanks, I'm sorry that I—"

"Never mind," the doctor said gruffly, and the line went dead.

When he returned to the bedroom, Torey had fallen asleep, propped on her pillow. Her head lolled to one side, so the swelling on the left cheek was hidden in shadow. With only the unaffected side of her face lit by a bedlamp, she hardly seemed ill. He put his hand to her forehead. There wasn't even a fever.

Naturally she'd been panicked. What woman wouldn't be by an affliction that destroyed her appearance? And so soon before the wedding. But it would be all right now, he was sure.

He didn't think he could sleep, so he pulled the chair from her vanity table alongside the bed. On the nightstand he found a recent *New Yorker* and sat down to read—a profile of a microbiologist. He checked Torey with a glance. She had changed position, rolling onto her side to face him. The pustulous swelling was visible now, but she slept on peacefully.

The earliest dawn light turned the background of the room to purple. Cal's eyes ran across the words on the page without assembling them into meanings. He was on the point of nodding off when a sound woke him, tiny, yet magnified in the dawn stillness. A little "pop," as if a soap bubble had burst. And then a short hiss like the air rushing into a freshly opened can of vacuum-packed coffee. He sat up and looked around. The radiator, perhaps, the furnace going on.

Then another hitch in the silence. *Click.* From the bed, barely audible. Did Torey click her teeth when she slept? He'd never noticed before.

He glanced over. Fatigue fuzzed his vision and he rubbed his hands across his eyes.

Then he noticed the trickle of viscous fluid oozing down her cheek and along the line of her chin.

The boil had burst.

He turned to the nightstand looking for a tissue, something to wipe away the excrescence. Nothing there. He started toward the bathroom when he heard it again—the faintest click—and his eyes were drawn back to the bed.

From the wound, was it? The head of the boil had opened wider, he saw, and the pus was pouring out faster, like yellowish lava streaming from a miniature red volcano. Cal could smell it now, an odor of sickness and rot that made him gag. And there was something *else* at the point of flow, a minuscule dark filament poking up. *Twitching*. The movement magnetized his eye, pulled him closer. A hair, a thread, what *was* it? He leaned toward her.

The tiny black thread disappeared, covered by the fluid from the suppurating sore. Impulsively, Cal grabbed a corner of the sheet and dabbed away the pus.

There it was. Yes, a hair—

But as he watched, the little stalk pushed upward. Lengthened. And he saw it was bent, jointed, like—

Like.

The thing it was.

A sound broke from his lips, a moan of horror and disgust and anguish. The tiny articulated leg was probing the skin around the wound, looking for a hold. It found it, and climbed out further. In a second another twitching stalk came through the break in the skin. The two legs quickly dragged out the living thing of which they were a part.

A grayish brown spider, no bigger than a tomato seed. Legs sticky with pus, the tiny speck crawled sluggishly along the skin. Then stopped, stretched its legs, rubbed them together—cleaning them.

Cal stared, every detail in his scope now part of a surreal painting he was sure his mind had created. Dawn sky in the window across the room. The woman asleep. And the spider.

And as he watched, frozen, unable to move or scream, sure of his madness and sure he must keep it secret, another one came out. The flow of pus had thinned and the tiny spider emerged faster.

With another behind it.

And another.

Cal shrank back, closed his eyes against the deviltry of illusion like a drunk retreating from the DTs.

But when he opened his eyes again, they were exploding from her skin.

He snapped out of it. Leaping forward, he slapped at the spreading blotch of gray-brown specks.

The crack of his hand against her cheek woke her.

"What—?"

Seeing her wake, sharing consciousness with her, strengthened his hold on the real.

But the spiders were still there.

And she didn't realize it, looked at him with sleepily questioning eyes.

"Don't move," he said in a hush, reaching out slowly to brush at her cheek.

Puzzled by this motion, she brought her hand up slowly to her cheek, too, and felt the wetness first.

"It's broken," she said with relief.

Then a tickle in her palm made her bring the hand down, and she saw the small dots speckling her fingers. She looked closely at them. There was an instant of disbelief, then she started clawing at her face as though she might tear the skin from the bone. Cal grabbed her hand in one of his, and with the other swiped at her face, brushing spiders away. Dozens now. They landed on the blanket, the floor, and fled away.

She watched them, in paralysis.

And then the scream ripped out of her throat, a sound of strangled fear and despair like none the night had ever heard. It went on, the shrieking note itself like the expulsion of her very soul through her mouth. Cal trembled, wavering between covering his ears and striking her.

But the scream ended before he made either move, and Torey tumbled sideways, and fell.

Ͻ ● ⊂

In the speeding ambulance he watched the intern giving her an injection.

"She's not going to die, is she?"

The intern glanced at him. "We'll do what we can. What happened to her, anyway?"

Cal hesitated. "I don't know. I thought it was that infection . . ."

The intern scrutinized him, obviously doubting. "If it was an infection, she'd be running a fever. And she's not. The symptoms go the other way. Blood pressure and pulse way down. Something blew out her system, pal, something sudden." He lowered his voice, as if imparting a friendly confidence. "If you know what it was, you oughtta talk. Information helps the treatment, and it keeps you in the clear."

So they thought he had done something to her.

But what could he say to assuage their doubts?

She collapsed because of the spiders.

What spiders?

The ones that were coming out of her skin, out of a hole in her face.

He said nothing. The intern shrugged and looked away.

Then Torey mumbled something, her eyes fluttered open and she struggled to raise herself from the stretcher.

"Lie back, ma'am," the intern soothed her. "Don't try to talk."

But she wouldn't be calmed. "Cal?" she cried softly.

Cal nudged the intern aside and leaned over her. "Relax, hon'. I'm here. We're going to the hospital." He brushed a strand of hair off her face.

She stared at him, eyes still dull. Her lips quivered, working to frame another word. It was only a pantomime of speech. He brought his ear over to her lips.

"Leg," she whispered. Then another faint incomplete word.

Cal spun to the ambulance attendant. "She's complaining about her leg."

The doctor pulled away the blanket for a look. Whatever the problem, there was nothing to be seen. He covered her again.

Torey shook her head weakly. Cal leaned over her again.

"Leg," she repeated, mustering a bit more volume. And again came another choked syllable—like the distant bleat of a sheep. "Baaaaa . . ."

"Bad," he guessed she meant. Leg bad.

"There must be some pain in her leg," Cal insisted to the intern.

"We'll be at the hospital any minute," the intern said.

Torey looked at Cal beseechingly. "Mus' unnerstan' . . . ," she mumbled. And once more came the two words telling him her leg was bad.

The ambulance screamed into the emergency loading bay of the hospital. All the helter-skelter activity of receiving a critical case roiled around Cal—the door being flung open from the outside, white-coated men. In seconds Torey was on a gurney being wheeled into the emergency room. Cal tried to stay with her, but he was elbowed aside by doctors; then a nurse took him firmly by the arm and pointed him toward a door.

"Wait outside," she commanded.

He paced for forty minutes before a tall resident in a white gown came out. He had a long narrow face, the kind that might seem grim even in repose.

"Mr. Jamison, I'm Doctor Meranze."

"How is Mrs. Halowell?"

"Holding her own," Meranze said.

Doctor-talk! "What the hell does that mean?" Cal demanded impatiently.

"She's suffered a massive insult to the central nervous system," the doctor explained. "The effects are not minor. Her blood pressure is low and her heartbeat is irregular. Her condition is stable, but she's still in danger. Of course," he added heavily, "it would be easier to know where we stand if you'd tell us exactly what brought this on."

There was a pause. Cal looked toward the end of the corridor, watched a limping old man being supported by a nurse.

"Our ambulance intern mentioned that you were reluctant to give him details," Dr. Meranze went on. "I should advise you, Mr. Jamison, that if you continue to withhold such information, it might be necessary to . . . refer this to other authorities."

They would suspect him either way, Cal thought. Might as well go with the truth.

At the beginning, at least, he made it sound sensible—describing the appearance of the swelling, its slow growth, leading up to her phone call begging for help. Then he could report only the unbelievable—the kind of scourge you could read about in biblical tales where divine wrath was visited on the wicked. Plagues of locusts. Oceans parting to drown pursuing armies.

And an infestation of spiders springing forth from within the body.

The long-faced doctor listened attentively without scoffing. Cal imagined that the doctor was studying him as a case history: what sort of man could invent such a tale? No hope, of course, that he believed.

Yet in the telling, Cal relived the horror, and ceased caring what the doctor thought.

The doctor said nothing for a moment when Cal finished, then nodded thoughtfully. "You're asking rather a lot to expect anyone to believe that, Mr. Jamison."

"I know."

"But you stand by the story?"

"It's the truth," Cal replied.

"What are your plans right now?" the doctor asked.

So they'd know, Cal thought, where to send the police. "I want to wait here until Mrs. Halowell's out of danger," Cal said. "Is it okay if I stick around?"

"Certainly," the doctor said. "The staff cafeteria on the third floor is open all night. You can wait there. I'll send word as soon as there's any change."

⊐ ● ⊏

Doctors and nurses coming off shift, orderlies on coffee breaks came and went while Cal lingered, returning to the counter again and again for one more cup of black coffee.

Staring into the well of black liquid, he could think of nothing but the spell. Who could have done it to Torey? And why? Was it an act of vengeance? What could Torey have done to deserve such punishment? According to the tenets of the religion, didn't she have to *deserve* it for the spell to work? The religion did not tolerate spells that were done only out of malevolence.

"Mr. Jamison."

Dr. Meranze stood over the table. There were no policemen with him.

Cal motioned him to the chair opposite.

"Mrs. Halowell is much better. You won't be able to see her right now, she's still under sedation. But after that she'll be fine. Physically. As for her emotional state, I'd expect that'll settle down as soon as she understands what happened."

"Understands?" Cal said derisively. "I'll tell you what happened. Somebody did a spell on her." He saw the doctor's eyes widen with astonishment. "A spell," Cal went on. "How the hell does she deal with that? Gods putting snakes and spiders inside—"

"Mr. Jamison," the doctor interrupted, then paused to give Cal a long searching glance. "I hope you're aware that you've suffered a shock, too. If what had happened to Mrs. Halowell had happened to you, then I think you would have reacted as she did. As it is, I strongly suggest you go home and try to relax, give yourself a day off. And I want you to understand this: there is nothing supernatural—or even without medical precedent—about what you saw this morning."

"Oh sure," Cal said tartly. "It's just some new kind of acne."

The doctor raised an eyebrow at the tastelessness of Cal's remark. "When we spoke earlier," he said, "you were sufficiently convincing that I decided to look into your story. As it turns out, there's nothing rare about parasites using the skin of warm-blooded animals as a medium for egg-laying and hatching. I called our staff specialist on parasitology, got him out of bed, and he referred me to more of an authority, a man named Traynor attached to the World Health Organization. I've just come from talking on the phone with Dr. Traynor."

"Don't tell me it's a common condition," Cal said sarcastically.

"As a matter of fact, in some countries it is. Mrs. Halowell was in South America recently, wasn't she?"

"No, she wasn't."

The doctor looked puzzled. "When you supplied information on the admission forms, didn't you tell a nurse that Mrs. Halowell was in the importing business? Are you *sure* she hasn't travelled to South America recently?"

What was he sure of anymore? Could Torey have been there and back in a day?

"Why?" Cal asked.

"Well, Dr. Traynor is familiar with a species of parasitic spider native to some tropical countries. It usually lays its eggs in the skin of domestic animals, but it has been known to infest human skin. In Brazil and Peru, the condition is common enough that it would have been diagnosed instantly, instead of being allowed to get to the point . . . that it did here." The doctor shook his head. "But that still leaves the question of where she could have picked it up."

Cal thought of it suddenly: the shipments of decorative art coming in from the tropics. The packing cases and protective cellulose were common carriers of vermin.

He mentioned the connection to the doctor.

"Well, there you are," Meranze said. "One of these parasitic spiders stowed away, and Mrs. Halowell had the bad luck to pick it up." He stood. "I've got to get back to my floor. I hope my research has made this ordeal a little easier for you and your ladyfriend to get through. She's a beautiful woman."

Cal thanked the doctor and left.

So that's all it was, according to the experts: a critical case of bad luck.

But Cal diagnosed it as something different.

He looked up at the cracked cafeteria ceiling, and for a moment nearly succumbed to the impulse to shake his fist toward heaven. What had Torey done to bring down the wrath of the gods? What had he done, or Chris, or Laurie?

"Tell me!" he screamed suddenly.

A chair scraped on the floor, and Cal became aware of a nurse at a table across the room who had turned toward him. From her wide wary stare and the tense set of her body, Cal realized instantly the professional judgment she had made: she might have a hysteric on her hands, a madman. Cal raised his open palms in an awkward gesture of apology and reassurance. Then, as steadily as he could, he walked from the cafeteria.

Of course, he thought as he stepped out the hospital doors, it could be said that he was mad. Because now, finally and irrevocably, he was a believer. But how did you explain that *they* were the mad ones, all those who did not believe in the gods and their wrath and the fine invisible edge on which human survival was balanced —*held* in balance by the mightiest forces with the same whimsical ease as the juggler spinning a ball on the end of his finger.

Cal's pace quickened. He had no idea why Torey had been punished, what crime she had committed in the pitiless view of the all-seeing eyes. Yet he knew somehow that his only hope of saving Chris would depend on understanding that mystery.

And he walked faster then, finally breaking into a breathless run, desperate to reach the one place where he thought he might find the answers.

Chapter 39

THE TAXI CROSSED Ninety-sixth street, the frontier, and rattled into the barren dawn of the *barrio*. Cal sat on the edge of the rear seat and peered out at the ominous desolation. Tin-windowed tenements. Garbage-strewn pavements. Tufts of newsprint drifting across gray deserted streets like swans in the morning haze. Bars of dusty sunlight, split by the elevated railroad tracks, lit the vaults beneath the rickety girders, and here and there Cal caught a glimpse of a sleeping body. Sleeping or dead.

What had Voodoo done for these people? Had their gods given them wealth?

His haunted eyes were drawn as though by a magnet to the steel-gated stores: a shop window full of candles, and on the next block another full of saints, then another with packets of herbs strung on wires and animal skins dangling in the recesses of darkness. Beads, statues, glowing bottles, their shadowed colors spun circles in his brain.

Harmless objects.

Harmless, but with the power to turn his life upside down.

Why had Torey been struck down? *Why?*

He felt light-headed from lack of sleep. A muscle twitched behind his eye.

The cab turned off Park Avenue, passing a corner store with a neatly arrayed display of plaster saints. Saint Isidro in brown robes: Ochosi. Saint Christopher with a cross: Bacoso. A blue-eyed Saint Barbara: Chango. The gods hid behind the statues, disguised in the rituals of Christianity. Syncretism. Masks. Which mask protected the god who had punished Torey? Cal thought of her as she'd looked on the stretcher in the ambulance. Saw her pale face, felt her reaching grasp, recalled her faintly murmuring about a pain in her leg.

"Leg bad . . ."

Then, with a force so strong it knocked him back against the seat, the realization broke.

She hadn't been talking about her leg at all! It wasn't "leg bad" she'd been saying—but Leg-ba. She had been telling him that her misfortune came from Legba, the Divine Trickster, that Voodoo god who punished anyone attempting to use the religion for evil purposes. Who "turned the trick," as believers put it. Torey's message had been almost the same as Mrs. Ruiz's final word: "*engañador.*"

But why would the trick be turned against Torey? What had she done that was evil? Yes, Carmen Ruiz had been trying to do some kind of spell against Chris. But Torey loved him, had helped Cal to save him. If the trick had been turned against Torey, that meant doing a spell to save Chris was evil.

Impossible.

"Legba," Cal murmured to himself, confounded.

He looked out the window at the brightening sky. The sun burned through the haze. Now the puzzle was magnified, and Cal searched its meaning with a different eye. Mrs. Ruiz, too, had been fond of Chris. Suppose her spell, like Torey's, had not been meant to hurt Chris, but to protect him. And, for attempting to arrange that protection, the trick had been turned against her.

Punished for doing *good?* Within the logic of the religion, it made no sense. By what reasoning could guarding a boy's life be designated evil?

Darker and darker circles. Could it have been Oscar's spell? Suppose Cal had not been provided with a spell to save Chris, but Oscar had tricked him into performing an evil ritual—and then the gods had condemned those who enacted it?

But why then hadn't Oscar been punished, too? Why, Cal wondered, wouldn't he be punished? Why only Torey?

And what motive did Oscar have to dispense an evil spell?

Questions within questions.

The cab screeched to a halt in front of the A.C.H.E.'s double brownstones. Cal fed a twenty-dollar bill through the partition and bolted out the door without waiting for change.

The building's front entrance was locked. Cal banged on the

wired-glass panel, shaking the door in its frame. For a moment the hall inside remained empty, and then from nowhere a sleepy-eyed teenage boy with a pencil mustache appeared. He peered intently through the glass at Cal, his dark suspicious eyes outlined in their sockets.

"I'm here to see Oscar," Cal shouted.

After a hesitation the young watchman turned the double locks. "Mr. Sezine is not—"

Cal rushed past and hurtled up the stairs, leaving the shocked boy in his wake. He took the steps three at a time, stopping only when he reached the fourth landing to catch his breath. Glancing first down a hall to his left, then to his right, Cal tried to remember where Oscar kept his private apartment.

A radio was playing somewhere in the morning calm, dispensing the news followed by a beeping musical tag: "You give us twenty-two minutes, we'll give you the world." It seemed to be coming from the far end of the hallway to the right. He walked down the hall, and the sound of the radio got louder. "A car went out of control in lower Manhattan last night and two people were killed . . ."

And what had they been punished for? Cal thought. Nothing. The good and the innocent died every day in accidents, of illnesses, shot down in brutal crimes.

But that was life as the gods had designed it, too. Accident and chance were built in. Life ran its course . . . until the gods chose to intervene.

Cal paused outside the door at the end of the hall. Suddenly it opened. Oscar stood before him in a bathrobe, a towel over his shoulder.

"You gave quite a scare to the boy downstairs," he said. "He phoned up on the intercom . . . to warn me. Said a man who looked dangerous was on the way up." He stood back from the door to let Cal in. Cal charged into the apartment.

"But that never worried you, eh? You walk right over and open the door. You didn't think that I might have a reason to come here and—"

"Cal, I never imagined it would be you. I don't know what you think I could have done." He closed the door. "As for worrying about myself, my life is completely in the hands of the gods. They will help me or harm me as they see fit."

"And Torey?" Cal shouted. "Why did they 'see fit' to harm her? Damn you, Oscar, what kind of spell did you give me?"

326

Freshly awakened, draped in his faded terry robe, Oscar seemed a bit like a befuddled old man. Shaking his head slowly, he said, "What's happened, Cal? Why are you here? Rushing in at this hour . . . accusing me . . ."

"Torey Halowell almost died a few hours ago, Oscar. A healthy young woman, and she almost died. Of a tropical parasite, the doctors say. But we know different, don't we? The trick was turned against her."

Oscar stared at Cal and moved slowly across the room. His lips moved slightly as he whispered the words to himself: "The trick was turned . . ."

"It means the spell we did was evil, Oscar. You weren't trying to help me save Chris, were you? The spell you gave me was for something else—something that offended . . . the gods."

"No, Cal," Oscar said, still shuffling slowly over the carpet, past Cal. "I wanted to help you. Believe me. I tried."

Cal was seething, and Oscar's sanctimonious tone, his plea for belief only enraged him further. Cal stepped up behind Oscar, grabbed the loose material of his robe, and pulled him around.

"No sale, Oscar. I don't buy the whole routine. Your goodness and generosity and benevolence. You know what you're into here —the *aché*, the power of the gods. Whatever else you've done, you've also used it to hurt someone I love."

"No, Cal, no," Oscar replied, and his vehemence almost convinced Cal again. "I've told you the truth always. You've *seen* the truth of my work. I've used the religion only for the good of the *barrio* people—indeed for *all* people, for the good of the world!"

It was a madly overblown claim. From anyone else it would have sounded megalomaniacal, even messianic, the ravings of a fanatic. Yet Oscar's earnest conviction, his consuming sincerity seemed utterly genuine, and they blunted Cal's anger.

"All right, Oscar," Cal said quietly. "If I'm wrong, and you do want to help, then get me another spell. Something that works."

Oscar tossed his hands up, a gesture of helplessness. "There is nothing, Cal."

Cal took another threatening step toward Oscar. "Nothing? Bullshit! There are spells for everything. To win a lover. Win a lawsuit. Make money. Lower the rent, cure a backache, kill an enemy, expand a business. Goddamn it, Oscar. Open your fucking book of spells and *give me*—"

"I'm sorry, Cal. But you see, we've been given a signal. What happened to Miss Halowell is a sign. The gods have their plan, and we must not interfere."

"No, Oscar! They can't have him. If the plan is to take my son for a sacrifice, I'll never let them." Cal backed away, shaking his head in denial.

Oscar stepped forward, put his hand gently on Cal's shoulder. "We haven't the power, Cal. It is theirs—theirs alone. But you will understand that soon. You will see that what they ask is really very little, and their wishes are for the best. The gods are not unkind, Cal. But they do expect us to honor them."

"By giving lives to them?" The fury welled up again in Cal. He wrenched away from Oscar's grasp. "I won't let it happen! If you can't help me, then I'll go somewhere else." He turned toward the door.

"Where can you go, Cal? The *santeros* cannot help, you went there before you came to me."

Where could he go? It seemed to Cal there had been some vague notion of an alternative in mind when he made his declaration. But what weapon did he have against the Voodoo gods if not their own magic?

And then it came to him: the magic he needed was the kind that Oscar himself had once said could be more powerful than Voodoo. *Mayombe.*

"I'll find a *mayombero,*" Cal said, and reached toward the door handle.

Oscar came at him in a rush. "You mustn't do that, Cal! For your own good. *Mayombe* is black magic. Commit yourself to the gods of *mayombe* and you will surrender your *soul.*"

Cal faced Oscar defiantly. "Is that what it would take to save my son? A deal with the devil? Then I say amen to it. I'm not worried about my soul, Oscar—I'm not even sure I have a soul. It's just Chris I've got to save."

"No, Cal, it's more. A billion times more. Don't you understand? These sacrifices have been done to save the world."

Cal stared at Oscar. So he knew, had always known—and had denied it as he must. They *were* happening again, as in Kimball's time, as in the darkest ages of men. Lives being offered to the gods. The lives of children.

"The dedication is almost finished," Oscar went on. "Six have been done, one remains. Seven. For the Seven Powers. Only Chango must have his offering. Then the gods will relent. The fate we have read in the Table may be changed . . ."

All as he had known. They wanted Chris for the seventh. *On the eve of the sixth*—the phrase shot through his mind, and now it made sense! One had been done then, after the *guëmilere*. And one remained.

But he would not let them have Chris.

Never!

Cal whirled to the door and pulled it open.

Suddenly Oscar's powerful arms were around him, pulling him backward. Cal jabbed his elbows hard into Oscar's ribs and managed to break away again. But Oscar recovered fast enough to lunge at the door and slam it shut before Cal could escape.

"I can't let you go, Cal. *Mayombe* is the way of evil. Its priests would like to stop us, yes. They want our gods to be angry, to destroy all that is good. But it mustn't be allowed to happen."

Oscar came toward Cal again.

Desperate, Cal brought his arm back, balled his hand into a fist and swung it in a full, fast arc. He had never hit a man before, had never even tried. He could only approximate the act from what he had seen on movie and television screens.

In life it didn't work so well. Cal's fist flew free past Oscar's jaw, missing by inches as the big man dodged backward. Cal was thrown off balance by his own momentum, and he went reeling when Oscar put a hand on his chest and shoved him away. Stumbling clumsily backward, one foot tripped over the other—or a heel snagged on the carpet, he wasn't sure—and he tumbled onto the floor. His head collided with the sharp corner of the coffee table, and a pain speared through the bone, the shaft of agony traveling through his brain, reaching to his forehead, feeling almost like some tangible thing as it emerged through his eyes. For a moment the pain actually blinded him. Then sight returned, but blurry. He could make out Oscar's figure moving toward him, bending down.

"Cal, I'm sorry," said the voice that went with the blurred image, that always solicitous and sincere voice. "But when you tried to hit me, I . . . well, I do have to stop you . . ."

The goals still hadn't changed. On either side. Oscar still wanted to stop him. Still wanted the gods to have Chris.

A wave of nausea and dizziness swept through Cal. The dark blur that was Oscar floated lower, descending over him.

Cal edged backward, sliding himself along the carpet, guiding his hand along the edge of the coffee table.

"I won't hurt you, Cal. I'm only going to keep you here awhile. Until you feel better."

Cal's hand connected with something on the coffee table. His fingers crawled over the object, defining it. An ashtray. Smooth sides, sharp corners. He'd seen a crystal ashtray there, he thought. Groping over it, he curled his hand around it. Picked it up. Solid. Heavy.

Oscar was right over him now, close.

"You'll understand soon, Cal. You'll know it had to be done."

With every cell, every sinew, commanded by the single loving need to save his son, flesh of his flesh, Cal swept up the cool heaviness in his hand and rammed it into the side of Oscar's head.

Oscar grunted. Cal saw the face hovering close over him contort with pain, and then the full weight of Oscar's body fell over him.

Cal lay back for a moment and breathed deeply. Oscar's dead weight pressed on Cal's chest, constricting his lungs. Cal tried to push Oscar off. As he struggled, a warm trickle went down Cal's neck. He thought for a moment it was blood from the back of his own head, where it had hit the table. Then he saw it was coming from a gash over Oscar's ear. Jesus, had he killed him?

Cal pushed harder at the body and it tumbled back onto the floor, face up.

Oscar groaned.

Thank God. Alive. Cal stared at Oscar a moment, mesmerized by what he had wrought by his own violence.

Oscar's eyes flickered open. "Don't," he whispered. "Please, Cal, don't go . . ."

He started to push himself up.

In a few more seconds, Cal thought, Oscar might recover, would be able to summon help from his students, or the watchman.

Cal took a slow step backward, hesitated one more second. Then he turned and ran from the room without even a backward glance.

Chapter 40

HE WAS TOTALLY winded when he reached Lexington Avenue. He rounded a corner and stopped to lean against the side of a building and recover his breath. How long before Oscar would rally his students and order them in pursuit? Or did he dare? To whom else had Oscar confessed his ritual murders? Cal stole a glance back around the corner toward the A.C.H.E. No running figures surged toward him. The street was quiet.

He rubbed at a stitch in his side. The pain wouldn't go away, his heart kept beating furiously, but he moved on down the avenue. One block. Then he turned another corner into a side street. He took deep breaths and rested again, frequently glancing back to be sure he was not being chased. After a minute the painful stitch went away.

Where did he go now? A *mayombero*, he had said to Oscar; he would seek a more powerful magic to save Chris. But how did you find a black-magic sorcerer in this alien land?

The landscape of ruined buildings and trash-littered alleys offered no hope. Whom did he dare to ask?

An orange Cadillac with a woman at the wheel pulled up across the street by the doorway of a burnt-out tenement. As Cal watched, a bearded man in mirrored sunglasses stepped out of the doorway and walked over to the car. He handed the woman an envelope, she pushed some money at him and drove away.

Cal felt dizzy again. He closed his eyes. Spiders squirmed in the blackness. Voices shouted. Sleep, he thought, I need sleep. But I must find the sorcerer.

"Hey man, you sick?"

Cal opened his eyes. Two images of himself stared back at him. Faces in the pimp's mirrored sunglasses.

"I'm okay," Cal said. And saw in the small mirrors that he was not. He looked anything but okay.

"I'd get your ass outta here, man," the pimp said. "Don't you know white folks get in trouble up here all alone?" He shrugged and then walked away.

Cal almost called him back. A creature of the streets, a dweller in the *barrio*'s dark places. The pimp might know . . . Then the absurdity of asking struck him. No, it was hopeless. Cal straightened, fought for balance, and walked toward the corner. Magic wasn't the way to save Chris. The answer was simpler. Go home, pack, get out of the city, take Chris away. Leave the madness behind.

He searched the avenue for a taxi, but saw none. The drivers didn't cruise this neighborhood. They brought their fares and left, fast. Easier to find one farther downtown—across the border. Cal turned along the avenue and took a few steps.

"Señor . . ."

The sibilant hiss came from very near. Cal looked around, but saw no one. He was about to continue walking when the flash of white caught his eye. Then he saw the girl. She wasn't near at all, but twenty or thirty yards away. Was it her voice he'd heard? The whisper had seemed to be right next to his ear. He couldn't take his eyes from her. She was wearing a white frilly dress, like a communion dress, that looked luminous in the early morning sun. The glaring whiteness contrasted sharply with her dark hair and eyes and skin.

She beckoned to him, a slow provocative gesture.

One of the pimp's girls. No, Cal thought, something about her looked familiar.

She was moving toward him now, in a swaying walk, naive and yet provocative. She was no more than fourteen or fifteen, he thought, very young but exuding an aura of sex.

Then she was close enough for him to see the amulet on a chain around her neck.

A tiny claw.

Mayombe.

He remembered now: the girl Oscar had scolded, Teresa.

She came to within eight or nine feet and stopped. Facing him, she smiled faintly and beckoned again.

Where had she come from? She must have been somewhere in

the A.C.H.E. this morning, had overheard him fighting with Oscar. Why else would she be here?

"You'll take me to a *mayombero?*" he asked.

As though unable to understand him, she only smiled and gestured again.

He had to go with her. But where? How far?

There was a public telephone in a glass-walled booth on the corner. Cal went to it and stepped in. The girl kept looking at him, circling around to stand outside the door of the booth. Cal put a dime in the phone and dialed Ricki's number.

Ricki answered sleepily.

"Ricki, it's Cal," he said urgently.

"Cal?"

"Listen, Ricki. You've got to help me out. Torey was taken to the hospital last night—"

"Oh dear God!" she gasped. "What happened?"

"I can't explain now," he raced on, "but she'll be all right. The thing is, I can't get home and I need someone to stay with Chris. He's with an upstairs neighbor, but it'd help if you were there when he woke up."

There was a fractional pause. "All right, Cal. If you need me. But I think I should know about Torey—I mean, if Chris asks."

"Just say she . . . got food poisoning. The main thing is that you stay with Chris until I get back there. Don't go out with him. And don't let anyone in."

"Cal, what's going on? I don't like the sound of any of—"

"Ricki," he begged, "do this for me, please. I can't explain, except that Chris's life could depend on it."

"Chris? Cal—"

"Please, Ricki, just *do* it! I can't answer any more questions." Cal's eyes were on the girl, who had beckoned again and taken a step backward as though about to leave. "Just tell me you'll do it."

"I said I would," Ricki snapped, sounding more hurt and upset than angry. "I just wish I knew—"

"I've got to go," Cal said, and hung up before Ricki could ask another question.

The girl in the white dress smiled and walked away.

And he followed.

⊃ ● ⊂

She headed north, where the *barrio* grew more desolate. The apartment buildings no longer presented any illusion of being livable: no doors, no windows, not even tin sheets to exclude squatters. From a third-floor hole that had once been a window a boy dangled a cat by its tail. Cal turned away, and hurried to maintain the girl's pace. His head throbbed, his vision seemed clouded. Was she ten feet in front of him or a hundred? He couldn't tell.

She never looked back.

The streets teemed with dogs and children and women carrying babies. A funeral procession came down an avenue, a shiny black hearse surrounded by people walking, all dressed in somber blue and black, the women in boxy white hats. A pockmarked man, gaunt and emaciated, shoved a cigar box at anyone who paused by the curb to watch the procession—collecting funeral expenses.

The girl threaded a path among the mourners, and Cal would have lost her except that the white of her dress shone like a light amid all the funereal black.

She led him past a rubbled lot, an entire square block, where children danced barefoot through shards of broken bottles, playing what seemed to be a grisly game.

She led him across a street and into an alley where light fell in filament-like strips over a beggar in multicolored rags. Cal stared at the man long enough to see that he was wielding a rusty knife over the corpse of a dog, tearing hunks of flesh from the bones.

The girl ducked suddenly into a building through a battered Gothic archway. *"Puerto Rico Libre,"* said the Day-Glo anthem over the door. Cal quickened his pace to keep up with the girl. She darted down a hall putrid with the smell of urine and rotting food. Rats scampered in the darkness. Chunks of plaster dislodged and fell with muffled thumps.

She paused once to look back, and smiled incongruously, that same smile Cal had seen on the street corner, at once provocative and naive.

The hallway ended at a gaping hole in the wall. Following his guide, Cal exited into another alley. He glanced both ways but didn't see her. He panicked for an instant, then caught the flash of her white hem fluttering around a corner. He ran to catch up and found that she had actually darted down a narrow stairway. The metal steps led down into a dimly lit railway tunnel. Broken fragments of track clogged his path. He stumbled over them, and stopped to get his bearings. He heard voices and made his way toward them, his feet splashing in and out of stagnant puddles. The voices rose, shouted, all in Spanish. Cal passed a door off the main passage of the tunnel and looked in. A cockfight was in progress in a vaulted room. Money covered the ground, the cries of excited spectators bounced off the stone walls. Two roosters were fighting, their iridescent plumage a whirling blur. The animals separated for a moment, crowed, and flailed their clipped wings. One bird shot a claw into the other, and Cal saw a bloodied eye fly through the air. He moved on.

The girl turned from the wider part of the tunnel into a stone corridor lined with niches, cells of no more than several square feet. Passing one, Cal saw a group of men surrounding a girl who seemed little more than a child. One of the men mounted her as the others watched, and a sound echoed out of the niche, like the child giggling.

Hell, Cal thought. He was in hell.

They emerged suddenly from the tunnel into the sunlight. Cal blinked, his eyes slow to adjust. Where was the girl?

There.

She had climbed a mound of rubble in a vacant lot and stood gesturing to him from the low summit. Then she disappeared down the other side.

Cal clambered after her and, as he reached the top, saw a vast cathedral-like building rise up in front of his eyes. High on the front wall was a blank three-sided marquee. Granite rosettes studded the pillared entrances, and two concrete gargoyles, pitted and chipped by decades of weather, decorated the enormous facade.

A theater, a grand old vaudeville palace, long since fallen into decay.

The girl disappeared around the building to the rear and through a narrow doorway. Above it, a sign read ST GE OOR.

He stepped in. The door closed behind him with a creak.

He was standing in the wings of a great tabernacle, musty with the smell of age. Craning his neck, he looked out past the proscenium. High above him was a domed ceiling several stories high. It had once been an intricately carved plaster masterpiece, sunflower medallions linked by the spokes of a seven-pointed star. Now the plaster was cracked, the pattern barely visible. Overhanging the cavernous auditorium were three precariously tiered balconies, their balustrades sheathed in tarnished brass. Mirrors rimmed in prancing Cupids covered the walls. It was the kind of place Cal could remember attending as a child, watching Flash Gordon serials on Saturday afternoons, a movie temple. There were a thousand seats or more.

The stage was long and deep, and seemed outfitted for some roadshow production of *Tarzan*. Pots of trees and tropical plants were lined up across the rear, and animals skins of every kind covered the floor. At the center a large throne-like chair faced the audience. The chair had arms formed of bones, and a polished animal skull adorned the upright peak of the back.

Cal's head felt better, but he was cold. He shivered and pulled his coat tight. Suddenly the girl came toward him out of the shadows. Moving with ethereal grace, she reached to take his hand, and pulled him gently across the stage. A sound of light drumming faded in from hidden loudspeakers.

Abruptly, from the darkened wings on the far side of the stage, a tall figure materialized, swathed in animal hides and furry pelts. Cal recognized the costume, the traditional garb of a tribal shaman.

The face of the figure was hidden behind a carved African mask, an elongated oval of ebony. Brown bark circled the eyes. The mouth was painted opalescent yellow, and a black raven-like beak of exaggerated proportions jutted from the center. Covering the figure's arms were flaps of animal skin fastened at the shoulders and the waist.

The shaman moved sinuously forward and circled Cal, examining him, the mask moving around him as if in a dance.

Teresa spoke in a quavering voice: *"Padrino Tata, este es el hombre que busca la verdad de mayombe. Él quiere que usted haga un trabajo porque ellos lo han insultado."*

So this was Dr. Tata, the fabled priest he had heard about from the ASPCA man, Landers. This was the high priest of *mayombe*. Cal wished he could see the face behind the fixed staring mask.

Dr. Tata lowered himself onto the chair-like throne, spewing a stream of rapid Spanish and occasional words that sounded to Cal like a tribal African dialect. Yoruban.

Cal turned to Teresa. "What did he say?"

"He asked what you need."

"Protection for my son," Cal said. "They want him . . . the gods want him." He paused, heard the unearthly echo of his own voice coming back from the far recesses of the auditorium. "They want him to be sacrificed to Chango."

Teresa translated for the priest, but for several moments he made no sound. It was as though he already knew what Cal had come to ask, already knew about the other sacrifices. At last, he spoke a few words in Cal's direction. Cal understood only one word: Chango.

"He agrees," the girl said. "He will help you."

Through the slits in the mask, Cal saw the eyes blink. A man was in there. An ordinary man.

The girl continued speaking in English. The priest, she said, would cast a *ndoki nganga* to conjure up the *mbua*—the most powerful spell used only to call up the most powerful spirits of *mayombe*. The will of the Seven African Powers might be too strong to be swayed even by the *mbua*. Against Chango, the greatest of the African gods, even these spirits would be fiercely challenged.

"And this week," the girl said, "Chango is most strong. Tomorrow is his feast day, the day he was born in the stars."

Feast. Like the *guëmilere. The eve of the sixth.* That too had been on the eve of a god's birthday.

So tonight would be the eve of the seventh! They wanted Chris *tonight!*

"But," the girl said, "there is something you must give to Dr. Tata before he can cast his spell."

"Anything," Cal agreed quickly.

"Dr. Tata asks for the gift of your *owo*."

Cal shook his head blankly. *Owo?* Soul? Was the sorcerer literally asking—

"Money," the girl explained.

Cal was almost relieved. Oscar had said the *mayombero* would want a soul in payment.

"How much?" Cal asked anxiously.

"Fifteen hundred dollars," the girl replied.

Fifteen hundred dollars? To turn back the forces of the universe?

He was in the grip of a charlatan, of course, not a true chosen representative of the gods of *mayombe*.

Cal wavered. "I don't have that kind of money with me," he said, half seeking a way out.

The girl translated. Dr. Tata reached for a thin pole fastened to the throne and pointed with it to Cal's gold watch, then his wedding band. He spoke to Teresa and she turned to Cal.

"He wants to know the value of your gold," she said.

"The watch is worth five hundred dollars," Cal replied sharply. "The ring he can't have at any price."

Teresa passed along the answer, and came back with Dr. Tata's response. "He likes the ring. If you want the spell, you must give it. He will accept that and the watch instead of a thousand dollars." For the other five hundred dollars, she added, Cal could write a check. She would go to the bank and cash the check; the spell would be done when she returned with the money.

For a long moment, Cal said nothing. The plain gold wedding band was the most precious symbolic vestige of his love for Laurie.

Dr. Tata's insistence on having it was cruel and arbitrary, and stirred an impulse in Cal to walk out.

But he was too vulnerable. He had to see it through to the end. Perhaps Dr. Tata's hard conditions were no less than proof of kinship with gods who could be equally cruel and arbitrary. Cal opened the clasp on his watch and gave it to Teresa. Then, with some effort, he twisted off the ring. His heart ached as he watched the girl drop it with the watch into a receptacle in one arm of the throne.

Fool. Victim. Gulled like any desperate widow needing the gypsy's promise of a tall handsome stranger.

But then he wrote the check, and handed it to Teresa, who left immediately.

And all the while he was aware of the sorcerer's hard unblinking stare behind the mask.

⊃ ● ⊂

The wait seemed endless.

Dr. Tata had indicated with his pointer that Cal was to sit in the front row of orchestra seats until the girl returned from the bank.

Cal fidgeted in his seat like a moviegoer impatiently waiting for the show to start. He scratched nervously at the velvet nap of the seat until his fingertips had been grated raw.

But on the throne Dr. Tata remained absolutely immobile. No movement except for the masked eyes, glittering like sequins.

Once, Cal challenged the figure to speak. "How much longer?" he demanded.

But the man on the throne said nothing, did not move.

There was a noise at the back of the theater. When Cal turned, he saw four young men and two women, one a slightly built pubescent girl, taking seats several rows behind him. Cal tried to make out their faces, but the features were indistinguishable in the half light. They sat wordlessly waiting, like him. Except that they knew what they were waiting for.

Without his watch, Cal lost track of time. It could have been an hour later, or four, when the girl finally returned. She came purposefully out of the wings and crossed the stage to Dr. Tata. She held out one hand, presenting a manila bank envelope. Dr. Tata nodded, and the girl dropped it into the compartment in the throne. Then she knelt.

Now the sorcerer stood. Slowly he shed his fur wraps, revealing nothing underneath but an animal-hide loincloth and a muscular body the color of mahogany.

338

The four men seated behind Cal came down the aisle. They stopped at his seat, but said nothing, until he realized he was to go with them.

After escorting Cal to the stage, the four men surrounded the sorcerer while Teresa and the other girls brought out clay pots and brushes, and daubed the priest's body in streaks of orange and green and red.

Cal watched it all with split vision. Desperate for help, and yet unable to surrender completely his hold on reality, he remained the anthropologist, recording every detail in his mind, drawing parallels to the hundreds of other tribal rituals he had witnessed.

As soon as the girls finished painting the sorcerer's body and carried the pots away, one of the four men came forward. He held a sack of translucent hide, clearly the dried and stretched internal organs of some animal. From the bag, Dr. Tata drew a collection of bones, all shapes and sizes and polished by much use. Then he squatted on his haunches and tossed the bones onto the hides covering the floor. Once, twice, and again he threw the ivory-like shapes, forming designs with them seven times, similar to the santero's procedure with the shells. The number of tosses was not accidental, Cal thought. Seven. A mystical number. Seven, as in the play of dice. Seven days of the week. The Seven Deadly Sins.

And the Seven African Powers.

And the children, he realized now—each of those sacrificed had lived just seven years.

A Coleman stove was brought from the wings, a fire was lit, and the sorcerer mixed powders and oils over the flame. Teresa and the three other women had moved into the wings. They huddled together just offstage. Cal thought he heard giggling and glanced over toward the girls. The youngest was naked, and the others were holding a bowl between her legs. At a sign from Dr. Tata, the bowl was carried past Cal and its reddish-brown contents poured into the brew on the portable stove.

The sorcerer put his hands on Cal's shoulders and pushed him down, forcing him to kneel before the now bubbling pot. Faster than Cal could see, the *mayombero* swung a white pointed object through the air and, with a sudden violent flick of the hand, raked the tip across Cal's face.

There was an excruciating pain. Cal's hand went to his cheek. He felt the blood.

Cal reeled backward.

But Dr. Tata had grabbed him again, reached around his neck.

339

With surprising strength he forced Cal's head down over the simmering pot as the blood dripped into it. Cal felt the steam rising, beads of thick filmy moisture coating his skin. He heard the sorcerer murmuring an incantation over the liquid. Then, grasping the scalding pot with his bare hands, the *mayombero* lifted it slowly from the stove and set it aside.

Now he spoke directly to Cal, a stream of rapid Spanish. Teresa translated:

"If Chango would take your son he must first mount his horse. There is only one way to stop it from happening. Another god must take Chango's place. Our god, a spirit of *mayombe*, the *mbua*. The body of the horse must be closed to Chango, and opened only to the *mbua*. You understand?"

Cal tried. The mounting of the horse was possession. Only someone who was possessed could kill Chris. But if the *mayombe* gods could drive out Chango, take possession of this person instead, the sacrifice could be stopped.

Teresa continued, "The spirits will fight for the horse, and Chango is strong; the *orisha* will try with every trick to keep his *omo*. He may win. Or he may lose. But this is the only way."

Dr. Tata picked up the steaming clay pot and thrust it to Cal's lips.

"*Omo!*" he bellowed. "*Bebe! Que puedes recibir los espíritus!*"

"Man," Teresa said, "you must drink so the spirits of *mbua* can enter you, fill your soul, and leave no door open to Chango!"

Dr. Tata prodded the cup to Cal's lips, arms outstretched.

What had the girl said? The words replayed in Cal's mind. Fill *his* soul? So that the spirits could enter *him*?

So Chango could not enter his *omo*.

He was to be the *omo-orisha*.

If he had a soul, it seemed gutted by the unholy fire of this realization.

The powers of the universe wanted him to sacrifice his own son!

Dr. Tata's shielded eyes moved, flicking from Cal to the liquid. He pushed the earthenware pot harder against Cal's mouth.

Cal drank, numb to all but the horror of what he now knew.

He was meant to sacrifice Chris.

Leon Farber, Quentin Kimball, the picture on Kate's wall of a boy in knickers and peaked cap, all tumbled through Cal's mind as he drank.

Kimball had done it forty years ago, had sacrificed his son believing it might change history!

No one will take him from you. Now the santero's meaning was clear. Chris would not be *taken*. Cal himself would give the boy to the gods.

The pot was empty. Dr. Tata pulled it away. A chill entered Cal's heart like fingers slipping into a glove. He sucked in air, straining to breathe. His skin went cold, his hands felt numb. A sound exploded in his head, a deafening roar, the coursing of his own blood. Then he was overwhelmed by dizziness.

Oh no, it was a drug. They've drugged me.

Cal slumped forward on his knees. The lights above the stage fragmented his vision like reflected stars. His hands scraped over the bristled hides on the floor, his arms gave out under his weight, and he sprawled. He fought the creeping numbness. Around him the eight figures melted away—Dr. Tata removing the envelope of money and the gold objects from the throne, stuffing them into his furry robes, the men and women carrying the throne away like a stage prop no longer needed for the next scene.

Cal pushed himself onto his arms and lifted his head. Something more important than the simple desire to be aware impelled him to rise to his knees. He had to get to Chris.

He had a blurred glimpse of Dr. Tata watching from the wings, his hide-covered arms at his waist. The sorcerer was smiling. A fierce smile, all teeth.

And then he was gone, into the wings.

Cal slipped back to the floor, unable to rise again.

Ə ● Ɛ

He awoke with a headache that filled his skull. He sat up. His eyes itched. Legs aching with stiffness, he stood. The theater was empty, the stage was bare. There were no trees, no animal skins, no sorcerer's props. Had he dreamed it all?

He touched his cheek. The cut was still there, a dried patch of blood.

He staggered outside. It was dark. But at the alley's end he could see light. Cal made his way to the street. In the window of a drugstore on the corner the neon face of a clock showed ten after seven.

Had he slept all day? Or two days? He flagged a passing gypsy cab, practically had to run into its path to force the driver to stop, and called out his address before he had even closed the door.

"Hurry. Please!"

"Yeah, everybody's in a hurry," the driver said, and the cab took off into the night, scattering pedestrians in its path.

Chapter 41

THE APARTMENT was empty. Where was Ricki? Cal flicked on the desk lamp in Chris's bedroom. The boy's yellow windbreaker was draped over his chair. The shell was on the desk.

Chris was gone.

Gone where? Cal ordered himself not to panic. There were obvious explanations. Ricki had taken Chris home with her or she had taken him to dinner in the neighborhood. He'd told her not to, but in their rushed conversation maybe he hadn't emphasized it enough . . .

He telephoned her apartment. The phone rang and rang. *Why didn't she have her machine on?* Her machine was always on. Maybe she was in the shower. But then Chris would have answered the phone. Cal's mind took off on a crazed flight of paranoid thoughts. They had gotten her, too. She was another victim. The dreadful idea struck him that while he had been diverted by Dr. Tata, they had killed Ricki, cursed her and murdered her. *They?* Who were they? He dialed the number for *New York* magazine, but the switchboard was closed. He grabbed at the personal phone list hanging from a string next to the phone, fumbled through it. Halstead. Hammerman. Hanauer—Ricki's direct-dial number.

After four rings, she answered: "Editorial."

"Ricki, it's me," he panted. He was no less out of breath than if he had sprinted a hundred yards. "Where the hell is Chris? Is he there with you?"

"Cal, where've you been? I tried your office and—"

He screamed. "Goddamnit, where's Chris?"

"Cal, relax. Everything's fine. I stayed with Chris until your new housekeeper—what's her name? Mrs. Griffin?—showed up. Chris seemed perfectly comfortable with her, so I thought I could go."

Cal's mind raced. Celestine Griffin was Jamaican. They had their own kind of Voodoo, didn't they?

Ricki's voice filled the silence. "Cal, it's all right, isn't it? I mean, Mrs. Griffin works for you—"

"I told you to *stay* with him," he said simply, yet his voice conveyed all his rage and terror and even a threat.

"Cal, I'm sorry," Ricki wailed. "But for God's sake, what's happening?"

He had no answer for her, and no forgiveness. He hung up and started searching the kitchen for a note from Celestine Griffin.

She couldn't really be . . .

But there was nothing.

Chris was gone.

Taken.

For sacrifice.

Cal had a moment of being lost, totally without direction. The fear in his gut was a solid leaden weight, so massive that he felt for a moment it would drag him to his knees.

MacTaggart!

Hope.

MacTaggart would get help, scour the city, turn the *barrio* upside down.

"Twenty-third, Anderson."

"Lieutenant MacTaggart, please."

There was a click, a series of rings in double-tone sequence.

"Captain Blaine," the answering voice said.

"I want MacTaggart," Cal said abruptly. "I *asked* for Mac-Taggart."

There was a pause at the other end. "Can I help you?" the voice said.

"I *said* I wanted MacTaggart."

"Who's calling?"

"Is there a number where I can reach him? It's urgent."

"Who's calling?" the voice repeated.

"Just leave a message for him," Cal said. "Tell him Cal called and I need him—"

"Just a minute," the voice placated. A hand was cupped over the phone and Cal heard a muffled conversation, but couldn't make out the words.

"I'm afraid I can't take a message for him," the cop said, unchar-

343

acteristically apologetic, when he came back on the line. "Now if you'll tell me why you want him, maybe I can be—"

"My name is Cal Jamison. I'm a professor at Columbia. Will you tell me where I can reach him? It's an emergency."

"Mr. Jamison, this is Captain Edward Blaine. I've taken Lieutenant MacTaggart's place. Are you a friend of his?"

"We've been . . . working on something together."

"Oh. Well, I'm sorry to tell you this, sir, but Lieutenant MacTaggart passed away yesterday. If you'd like to attend the service, it's scheduled for—"

"Dennis? *Dead?* How?"

"Cerebral hemorrhage. I'm sorry to be the one to tell you."

MacTaggart. Dead. Cal closed his eyes and recited to himself all the pieties: a good and decent man, drove himself too hard, on the edge of a breakdown anyway, it had been too much for him.

No. He knew all the logic. But logic did not explain this death any more than the children's.

"Do you know this case he was working on?" Cal asked. "The missing kids? The murders."

"Yes, I've taken over his whole case load. That's one of—"

"I think my son's been kidnapped and it's tied in with the others and we have to find him before they—"

"What's your address?" Blaine snapped quickly.

Cal gave it to him.

"I'm on my way."

∋ ● ∈

By the time the cop arrived Cal had called the Hacketts and most of the other parents of Chris's friends. None of them had seen Chris or Celestine.

Captain Edward Blaine was a husky sweet-faced redhead. Cal led him into the living room. Blaine sat on the couch and held a notebook on his lap. "Tell me about it," he said. "When did you last see your son?"

Cal spilled it out—about the spell and Mrs. Ruiz and his research and Torey and doing the spell in the cemetery. He sat still so he wouldn't be tempted to pace, and tried not to sound deranged. He was aware that no matter how lucid the explanation, he did indeed sound like a madman, so he kept reminding Blaine that he was an anthropologist at Columbia, that he was respected in his field, and that his knowledge of primitive religions convinced him he was right about what was happening.

344

"Now let me get this straight," the cop said when Cal had gone through it once. "You think your son's in danger of being killed."

"Sacrificed," Cal said. "Torey and I tried to save him, and Carmen did, too."

"With a spell," Blaine said. "I got that."

"Yes, that's why the trick was turned. It all goes back to the reading."

"The shell thing," the cop said matter-of-factly. "The Table of . . . something."

"Ifa," Cal said. "So you see, this isn't an ordinary kidnapping."

The policeman had been listening attentively. "Mr. Jamison, let's get some facts down, okay? Now, can you give me a photograph of your son, a snapshot'll do, and a description of your housekeeper and where she lives."

Cal took a deep breath. It seemed the detective had believed him. "Captain Blaine, please, you don't know what you're dealing with. There's no time for sending out pictures. You've got to bring Oscar Sezine in, and force him to talk. You have to interrogate him, break him. MacTaggart knew that. He would've—"

"Mr. Jamison," the cop interrupted, "do you have a picture of your son?" The cop talked in the patient tones of a psychiatrist with a hysteric.

It was hopeless. Blaine would never understand.

Cal hung his head and began to cry. The cop reached out a hand.

"Mr. Jamison, really, I'm trying to help you. If you'll—"

The telephone rang. Blaine glanced toward the phone, but Cal was already out of his chair and across the room.

"Hello?"

"Hi, Daddy."

Tears sprang again to Cal's eyes, tears of relief and gratitude. *Safe! Chris was safe.*

Cal had to catch his breath before he could speak. "Bean, where are you?"

"At Kate's."

"And you're okay?"

"Sure. Great. Kate took me to a movie, and then we had Chinese food and—"

"Bean, can you put Kate on now? I'll see you soon."

Kate. She'd been away. Now suddenly she was back and had taken Chris without letting him know . . .

There was a rustling by the phone, then her voice came on, full of concern.

"Cal, dear. Chris told me about Victoria, and I tried to reach you at the hospital, but you weren't—"

"Kate," he broke in sharply. "I've been out of my mind about Chris. Couldn't you have left a note or something?"

"Well, I never thought it would be so hard to reach you. Please don't be angry. I dropped by earlier and Chris was there with Celestine and she told me she had to go. I thought I was helping. I did call you at home, but your line was busy before . . ."

Of course. It all made sense.

And it still bothered him.

"Kate, I'll be right over," Cal said. "Now listen to me: I want you to lock your door and not let anyone else in. Only me. Okay?"

"Well, it's already locked, but I certainly won't open it until you get here."

Cal thanked her and hung up the phone. Captain Blaine stood and put his notebook back in his pocket.

"You found your son," the detective said as though he'd been through this a thousand times before. He headed for the door.

"No, wait," Cal pleaded. "Come with me. He needs protection."

The policeman paused. "Protection?" he said quietly. "But he's with a friend, isn't he?"

But the gods still want him, Cal was going to say. Then he realized it was no use. The cop was at the door.

"You go to your son, Mr. Jamison, and bring him home, and then get a good night's sleep. Come up to the precinct when you have a chance and we'll talk about what you and Dennis were working on."

He tipped his hat and went out the front door, closing it softly behind him.

Cal almost called out, then he shook his head and sat down for a minute on the couch, motionless, unable to think. At last he got up and walked down the hall to his bedroom. He took off his shirt and dropped it into the hamper. Putting on a fresh one, he thought about Kate. Trying to help by taking over from Celestine. Only helping. As she always did. And it was Kate who had suggested that Celestine work for him.

He smoothed out the wrinkles in his tie and looped it onto the rack.

Then he remembered how interested Kate had been in Chris's shell. That first day, the minute she saw it.

No, of course it couldn't be Kate.

He buttoned his shirt.

But Kate had brought him to New York, used her influence to get him a job. Kate, the quintessential scientist, had said she believed in destiny, even in the inevitability of Laurie's death.

But she had also said the same thing to millions on television. And hadn't she discouraged him from his interest in Voodoo? Hadn't she said it was dangerous?

He put on his tan corduroy jacket and adjusted his collar in the mirror.

Or had she really discouraged him?

Cal's heart raced. Wasn't it Kimball's manuscript that led him deeper into Voodoo? Quentin Kimball had killed his own son. Could Kate not have known? Kate, whose own son had been killed. Could her husband have hidden the truth from her?

Cal's palms were cold and clammy. He picked up his wallet.

But would Kate hurt Chris? If anything, she had been grandmotherly and concerned as always. She had even come running that day with salve for his poison ivy.

Cal looked at himself in the mirror. He looked unreal, his skin white and waxy. He rubbed his forehead for a moment.

The poison ivy! What had Carmen said? "*Guao* is good." Poison ivy was used by believers to ward off evil. Carmen had wanted to save Chris. And Kate had cured the rash, torn up the plant by its roots and thrown it away.

Cal switched off the bedroom lamp, and stood motionless in the darkness, and he knew.

Kate believed.

Believed that the sacrifice of seven children would save the world.

Yet every part of him that could love and respect and *feel* fought against the warnings of his reason. Kate? Impossible. He was stunned and shamed by his own suspicion.

Yet six children had been killed, and now one was left. To be done tonight, on the eve of Chango's feast day.

And where was Chris?

Cal raced to the front door. Then, with his hand on the knob, about to leave, he stopped.

The gods wanted *him* to do it, to give his own son. He was the horse to be mounted. The *omo*.

But if he didn't go . . .

The course of fate could be changed. If he wasn't near Chris there was no way he could be the one to hurt him.

But could he forsake his son? Leave him with Kate? He stood by the door for a second, an eternity, deciding which way to turn.

Chris needed him. Was waiting for him.

He had to go.

Chapter 42

THE CAB RIDE to Kate's required a convoluted trip down Seventh Avenue into a warehouse district, and even now, after two seasons in the city, the neighborhood felt foreign. Mars. He rode down West Broadway through the fashionable dark district of Soho, where industrial lofts became bankers' homes and marine supply depots turned into restaurants with names like Central Falls and Odeon. You could have Paris in New York. Or Montana.

Or Africa.

Could Kate really be a part of it? He couldn't bear to think so. He couldn't bear to imagine such a betrayal, such an evil.

The cab passed a lumberyard. Cal thought he heard thunder.

Thunder?

But the sky was clear, he could see stars, the Little Dipper. He could have sworn he'd heard thunder. Maybe it was from New Jersey, a storm over the Hudson.

"Six bucks even," the cabdriver said, and Cal paid.

He got out and paused on the sidewalk, looking west. He heard thunder again. There wasn't a cloud.

∋ • ∈

The industrial-size elevator car crept slowly upward, its pulley system shimmying as though it might crack apart at any moment. He would be instantly killed when it crashed to the basement. Had it been rigged? Had they seen him talking to Blaine?

The car thumped to a stop, but the doors didn't open. Cal told himself to be patient, it was an old elevator. He pushed the button marked "Door Open," and the doors parted, leaving him on Kate's doorstep, staring at the fake rusticated stucco hallway.

He closed his eyes.

Nobody wants to hurt you. Or Chris. Kate is your oldest and dearest friend in the world.

He realized with a start that he had his finger on the bell, and the door was opening. He had never stopped ringing.

Kate was stunning as only an old woman can be, her engine-gray hair swept back, her warm lined face lifted toward him in concern. The caftan she wore was fancier than usual, all black and trimmed in sparkling silver thread.

"Cal, my dear, you look all worn out. Come in, come in."

He felt himself staring at her suspiciously, but she smiled and led him into the spacious loft. The wall of fifteen-foot windows was almost entirely obscured by heavy drapes. Dim shafts of moonlight penetrated the seams, reflecting a luminous gold from the polished floor.

Cal heard the television from the far end of the loft and peered into the darkness, searching for Chris. In shadows cast by the flickering screen he could make out a dim figure—yes, it was Chris, lying on his stomach, one arm propped on his elbow.

Cal's heart leapt and he stared so hard that his jaws involuntarily clenched. Chris was fine, Chris was safe, nothing was wrong, the television set was on and Chris was resting his head in his hands facing the screen and everything was all right and there was a can of soda near his elbow and nothing was wrong.

With a long fast stride, Cal hurried across the room toward the boy. Kate followed beside him.

"You must be in awful shape," she said, her voice gentle and concerned. "I called the hospital three times to ask about Victoria, but they wouldn't tell me a thing. What's wrong with her, dear?"

Someone did a spell on her.

"It was . . . it's an infection," he managed to say as he reached Chris and bent down next to him. The boy's attention was being held by a peculiar game show called "Family Feud," in which two families competed to win money. Chris rolled onto his back when he heard Cal approach.

"Daddy!"

"Bean, you okay?"

"Sure."

Cal touched Chris's forehead, hesitated a moment, then leaned over and hugged him, overwhelmed by the simple fact that the boy was safe and unharmed.

350

"Daddy, where were you all day?"

"I was at the hospital with Torey."

"Aunt Ricki told me she ate some bad food. But she's going to be okay, isn't she?"

"She's going to be fine, Bean."

"I missed school today," Chris said. "Aunt Ricki said I couldn't go. But I got to read *Charlotte's Web*. It's nice to stay home from school."

Cal smiled, then looked up and saw Kate observing them benevolently, full of pride and pleasure and beaming with love. What had he been thinking of her? He stared at her for another second, and her placid demeanor frightened him.

He turned back to Chris. "Let's go, Bean, get your jacket and I'll take you home."

"You'll do no such thing," Kate said authoritatively. "I'll bet you haven't eaten a thing all day. Come and put some hot food in your stomach. I've been saving it for you."

She took his arm, brooking no argument, and marched him toward the kitchen. He still wanted to leave. How long since he'd slept? He glanced down at his wrist.

The watch, of course, was gone. In payment to a sorcerer.

Cal felt a wave of self-loathing at having been played for a fool. He had been conned. He looked back over his shoulder, stiff-necked and turning with some difficulty. Chris had returned to lying peacefully on his stomach.

"Goodness, dear, you're perspiring," Kate said. "Let me have your coat. It's warm in here."

She was already behind him, pulling him out of the sleeves. She scurried to the hallway closet with his overcoat. As she was slipping it onto a hanger, Cal shot a glance down the hallway toward the rear of the apartment; the doors to all the rooms were closed.

They went into the kitchen. Cal felt a spasm in his leg, a great weight on his back. Tension. Exhaustion. He sat down at the slab butcher-block table and crossed his hands in front of him. Kate, taking a plate from the dishwasher, looked across the table at him.

"Where's your wedding ring, Cal? Didn't you use to wear a gold band?"

"I . . . I've stopped wearing it," he said shakily.

"Oh," she smiled, "for Victoria. That's very considerate." She busied herself at the stove, standing over a steaming iron pot of stew, stirring with a wood spoon.

"Kate, on the way over here in the cab . . . well, I know this doesn't exactly sound reasonable . . . but I had this feeling that . . ."

She finished pouring some broth from a saucepan into the larger dish, and turned to look at him, bright-eyed.

"Yes, Cal?"

That you were sacrificing children.

Christ, how could he get into this? Why should he—the fevered imaginings of his exhausted mind.

He shook his head, and Kate went on as though he had given her an answer:

"You'll like this *paella*," she said. "Oysters and lobster and clams, it's marvelous. Give me a minute here and I'll fix you some coffee. With brandy, maybe? Then we can talk."

Cal's chair was facing the high window at the end of the kitchen, the glass with tiny strands of wire threaded through it, a remnant of when the building was industrial. In the center panel, Cal saw his own reflection against the blackness of night. The mirrored image of his face surprised him, made him corporeal, fixed reality. The day had seemed so *un*real, the last twenty-four hours a return of the hallucinatory nightmare that he had thought was ended.

Yes, he had to confront her.

"Kate," he said, "why didn't you tell me the truth about Scotty? That he . . . he didn't die from an illness?"

She turned from the stove holding a plate heaped with the *paella* over rice, and brought it to the table, setting it on a linen placemat with a damask napkin and a silver fork with a bone handle. Everything in high style. Then she moved back to the stove, poured two cups of coffee, and added a splash of Remy Martin.

Had she heard him? He thought of the moment with Mac-Taggart when the cop had been invisibly encapsulated.

"Kate," he repeated, raising his voice. "Why did you lie about what happened to your child?"

She brought the coffee mugs over to the table, set one in front of Cal and sat down across from him. She smiled at him, and then looked down into her mug, and for a few moments he was sure that she had heard nothing.

Then she said evenly, "I should think you'd understand, dear. It's always been too painful to talk about."

It was as though she were pleading for his mercy, Cal thought, to drop the subject now.

But he couldn't. "Quentin committed suicide," he said. "You never told me that, either."

352

She breathed deeply, then looked up at him. "Who told you that?" she asked.

"Farber," he said. "He told me what happened in New Orleans when you and Quentin lived there. When he researched Voodoo —wrote the notes that you gave me. You did read those notes, didn't you, Kate? You knew exactly what happened to Quentin and Scotty."

She gazed back at him steadily for another second. Then the pain began to creep into her expression, as slowly as a fog over the coast of a forsaken island.

"I love you, Cal," she said. "You know that. You're like a son to me."

She kept staring at him, and through the pain he could see something defiant in her eyes.

"Kate," he said, and his voice broke and he felt crushed by a surging wave of love and fear and hatred and despair. "Kate," he repeated, his voice dying to a shocked whisper, "what have you done?"

There was a long silence. She turned away, and Cal could tell from the cast of her eyes that she was looking back, all the way back.

"I should tell you about that summer," she said at last, and her tone was eerily normal and conversational, "the time just before I met Quentin. That's where it really begins." She paused, and frowned, as though trying to remember, to be sure. "Yes, the summer of 1931, it was. My first book had been published and I'd spent a year basking in all the glory, and it was time to get back out into the field. Well, I had all the fame and money I could ever use, and I realized I could go *anywhere*. And it was then I decided I wouldn't specialize in just one culture, I didn't have to go back to where I'd been. I wanted to see them all, to tell people about the wonders of every ancient people. 'So where next, Katie?' I said to myself." She flicked a glance at Cal, sparkling and affectionate. "It was almost like that, dear. Spin the globe, see where your finger lands. I decided to go to Africa, to some of the unexplored jungle around Dahomey. At least, I thought at the time it was my decision."

Cal wondered for a moment if she'd started so far back to answer his questions about Scotty and Kimball—or to avoid them. But he didn't interrupt. As always, from the first day he'd ever seen her, she had the power to hold him spellbound with her adventures.

"I stopped over first in a coastal town, and the French who

353

administered the territory supplied me with an escort, a Major Dreyfus. Lovely man, he'd always joke that he was the one that had been court-martialed in the Dreyfus case and that his punishment was to serve out his term in Porto Novo. I spent a few weeks there while the expedition to the interior was arranged, and also to learn the Fon languages of the natives. And that was where I got the first inkling that this trip was . . . was part of my karma." She glanced at Cal again, as if remembering his surprise at the word once before, and expecting another objection.

But Cal only listened.

"I'd always had to work at languages," Kate went on. "Hard as it was, of course, I'd learn the dialects wherever I went—there was no hope of reaching the heart of the primitives without knowing their speech. Yet this time, with the African tribal dialects, I had no trouble at all. It was as though I'd been born with them in my head, engraved somewhere in my memory, waiting to be used. I only had to blow the dust off the chiseled words, and I could speak. It was enough to make me start wondering then if there wasn't such a thing as reincarnation, as if I wasn't some tribal chieftain's wife reborn," she fluttered her hand over her caftan, "in this old body."

Cal gazed at her, admiration oddly mingled with his fear of her. She had yet to offer a defense, but she could still turn on the charm and make it work.

"Well, at the end of June, my Major Dreyfus took me up country, along with forty bearer-boys. It was staggeringly hot, and after a week out the major became sick. I thought we'd turn around, bring the old boy back, but he said if we continued there was a village not more than a day's walk ahead where he could rest—and perhaps be cured. There was a witch doctor there, the major told me, who'd acquired quite a reputation for performing miracles. We expected he could make light work of dysentery. So we went on, walked for a day and found nothing. The major was much worse, but by then the only choice was to locate the village. We went for another half day . . . and then Dreyfus died." She shook her head, a respectful moment of mourning for a companion. "So there I was, in the middle of the jungle, with forty bearer-boys. Dreyfus had known something of the area, but I knew nothing. Perhaps you won't believe me when I tell you this, dear, but my will almost failed me. I thought of turning back, reorganizing, or perhaps abandoning the expedition. And yet something held me. We buried Dreyfus—we couldn't bring him back in that heat—and I re-

354

member kneeling for a minute over his grave, and saying the Lord's Prayer because that was all I could think of in the way of a ceremony, and at the moment I finished I had . . . a kind of revelation. 'This is the crossroads for you, Katie,' I thought. 'Right here at this spot, in this time and place, your real mission begins.' And that was it: I simply knew if I turned back, it was to the ordinary —to the predictable and banal. And if I went forward, I would walk into . . . into a kind of glory. Can you understand any of this, dear?" she said to Cal.

"I guess I know the sort of feeling you're talking about," he said.

She continued: "So I told the carriers we would go deeper. Naturally, some turned back—the idea of a woman leading an expedition alone into uncharted territory was more fearsome to them than dropping into a pit of cobras. But there were enough who stayed. And when we'd gone only another two hours beyond the point where Dreyfus had been buried, we reached a village. I believe you'll find something more like a town there now, but then it was almost nothing, a place called Akoyú—which is also the Yoruban for 'wise man.' I don't suppose there were more than twenty grass huts. But, oh Cal, the people—they were the most extraordinarily beautiful human beings I'd ever seen. They lined up to greet us when my caravan walked in, and I was just stunned by . . . by their nobility. The men were lean and muscular, the women with perfect bodies, full and round with the most breathtaking faces. And all of them the most unbelievable shade of black you can imagine—the blue-black of the infinite. It was as if the gods had actually painted them."

The reference struck Cal: it was the first time she had mentioned the gods.

Then there was a peal of rolling thunder again, and Cal turned to the window. Kate glanced at him expectantly, and resumed the story only when he turned back to her.

"I was received into the village as I've never been taken in anywhere, before or since. I thought at first it might be only that I was a white woman, a curiosity, especially appreciated perhaps because I spoke the language. But then I detected something different in their attitude . . . a reverence, and at the same time a feeling of true kinship. It was as if they'd been expecting me. Oh yes, I know anthropologists have had that feeling before, that egotistical longing to be totally accepted. But this *was* different. These people loved me, made me feel honored. The chief, the children, the old people, the hunters, the fire-tenders—all of them spoke openly to me in a way I've never experienced elsewhere. All . . . but one. There was an old man who lived in a hut slightly separated from the rest of the village. I hadn't even known he was there at first. Then one day I saw him walk into the village and visit the chief's hut, and walk out again. The chief had been sick, I knew, but after the old man left he was well again. Once I'd seen the old man, of course, I asked the others about him. But they put me off, they wouldn't speak about it. After they'd been so free with me about everything else, I thought it was odd they would say nothing on this one subject. But I didn't press them. I began keeping a watch on the old man's hut; and, in fact, I let him see that I was watching. It didn't seem to bother him. He used to sit cross-legged outside his hut for hours at a time—like a sort of African Zen Buddhist—just watching the river that flowed by not far from his door. He'd sit there, and I'd stand in the trees—and later I took to sitting myself—and I don't know how to explain this, but there was an absolute . . . communion. I knew I must never try to speak until he wanted me to, gestured me closer. And though day after day went by and he said nothing, I knew with absolute certainty that the moment would come."

Cal was entranced by the narrative. Yet there were moments when the symptoms of exhaustion intruded. The muscle at the back of his neck constricted. And he heard something like the rush of wind, or a metallic noise faintly stirred his ear drum, like the clank of armor from a distant army.

"And then it did. It was at the end of a day after I'd been there several weeks. A magnificent evening. The sun setting over the river, and the orange light making the dried grass of the crude huts seem to be spun from gold. Well, the beauty of the day, the emptiness of the horizon—I never felt as I did that night so connected to . . . to Creation itself. It was as though this was the very dawn of it, and I was there with the very first human creatures who'd been set on the earth. The tribe had finished their evening meal, sitting in a circle at the center of the village as they did when it didn't rain, and then they began to sing. And how can I describe the song? Slow, and much sweeter than most of the African music you hear, this was . . . oh goodness, there isn't a word, just transcendent. And as they sang, I knew—Cal, I *knew*—this was the night the old man would send for me. This hour, this place, this experience had been destined for me, written in the stars, as surely as if I could read it in the sky under the Big Dipper. The sun went down, the stars came out, and one by one the rest of the tribe drifted away. But I sat there. And then when a cloud drifted across the moon, and the night was its blackest, I saw a light shining through the trees from the old man's hut. His silhouette stood in the door motioning me to come to him.

"When I entered the hut he was already seated on the floor, and he indicated with a nod that I was to sit across from him. A fire was going between us. Then he began to speak. He said that he was the *babalao* of the village, the priest, and that from the day I arrived he'd been asking his gods about me. They said that I was part of the *iré*—the destiny—of the Great Tribe of Men, and that I was a *maputo mendele;* the closest translation I can give you is 'noble animal.' He told me, too, that only once before in his own lifetime had he heard of the gods bestowing such a designation, and that had happened forty years earlier. Then he said there was a ceremony we would have to perform together. The priest asked me to cut off three hanks of my hair, and handed me a special ceremonial knife. When he had the hair, he placed it into three bowls—gourds, really, sliced in half. Then he took three embers from the fire, lifted them with his fingers, actually, and dropped them one by one into the bowls. The first one cracked instantly, and fell apart. Then the second one. And the third one exploded, was gone instantly in a flash of light. But my hair wasn't burned at all. It lay in the ashes of the gourds, not even singed. Then the old man dipped his fingers in the ashes of the gourds and drew three lines across my forehead. He told me that I was a messenger of the gods without doubt, that through me, and those I loved most, the gods would exercise their power and make their glorious and merciful presence known on earth. I'd been silent through it all, half stunned, half simply . . . tranquil, accepting it all some- how unquestioningly. But when he said that the gods would make themselves known through me, I cried out, 'How? Tell me how?' "

She cried it out now as she must have then, pleading intensely, and Cal felt he was there in the hut with her, that he, too, was hearing the message of the *babalao.*

"But he wouldn't tell me," Kate said, becoming quiet again. "He said only that I had no choice. That it was my destiny, and all would one day be clear to me."

She stopped and looked for a long time at her hands. "And then . . ." She paused again, choked up, and tears began to spill slowly out of her eyes. But she wiped the tears, and squared her shoul- ders, and when she spoke her voice was firm.

357

"Then I went away from the village. I knew, as I'd known to come, that I had to go. I marched back to Porto Novo, and it was there I met Quentin. For a while life was so good, and so normal —for years, in fact—that I thought the whole experience was . . . well, perhaps I'd caught a touch of the same fever that killed the major. But then it happened that Quentin and I went to New Orleans, and he began to study Obeah . . . and finally the old man's meaning was revealed. All the terror of it . . . and, as I've come to understand, the wonder of it."

Kate was silent. Cal felt as if he should say something, but there was nothing to say. He understood.

And he believed.

He wanted now only to run. From his own fate.

But he couldn't move. The air around him grew dense, and he could hear again the sound of armor, the army advancing, closer now. Then the hard metallic noises were washed away by the soft rush of surf, followed by the pounding of waves. A lightning bolt crashed through his vision, seemed to split his eyes open, a stream of flashes one right after the other, shivering and hovering in the air and entirely blocking his sight.

He shut his eyes. The lightning remained, streaks of yellow exploding with red coronas. A form took shape around them, a swirling cloud of blue-black smoke.

And then suddenly was gone.

He opened his eyes. Kate was across from him.

"Chango is with you now," she said. "Isn't he?"

Cal saw his reflection in the window, his face white against the black. And yet, at the same moment, the black cloud took shape again, lightning erupted and shot through it, and the cloud became more solid, it seemed to be a face. Not a face, but only eyes, golden glittering eyes. The sounds of clashing metal were coming from the cloud itself, with the semblance of speech.

Kate had not moved. Cal felt himself rocking in his chair, his arms jerking as though he'd been electrically shocked.

"Yes," Kate said, "he's with you now." She brushed a hand against her cheek. There were tears in her eyes. "Cal, I want you to know, you must believe me, if it could have been any other way . . . but there was never any choice. I knew that Chris had been called when he found his *otane*—that shell from the reading of the Table of Ifa. I knew that the gods wanted him, knew that I had no choice but to give him. None of us does. You know what happened the last time we denied the gods."

And then she was gone. The black cloud had turned even darker, its gold eyes brighter.

Cal shouted into the void, soundless words *save me* a shout only in his mind.

Then, without warning, a weight slammed onto his shoulders, and he was knocked from his chair, thrown to the floor, bent over like a dog on all fours. His head went forward, then whiplashed back, then down again, snapping back and forth. His back arched and bucked.

It was happening, he knew. Happening to *him*.

The god had mounted his horse.

Chapter 43

HE WAS IN a vast ocean, a bottomless sea.

He was a speck, a spot of dust, the tiniest particle in the universe. And then he was split in two, and then split again, and again, until he was nothing. The ocean washed over him, and he was a corpse on a circle of water surrounded by greater and greater circles radiating out from his arms until they were no longer in sight. The mandala, the world. There was a great citadel of seven angles and seven peaks, and above the citadel a pulsing force that was neither light nor heat nor sound, but a collection of infinite shapes, always changing but always recognizably the same. Cal knew he was on the verge of witnessing his own soul. He had never believed in a soul, and even now could not see it or touch it, but on the shore of the ocean where he stood beneath the citadel he watched the water swirl upward, and deep inside himself, where he could find in man what was pure and innocent and eternal, he saw that it was seeping out of him, that his soul was leaking away into the water and being drawn into the infinite series of shapes above the citadel, always changing, always the same.

He was losing his soul. And something he could not define was taking its place.

He felt the pain in his head.

He had blacked out.

I am Chango

His head was on the floor, and his eyes opened to threads of light on the hairs of his arm. He blinked, saw Kate above him, looking down with concern.

360

His back arched again.

Instinctively he fought, fought as though he were locked in battle, wrestling with an attacker, the black cloud swirling in front of his eyes. Inside him? Around him? He was stupefied by the strength of the grasp on his body, as though a snake were encircling him, a boa tightening around his middle.

He grabbed blindly for the table, flailing, and shouted again into the void.

He could hear his own voice now, calling for help aloud, and it was a cry of rage. Accusation. Agony. Echoing as though it would never stop, the scream of a man dying, being crushed alive at the bottom of a pit.

"Kaaaaaaaaaaattte!"

He clung to the table, and then was torn away, thrown onto the floor again by the awesome weight. Thrown into a void, into space. He was traveling through a tunnel drilled into time. He could not remember how he had come to be in this place, or how long he had been there. It was a long tunnel, then a field of gray, a sun rising, or was it setting? An army unfolded in front of him, an ancient army led by the black cloud form, with floating eyes and the sound of clanking armor. Cal looked down at himself and saw that his body was gone. He was pure spirit, pure mind.

Soul.

He shouted *No!*

And was seated at the table again, Kate gently easing him into the chair.

"Cal?"

His face reflected back at him from the window, but his features were flowing, changing shape, becoming amorphous and cloudy. Then it was no longer his face, but the black cloud form in front of his eyes. From inside the cloud came a voice with the resonance of wind coming down the tunnel, not as

> *mine horse*
> *stronger*
> *in name Olofi ruler of*
> *heavens Obatala the father*

words, but rhythms. Where did the voices come from? Where was the language? At a level below consciousness.

Down the tunnel came another figure, a towering wall of fire, flames licking at his eyes, a wall that seemed to walk

OF THE EARTH
BOY
MBUA RIDE

and speak, the voice in a loud whisper, a screaming furious whisper

OUT OF FLESH
HE IS FLESH BOY
OUT CHANGO
OUT
OUT

and then the voice of the cloud, the howling wind

Olofi banished you
horse I ride

raging in the tunnel, the cloud surrounding the fire now, engulfing it. The fire voice faded, the fire was enveloped in blackness.

Light dimmed in the kitchen. Cal could see his reflection in the window again, his face his own for a moment, then melding with the fire and smoke, his own eyes glittering gold. Behind him, in the reflection, he saw Oscar Sezine, and Celestine and Raymond Suares and faces from the *guëmilere*. Oscar was lifting him from the chair, draping something over him; there were bandages on Oscar's head. He remembered hitting him. In another life?

Oscar's voice broke through. "Cal, you are meeting your destiny. This is your mission for the gods."

Cal felt himself losing touch again. Now there was the image of the room in front of him, the hallway, the living room, and moving with him, as the moon moves when you walk, the black cloud and the fire. As long as he struggled to remain aware, their voices were drowned in the loudness of his breathing. But the mirage remained, and expanded, filled his field of vision. The black cloud and the flame merged, pulled apart, became one, separated, and between them Cal could see sprawled like a rug on the floor Chris's sleeping body, legs spread, his head nestled against the chair's leg, the can of soda nearby. An artifact from an ancient and vanished civilization.

He picked up his son, held him in his arms. The front door of the loft beckoned, take him out

OUT CHANGO
HE IS OF THE EARTH
GOD LU GOD OGU SENT YOU

OUT OF THE EARTH
BOY IS NOT YOURS BOY
OF THE EARTH
OF THE FLESH

And the cloud swarmed over the flame, burying it, the shrieking voice of the wind a

> *no no no no*
> *give unto Chango*
> *give unto Chango*
> *the flesh the blood*
> *the blood*

chant, song, rhythms, not words.

Chris lay before him in a pool of water. A bathtub. Oscar was chanting and adding herbs, colored oils.

The fire swept over the cloud.

Chris's eyes were closed, his smile deliriously wide. On the surface of the water in the tub, the herbs drifted over his pink flesh. His hair glistened, fragrant soap oozed down his flesh.

The boy's eyes opened.

"Daddy, I'm going to Mommy. Take me. You and Chango."

Cal bathed him.

The gods fought, the fire of *mbua* and Chango. Cal watched their spirits in the air before him, then inside his head, then himself.

He was standing over himself!

High above his own head, near the ceiling. He had departed his own body while the fire and cloud raged inside him. He was their battlefield.

He watched himself carry Chris toward the back of the apartment. The door to the storeroom opened. Down the middle an aisle of trees and

> *mine! blood! mine!*

OUT CHANGO OUT

> *give him to me the*
> *Powers! Cut him cut cut*

I CAST YOU OUT CHANGO

plants, the filing cabinets pushed aside. At the end of the aisle an altar. Masks above it, suspended by chains. They had been in packing crates. But the crates were gone. Now in their place was a table laden with platters of food and a large wooden bowl.

363

Cal started toward the altar at the end of the aisle. Far away. He looked to his side and saw the woman in the brown dress, the *akronin*, Mrs. Escobar. The man with silver hair, the dentist. And the model's boyfriend. There were dozens of them, crowded to the edges of the room.

Cal faltered when he reached the end of the aisle. He stared down. Chris's eyes were closed now. Cal looked up. He could see on the altar's lower tiers strings of beads, black and yellow, and amid these, bottles and jars and pots.

He could see himself from above.

A shout came to his lips: *No I won't give him No*

It was his own voice, now entering the fray between the cloud and the fire, taking shape as . . . as a white obelisk enshrouded by fire and smoke.

The cloud enveloped the obelisk.

> *quiet!*

Cal fought. The obelisk pushed through the cloud.

> *give give him*
> *I am you we are one*

The altar was wide and deep, made of stone. Lashed to its legs hung a rich straw tapestry, black and gold. Cal set Chris on the stone, and the boy lay down, stretched out, his eyes open again and his smile beatific, the anticipation of holiness. Oscar stood behind Cal and raised a goblet in the air. On his robe, red swords mingled against a field of black.

"To Chango," he intoned, "god of war, god of lightning and thunder, god of passion and god of enemies, god of the sword, we make this offering. We have heard your command. We grant what you ask, we ask nothing in return but your blessing. Yours is the power of Olodomare, yours is the kingdom of Obatala, yours is the strength."

The congregation responded. "Yours is the power and the kingdom, yours is the strength—"

> *give him unto Chango*
> *stop final*
> *stop final fire*

Yes, Cal thought, to sway the gods from destruction. To save the earth. Millions of lives. From destruction—

364

LEAVE HIM!
LEAVE HIM!

The fire's whisper bellowed into the tunnel.

Oscar passed the cup. Cal drank the burning liquid and passed the wooden goblet to Kate, who sipped and then handed it into the crowd. Cal watched as the cup made its way around the room from hand to hand, everyone taking a sip.

Oscar placed a fringed strip

> *blood blood*

of cloth across Chris's body, black fringed in gold, African words unreadable in the fabric. Cal looked down and saw woven into the cloth the face of the black cloud, the golden eyes, Chango's face—

No, it was his own. No

NO POWER FROM CHANGO
POWER YOURS

> *give me! give me! unto me*

NO GIFT HE IS OF
EARTH DOMAIN MBUA

No, Cal said to himself, *No*.

Oscar reached under the altar and brought out a glinting blade, its handle richly carved and inlaid with strips of gold. It was just as in the dream, the sunset and sunrise, the sound of thunder, the knife in his hand. Smoke rose from the congregation. Cigars. The knife was in Cal's hand, a cloak hung from his shoulders.

> *now now*
> *in his ripeness*
> *give*
> *give*
> *give*
> *give*

"No," Cal whispered aloud.

He grasped the iridescent handle of the knife with both hands and held it at full arm's length above his son's body. Chris was a beam of radiant light, an incarnation of joy. His chest undulated in a rhythmic inhaling and expelling of perfumed air. The whispering fire

BLOOD OF THE MAN
IS BLOOD OF THE EARTH
NO FINAL FIRE
NO FINAL FIRE

called to Cal. Kate joined Oscar's chant, her hand on Cal's arm. He turned to look at her. She was weeping. From joy? Sadness?

The knife lowered of its own will. In the reflection of the burnished oiled steel Cal saw flickering candle auras, the silver of Kate's hair, and the opalescent mahogany of Oscar's face dappled in red and black shadows.

The voices in his head were clearer, the fire and the cloud, clanging armor, whispering howling wind, whispering fire, whirling around each other

> *to live in the house*
> *of the gods*
> *to live*
> *to live forever*
> *forever forever forever forever*
> *all is mine*

as the knife came down. Cal struggled. The blade veered aside.

"I love you, Daddy," Chris crooned. "Send me now to Mommy."

Cal's shout died in his brain, never trod beyond the idea of a sound.

The blade resumed its course.

Oscar chanted, and the song reached Cal as a swell of sounds in the rush of surf and clanging metal but not

NOT YOURS CHANGO
NO BLOOD GIVE NO BLOOD
TAKE HIM AWAY NOW NOW NOW

to be heard. The knife swung in a wide arc to begin the long low stroke down to Chris's body. Cal could see the knife now. Something in him, something he could neither hear nor find nor see, stung his hands. The knife budged from its path, swerved upward, out over the edge of the altar.

In his hands Cal felt his own force veering the blade away from his son. It soared high past his own face

MINE!

and he heard the crowd gasp.

There were shouts. Screams.

"Stop him! Stop him!"

Cal went rigid, dimly aware of the knife moving past his eyes, each second breaking up, a series of pictures. Knife. Hands. Oscar's face. Candle.

His own will, his own strength swung the blade low, and he turned on the balls of his feet and drove it home into the man beside him.

Oscar. His mouth gaped, the blackness of space within.

Ripping and pulling downward, Cal dragged the blade through Oscar's gut. Blood spurted onto Cal's hands, rivers of blood. Crimson patches seeped across Oscar's chest. Oscar swayed, his body pitched forward, his hands clasped his stomach. His insides slipped out between his fingers from the wound in his gut, his life spilling onto the floor.

Cal loosened his grip, stumbled, skidded backward into Kate.

She held him for a moment, looked at him with infinite sadness. "May they have mercy on you, Cal. May you forgive yourself for what you have done."

Cal turned. The rest of the congregation had gone silent, stared at him emptily. In trances. Not one of them moved to imprison him. He had killed their high priest, doomed them all to the gods' wrath. Silent faces taking in the unmentionable, the unbelievable. In their moment of surprise and terror, Cal swept Chris from the altar and hugged him to his chest.

He walked slowly at first, edging his way up the aisle. They parted in awe, let him through.

He passed through the living room.

Can of Coke on the floor.

Television set on.

Real. He hugged Chris tighter.

Then he lost control, broke into a panicked run through the front door, his legs pumping desperately past the elevator and down the steps, out into the street. The sidewalks were empty, the stores shuttered. The world cared not, knew not what rites unfolded in secret havens.

∋ ● ∈

He ran and ran—through the concrete canyon, ignorant of direction, knowing only it was *away*, and that was good. Chris lay quietly in his arms, asleep, though his naked skin was cooled by the night. But still Cal could not stop. He pounded on, though he felt not only the weight of his son in his arms, but a heaviness over his back and shoulders. The god was still riding him—the saving god, the *mbua*. His lungs burned, and periodically his sides ached, almost as if he were being spurred. And on he ran, unable to stop.

Then suddenly the weight lifted from his back, and with the burden gone, Cal felt almost as though he could fly. He could run faster and faster.

But almost at the same moment he realized that the sound of reverberating footsteps in the street was only the echo of his own.

No one was chasing him. Of course—they had to let him go.

He stopped and knelt on the sidewalk. Chris was shivering now, though his eyes were still closed. Cal rested the boy on his knee, wriggled out of his blood-spattered jacket, and wrapped it around Chris. Then he started walking again, forward, away.

He heard Chris murmuring in his arms and stopped under a street lamp. Chris's eyes were open.

"Where are we, Daddy?" he said sleepily, not alarmed.

Cal hugged him tighter. "We're . . . we're together, Bean," was all he could say. "Don't worry. We're safe, and we're together."

But still, under the glare of the streetlamp, Cal felt too exposed. He moved out of it, but walking now.

At a corner he paused, contemplating directions. For a moment he looked up. His eyes took in the streaking light of a shooting star scoring the deep blue sky. For a long time Cal stood looking up, his gaze held by the heavens, the enveloping darkness of the universe.

Then he took the next step forward.

Aché

(The Power)

Chapter 44

CAL STOPPED outside the back door, wiped his boots on the thick sisal mat, and went into the kitchen. The field behind the big colonial house was no longer muddy from the spring thaw, but the dew was heavy at this hour of the morning, and the thick rubber soles of his boots were covered with blades of wet grass.

He knelt by the open hearth and dumped his armload of logs into the bin. It might be the last morning fire he'd make before next autumn, he thought. The weather was warming up; there was hardly a chill in the air at all now. In fact, he could have stopped making fires a week or two ago, but the novelty of the fireplace in the old-fashioned kitchen hadn't yet worn off. He loved using it, and knew how much Torey liked to see a fire going when she came down to breakfast. Something about having a fire made you feel safe, protected—perhaps an atavistic impulse passed down through the genes all the way from the primitives, for whom fire was the source of warmth, the shield against darkness, a beacon of life.

He finished building the fire, lit the crumpled pages of last week's Amherst *Record*, and watched the flames rise. The smell of hickory smoke crept over the kitchen. Cal started preparing coffee.

A flurry of rapid footsteps were heard on the stairs.

"Chris?" Cal called.

The feet landed with a jump on the hardwood floor at the base of the steps, went clattering away, then a door slammed. Must have gone through the sunporch and out the side door, Cal thought. Sure enough, a moment later there Chris was in the new-mown area of the rear field, dressed in his new Little League uni-

371

form. Of course he hadn't been able to wait to try it on; the first game was today.

Cal opened a kitchen window and called. "Hey, Bean—how about some breakfast before you warm up?"

"In a minute, Dad. Just gonna loosen my arm up first."

Dad. Not Daddy. Only three weeks past his eighth birthday, and somehow he suddenly seemed twelve.

Cal closed the window, but stood watching. Chris was making quite a show of it, tossing pitches against the side of the woodshed, doing all the exaggerated dramatics of a big-league hurler. Bending over, peering out from under his cap to read the signs of his imaginary catcher, then going into the windup. Windmilling his arms, leg kicked high. The rubber ball was unleashed toward the wall of the shed, and Chris ran to get the rebound.

Strike one, Cal called silently.

And then it came over him in a wave, catching him totally unaware as it always did. How close he had come to losing Chris, to being lost himself. Lost in madness, superstition, caught in a chaos of ideas with no meaning or reference.

There were more sounds in the house. The floorboards above creaked as Torey moved around. He heard the toilet flush in the upstairs bathroom, then the old pipes jangled as she ran water into the sink. He wondered if she'd had morning sickness again, and moved toward the hall to call up and ask if she needed help. But then there was the scuff of her slippers on the floor, and she started downstairs. He moved out into the hall, looked up at her. Her hair was still hanging over her eyes, yet disheveled she looked all the more adorable.

They met and kissed at the bottom of the steps.

He brushed the hair back from her face. "Everything okay?" he said.

"Fit as a fiddle." She patted her stomach. "Fit as a fat fiddle."

He put his arm around her and they walked along the hall into the kitchen.

"You were up early," she said.

"So are you."

"Smelled the coffee. What's your excuse?"

"I don't know . . . couldn't sleep. Country air. You know . . ."

He could see by the color of the coffee that it was almost finished perking, and went to the stove, ready to turn off the flame. Then he caught Torey examining him.

He knew what she was thinking. That he'd dreamed about it

again. There *had* been some terrible dreams, and he supposed there would be again. But he couldn't be expected to get over the fact that he had murdered a man. He might excuse it to himself as justice, or a necessary act to save Chris. Yet he could only pretend that he was not a kind of fugitive. Of course, he'd had no choice. Should he have confessed to killing Oscar Sezine? Tried to convince the police there had been good cause? No explanation would work. Kate had certainly understood that. She'd felt no need, no need at all, to go into hiding. A report had appeared in the newspapers that Oscar Sezine was killed in a fire, and that took care of that. Kate was still at Columbia, still making her appearances on television talk shows. She had a more doomladen message these days, kept saying the world was on the brink of destruction; but she wasn't running away. No, he was the only one who'd had to run. Run to reality, run to happiness and peace. Most of the time he had everything he'd come to find. But of course there would always be nightmares.

Not last night, though. "I'm fine, darling," he reassured Torey. "I got up early so I could finish marking those term papers. I didn't want them hanging over me when I took Chris to Little League. First game today, remember? He's up already." Cal nodded to the window. "Take a look."

Torey moved to the window, watched Chris perform one of his big-league windups, and laughed gently.

"And I suppose you gave him coffee for breakfast, too," she chided Cal. She pushed up the window. "Hey, number ten! Breakfast in the bullpen in five minutes. Bacon or sausages with your eggs?"

"No eggs, Mom," Chris called back. "Just Wheaties."

Torey turned from the window. "What else!"

"Bacon with mine," Cal said. He sat down at the table, where he had left a stack of term papers the night before.

Torey began putting breakfast together. She poured out three glasses of orange juice, put six strips of bacon into a pan. Passing one end of the counter as she carried some eggs from the refrigerator, she flipped on the radio, then moved quickly on to a cabinet and brought out a mixing bowl.

She whipped up the eggs, and was about to pour them into a pan when she realized that nothing more than a faint hum of static was coming from the radio speaker. The tuner had obviously drifted off her favorite classical music station. With the pan in one hand, she moved back to the radio and reached for the tuner. Before she touched the dial, the pan knocked against a glass of orange juice and it spilled onto the floor. "Oh shit," she muttered. Putting down the pan, she got a sponge out of the sink and swiped it over the floor. When the floor was clean she started the eggs, then returned to the radio. As much as she fiddled with the tuning knob, however, nothing but static came from the speaker.

"Darn it."

"What's wrong?" Cal said absently.

"Radio's gone on the fritz."

She picked up the small radio and turned it around in her hands.

"Loose wire, maybe," she said. She put it back down on the counter and studied it, then pulled out a drawer where some tools were kept.

The sound of metal rattling in the drawer made Cal look up. Then suddenly the memories detonated in his head. Wet floor. Bare feet. Electrical fault.

He flew out of his chair. "Don't touch it!" he screamed.

Torey backed off, startled. Then she read Cal's face. "It uses batteries," she said quietly, and picked up the radio in one hand. "All of nine volts."

Cal shook his head—tried to laugh, failed. "Sorry . . . I . . ."

"I know, darling. Oh—"

The pan on the stove had begun smoking. Torey put down the radio and walked over to the stove. "Well," she said, seeing the burnt eggs, "it won't hurt any of us to have the Breakfast of Champions." She put the pan in the sink and got out the cereal.

The radio was still putting out static. Now Cal was curious. He went over and picked it up. He turned the tuning dial through all the frequencies. Nothing. No news, no music anywhere.

Nada, he thought, and remembered MacTaggart—then wondered at the memory of the word. So long since he'd heard Spanish . . .

A high-pitched whistle broke through his thoughts. Cal had continued turning the dial. A station? Playing only this whistle?

The shrill noise ended abruptly and a voice came on. Speaking slowly, calmly.

"This is the emergency broadcast system. In accordance with civil defense regulations, all regular broadcasts have been terminated. Please turn to your emergency broadcast stations at 850 and 1130 on your dial, and you will be instructed in emergency civil defense procedures. This is not a test. Repeat. This is not a test. Turn at once to the emergency civil defense frequencies."

374

For a moment Cal and Torey stared at each other. Then they embraced, clinging tightly, and Torey began quietly to cry.

Outside in the green and sunny field, Chris went into his windup and threw another pitch, a perfect strike.